T0030084

CAVE 13

ALSO BY
JONATHAN MABERRY

Son of the Poison Rose

Kagen the Damned

Relentless

Ink

Rage

Deep Silence

Dogs of War

Kill Switch

Predator One

Code Zero

Extinction Machine

Assassin's Code

The King of Plagues

The Dragon Factory

Patient Zero

Joe Ledger: Special Ops

Still of Night

Dark of Night

Fall of Night

Dead of Night

The Wolfman

The Nightsiders: The
Orphan Army

The Nightsiders: Vault
of Shadows

Ghostwalkers: A
Deadlands Novel

Lost Roads

Broken Lands

Bits & Pieces

Fire & Ash

Flesh & Bone

Dust & Decay

Rot & Ruin

Bad Moon Rising

Dead Man's Song

Ghost Road Blues

Bewilderness

Glimpse

Mars One

ANTHOLOGIES
(AS EDITOR)

Don't Turn Out the
Lights: A Tribute to Alvin
Schwartz's Scary Stories
to Tell in the Dark

Joe Ledger: Unstoppable
(with Bryan Thomas Schmidt)

Nights of the Living Dead
(with George A. Romero)

V-Wars

V-Wars: Blood and Fire

V-Wars: Night Terrors

V-Wars: Shockwaves

Out of Tune Vol. I

Out of Tune Vol. II

The X-Files: Trust No One

The X-Files: The Truth
Is Out There

The X-Files: Secret Agendas

Hardboiled Horror

Aliens: Big Hunt

Baker Street Irregulars
(with Michael A. Ventrella)

The Game's Afoot: Baker
Street Irregulars II
(with Michael A. Ventrella)

Scary Out There

JONATHAN MABERRY

CAVE 13

A JOE LEDGER AND ROGUE TEAM INTERNATIONAL NOVEL

 ST. MARTIN'S GRIFFIN
NEW YORK

This is a work of fiction. All of the characters, organizations, and events portrayed in this novel are either products of the author's imagination or are used fictitiously.

First published in the United States by St. Martin's Griffin, an imprint of St. Martin's Publishing Group

CAVE 13. Copyright © 2023 by Jonathan Maberry. All rights reserved. Printed in the United States of America. For information, address St. Martin's Publishing Group, 120 Broadway, New York, NY 10271.

www.stmartins.com

Designed by Jonathan Bennett

The Library of Congress Cataloging-in-Publication Data is available upon request.

ISBN 978-1-250-61932-7 (trade paperback)
ISBN 978-1-250-61933-4 (ebook)

Our books may be purchased in bulk for promotional, educational, or business use. Please contact your local bookseller or the Macmillan Corporate and Premium Sales Department at 1-800-221-7945, extension 5442, or by email at MacmillanSpecialMarkets@macmillan.com.

First Edition: 2023

10 9 8 7 6 5 4 3 2 1

This is for two family members who passed this year.

Alan F. Maberry (6/5/1948–1/30/2022).
My brother.
Vietnam veteran. Served two brutal tours.
Struggled with PTSD for all those years.

And

Alison Prenner (3/27/1980–10/7/2022).
My niece.
Fellow pop-culture nerd. Joyful.

And, as always, for Sara Jo.

PROLOGUE

(1)

Jason Aydelotte is the scariest man you never heard of.

Well, you *have* heard of him, but like everyone, you thought he was great. He's the smiling face on so many Nat Geo and History Channel shows about the treasures of ancient Egypt and the Holy Land.

Or you know him because of all the ultra-rare ancient artifacts he's brought to public light, like rare books of old magic and burial goods from the tombs of pharaohs. Stuff he discovered through his funding of archaeological digs. Or because he helped recover lost fragments of the Dead Sea Scrolls. That's who he is to nearly everyone.

They call him Mr. Miracle.

He looks like a slightly slimmer Santa Claus, from the white beard to the broad smile to the twinkling blueberry-blue eyes. The kind of guy you'd happily leave your kids with, believing they could not be safer.

Yeah.

No.

He's a monster.

I didn't know it going into this and found it hard to buy even when things were going south and there was blood on the walls. Some things you just don't want to believe. Some things you can't easily accept. Mr. Miracle being a bad guy wasn't just hard to swallow, it was laughable. Like the punch line of a joke.

Except now . . . ? No one's laughing now.

By the time they put me in play, there were so many things going on. It was like trying to solve five jigsaw puzzles at once with no pictures for reference. The difference is, if you don't finish an actual jigsaw puzzle the ass doesn't fall off the whole damn world. So, yeah, this was in motion and getting really bad long before I knew anything about it.

And things are about to get a whole lot worse.

Because I don't know if there's enough time left to stop him. I don't know if, under any circumstances, I *can* stop him.

I don't.

I don't know if anyone can.

(2)

I hid in the darkness and tried not to scream.

Tried.

Failed sometimes, and then I had to bury my mouth in the crook of my arm and muffle the sounds.

Things were bad. I was hurt. Bleeding in more places than I could count. Pretty sure something was broken inside. In my body. In my head.

I crouched there on one side of a door.

They were on the other side.

I had my knife. I had my combat dog, Ghost. I had a pistol with two bullets. Maybe I could use them to take the first two down. Or maybe I should save them. One for Ghost, one for me.

My head was filled with monsters, and I couldn't think straight.

There were monsters on the other side of the door, too. Some of them used to be people I knew. People I loved and trusted. Top and Bunny. Or what had once been Top and Bunny.

Pounding on the door.

The wood was splintering. My time was running out.

The pounding was getting louder.

I stood. Blood flowed down my arms and legs and body. The world spun, and I knew that I was at the end of what strength I had. Maybe there was enough for one more fight. One last try.

The door began to buckle. Ghost got shakily, weakly to his feet. His white fur was painted in red. He looked up at me, at his master, his pack leader. Looking for comfort, for direction, for strength.

"It'll be okay, boy," I said.

He knew I was lying.

It wasn't going to be okay.

The wood around the lock began to splinter.

I raised the gun.

"Come on," I growled. *"Come on!"*

And, damn it to hell, they came.

A DAY AT THE LAKE

PART 1

TWO WEEKS AGO

We are little flames poorly sheltered by frail walls against the storm of dissolution and madness, in which we flicker and sometimes almost go out.

—*ALL QUIET ON THE WESTERN FRONT,*
ERICH MARIA REMARQUE

CHAPTER 1

RÉGION DU LAC
REPUBLIC OF CHAD

It was a snatch-and-grab job.

No good guys believed to be in the target area. Lots of bad ones, though.

Plenty.

Havoc Team was on the ground near the shores of Lake Chad, right at the crossroads of north and central Africa. Once upon a time, it was a beautiful place to live. A lovely desert, lush forests, and a sparkling blue lake. Probably be nice again one of these days. Not so much right now.

Real damn short history lesson: ISIS and al-Qaeda are the most dangerous active terrorist groups in the world. The US and its allies have done a pretty good job spanking them, but the thing with fanatics is that they view every loss as a rallying cry. Special Forces have scored some serious wins that with other enemies might have had a demoralizing effect.

During one raid by US Special Operations forces in Syria in 2019, ISIS leader Abu Bakr al-Baghdadi detonated a suicide vest rather than allow himself to be taken. Abu Ibrahim al-Hashimi al-Quraishi, the successor to al-Baghdadi, was killed in a US raid in Idlib province in Syria in 2022. And Ayman al-Zawahiri, the leader of al-Qaeda after the assassination of Osama bin Laden, was taken out by a drone attack in Afghanistan in 2022.

But with people like these, every death saw the birth of a new martyr. Martyrs are excellent recruiting tools. Western military is often a step behind the learning curve in thinking these strikes will take the heart out of the fighters. I mean, sure, they're useful strategic hits, but they don't stop the war.

Nothing so far seems able to do that. The war is the war, and it will always rage. Here and there. Under different flags, fueled by different kinds of hate. Rationalized by the ideology du jour. Guys like me aren't fighting for the big win. We're either fighting holding actions in whatever shape they take, or we're looking for small wins, taking what we can. Making whatever difference we can.

And, as jihadist groups in the Middle East are weakened through attrition, splinter groups tend to pop up anywhere the organizers view as fertile ground. In Africa, amidst the rampant poverty in certain nations, and with culture wars and ethnic genocide, the pickings are ripe. These extremists have established serious footholds in Somalia, the western Sahel region, the Lake Chad basin, northern Mozambique, and the Sinai Peninsula. In Chad, there's a group that thinks ISIS has taken losses because they weren't extreme enough. Yeah, sit with that one for a moment.

What makes them even scarier is that they have focused less on suicide bombings and more on acquiring technology that gives their small group a fighting chance against the superpowers. Since late 2022, there have been dozens of hits against US and UN drones and surveillance helicopters. Not just teenagers with RPGs, but weirdly sophisticated strikes that suggest someone with deep knowledge of combat software.

And that's where Havoc Team joins the party.

We were hunting a man named Marco Russo, an Italian national who worked as a freelance military systems software engineer for Italy, Germany, and France. He's one of those computer super nerds who probably thinks in code. Software and hardware genius. For the first eleven years of his career, he was considered a safe bet by any nation's vetting teams. Squeaky-clean life except for some parking tickets near the better museums in Rome and Florence; no politics at all, and no red flags like deep debt or known addictions.

Then one day Russo went missing. His wallet, passport, keys, and shoes were found on the Grand Duchess Charlotte Bridge in Luxembourg City. No note, no known reason for suicide, and no trace of him was ever found. Missing, presumed drowned.

Now here's the scary part: When forensic computer whiz kids tore apart his emails and text messages and computers, they discovered hints of what he was working on. Not full details, but enough to suggest that he was edging toward several variations of new software packages that could turn the randomness of LAW rockets and RPGs into very precise and nearly unshakeable laser-guided missiles.

That was when drones and choppers started falling out of the sky.

Around that time, rumors began whispering down the lane through various communities tied to ISIS. The rumors hinted that Russo was alive, well, and working on something even more dangerous for an extreme splinter group.

A lot of covert ops teams were out hunting for him. Everybody wanted his scalp, but rumors or not, Russo seemed to be unfindable.

Then we caught a break.

Ali Hissein, a local Muslim working as a ground man for a central African Islamic counterterrorism group, took photos of everyone going in and coming out of an ISIS camp by Lake Chad. It was a place that used to be a school. Hissein's computer team ran every surveillance photo they took through facial recognition software and pinged Russo. Very much alive and well and laughing it up with two men known to be leaders of a Boko Haram group overseeing the ISIS recruits.

Russo, being an Italian national, was hands-off for American Special Forces. Lots of red tape, some political challenges with the new government in Italy, and outstanding warnings from the government of Chad against any incursion by the US of A.

Which is why Mr. Hissein reached out through his group's network of contacts, and a phone rang on the desk of my boss, Mr. Church. We at Rogue Team International don't fly anyone's flag. We're autonomous, although we will occasionally do jobs over or under the table for the UN and other allies who ask nicely. Hissein was a trusted friend, and Church took his intel very seriously.

Thirty-seven hours later, Havoc Team was in Chad.

Hunting.

CHAPTER 2
THE TOC—TACTICAL OPERATIONS CENTER
PHOENIX HOUSE
OMFORI ISLAND, GREECE

There were forty people in the TOC.

Most were technicians focused on their individual tasks—comms, satellite feeds, news feeds from the region, chatter on local bands, eavesdropping on police and military channels in Niger, Nigeria, and Chad, scanning cell signals. Others worked the logistics desks, making sure that support craft were in position, adjusting them as needed to ensure that extraction was always a viable option.

Seated at one big desk was Leroy Jerome Williams, known to everyone as Bug. Several of his senior department heads were at nearby workstations. Their jobs were to provide any real-time information, deep background on people and places, and to answer any questions Joe Ledger and Havoc Team might have.

In the back of the room, shrouded in soft shadows, stood three people. One was a tall, blocky man with dark hair shot through with gray, wearing a beautiful Italian suit with a crisp white shirt and hand-painted silk tie. Mr. Church. This was his island, his organization, his war. These were his people. His face gave away nothing about what emotions he might be feeling.

To his left was Scott Wilson, the chief of operations for RTI. He was a thin, angular, uncomfortable-looking man who gave the impression of always being ready to sprout wings and flap away in annoyance across a marsh. His face was perpetually pinched with disapproval.

To Church's right was the outrageous and flamboyant Joan "Doc" Holliday, chief science officer for RTI. She was nearly as tall as Church and dressed in an embroidered western shirt with hummingbirds flitting across the expanse of an improbably large bosom. Her hair was a towering mass of carefully coifed and sprayed blond waves, and her lipstick was a murderous red. She was an actual descendant of John Henry "Doc" Holliday, who had drawn guns with Wyatt Earp at the OK Corral. The clothing, the push-up bra, the hair, and the Dolly-Parton-on-steroids vibe she constructed were deliberate, and the reactions she received were very amusing. Behind all of that was a mind like a supercomputer, and, before signing on with Church, she had made billions with patents in a remarkable range of scientific fields.

The three of them were each powerful in their own unique way. Even Wilson, who once went into the field on missions very much like the one they were watching. Each of the three of them had their own view on Ledger's recovery and the dangers of using so unstable a tool. Ledger had fallen into darkness a year ago. Wilson thought the man should be, at least, assigned to a desk from now on, and at worst discharged back to a less stressful civilian life. Doc Holliday approved of Ledger going back to the field, but she had insisted on speaking with Top Sims for a good long while before they were wheels up.

As for Church . . . the war was the war. The war never ended, and if only the enemy was ruthless, then there was no chance of survival. In the course of a long career, he had made choices that would have shocked both of his companions. There were a few choices he wished could be undone but many more that proved his judgment and vision were sound.

This mission, though, had been a roll of the dice. Even for him.

CHAPTER 3
RÉGION DU LAC
REPUBLIC OF CHAD

We entered Nigeria using different routes and made our way to the shores of Lake Chad. As night fell, we suited up in waterproof gear, slipped into the ink-black waters, and used Hoverstar Aquajet diving scooters to move unseen beneath the surface. Silent as barracudas.

Everyone was in lightweight waterproof black trousers and jackets. Lots of sealed pockets filled with goodies. Gear bags on our backs with even more toys. Most of us had M4A1 assault rifles with high-end sound suppressors along with sidearms. Lots and lots of magazines because sometimes things get weird. Belle had a Sako TRG 42, a superb Finnish bolt-action long-range sniper rifle. Bunny had his Atchisson assault shotgun with a thirty-two-round drum magazine slung over his back just in case things needed to get real damn loud.

And they usually did.

We came up through tangles of water lilies, climbed the sloping beach, and faded into dense foliage. I triggered the distance switches on the scooters. Once we were five miles away from where they lay on the lake floor, thermite explosive charges would quickly and quietly turn them into unrecognizable slag.

The beach and jungle were pitch black on that stretch of deserted lakefront, so we put on our Scout glasses, which were designed especially for Church by one of his many friends in the industry. Pick an industry, and he has someone on speed dial. The glasses—goggles, really—were lightweight and more useful than standard military-issue night vision goggles in that they could be cycled from normal lenses to zoom to infrared and ultraviolet. Real-time mission intel was fed to us across the inside of one lens. Currently, we had ours switched to ultra-low-light night vision, which plunged us into a world of luminous green, bright white, and dense black.

Then we were in motion.

The two kilometers melted away, and soon we saw lights ahead. I signaled the team to stop, and we all knelt in a thicket of ambatch bushes withered by recent drought. A pair of big and leafy old ebony trees protected us from above. From that vantage point we could see a big chain-link fence encircling a cluster of small buildings. Kapok and jujube trees grew inside the fence but had been harshly pruned back.

"Jackpot," I said, using Andrea's combat call sign, "let's get some birds in the air."

"Copy that, Outlaw."

Andrea was a lean Italian on semi-permanent loan to us from the GIS—Gruppo di Intervento Speciale—an elite division of Italy's Carabinieri. His combat call sign was one of those truth-in-advertising things, because he had a penchant for gambling.

More usefully, he had a genius for sneaky tech. Andrea opened a pouch and removed a half dozen cicada drones. Small and—unlike their singing counterparts in that part of Chad—silent. He tossed the little machines into the air and then bent over the screen display of his forearm-mounted tactical computer. The cicadas rose up and circled, feeding us different views and angles of the compound.

Belle leaned her head against his shoulder as she studied the feeds. "Eight guards on patrol. Machine guns on the northeast and southwest towers."

"Switching to thermal imaging," said Andrea. "Here we go."

Immediately the buildings faded to gray, and dark red silhouettes appeared.

Andrea frowned. "*Accidenti!* There are close to forty unique signatures in there."

"More than we thought," agreed Top.

Bunny sighed. "Fun times."

"What are those?" asked Remy, tapping one cluster of signals. "Depth-finder on the thermals say they're in the basement."

This was Remy's first field op with Havoc. Top had scouted him. At twenty-four, Remy was the youngest on the team. He was a Cajun kid from New Orleans and looked it. Combat call sign was Gator Bait. He had intelligent brown eyes under a mop of coal-black hair. A good smile, but you had to earn one from him. My height, but bigger in the chest and shoulders. I looked like a third baseman, and he was built for first base.

We all studied that image.

"Could be tangos bedded down," suggested Andrea. "They're all lying down. Curled up in different parts of the room."

Top tapped the screen. "Looks odd to me. Most are curled up on the floor near one another, looks like. But see, over here . . . ?" He tapped a room on a higher floor of the same building. "More people lying down—count nine—but these signatures are all in neat rows, the bodies shaped the way they would be on beds or cots. And the blank spaces between some of them are empty beds. Completely different from whoever's in the basement."

"What are you thinking about that other group, Pappy?" asked Bunny.

Top and Belle answered at the same time. "Prisoners."

"There's a heat signature outside that room," said Remy. "Could be a guard on a chair."

We studied the image of the bodies curled on the floor.

Andrea frowned. "They're smaller than most of the others. Women, maybe? Or teens conscripted to be fighters?"

That was always a possibility in radicalized parts of Africa. I heard Belle give an ugly little growl. She'd been in a camp in Mauritania, one set aside for genital mutilation and other horrors. An Arklight team raided the camp and recruited Belle, training her to fight back against that kind of tyranny.

"We keep that as a working theory," I said.

Bunny used his fingertip to draw a small circle around something on the roof of one of the buildings. "Is that an antenna array?"

"Yes, it is," confirmed Andrea. "Cell phone, radio, probably long-range Wi-Fi. "Want to bet that's where we find our boy Russo?"

"Sucker's bet," said Bunny.

Belle looked at me. She was thin, wiry, unsmiling, and deliberately unpleasant most of the time. That was her shield; it was armor over the terrible personal scars inflicted upon her. The only time I ever saw her relaxed was in a combat situation. "What do we do if those *are* prisoners?"

"Our mission is to get Russo and get out," I said.

Her eyes never wavered. "That is not the question I asked, Outlaw."

"I know. I can't make promises. If we can extract them without endangering our primary goal, then we give it a try."

"There's some trucks over by the east gate," said Remy. "Might be the easiest way to move all those people to the extraction point."

Top's face was uninformative. Bunny cocked a single eyebrow but left it unsaid. Field ops were not run according to any democratic process. The boss called the shots before we left, and I dealt the play on the ground. That said, none of us bought into the idea of collateral damage. That was too often a political exigency, and we weren't political.

In a very firm, let's-have-no-debate tone of voice I said, "We extract them if we can. But that is still a secondary objective. Are we clear?"

"Hooah," said Belle. If there was a small pause before that reply, I chose not to acknowledge it.

"Either way," I added, "we have to accept that there may be civilians, so pick your targets. Controlled fire."

They each very quietly replied with a heartfelt "Hooah."

I sent Belle off to find an elevated shooting position, then told Andrea and Remy to see what mischief they could get up to with the toys they carried in their backpacks. From the way they grinned you'd have thought they were setting up a particularly wild frat party.

When we were alone, Top and Bunny leaned close. Our team comms were on the mission channel, so everyone else could hear.

"The thermal scans didn't show any active current in the fence," I said. "So, we go here and cut in." There was a section of that fence far away from anything useful.

"Rules of engagement?" asked Top, a habit of his at moments like this, even though that had already been discussed before we went into the water. He was big on clarity, especially now that we knew there might be prisoners in play. And besides, the whole team was on the shared mission channel of our comms.

"Everyone gets into position," I said. "On my go order, we start taking down the tangos."

"Tangos" was useful shorthand for terrorists.

"Guards first," I continued. "Don't take a shot unless you're sure it can be a silent kill. We don't want anyone inside to turn this into a siege. Once we have the guards neutralized, then we hit at the points discussed in the mission briefing. We want Russo with a pulse."

"Hooah," they said softly.

"Then let's go to work."

CHAPTER 4
THE TOC
PHOENIX HOUSE

"Here we go," said Scott Wilson, snapping his fingers several times over his head.

The members of the technicians and logistics teams did not turn or flinch. They were used to his ways by now. Bug, however, found it deeply irritating and wished the COO would stop doing that. It was distracting and rude.

Jackass, he thought, and—as he had more than once—contemplated doing something nasty to Wilson's cell phone. Videos of explicit animal sex, maybe. Or something with lots of photos of really disgusting diseases.

But no. Wilson would know who sent it, even if the stuff carried no telltale metadata. And Church would disapprove.

Nice to think about, though.

Bug reclaimed his focus and bent over a satellite image of Havoc Team making its way through night-dark forest toward the ISIS compound.

"Here we go," he said, echoing Wilson's comment, but only to himself.

Like everyone in the room, he was sweating bullets because this was the first time since the Darkness that Joe Ledger was back in the field.

Come on, Joe, he thought, *don't get weird on us.*

INTERLUDE 1
UNKNOWN TOMB
NEAR THE RUINS OF THEBES
CITY OF LUXOR, EGYPT

THREE YEARS AGO

The leaders of the tomb robbers did not look like what they were.

One was a slim woman with shocking red hair, a pretty American face that looked like it belonged on an East Coast college campus, ideally somewhere in the theater arts department. Everyone who knew her called her Shock.

Her companion looked like Santa Claus dressed up as Indiana Jones, with khaki pants, a leather jacket against the chill of the desert night, and a brown felt hat crammed down on his head.

Shock and Jason Aydelotte.

Their team, on the other hand, looked like they robbed tombs for a living, and that was truth in advertising.

Aydelotte was the overall boss, and he was unused to being in the field. Until recently, he had always been the face on TV or magazines or at big-ticket events celebrating the discovery of this or that artifact of historical importance, mostly religious antiquities, which he seemed able to find when generations of professional diggers could not. Fragments of Dead Sea Scrolls, rare burial goods from Egypt and Israel, relics of the Crusades. Someone in the press had hung the nickname Mr. Miracle on him, and Aydelotte grabbed it with both hands, trademarked it, and made it his public face.

Venturing into the field with Shock was new, and he was terrified and excited in exactly equal measures. It was, as he explained to Shock, his way of showing confidence in her and of deepening his own understanding of what they sometimes had to do in order to make those astounding discoveries. It was also fun.

"We are almost there," said Shock.

Aydelotte watched her as she worked with the diggers to move the hundreds of pounds of sand from what they both hoped was a tomb of real importance.

Shock was a lean, wiry scorpion of a woman. Unsmiling, unforgiving, unimpressed, and unencumbered by adherence to laws, rules, or any need for approval. Apart from the cap of spiky hair, she had a woodpecker beak of a nose and hands with the long, spatulate fingers of an artist. She had let her true name—Jennifer Rose—melt away over the years and had used "Shock" since before committing her first crimes. First *major* crimes, at least. The name echoed throughout the entirety of the black market for antiquities. And it described her quite precisely when she was in gear.

"Let me look," said Aydelotte.

He went over and squatted on his heels, looking down into the hole. It was ten feet long, five wide, and five deep. Three weeks ago, this part of the desert was a different place, with dunes as much as fourteen feet high in this very area. But the sandstorm—a real mother of a blow—had come in and swept a few billion tons of sand into another part of the desert. Two new archaeological sites of interest had already been roped off less than a half mile from where he squatted. Those sites were previously unknown tombs in what the scientists hoped and prayed might be a new royal cemetery.

The Egyptian government and the Ministry of Tourism and Antiquities wasted no time in declaring the entire region off-limits. Guards were posted and all digging forbidden pending official investigation. The red tape unspooled everywhere as universities and museums around the world applied for permits. Until all of the paperwork, ego-massaging, backbiting, and bribery were settled, no one was allowed to so much as build a sandcastle, let alone launch a major excavation.

Aydelotte absolutely loved red tape. It was very useful, and it had opened so many windows of opportunity—admittedly narrow windows, but he was always ready. That was another quality, every bit as beneficial as patience.

He had Shock launch a dozen drones outfitted with the most compact and sophisticated ground-penetrating radar. They flew every night, soaring silently on special rotors designed to muffle the whine. Very expensive and worth every penny.

The drones found very little the first eleven nights. And then they began quartering a new section, and the *pings* were nearly constant. Not only the two sites already revealed by the storm—which Aydelotte would not dare touch for all the obvious reasons—but also because he wanted privacy.

On the twelfth night, the drones found three new sites, each relatively close to the surface.

Before dawn had broken the following morning, Aydelotte and Shock were busy assembling their team: government diggers whose loyalty could be bought at a reasonable price, some hired muscle, and Shock.

After an hour of furious labor, a tomb emerged from the sand.

There was a strong breeze, and it brushed away much of the sand as if it conspired with fate to uncover what had been buried all those years ago. It was as if the tomb wanted to be found.

That thought—that *belief*—made Jason Aydelotte a very happy man.

CHAPTER 5
MADRASAT ALMAZRAEA SCHOOL
RÉGION DU LAC, REPUBLIC OF CHAD

Top, Bunny, and I moved in a line along a footpath in the woods, emerging at an angle where the cicada drones told us no guard was looking. The closest watchtower was forty yards to our right, and I could see the small flare of a cigarette as the guard took a drag.

"Mother Mercy," I murmured.

"In position," came Belle's reply.

"Tower guard," I said. "Southeast corner."

I never heard the shot. But the guard puddled down out of sight.

"Moving," I said. The three of us ran to the fence. Bunny had the nippers out of his bag and began cutting while Top and I knelt, guns up, pivoting slowly. The few lights on in the compound seemed unable to force back the sheer weight of the shadows. The place was alive with insect noise and the strange cries of unseen night birds.

Bunny tapped my shoulder and held the severed folds of the fence back as I went through, crouching, moving fast and light. Top was behind me, his footsteps barely making a sound. We ran to the closest wall and paused, watching the area.

"Two on foot," said Andrea. "On your three o'clock. Ten seconds."

Top had his rifle up and, as the pair of guards rounded the corner, he took them center-mass. Quick, quiet, and certain, the suppressor reducing the sound of the shots to vague whispers. One guard fell outside the line of shadows thrown by the building, but Bunny grabbed him and dragged him into darkness.

This building was one with the fewest heat signatures, so we entered that through a door that led us into a kitchen. Everything was dark. Top held his hand above the burners on the stove, but they were cold. We moved as fast as care allowed. Last thing anyone needed was someone's elbow hitting a goddamn frying pan handle and turning this all into a rather tragic comedy skit.

You'd be amazed at how much of the training in covert ops is dedicated to not being a klutz. I will freely admit that there have been times I've needed to repeat certain drills while my own team members watched and tried not to laugh. Tried, not succeeded.

Top took point as we neared the door to the mess hall. It was empty except for one man bent forward onto the tabletop, face on his folded arms, sleeping. Top put two in his back without a pause.

That's a weird thing about our business. On one hand, there are actions taken that appall the noncombatant and the more civilized parts of people like us. Shooting a sleeping man in the back sounds cruel and harsh. But what are the options? Trying to knock him out and managing that quietly was a risk, and we believed there might be civilian prisoners in the compound. Leaving him behind without waking him ensured danger behind us.

The moral part of the mind offers alternative suggestions; the pragmatic part insists on eliminating all possible threats. Mind you, this isn't a debate guys like us have in the field, but it does come back to haunt our thoughts in those quiet downtime hours. A lot of PTSD is born there. I know something about that. Too much, and by any metric by which mental health is measured. This was my first field op since I went a little crazy last year.

Well, crazi-*er*.

Took a lot of work to get my head screwed back on the right way. A lot of work.

As we left the mess hall, some part of me filed that necessary kill away, and I knew I'd have homework to do later.

Not now, though.

Reports came in, soft and brief, from Andrea and Remy. They had so far taken down four tangos, and Belle had taken out the guard in the second tower. That left four more walking the perimeter. I left them to Belle and the boys.

Top, Bunny, and I moved through the building. We found the bunkhouse and very quietly opened the door about three inches. Nine sleeping men. Too many to take out silently. We'd get some, and the others would start yelling. So I eased the door shut and moved aside, nodding to Top. He removed a blaster-plaster from a pouch, tore off the film on the back, applied it very gently to the jamb, inserted a trigger, and backed away. That plaster would sit there and do nothing until someone opened that door. And then it would go boom in a really big way.

We left and went to the next one. That was the structure with the antenna array on the roof, the one in which we hoped to find Russo. It was also where the presumed prisoners were kept.

"Going for the target now," I said, and ran low and fast with Top and Bunny behind me.

The building was the only two-story affair on the property and had been the main part of the school. From the old floor plans Bug had pulled for us, there was a single hall that ran front to back, with classrooms on either side, a bathroom each for girls and boys, a storeroom, a small dining room, and a mud room leading to the back door. The second floor had offices for the faculty, a small room for daily prayer, and some unspecified smaller rooms. Once we were again in shadows, I used my tactical computer to view the feeds from the cicada drones. Two heat signatures on the ground floor, both in the dining room; seven on the second floor. Basements are uncommon in these kinds of structures, but the depth-finder on the thermal scans indicated that the prisoners were below us. A dozen clustered together and one slightly larger one separated from them by a wall.

The challenge here was taking Russo without a ruckus, but planning for the unexpected. The old saying that no plan survives contact with the enemy is the truest thing I ever learned.

I pointed to the ground and then at Bunny. He nodded and faded off to the back of the building. It would be his job to eliminate the guard downstairs outside of the room where the presumed prisoners were sleeping. He slung his rifle and drew his FNX-45 Tactical handgun, which already had an Osprey sound suppressor screwed in place. For a man who was six-six and packed with more muscle than is reasonable for anyone other than King Kong, the boy moved like a ghost.

Top and I went to a side door. While I kept guard, he ran an

Anteater over the frame and determined that there were no active alarms. The lock was a piece of shit that rolled over at the first touch, and we were inside.

The place was quiet but not silent. A TV I hadn't heard from outside was playing upstairs. I could hear canned voices but was unable to pick out the words. That made things easier, but not so easy we could be complacent.

We checked and cleared the classrooms and then went up the stairs. I took point to the first landing and then covered Top as he passed me and led the way up to the second floor. The TV sound resolved into a drama in Italian. Two men, apparently investment bankers, arguing about some kind of worldwide financial crisis. The noise came from the room that had a single heat signature. At that moment I would have bet my 1974 Topps Dave McNally #235 Baltimore Orioles baseball card that the guy watching that show was Russo. I slung my rifle and drew a Snellig 22A-Max gas dart gun with a full magazine of Sandman.

The gun is nearly silent. Just a soft *whiff*. The darts are thin-walled, gelatin-filled with a cocktail of chemicals designed around the veterinary drug ketamine, but with BZ—3-Quinuclidinyl benzilate—to cause intense and immediate confusion and DMHP—Dimethylheptylpyran, a derivative of THC—for muscle failure. And it has some benzodiazepines and chloral hydrate and some other surprises. We call it Sandman. When you get hit with one, you go down. No one bulls through it, no one has immunity. One shot and you fall, and then your brain wanders through Alice's looking glass into a world of the most disturbing hallucinations you never want to experience.

We try not to use it on the good guys.

Russo wasn't on our list of people we consider "good."

Mind you, there are times with an infiltration of this kind where everyone gets a dose of Sandman, but that's when the targets are friendlies—such as if we need to sneak onto an ally's military base—so all they get are bad dreams. This was a Boko Haram camp. No one here was on Santa's nice list. Except the prisoners downstairs and Russo—and his survival was all about the information he had, not his value as a carbon-based life-form.

I tapped lightly on his door, heard someone mutter in annoyance, then bare feet on the hardwood floor. There was no peephole on the door, so he had to open it. He was a geeky, seedy man with a lot of black hair tied in a retro nineties ponytail, a thick mat of chest hair, and he wore only green boxer shorts and a T-shirt with the name of a thrash metal band I had never heard of. He smelled of indifferent hygiene, pot, testosterone, and fried meat.

"What the fuck?" groused Marco Russo in slurred Italian.

Sandman answered with its typical eloquence. Top rushed past me and caught Russo as he fell.

I tapped my earbud. "Package secured."

Instead of team responses, it was Mr. Church's voice in my ear.

"Proceed to the extraction point," he said. "Osprey is inbound. Thirty minutes."

CHAPTER 6
THE TOC
PHOENIX HOUSE

Mr. Church stood in the back of the TOC, watching the drama unfold on large screens fed by live streams from the body cams of Havoc Team. Scott Wilson stood beside him, hands clasped tightly behind his back, his pointed chin outthrust, small muscles at the corners of his jaws clenching and unclenching.

"Perhaps now you can stop fidgeting," he said quietly. "Colonel Ledger is doing well, don't you think?"

Wilson's head snapped around, and his tight lips began to form a retort. It was a long five seconds before Wilson trusted his control enough to answer. "I rather think that's because Top Sims is babysitting him."

"You've never understood Colonel Ledger, Scott."

"I understand that he is a walking time bomb."

Church's reply was a small, bland smile that said everything and nothing. Wilson turned away again. The muscles at the corners of his jaw continued to bunch and flex.

CHAPTER 7
MADRASAT ALMAZRAEA SCHOOL
RÉGION DU LAC, REPUBLIC OF CHAD

Bunny crept down the stairs to the basement, his pistol clutched in two hands but held close to his chest in the narrow stairwell. There was a dingy yellow light bulb hanging from a dusty cord. Because it was down at floor level, it pushed his shadow behind him and up the stairs rather than paint the cellar floor ahead of him.

At the bottom of the stairs there were rows of metal shelves on which were stacked cases of canned goods, big bottles of water, and boxes of miscellaneous supplies. The last shelf in the row was at the end of a short corridor and provided good cover for him to kneel and peer around the corner.

As anticipated, there was a single guard on a chair. He was reading a newspaper. There was a coffee cup and the leavings of a meal on a metal plate on the floor next to him.

The door he guarded was a surprise. Instead of an ordinary door of the kind one might expect in a school in a third world country—or, more typically, a cloth nailed to the frame and draped across the doorway—the one he saw was impressive. It looked to have been made of sheets of heavy aluminum nailed over plywood—evident because the metal sheeting was an inch or so shorter than the door itself. Longer two-by-fours were slotted through heavy metal bands bolted to the wall on either side. And there was also a very strong-looking lock.

They don't want whoever's in there to get out, he thought. *Must be valuable prisoners.*

Bunny raised his pistol as he stepped into the hall and shot the guard twice through the newspaper, the rounds taking him in the sternum. He put one more in his head, splashing the wall behind him with red.

He stepped forward and pulled the corpse away from the door, then paused and listened for any sounds—upstairs or down there. The wind outside had picked up, and the whole building was an orchestra of sinister creaks and strange groans.

But . . .

JONATHAN MABERRY

There were sounds inside that room, too.

Soft noises. The rustle of cloth. Some low murmurs. Then abruptly one voice spoke at normal volume. Bunny's Arabic was rusty at the best of times, and he could only pick out a word or two, but they did not fit together in any useful way.

Scorpion and *baby*.

He holstered his pistol and quietly slid the restraining bars out of their slots. Then he patted down the guard for the keys. He found them, but also found a small case about the size of a cigarette pack; inside was a set of syrettes. Seven, and each was nestled into a slot marked for a day of the week. It was a Friday, and the only unused syrettes were for Saturday and Sunday. The liquid inside was clear, and Bunny thought it might be insulin. When he pushed up the guard's sleeve, he saw track marks. They were orderly, following the line of a vein near the inner elbow. There was nothing particularly sinister or important-looking about the stuff, so he left it and took the key instead.

The door opened easily, and he took a quick look through a narrow gap. The scene inside was not what he expected.

There were, indeed, a dozen young people inside. All younger teens, but not all females. Seven girls, five boys. They each wore institutional-looking pajamas. They were filthy. Some were caked with dried blood. All had obvious wounds—bruises, scratches, cuts, and some wounds that looked like bites.

Some were asleep, though they twitched and shuddered as if lost in the dark drama of nightmares. The rest were awake—if that word applied. They seemed drugged, their eyes jumpy and unfocused. One, a girl of about thirteen, was punching herself in the chest; her shirt was ragged, and her breasts and sternum swollen with tissue damage. She moved to a grotesque pattern—two punches, then a pause to listen, a nod as if in reply, two more punches.

Nearby, a slender boy of about the same age was slowly, systematically tearing out the hairs on his head and eating them. Half of his scalp was raw and bleeding. He looked very happy with his progress and kept telling himself something after swallowing each hair. Bunny tapped the translate function on his Scout glasses, and the boy's words scrolled across one eyepiece.

"That will feed the scorpions. The baby will like that. That will feed the scorpions. The baby will like that."

He rocked as he plucked and swallowed and recited. It had clearly been going on for hours, and he made no signs of stopping. It was an activity assigned in some private hell, and his entire being was dedicated to it. And yet . . . he was smiling. He was happy in his work.

One other, a girl of about fifteen, knelt beside a sleeping boy and kept slapping him. She spoke only a single word as she did so. "Alghul." The name, Bunny knew, was of a desert demon from Arabian myth. What chilled Bunny was that her voice was completely normal. Unstressed, conversational, even pleasant in tone.

The sight of those kids and their casual violence triggered an atavistic dread in him. He'd been with Joe Ledger long enough to have seen a lot of extreme things, and recently that included a dreadful behavior-warping bioweapon called Rage. The complete dissociation from reality was similar. And yet . . . not. Rage was utterly, appallingly violent. What he was seeing in that room was violent but without the passion.

Then, far back in the gloomy rear of the room, he saw another woman. She was older than the others and had lighter skin, the color of coffee with a large dollop of milk. She stood with her back to Bunny, though her face was turned just enough for him to see a curve of brow and cheek. She held a bundle in her arms and rocked it back and forth.

Bunny's heart nearly stopped in his chest.

In the bad light and at that distance, the woman looked like . . .

"Lydia," he gasped.

The sound of her name jolted Bunny because he did not at first realize he was going to speak aloud. He had not expected to speak his wife's name.

At the sound, the woman turned a little more. The face was not in any way African. It was a Latina face. The hair was long and sleek and glossy. The eyes were *her* eyes. And the bundle she held . . .

"No . . . !" The word was a denial of what he saw. A refutation. A demand and a prayer that what she was holding—that ragged, red, torn, dripping, savaged thing—was not a baby.

Not his baby.

JONATHAN MABERRY

Not *their* baby.

"God . . . no . . ."

The words were pulled from his throat with rusty pliers. Small words that ripped his throat and tore his mind.

Lydia Ruiz stood there with the murdered and desecrated remains of their baby.

"No . . . no . . . no . . . no . . ."

He blinked as burning tears filled his eyes.

Blinked and . . .

The back of the room was empty. No figure. No woman. No bloody bundle. Not his wife. Not his child. Nothing at all but shadows.

"I . . . " he began but did not dare to finish that sentence.

Scott Wilson's voice broke through the horrified trance.

"Donnie Darko, say again."

Bunny did not reply. He didn't move. He wasn't sure he could. Inside the room, the teenagers slept or beat themselves or stared with wide, empty, mad eyes.

"That will feed the scorpions. The baby will like that," said the boy as he tore his hair out and fed on it. "That will feed the scorpions. The baby will like that."

"Donnie Darko," repeated Wilson. "What is your status? Do you require assistance?"

Bunny backed slowly out of the room. His eyes kept blinking. Lydia and the baby did not reappear. The other horrors refused to vanish.

"Donnie Darko to Grendel," he said, getting the words out more by reflex than deliberate action. "All good."

He knew it was a lie. There was nothing good about any of this. His pulse was faster and louder than automatic gunfire. The fear was a monster that slashed at him. He backed slowly out of the room and closed the door. Those poor kids had not noticed him. He knew that he would never forget the things he had seen there. Never.

He leaned back against the far wall of the corridor, his pistol hanging slack at the end of a loose arm. Sweat poured down his face, and it had no origin in the heat or humidity. It was ice cold and greasy with terror.

"God," he breathed again.

INTERLUDE 2
UNKNOWN TOMB
NEAR THE RUINS OF THEBES
CITY OF LUXOR, EGYPT

THREE YEARS AGO

"Boss," said Shock, "*look!*"

Her voice was charged with electricity as she turned a flashlight beam on a section of exposed stone and moved aside to afford him the best view. Two of the diggers brought their lights to bear as well.

"Is that a cartouche?" gasped Aydelotte.

"It . . . is . . ." said Shock, though she sounded unsure.

"What's wrong? Can you read it?"

He watched her trace the symbols. Ancient Egyptian was not one of the languages Aydelotte could read—his skills tended more toward Greek, ancient Hebrew, Latin, and Aramaic. He saw Shock's lips move as she translated symbols into Egyptian and then those words into English.

"What does it say?" he prompted. "Is it Siamun? Please say it is."

But after a long pause, Shock shook her head. "I can't tell. And it's . . . strange."

"Strange *how?*"

She was kneeling and pivoted to look up at him. "Cartouches are most commonly used to name the king or royal person entombed there. Napoleon's people coined the word because the symbol resembled the cartridges—cartouches—they used in their guns. The Egyptian word is *shenu*."

"Okay. And . . . ?"

"This cartouche names someone by description only. The rough translation is 'the Mad King.' But it doesn't actually give the name of whoever is buried here."

"The Mad King . . . ? That's a bit lurid, isn't it? Even for the ancients."

"It's not even exactly that," said Shock, brow furrowed. "Never quite seen this phrasing before. Wait, let me look at it again. Yes . . .

it's closer to the 'King Who Went Mad' or the 'King Who Saw Shadows.' Something like that. Maybe Dr. Hegazy will know once we get back to Cairo."

Hegazy was the director and chief expert on the languages and dialects of ancient Egypt for the newly opened Grand Egyptian Museum in Giza. He was a world-class scientist, but privately a gambler whose debts were enormous. Aydelotte—as well as some competitors and even special clients—used the knowledge of those debts, and offers of under-the-table payments, to turn dials on Hegazy.

"Very well," said Aydelotte.

Something howled out in the blackness of the desert. Shock and Aydelotte turned in that direction. The howl rose and rose, shrill and thin, and finally faded out.

Aydelotte gave his lips a nervous little lick. "Could have done without that."

Shock shivered and nodded. "There's one more thing, boss."

"Do I want to know?"

Shock gave one of those there-and-gone smiles. "We've uncovered most of the door. The seals are all intact, which is awesome. But those seals themselves bother me, too. They bother me a lot. Look." She played the light over them, and the beam revealed the image of a coiling serpent. "They're named after Apep, a minor god from the Fourth Dynasty, right at the end of the Old Kingdom. Call it forty-two hundred years ago."

"What was he the god of . . . ?" asked Aydelotte.

Her eyes were lost in shadows. "Chaos."

Aydelotte paused and gave the entrance a long reappraisal. Icy sweat was wriggling its way down his back under his shirt. And the hot night seemed to have gone colder.

"That isn't disturbing at all," he said weakly.

"It's more than that," insisted Shock. "The seals . . ."

"What about them?"

"Look . . . these doors aren't just marked with Apep's symbol, they are literally *sealed*. Like airtight. And this is different from any necropolis seal I've ever seen."

Aydelotte moved down into the pit and studied them closely. He had seen a number of sealed tombs, though mostly in photos displayed in museums or on websites. The heavy metal handles were usually bound by a rope looped through them and knotted in ritual fashion. The knotted binding was accompanied by a delicate clay seal featuring Anubis, the ancient Egyptians' jackal god entrusted with the protection of the cemetery. That was the standard.

What he saw here, though, was different. The handles were missing, though there was some evidence that they had been there originally but had been broken off. The chisel marks were evident, some having deeply gouged the wood. The doors were tightly shut, however, with beads of molten copper filling the cracks between the panels and the entire stone frame. Every few inches along those metal seals were the cartouches of Apep.

"What the hell?" he asked. "Why did they do that? What's it mean?"

"I don't know. This is unique in my experience," said Shock. "What I *do* know is that I don't like. No sir. Not at all. I've never seen anything even remotely like this. I've never even *heard* of this."

Aydelotte smiled. "Then that means we have found something truly unique, and that makes it all the more valuable. Make sure you take photos and videos of all of this. The unbroken seals, the king's cartouche and those of—what was his name? Apep? Get it all. We'll need proof that this tomb was untouched and therefore everything inside is inarguably unique. Provenance matters, even in our corner of the trade."

Shock did not immediately respond. She stayed still, eyeing those seals, apparently unwilling to touch them.

"Shock . . . ?" murmured Aydelotte. "Are we going to have a problem here?"

She turned slowly to look at him. In the utter silence he could hear her breathing.

"No," she said at last, her voice thin. "It's fine."

Aydelotte patted her shoulder. "That's what I like to hear."

CHAPTER 8
MADRASAT ALMAZRAEA SCHOOL
RÉGION DU LAC, REPUBLIC OF CHAD

"Donnie Darko to Outlaw," said Bunny.

"Go for Outlaw," I said.

"I'm in the basement. Civilians confirmed. Twelve prisoners. All teenagers, male and female."

"What condition are they in? Can they walk?"

The pause was oddly long. "I don't think so. Not without help. They're either all crazy or, more probably, they've been drugged. Lots of injuries. Self and mutual harm."

And my heart turned to ice. Top gave me a sharp look and mouthed the word even as I asked it of Bunny.

"Is it Rage?"

Rage was a bioweapon used in terrible ways by agents of the Kuga crime organization. We'd fought our way across a South Korean island where every single person had been infected. The level of violence, mutilation, and slaughter we saw was appalling. Beyond words, really. Later in that same operation, Rage was released at a big global de-nuclearization conference in Norway. I even got a dose of it. It wears off, but it leaves its mark on you. The memories of what we witnessed and the intensely ugly emotions it engendered in me will always haunt me.

"I don't think so," said Bunny. "But it's bad."

Church spoke from the TOC. "Can you exfil those prisoners?"

"Not without help and time," he said. "Some of them are in rough shape."

Bunny's voice was strange. Almost flat, but there was a lot of emotion trying to break through.

"Outlaw," said Church, "tell me if you can bring the civilians out *safely*." He leaned on that last word, and in doing so, turfed it to me to make a necessary call. Including a hard one.

I glanced at Top. His eyes looked angry and hard.

I said, "Not in the presence of active tangos."

Church's voice was cold. "Advise using Sandman if necessary to control the civilians."

"What if they're already drugged? What will Sandman do on top of that?"

"It's that or leave them, Outlaw," said Church. Then he added, "I'll arrange a full medical team to meet your aircraft."

Church was a hard-ass son of a bitch most of the time, but not actually callous. This was the war—and he had been fighting it for a very long time—and those kids downstairs were what we were fighting *for*. He knew it, I knew it. We all did. However, he wasn't on the ground, and I was.

"Copy that."

Top pointed to his earbud and then drew his hand across his throat. I tapped out of the channel for a moment, and he did the same.

"Don't like the idea of pumping those kids with something as nasty as Sandman," he said. "Also don't like the idea of carrying twelve sleeping bodies up the stairs and loading them on trucks. But we can't leave them."

We spoke in low tones, quieter than the TV chatter.

"No," I agreed. "We can't."

That said, mission creep—the modification of a plan in an operation—was dangerous. It upped the risks because instead of being focused purely on fighting and evasion, we now had to split focus to protect civilians.

Top gestured to the room across the hall. "Can't have these assholes dogging us while we're hauling bodies out of the basement."

"No."

He looked at me. "We can't allow anyone to sound an alarm. We lose control of the situation, and one of these fuckers makes a call or sends a text . . ."

"No," I said again.

His eyes bored into me. "This is going to get messy. Are you good?"

I knew what he was asking. He wanted to know if being back in the field and back to pulling triggers was going to shift me into the wrong headspace. I have three people in my skull at any given time, each emerging after some soul-crushing personal trauma when

I was a teen. The Modern Man was the part of me that was likely my default setting—optimistic, affable, civilized. The Cop was the professional aspect, and he was calculating, thorough, detail-oriented, and completely pragmatic. And then there was the Warrior, whom I sometimes called the Killer . . . and for years, that had been the worst aspect. Never being cruel to anyone who fell under the "innocent" category but being absolutely ruthless and merciless when it came to taking it to the bad guys. I've lost myself a few times in that feral headspace.

But that wasn't what Top was asking. A year ago, Kuga's henchman, Raphael Santoro, murdered my entire family. A bomb delivered as a Christmas present. I survived, barely. My lover, Junie Flynn, was badly injured. We've both recovered in body, but during that time a new personality emerged in my head. The Darkness. It stole my conscious control for days at a time while propelling me around Europe on a murder spree. For what it's worth, I never killed anyone who wasn't part of Kuga's empire. But the things I did to his people were appalling.

It took a lot to bring me back to me. I am nearly positive the Darkness is totally gone. Nearly. What mattered to me was that I felt completely in control. The Cop was driving the car, and I completely trust that part of me.

"I'm good, Pappy," I said, meeting his hard gaze and holding it until he finally gave a single small nod.

"Call the play," he said.

I tapped back into the team channel. "Jackpot, where are your toys?"

"Right where we need them, Outlaw. Locations have been sent to the team tac-computers. Take a tip—don't go anywhere near my toy box."

"Copy that," I replied. "Everyone Faraday your comms and weapons. Jackpot, pop an EMP in exactly three minutes."

"Copy that."

"EMP will take out the hostiles' phones," I continued, "but collect them anyway. Bug says he can retrieve data, contacts, emails, texts, and call logs even after they've been hit. Bunny, secure the prisoners with Sandman and then watch the first floor. Anyone shows up, send them to Jesus."

"Allah," corrected Belle.

"Whoever's taking DoorDash deliveries from fucktards," I amended.

"On it, Outlaw," said Bunny. His voice was closer to normal now, but there was still something off about him.

Top and I immediately pulled the bugs from our ears and stuffed them into our pockets. The equipment bags we all carried were designed to be Faraday bags—devices that will protect sensitive computer chips and other electronics from being destroyed by an electromagnetic pulse. The pockets on our combat clothes were the same.

Then Top and I went to work inside Russo's nest. We cracked open every computer and took the hard drives. We found at least thirty flash drives of various makes and storage capacities and swept them all into a bag. There were reams of notes in Italian, and they looked useful, so we took them, too. We moved very fast, listening all the time for sounds from the room across the hall.

Last thing I did was remove my watch. Then Top and I stepped very quietly out into the hall.

The EMP bomb we use is called a nightbird. It's not really bird shaped, but once it fires everything goes dark. All of the lights went out at the same time, darkening every building all across the compound.

We immediately replaced our comms, removed the rifles from the bags, and moved out into the hall. I finger counted down from three, and then we kicked the door. Almost at the same moment I heard the big *boom* of Bunny's combat shotgun two stories below.

The jihadists tried to make a fight of it as they swam up out of sleep and scrambled for their weapons.

They tried.

We were *not* firing Sandman at them.

CHAPTER 9
MADRASAT ALMAZRAEA SCHOOL
RÉGION DU LAC, REPUBLIC OF CHAD

Silence fell in the room, and I was aware of Top looking at me. Searching for some kind of psychic error message. It wasn't him questioning my authority as team leader. It was him being the world's finest wingman. If you can't trust Top's judgment, then you simply can't trust.

He said nothing, though, which told me that he felt there was nothing that needed saying. Hooray for sanity. I hope.

There was a sudden chatter of automatic gunfire from outside. AK-47s on full auto.

We hurried to the window and knelt on either side of it, activating the Scout glasses for night vision. But our angle was bad. That window looked out at an uninformative stretch of chain-link fence. We could not hear any answering fire, but those guns went silent. One, two, three, four.

Then nothing for one full second before a series of sharp explosions rippled through the night. There were screams buried within those blasts.

"The bad guys are in the toy box," said Andrea. "*Fa schifo essere loro.*" *Sucks to be them.*

I almost pitied the sons of bitches. The toy box is a euphemism for a kind of kill box that is an area in which there is no safe exit point if you're a bad guy. The idea is to understand the natural paths of men moving while under attack on known ground. Everywhere they think would be safe isn't. Andrea allowed for no safe exit routes. Run one way and you trip a wire that flings sparklers at your face. Sounds fun, and would be if it was the Fourth of July. Andrea's sparklers were miniature impact-charges that will blow a two-inch hole through anything short of titanium. Faces tend not to be titanium.

If the hostiles inside the toy box went another way, they stepped onto Andrea's version of a toe-popper, but instead of blowing off part of your foot—which it will do—it sends a fusillade of flechettes up into your groin. The flechettes are tipped with a neurotoxin. Very deadly and very fast.

All of the items in the toy box have self-destruct charges except for the wire. Andrea typically used analog tech for those toys because EMP bombs were becoming a bigger part of our infiltration process. Good old-fashioned short-wave radio signals were used to trigger detonation. Once we were clear of the area, he'd set off the cleanup charges. Nothing that could be recovered would be of any use in identifying who had been there.

Top walked quickly through the bunkhouse room, using single shots to make sure everyone who looked dead was dead. It was cold and without either mercy or remorse.

"Let's move." I scooped up Russo and slung him over my shoulder like the sack of shit he was. Top led the way, and as we reached the first floor, Bunny was there, his combat shotgun ready. I dumped Russo in a closet where no one would trip over him until we were ready to get out of Dodge.

"Jackpot," I called, "what's the count?"

"Including your numbers, we have twenty-eight up and twenty-eight down," he said. "All tangos accounted for. Cell phones collected."

"Do a sweep. Make sure. No surprises."

"Copy."

"Belle, watch for incoming foot, boat, or car. If it isn't ours, kill it."

"Hooah."

Bunny led Top and me downstairs. He did not go immediately to the door but instead knelt by the guard he'd killed, fished a package of syrettes out of the dead man's pocket, handed them to Top, and then showed us the inside of the guard's arm, revealing track marks.

"At first, I thought it was insulin. I don't know much about diabetes, but the more I thought about it the more I kind of remembered that insulin is clear. Like water."

Top removed a vial and held it up so we could both study it in the light. "My aunt was a diabetic. That's definitely not insulin."

"Could be treatment for anything," I said.

Top shook his head. "I don't think so. I saw some of this same stuff upstairs on the nightstand beside one of the guards."

I tapped the team channel. "Outlaw to Havoc. Check the bodies. Look for track marks on their arms, maybe inside of the elbow. And see if any of them have small packs of syrettes."

Less than a minute later, they each reported in. Every single guard had identical drugs. The needle marks, though, were on their thighs.

"Okay," I said. "Collect any syrettes you can find. We don't know what it is, so be careful."

As Bunny reached for the doorknob I said, "You good?"

He turned and looked at me. His face was wooden; he wore no smile of any kind. "Define *good*."

Then he opened the door.

The kids were in there. In a horror show. Trapped inside psychosis or drugs. I entered carefully and went to the first kid sleeping nearest the door, checking his arms and legs and throat. But I could find no needle marks on him. We checked the others. Nothing.

"Could be airborne," warned Top.

"Door wasn't airtight," I countered. "If it was in the air, that guard would have been doing something weirder than reading the sports pages."

They both looked at me. We hadn't brought biohazard suits or HAMMER suits or anything for biological warfare.

"Bunny, did you go into that room?"

"Yeah."

"You feeling anything?"

He paused a half second too long. "I'm good."

I was about to ask him again to make damn sure, but a voice stopped me.

I'll . . . never leave you . . .

It was a soft voice. Female. Familiar. An echo from a long time ago. And it was as achingly familiar as it was impossible.

I turned fast, but there was nothing and no one behind me.

"What's wrong?" asked Top, his gun barrel beginning to rise.

I'll . . . never leave you . . .

That voice. That promise. It reached out of the past and stabbed me right through the heart.

It was the voice of someone I loved for too brief a time. Someone I met during my first mission with Mr. Church. Someone who fought alongside me. Someone who saved the world.

Someone who died doing that.

I almost spoke her name aloud.

Grace.

Had I not been on active comms, I would have. Maybe before the whole Darkness thing I might have anyway.

When I turned—before I even began that movement—I knew that she wasn't there. She could not be there. Grace Courtland was buried in a hero's grave, and the world had moved on since then, turning and turning because she had made sure it could.

The air around me had turned cold. So deeply cold. The only warmth was my heart, and that was burning, melting, dripping down inside my chest.

I'll . . . never leave you.

"Outlaw?"

I heard Top's voice as if it came from a million miles away. And as an after-echo, I realized that it was not the first time he'd spoken my name. I took a breath and was in no way sure that what I would say would not come out as a scream, or a sob.

I said, "I'm good."

He gave me that look, asking without asking if the Darkness was once more taking hold. I forced a smile and shook my head.

"That will feed the scorpions. The baby will like that," said the one teen. "That will feed the scorpions. The baby will like that."

"Let's get this fucking job done and get these kids out of here," I said.

I drew my Snellig and waited until the others did as well. Top was the last to draw, and his eyes were still asking questions. I ignored them.

"Single shots," I said. "No double doses. Zip ties. Go."

Twelve kids, three of us. Four shots apiece.

No, these were not lethal rounds. But the effects of Sandman are terrifying and can leave a person emotionally traumatized for days. Inflicting that on top of whatever else these children were going through felt like the worse kind of abuse. We fired our dart guns. We secured their ankles and wrists with the zip ties. We carried them up the stairs and laid them in the entrance foyer.

But none of us could look each other in the eye.

INTERLUDE 3
UNKNOWN TOMB
NEAR THE RUINS OF THEBES
CITY OF LUXOR, EGYPT

THREE YEARS AGO

Opening the tomb door took a lot of time.

It would have taken all night if Aydelotte had wanted the door preserved. But the market for tomb doors was shallow and cheap. It wasn't something you built a museum exhibit or—more to the point—a private collection around. He never once had a buyer request a door.

Even so, even with Shock and the diggers chopping away at the copper seals, the door resisted them. Aydelotte found that amusing. The wind had helped uncover the tomb, but the actual tomb fought them. He almost mentioned this to Shock but left it. The inscriptions seemed to have rattled her, which was something he didn't think was possible.

"Here it comes," called Shock, and he shook himself from his musings to see the diggers removing a large chunk of the upper right corner. Shock then waved them back.

"What's wrong?" asked Aydelotte.

"Nothing," she said. "Just bugged about those warnings."

"What about them?"

"You remember the old story about the curse of King Tut's tomb?" she asked, speaking quietly so the diggers would not overhear. "How some of the people who entered the tomb died in unusual ways? One of the theories is that there were ancient pathogens trapped inside and that some people who entered became infected and got sick. Some even died."

"I heard about that, of course," said Aydelotte, "but I thought they disproved it."

She shook her head. "They proved that some of the deaths from the expedition financed by Lord Carnarvon and led by Howard Carter were not related to fungi. But some are still in doubt, and there have been verifiable infections." She made some small adjustments to the drone. "Look, when you think of Egyptian tombs like these, it's more than finding gold and other goodies. Remember there were corpses here, as well as other organic stuff like meats, vegetables, and fruits."

"Right. For the dead to feed on during their trip to the hereafter."

"Exactly. That stuff may have attracted insects, molds, bacteria, and those kinds of things. Well, some of the lab studies done here in Egypt and by university groups around the world have discovered that there are dangerous molds in there. *Aspergillus niger* and *Aspergillus flavus*, and they can cause allergic reactions ranging from congestion to bleeding in the lungs. Those are just the ones we know about. The Egyptian tourism board shut a lot of that stuff down in terms of what's gone out to the world press."

"So . . . ?"

"So let me send in the drone that has cameras and that portable BAMS unit."

"Wait? What? BAMS . . . ?"

"BioAerosol Monitoring System," she explained. "It's tech used for real-time environmental monitoring of microorganisms in the air."

"Like they have in some airports to prevent people from bringing anthrax on a flight?"

"Exactly like that. Except this is smaller, and you paid for it."

"I did? How clever of me."

"It was in Dr. Conti's budget. She gave this to me to bring."

"Ah. Smart lady."

Shock brought the drone over to the edge of the pit, activated it, and steered it with great delicacy in through the opening. Aydelotte stood close to her, both of them watching the live feed on a small high-def screen. She activated the drone's lights, and instantly the blackness of Pharaoh Siamun's tomb blazed in brilliant colors of car-

JONATHAN MABERRY

nelian red, lapis lazuli blue, and the untarnished and brilliant yellow of pure gold.

"God in his heaven," breathed Aydelotte. "This is amazing and . . . wait—go back. Turn it around. Look . . . *look!*"

There, half hidden by heaps of burial goods, was a granite slab of considerable size. Only when Shock steered the drone closer could they see that it was a box made from dull lead. There were markings all over it, and the corners and lid were sealed tight with copper.

"Damn," said Shock. "They really wanted this cat to stay locked away."

Aydelotte was impatient, and the night was burning off. "What does your scanner say about the air in there?"

Shock fiddled with the screen display and pulled up a smaller inset window. Her face creased into a worried frown. "Damn . . ." she said, drawing out the word. "It's a frigging soup in there. Fungi out the ass. Five, six . . . ten. Shit, it logged twelve kinds, and now it's saying there are some identified toxins in the atmosphere."

"How is fungi still active after all this time?"

"Not sure. It's damp in there, so maybe that's it. Dr. Conti will know. Not my field."

"Are we screwed, then?" groaned Aydelotte. "Is this all a waste of time and money?"

"Oh, ye of little faith." Shock laughed. "I told you, I spoke to Dr. Conti. She set me up. We have oxygen masks and those lightweight coveralls British cops use on crime scenes. And we have what Conti calls a bug box. It's a high-density particle collector. We'll be able to get all the goodies out—your antiquities and Conti's bugs. Christmas morning for everyone."

"That's excellent."

Shock paused. "You still haven't told me why Conti is in the mix. She's a biologist, and you set her up with a lab that would make any scientist pop a boner. I don't get it. Why her? And why would she want this stuff?"

Aydelotte's blue eyes settled on her for a long time. He wore a smile, but it did not reach as high as those eyes.

"I love you, kid, but this is above your pay grade."

That was all he said, and Shock knew better than to press it. Not when he used *that* tone of voice.

"You're the boss," she said, and turned away to begin telling the diggers to suit up.

Aydelotte stepped back and watched.

He never stopped smiling.

CHAPTER 10
RÉGION DU LAC
REPUBLIC OF CHAD

It took twenty minutes and about a gallon of sweat each to get the unconscious prisoners out of the basement and into one of the trucks parked behind the compound. Russo was trussed like a Thanksgiving turkey and, because we didn't want him to wake up and—more to the point—because we disliked the traitorous asshole, Top shot him again with Sandman. Double doses are particularly unpleasant. He groaned in his surreal sleep.

I'll . . . never leave you.

Those words still burned in my mind.

Grace Courtland. She was gone so long ago that I no longer thought about her ten times a day. Maybe only three. Since her I'd been involved with Violin. Then I fell in love with Junie Flynn. Fell hard. And I know she is the purest, strongest, best thing in my life. I never used to believe in all that "soul mate" woo-woo horseshit.

"Used to" being the operative words.

I know that I will always love Junie. Always. She is my heart, my hope, my joy.

But . . . Grace was someone so special to me. So important. And there is a part of me that will always love her. Even Junie knows this. She accepts and honors it because Junie is that kind of evolved. Her empathy runs miles deep. And she isn't the kind to be jealous of a ghost.

As we loaded the rescued teens into the trucks, I wondered what it was that happened to me down there. I know—for *sure*—that I heard Grace's voice. That's not even in question. Even as psychologically screwed up as I am, I know the difference between a sharply defined memory and actual spoken words. At that moment I would have bet everything I owned that her voice had spoken in that basement room.

What *was* in question was whether I heard her ghost or whether my head was still fucked up. The Darkness was gone, but did that mean I was free? Fixed?

I'm not easily frightened. But right then I was as scared as I have ever been. I didn't want my mind to be losing ground. Fighting my way back from the Darkness was the hardest thing I've ever done. I needed that win.

I'll . . . never leave you.

Was that a sweet whisper or a threat? Fuck me, I don't know.

Bunny must have seen how rattled I was because he couldn't even meet my eyes. Only Top—my rock, our one fixed point of level-headed strength—kept watching me.

I let the necessities of the job carry me through.

Remy drove, with Bunny riding shotgun. Belle was in the back with the prisoners. Top, Andrea, and I rode in a second vehicle, a Toyota SUV that had seen better decades.

We drove through the ink-black night, all of us nervous and alert. We had completed a mission, but we were carrying with us so many unanswered questions. I had a feeling when we got those answers, we weren't going to like them.

Not one damn bit.

INTERLUDE 4
THE SHEPHERDS
QUMRAN, IN THE JUDEAN HILLS

1946

He was looking for a goat.

That's all.

It was chilly, even for November, and Muhammed edh-Dhib wanted to find him, bring him back home, and see if there was enough light left to play some football with his cousins, Jum'a Muhammed and Khalil Musa.

In most ways it seemed like another late autumn afternoon in Qumran.

In no way was it actually normal.

"Did you find him?" called Khalil from down the slope. He was never a fan of climbing if he didn't have to.

"I can see him," Muhammed yelled, cupping his hands around his mouth. Even so, his words echoed and bounced off the hills and rocks.

"Then what's taking so long?" asked Jum'a. "Don't tell me you've been outwitted by a goat."

"Again," added Khalil.

Muhammed considered a stinging retort, but he'd gotten in trouble a few times already for using words and phrases lifted from adults who had been in the war, and he did not relish another night without dinner. Or the extra chores that went with it.

Instead, he thought evil thoughts about the goat, muttering promises to the animal about how lovely smoked goat tastes and how he would nominate this particular animal for the cooking pot.

The goat, eyeing him with the placid indifference of its kind, casually walked a few yards higher and moved onto a promontory that would make being caught even more difficult.

Muhammed wondered if goats were actually as devious and manipulative as they seemed. He was sure they were. As he climbed, he waved his switch a few times in what he hoped was an appropriately threatening gesture.

The goat mocked him with a derisive cry and showed no sign of looking threatened or nervous.

The young goatherd picked his way among the stones, avoided slipping on the loose pebbles half-buried in dry dust, winding his own way upward rather than falling for the trap of taking the goat's path. They had smaller, surer feet and could mince delicately through places that would have sent Muhammed tumbling down.

"It would be faster if you two helped," he called over his shoulder.

"No doubt," agreed Khalil.

"We're enjoying watching you show us how it's done," said Jum'a. "Very useful."

Muhammed bit back more curses and then cut a look heavenward and apologized to Allah. No fiery lightning bolts struck him down, so he figured foul language no one could actually *hear* was a relatively minor sin.

When he reached the top, the goat, contrary as they so often are, did not scamper away, but waited docilely while the boy looped a lead around its neck.

"Come on, you brat. Let's get back down to the—"

He stopped, noticing something he hadn't seen before. The hills on that part of the northeastern shore of the Dead Sea were deceptive—they looked solid but so often that was a sham, hiding dangerous deadfalls or caves in which scorpions waited out the hottest parts of the day, or where poisonous snakes coiled around their eggs.

This particular hill had been unmarked the last time he was there, but now there was a hole in it. A large one, easily big enough to stick his hand through—though he was too wise, even at his age, to do something like that. Instead, on a whim, he picked up a rock just a little smaller than a hen's egg and tossed it sidearm into the hole, a good throw that plunged through the center of the space and vanished immediately into blackness. Muhammed grabbed a second rock just in case something scuttled or slithered out.

Then he froze, head cocked to listen.

The rock had hit something. That was obvious, but the sound was strange. It wasn't the dull thud of rock on a cave wall. No, this was a thinner, higher sound. Like plates breaking. Or perhaps clay pottery.

He stood there, regarding the hole, trying to make sense of what he had heard. What could be inside that would make that kind of sound?

He tossed in a second rock and heard a similar sound. Not as loud or distinct.

"Are you planning on staying the night up there?" yelled Jum'a.

It snapped Muhammed back to the moment, and he turned and

looked down the slope. Jum'a had a football—old, dusty, scarred, poorly inflated—and was bouncing it from palm to palm.

He glanced once more at the hole, frowned, shrugged, took the goat by the lead, and climbed down.

In the morning, the three boys returned to the spot.

"I think this is a silly waste of time," complained Khalil.

"You think everything is a waste of time."

"Except football," said Khalil.

Muhammed ignored that. "It's just up here. Where I found the goat."

"I'm not sure I get why this is so important," said Jum'a. "So you heard a rock break something. Or *thought* you did. So what? Maybe it's shale. That breaks easy."

"Or maybe it just sounded like that," said Khalil, grunting as he followed the more nimble boys up the slope. "You know caves. Echoes and all. Could be anything."

"Or it could be hidden treasure," said Muhammed.

The other two boys shared a *here we go again* look.

"Sure," said Jum'a. "Mountains of gold waiting for us to find it so we can be rich. That's exactly what's in your cave."

"Don't make fun. You know what Uncle Abdel said about how they buried stuff all over this place."

"Your uncle Abdel found exactly one Roman coin," said Khalil. "And my dad said he probably bought it somewhere."

"Why would my uncle buy a Roman coin and then swear to Allah that he found it in a cave not half a mile from here?" demanded Muhammed.

"Because your uncle is always making up stories," said Jum'a. Since that wasn't entirely a lie, Muhammed let it be.

Instead, he said, "Stop complaining, we're almost there."

When they reached the top, the boys stood looking at the hole.

"It's bigger than it was last night," said Muhammed.

Jum'a touched the rim, and a chunk fell inward. "Not very strong. I bet we could open it up pretty easy."

They grinned at one another and began pulling at the edges, tearing away chunks of limestone. The hole grew and grew until they had an opening easily big enough for any of them to enter.

The day was bright and cloudless, and sunlight streamed past them and filled the entrance, revealing a much bigger cave than any of them had expected. They exchanged looks in which nervous uncertainty was only a thin veneer atop excitement.

Muhammed, having made the discovery, entered first, with Jum'a and Khalil close behind. They trod carefully, not entirely trusting the solidity of the floor. Suddenly he slipped and fell, tumbling down a steep slope to the bottom.

"Muhammed!" yelled his cousins. They plunged after him.

"I'm okay. Just bruised my knee. Ow!"

They pulled him to his feet and dusted him off; then they stood, looking around at the interior of the cave.

"What's that?" asked Jum'a, pointing.

Muhammed frowned. "What's what? Oh, wait, I see something. Khalil, move out of the light."

They crowded back to let the sun paint the cave with golden light.

"It's just old clay jars," said Khalil, disappointed. "See? That one's broken. I bet that's what you heard after you threw the rock."

They crept forward.

Their shadows fell across the contents of the shattered jars.

"What *is* that?" asked Khalil, nudging something with his toe.

"Well," said Jum'a, "it's not a bag of Roman coins."

They squatted down and poked around the debris.

"Just a bunch of old scrolls," said Muhammed, equally disappointed.

He tried to unroll one, but it tore in his hands, pieces fluttering down to the ground.

"Worthless junk," concluded Jum'a. "That's all."

They had found the first of what would come to be known as the Dead Sea Scrolls. That discovery would not change their lives very much.

They would, however, irrevocably change the lives of countless others.

CHAPTER 11
PHOENIX HOUSE

Getting our prisoner and the infected teens safely out of Chad airspace was time-consuming and difficult. Getting us all through Libyan airspace—where we were absolutely not allowed to be—was a nail-biter. The pilot skimmed the borders of Chad and Niger, shifting this way and that to follow a flight plan that was also *supposed* to take us through areas where sensor coverage was weakest. Even so, we were nervous as hell the whole way.

There was an experienced combat medic on board who had a scrambled sat-phone link to Doc Holliday. Once he had done a preliminary exam of the kids and treated the more serious wounds, Doc walked him through some other tests. Not sure what he was looking for, because he told me to leave him alone while he worked. So I sat with my team and watched his face grow less optimistic and more concerned with each minute.

At one point he looked at us. "And you have no idea what was done to them?"

"No."

"You found no medicines other than the syrettes the guards all carried?"

"That's right."

"There was no medical facility at the site? No lab or stores of medicines?"

"Not that we found," I said.

He blew out his cheeks, nodded, and went back to work. The teens groaned and writhed and twitched and wept in their drugged sleep.

Bunny looked pale and haunted and did not do a lot of talking. Belle, Andrea, and Remy were all silent, each of them probably taking emotional inventory as soldiers often do after an action of this severity. Lots of blank stares through the middle of nowhere.

Not too long after that, a call came in over comms. It was Church and Doc Holliday.

"Bunny," Holliday said, "Scott had me look at part of the footage from the body cams. When you were down in the room with those poor kids there was a moment when you looked—and here I use a

JONATHAN MABERRY

precise medical term—freaked out. You want to tell us what that was about?"

Bunny stalled for a moment, then blew out his cheeks. "It's nothing because it was nothing. I had this weird moment when I swear to God, I thought I saw Lydia and little Bradley." He paused. "Look, I saw those teens in there. They were all messed up and doing nasty stuff to each other and themselves and . . . I guess that hit me fast and hard."

"How long did that hallucination linger?"

"Oh, I wouldn't call it a hallucination, Doc. It was just a second. There and gone."

"You're sure about that? This isn't a time for macho displays of stoicism."

"Yeah. There and gone, like I said."

"Okay," she said uncertainly. "But when you get back, you come and see me and then you go and talk to Rudy Sanchez."

"I'm scheduled to go home for a bit."

"Wasn't a request, Bunny honey. You skip out on that and the next time I see you I'll kill you and swear you just up and died."

"Yes, ma'am," he said, and from the look on his face I knew he meant it.

"Good," she said. "Anyone else have a trippy moment?"

I asked the rest of the team, but everyone else shook their heads.

"What about you, Joe?" she asked. "Your heart rate was playing the conga drums, too."

"Just reacting to the kids," I lied.

"You wouldn't lie to me, would you?"

"Never," I said.

"Okay. See you boys back here."

The call ended. Bunny went back to where he was, and Top came over and sat down next to me.

"You good?"

I shrugged "The kids. That brought up some stuff."

"Too much stuff?"

I thought about that and answered truthfully. "No. I'm good. But there are a lot of questions I want answered."

He studied me, then nodded and simply said, "Yeah."

There was no more conversation the rest of the way. We slept—or pretended to sleep. I tried not to replay the sound of Grace Courtland speaking to me. I had not mentioned any of that to anyone. Church would bench me in a heartbeat. Somehow knowing that Bunny had had his own hallucination in a roomful of kids clearly tripping made me think it was just some side effect of whatever was done to them. The fact that the others weren't affected seemed—to me, at least—to be a result of the door being open for so long by then that anything in the air had simply thinned out.

It was a rationalization and probably too thin to stand up to scrutiny. Even so, I kept my own experience to myself.

I'll . . . never leave you.

It hadn't felt like anything conjured by some drug in the air. No way. It felt completely, terrifyingly real. I crossed my arms, nodded my chin down onto my chest, closed my eyes, and tried to sleep.

Tried.

The Osprey flew on and on.

CHAPTER 12
INTERVIEW ROOM C
PHOENIX HOUSE

Marco Russo sat in the room for hours.

Or it could have been days.

There was very little to help him mark the passage of time. Food was brought in with no recognizable pattern, and the menu was always the same. Quinoa and vegetables, water, coffee. Pushed through a slot near the floor.

Music played constantly, but it was a random and ever-shuffling series of classical pieces of varying length and style. No change of volume, and it was always just a bit too low for him to actually use as either entertainment or distraction. There was a cubicle with a steel toilet—no tank, no seat, no moving parts he could touch—and a steel basin for washing.

Russo was given no books, nothing to write on, nothing to fill the hours.

JONATHAN MABERRY

And the hours went on and on and on.

Several times Russo tried to tear the metal chair from the bolts that anchored it to the floor. And he failed each time.

He tried to kick the table loose, and failed, accomplishing only bruising on both feet.

The door was heavy steel, and any attempt to pull it open likewise failed.

There were no beams or struts or bars from which he could hang himself, had that been a choice. Russo had considered it.

Short of running headfirst into a wall, he had no out other than to wait for his captors to begin the interrogation. He sat and fretted. He yelled and screamed. He wept. He napped when he could. He rehearsed answers that would frustrate his captors. He rehearsed answers that would ingratiate him to them. He thought about the consequences of spilling everything. He wondered if he was going to end up in a black site and never be heard from again. He worried that his interrogators would wheel in a cart with power tools, bone saws, pliers, and a little generator with alligator-clip leads.

When the door finally opened, he nearly screamed.

The man who came into the room was a stranger. Tall, broad-shouldered, blocky, dressed in an excellent though understated suit. His face was impassive, with no expression of any kind.

The man brought a folding chair with him as there was only the one chair bolted to the floor. He unfolded it and sat on the far side of the small table.

"Who are you?" demanded Russo in Italian. "Where am I? I want my lawyer."

The big man said nothing.

In fact, he said nothing at all. Russo got up from his chair and once even charged around the table and made as if to grab the man. As if. Not actually. He stopped within inches of the act of commission. Then he withdrew his hands and stepped back.

The big man studied him, though his own eyes were hard to read. They were flat and gave nothing away. He made no threat, did not tell Russo to sit down again. He said nothing.

Russo eventually crept back and perched on the edge of his seat.

Waiting for the questions. The accusations. The threats.

He waited and waited.

After a long time—ten minutes or half an hour, Russo could not tell—the big man stood and folded his chair.

"Hey! Wait. Aren't you going to ask me anything?"

The big man knocked once on the door, and when it was open, he left.

Leaving Russo alone.

Again.

INTERLUDE 5
UNDISCLOSED LOCATION
AL-HASAKAH, SYRIA

FOUR YEARS AGO

Ayoob Alazaki agreed to meet the most important man in his life, and to do so in secret and under strange conditions. He agreed to all of this because their world was burning down.

Alazaki had been a schoolteacher in Yemen, but that seemed like a long time ago now. The last few years had changed his life so dramatically and completely that his old life seemed like it was decades past. He no longer taught school. Instead, he was the face and the voice of Al-zilal—the Shadows—a group of dedicated and uncompromising fighters who had split off from the main body of Daesh—Islamic State of Iraq and Syria—to act independently. Daesh, or ISIS, as the world press often called it, had been too thoroughly weakened, too frequently beaten, and too obviously unable to do what God required. Al-zilal would not accept defeat, no matter what degree of escalation was required of them. That was what drove Alazaki.

It's what made him proud to serve the will of God.

They met in a small house on an unimportant street in a village in Syria. The man he had traveled all this way to meet was a stranger to him, even though Alazaki would have gladly died for him. Would probably die at some point for that man.

Alazaki did not know his real name, only a Syrian nickname,

Harith al-Wazir, which meant "The Great Lion Who Digs in the Earth." It was his vision that had reignited the faith and, more critically, the optimism in the overall goals of the caliphate—to root out vice and enforce attendance at *salat* prayers; to crush out polytheism in all its forms; to tear down all churches and temples to false gods; and to promote the fundamental truths of the Sunni path. It was a hard life, and the road was often rocky and uphill, but what God required the faithful must undertake. Harith was steadfast in this, and he drew to himself the toughest, wisest, most dedicated fighters from various groups within the overall caliphate.

But Alazaki, despite being one of the most senior Al-zilal leaders, had never met Harith before, and even now did not meet him face-to-face. They sat on overstuffed chairs on opposite sides of a thin, opaque curtain. All Alazaki could see of the man he had sworn his life to follow was a stocky silhouette painted by lamplight onto the curtain.

Sentries and patrols kept them safe. The building had been thoroughly swept for bugs, and a portable radar kit mounted on the roof of a nearby grocery store watched the skies for combat and surveillance drones.

"Things are falling apart," said Alazaki.

"Things are always falling apart," said Harith. His accent was vaguely Syrian, but Alazaki guessed the leader had spent many years traveling or even living elsewhere. His wisdom and understanding of the Western mind were sophisticated in the way that only travel inspires. And there was the possibility that Harith wore a public face of some note and modified his accent to reinforce his anonymity when speaking frankly of matters of great importance to the cause. "But do not lose hope. A great storm is coming."

"Forgive me, my brother," said Alazaki, "but what does that even mean? *Al Assefa*. The Storm. We have heard rumors of something coming that will help us in these dark times. But so far it is only voices on the wind."

Harith chuckled and nodded. "Before I answer that . . . tell me, my friend, what do you feel is at the root of our recent defeats? Why have we been beaten back, crushed down, or chased away from so many places?"

"It is not lack of commitment," said Alazaki somewhat defensively. "Nor lack of numbers. We are recruiting more of the faithful all the time."

Harith spread his hands to acknowledge the point. "I agree. But are numbers what we most require?"

"It is important that we replace those lost in battle or arrest and . . ." He trailed off as he saw Harith's shoulders slump and heard a sigh. Alazaki cleared his throat and with more force said, "Fundraising in order to purchase weapons and equipment matters. Financial support from our most reliable sources, both private and national, has dropped. And prices rise all the time. Growing unrest in Europe, Central Asia, and America has dried up some sources; and other vendors are charging more because they know the supply has dwindled. We are increasing our fundraising in order to remain competitive."

"Ah," said Harith. "Money is always important. Tell me, how much do you care where that money comes from?"

Once again Alazaki did not directly answer the question. "There are many among the faithful who want to help but are afraid."

"Afraid or uncertain as to whether those donations are being used in the most effective way?" prodded Harith.

The schoolteacher stopped knotting his fingers and instead used one stiffened index finger to jab his palm as he made a series of points. "There are delays that become necessary when we have to educate people so that they understand the nature of what we are fighting for. Other sources of funding dry up when political situations change in their countries. Some important families or groups have had to use their funds to rebuild their own estates or towns or even countries. The American wars in Iraq and Afghanistan, and their actions in Pakistan and elsewhere, have frightened many away. The Syrian Defense Forces have relentlessly chopped away at our bases and strongholds throughout northeastern Syria. Key Daesh members have been captured or killed. Much has been done by their enemies to limit freedom of movement between our strategically placed bases, primarily by closing off smuggling routes that bring supplies and weapons to us. We—"

"Please," cut in Harith. "These are excuses, are they not? I am not blaming you, Ayoob Alazaki, but I have heard this defeatist rant from too many of our brothers."

"I am not being defeatist," protested Alazaki. "These are the facts. This is the position in which we find ourselves. Not just here in Syria but all over, and the heavy hand of the Americans can be felt everywhere."

"For now."

"Meaning what? You accuse me of making excuses, but what do you offer instead? Vague promises? Cryptic references?"

"Peace," laughed Harith. He leaned back and crossed his legs. "You are not wrong, my friend. Too many of our leaders have made grand promises and failed to deliver."

"What, then, do *you* offer?" asked Alazaki coldly.

"Much."

"Speak then," said the schoolteacher. "I am ready to listen and to hear."

Harith nodded and then paused for a moment, head cocked, as if he was the one who was listening, though from his physical attitude Alazaki wondered if the man was pretending to listen to some higher voice.

"Tell me, Ayoob Alazaki," said Harith quietly, "what do you know of the American known as Mr. Miracle?"

Alazaki thought the question random and bizarre. "He is a pest who is always on television telling the world what fiends we are for destroying what he calls 'precious and invaluable antiquities.' He calls us barbarians and savages."

"Yes, he says that. What *else* do you know of him?"

"What else is there to know? He or his agents are in every auction, in every market square from Cairo to Dubai to Jordan. Openly defying international laws, including those enforced by his own country. He claims that he is protecting those foul things that celebrate polytheism, that celebrate *shirk*. He says that we are wrong to destroy things that are an affront to Allah. He mocks us for *tawhid* even though he himself belongs to a monotheistic religion. He is Christian. He trots out his so-called friends among the Jews and even Islam to decry what we do."

"And yet," said Harith, "our own brothers in Daesh trade with him, and those like him, in order to raise the money we both know is necessary to do God's work."

"So, what if they do?" countered the schoolteacher. "If I was in a battle and lost my rifle, would I abhor an American gun found on the ground? The purpose to which I put it makes it a tool with which I serve God."

"Just so," agreed Harith. "So, you do not think very much of this Mr. Miracle?"

Alazaki sneered. "He is a rich American fool."

"Oh," said Harith, "I think you will find that he is much more than that. Very much more."

"And if he is? Why are we talking about him rather than how to acquire new and better weapons and technology?"

"Ah," said Harith. "You know as well as anyone how important it is to separate our public face from the truth of who we are."

Alazaki frowned. "What are you trying to tell me?"

"Mr. Miracle is not who he pretends to be," said Harith. "He is a man of great subtlety and resources. And it will surprise you to know that he has been a great friend to us in the past and will be an even better friend in the days to come."

"Are you making a joke?" asked Alazaki.

"I am not. I am going to arrange a meeting with you and a man named Sadiq who represents the American. This meeting will be of tremendous value to us."

"I do not understand."

"You will," said Harith. He paused, and when he spoke again his voice was charged with energy, with passion. *"Al Assefa*—the Storm—it is coming."

"Yes, so you have said many times, but what *is* it?"

Harith told him.

Ayoob Alazaki sat and stared at the curtain, at the silhouette of the Lion. He stared and said nothing because he was absolutely unable to force a single word out. His face felt bloodless, and his fingers felt as if they had turned to ice.

"Yes," said Harith, as if the schoolteacher had spoken, "the Storm is coming, and when it arrives it will sweep away the enemies of God."

Alazaki's heart was hammering in his chest with such force that he thought he was having a heart attack.

CHAPTER 13
UNNAMED ISLAND
EXUMA CAYS, THE BAHAMAS

The island probably had a name, but I didn't know or care to know what it was. We called it Leaf Island because there was a warm wind blowing exotic leaves across the sand.

It was small—about forty acres—with one house with a single large bedroom and a big bathroom, with a massive shower and a soaker tub built for two. The fridge was pre-stocked before we arrived. There was Wi-Fi, but it had an easy on/off switch. We left it off.

Junie and I flew to Grand Bahama and then rented a carbon-free electric seaplane of a kind I had never seen before. Something Free-Tech was developing for aid and rescue workers. This was, she said, a kind of shakedown flight. Just to make sure all the parts worked right.

If I felt, on some level, that it was a shakedown flight for me personally—to make sure all of my mental parts were still working right—then I could choose to ignore it. As often as I could.

Havoc team had delivered those poor kids from Chad. Doc Holliday gave everyone a physical that included blood work, body scans, and just about every other test she could come up with. I think they tested me for pregnancy, demonic possession, and brain gremlins, too.

"You're healthy as a goldurn horse," said Doc after the third day of tests. Then, with no trace of manners, hesitation, or deference, she asked, "How's your head? Any wires coming loose? Any dark shadows you want to tell me about?"

"Normally," I said, "I'd tell you to go fuck yourself."

"Oh, if I only could."

"But your question is fair."

"And . . . ?"

"Everything seems to be working fine," I lied.

I'll . . . never leave you.

Her outrageous appearance fools nearly everyone. The jokes, the cartoon hair and Dollywood clothes, the deliberately distracting curves. And she turned all of that up to eleven.

"You sure, honey? You know you can trust me."

"Doc," I said, "I can't trust you worth a damn."

Her smile was dazzling enough to give me a suntan. There was a warning in it, and I took it seriously. Even so, I wasn't going to tell her about hearing Grace Courtland's voice.

So she signed me out, and I flew to the Bahamas to meet Junie.

No matter where I meet her, it's not part of the real world.

Wait, hold on, that's not true. When I'm with her it's the only time I'm *in* the real world. Everything else—Havoc Team, RTI, Church, Doc, Bug, the things we do, the people we fight—is unreal. I work in Crazy Town; home is wherever I am with Junie Flynn.

When I saw Junie at the airport, even though I'd seen her ten days before, the sight of her took my breath away. You hear things like that in bad eighties rock songs and Victorian poetry, and I was always cynical about that. Until I met Junie. Now I get it. Now I understand what they've been trying to say all along.

It's not that there isn't enough air in the room, though it feels that way. It's that every molecule of my body wants to express something, say something, but words carried by breath aren't enough. So instead, it builds inside, as if fireworks are going off in my skin. My heart finds a new rhythm—a lot wilder but with control, without panic or fear. With love and longing that runs deeper than I can measure.

If you've been in love, you kind of get it. I've felt that in various frequencies with Helen and Grace and Violin. But that's not what it really is. I loved each of those women. Truly and without reserve.

But Junie is the woman I would want to be with for the rest of my

JONATHAN MABERRY

life. If there is any kind of afterlife, I want to be there with her, too. And you know what? I don't give a chrome-plated, rotating, nuclear-powered fuck if you think that's corny.

She came walking through a crowd of people going this way and that, and instantly those folks melted out of my perception. They vanished like ghosts, and I saw her. Tall, slim, with masses of wavy blond hair that looked as if she alone were being caressed by a summer breeze. A plain cream T-shirt and pale blue jeans under a gauzy print jacket thing that looked like it was designed for someone going to Woodstock. Rope sandals and toenails painted a different shade of coral than her fingernails. Oversize retro sunglasses with white frames pushed up on her head. No makeup, no jewelry.

She looked around the airport for a moment, her expression expectant but calm. And then she saw me, and that contact ignited her smile.

You can't stand in the presence of that smile and frown. It doesn't work like that. If you can read people and make any kind of accurate assessment of who they are, then that smile tells you what you need to know about her. The intelligence is obvious, the composure, the reserves of control are implied but not in play, the genuine empathy. The joy at being at peace in a world where she is both allowed and encouraged to do the kind of good work she does, the contentment of doing it well, and the delight in seeing the man who loves her.

And what did Junie see? A guy a bit over six feet. Gangly-looking, with a scuffle of blond hair that obeys no attempts at control and is seldom subject to any. Skeptical blue eyes filled with my full share of shadows, visible scars, a nose that has been broken more than once, big long-fingered hands, and a smile that probably looked like a skull's. I look like rough trade, and I am. I look like I've been through it, and I have. Not everyone sees it because not everyone can. Or wants to.

She can because she does.

Junie came to me without any of that slow-motion running. She walked up to me, her eyes seeing everything, knowing I hid nothing. Not from her.

"My love," she said, and I took her gently in my arms. We kissed, and neither of us cared a damn who else saw it.

One hell of a kiss, too.

A couple of hours later we were on Leaf Island.

The seaplane was secure between a pair of finger piers, with lots of soft fenders and properly tied lines to keep it snug. The forecast called for rain but not much in the way of heavy winds.

The island was leased from the Crown for ninety-nine years by Mr. Church, though as far as I know he has never stayed there. Never even bothered to name it. Not sure why he bought it, but he said that it was mine as often as I wanted it. He sent someone ahead to open the place up, air it out, stock it up, top off the fuel and water, tidy up the beach, make sure there were all the play toys we might want—sailboat, scuba and snorkeling gear, the works. That person was gone before we arrived, and for the next five days we were entirely alone there. That was as long as we could each get away. She had an important FreeTech job to do, and I had to go back and do some work related to Chad, Russo, and those kids.

I think Junie and I were dressed for maybe the first eight minutes we were on the island. Clothes began disappearing during our self-guided tour. We never did find my left sneaker or Junie's bra.

We made love on the floor of the living room. That's as far as we got.

Then we took a shower together. She is so beautifully made. Lean in the way strong women are—dancers, certain kinds of athletes. Not so honed down that the curves are gone, though. Under the fall of warm water, I soaped her all over until her pale, freckled skin glowed. Then I held her close as we kissed, the water sluicing down our bodies, washing away more than the residual oils and juices of our first round of lovemaking. I could feel tension draining away, melting like gray clay under the persistent spray.

We dried each other off and made some noises about going for a longer walk on the island. But as I blotted the water from her graceful shoulders and down between her breasts, I could feel the heat bloom in me again. It came on slower the second time, but no less intense. We stepped over the towels that had fallen to the tiled

JONATHAN MABERRY

floor, paused for a kiss in the doorway, and then lay down together on the big bed.

There are times it is all very adult, very erotic and intense.

And then there are times it is a ceremony of innocence so pure, so natural that it brings tears to the eyes. We lay for a timeless time and kissed. Then, without a word, she shifted and swung one leg over me. I helped with a guiding hand on her hip and as she settled down on me, we were joined. She was very wet and furnace hot, but neither of us felt the need for haste. This time it was about perceiving and knowing, sharing and understanding. This time it wasn't at all about sex. It was all about love.

She sat up, and I looked at her in the golden sunlight that slanted through the blinds. Her thighs and stomach were pale. She had scars from violence and those, too, had paled from the angry red of knitting wounds to a faint rose hue that somehow made those scars part of her beauty. Her pubic hair was a shade paler than straw and ten times paler than the wavy locks that fell around her shoulders and across her breasts. Her hips moved with an oiled grace that kept things building at a slow but steady pace. I didn't think I could come again so soon, but when I heard her breath catch as her orgasm began to build, and felt the reciprocal tightness within her, my body responded without pause. We came together with a shared gasp and then a full-throated cry of release that had so much more about it than sexual climax.

When we had toppled over the crest and ridden the aftershocks all the way to the last faint tremor, she collapsed down on me, doing it by degrees until she lay atop me. We kissed, sharing the same heated, ragged breath.

Sleep took us both.

I think we'd spoken maybe forty words since arriving on the island.

We hadn't needed any of those words.

CHAPTER 14
INTERVIEW ROOM C
PHOENIX HOUSE

Marco Russo had lost track of time.

After the big man's visit, he yelled for a while. Then he curled into a tight ball under the table and wept.

He slept.

He used the toilet, which was in a tiny cubicle in one corner.

He waited and talked to himself and pounded on the door.

When the big man returned, it was not in response to anything Russo did. The door opened, and the man came in with the folding chair, set it up, sat. All in silence.

"Please . . ." begged Russo.

After a long time, the man stood up and reached for the folding chair.

"No! For god's sake, *say* something. Ask me something. Anything." Russo's voice rose and rose until the last word was a shriek.

The big man left the room without a single word.

Russo beat on the door until his hands were throbbing lumps of pain. He sank down and leaned against it and prayed to a god he did not believe in. He prayed to his mother, whom he hated. He prayed and begged and sobbed.

Without context or any form of measurement, time becomes infinite.

Infinity is a concept the human mind is unable to properly grasp.

In that little room, time lost all of its meaning. Russo could not tell if it passed or if his own mind had snapped.

CHAPTER 15
UNNAMED ISLAND
EXUMA CAYS, THE BAHAMAS

Junie and I sat together on a big bamboo swing on the front deck of the house, watching the sun set. It was one of those evenings where the sun, feeling really sporty, decided to trot out all of its most dramatic colors. Maybe that big burning fusion reactor in the sky was stoned and we were seeing its hallucinations. If so, it was having a nice trip.

It was the fifth of October, and it was a day that should somehow be cut into stone on some lasting monument or marker. It occurred to me that I have had substantially fewer than forty October fifths. Somehow that didn't seem like a lot, or even enough. And this one was a classic. There are times you can feel the hammer and chisel cutting a particular date into that marker. Junie and I had not had that many of them. That seemed unfair. People in love like we were should have had many more behind us and uncountable days like this ahead.

Yes, I know that is saccharine-sweet romantic garbage. Add any dissenting opinions to my list of things I will never burn up calories worrying about. The setting sun agreed with my assessment. So did, I'm sure, my lady.

We sat saying nothing for a very long time and watched the sun spill its paintbox all over the ocean.

Later, Junie leaned sideways, her head resting on my shoulder.

"No Darkness," she said.

"No Darkness," I agreed.

It was a new part of our shared vocabulary. Not a question. It was a statement that I knew meant she could see none in me. It was my way of saying I felt none. Not even when I heard the faint and receding echo of Grace Courtland's words.

Much later, when the sun was just resting on the horizon, she turned and looked up at me.

"Did you tell Rudy that you went back into the field? About hearing Grace's voice?"

I hesitated. "Not really."

"Not really meaning 'no'?"

"Yeah."

"Why not?"

I smiled. Almost a wince. "Because he would freak out, and that vein in his head would start throbbing."

"And you think that's fair?"

I laughed. "No. I am being a total chickenshit coward."

She punched my arm. Pretty hard.

"Hey!"

"Rudy is your best friend, Joe," she said. "He's stood by you through everything. Why close him out now?"

"You know why."

Junie sat up and half-turned to face me. "He can only *recommend* that you stay out of the field. Rogue Team isn't the military. Church makes up his own rules, and to a great degree so do you. Rudy can't force you to stand down."

"But he can make a big damn fuss about it."

"Don't be such a baby."

"Hit me again like that and I might cry and kick my little legs."

She *did* punch me again. Just a little bit harder, too.

"Some pacifist you turned out to be," I said.

"I'm peaceful by choice, Joseph Edwin Ledger. I am not incapable of kicking your ass."

I held up my hands in surrender. "Okay, okay, I'll tell Rudy."

Her blue eyes caught and held mine. "Truth?"

"Truth," I said. And, sadly, I meant it.

Junie studied me a moment longer, then settled back against my arm. She kissed the place she'd punched.

"It hurts," I said.

"Oh, grow a set, you sissy."

That started a tickle fight. It spilled off the porch. I chased her all the way around the house, down to the beach, through the surf, and back up onto the deck. She let me catch her as she was going into the living room. I fake-tackled her, and we fell into the hall in a kind of controlled/uncontrolled deliberate fall. I love how her freckles seem to glow when she is either turned on, angry, or laughing. She was two of those three things.

We made love right there.

And in bed.

And many more times in dreams . . .

CHAPTER 16
INTERVIEW ROOM C
PHOENIX HOUSE

Marco Russo twitched in his sleep.

He was caught inside a nightmare of chase and pursuit. Sometimes he was the hunter, but that kept flipping on him, turning him into the prey for longer and longer stretches of the dream, until all he dreamed was a hopeless, headlong flight from an enemy he could not see.

In the dream he crashed through forest foliage—leaves, branches, sticky vines—and then across endless fields of grass so tall he could not see what it was that pursued him. At one point in the dream, as he reached the end of that field, to his shock and horror, he saw that it terminated in a cliff that plunged thousands of feet to a rocky crevasse below. He teetered there on the edge, knowing that death was waiting for him no matter what he did.

It took what little courage was left in him to turn.

Behind him was a figure—tall, broad-shouldered, shrouded in shadows that erased any details except for two pinpoints of burning red light. Eyes of fire.

"*No! Leave me alone*," he screamed, and in screaming he woke.

To find the big man seated at the table across from him.

For a moment—just a fleeting, uncertain, semi-doze of a moment—he thought he saw red flames flickering behind the big man's tinted glasses.

CHAPTER 17
UNNAMED ISLAND
EXUMA CAYS, THE BAHAMAS

We flew back to Grand Bahama on the fifth day.

Even with the apprehension of what was going to happen when I fessed up to Rudy, I don't know if I was ever as relaxed as I was that day.

At the big airport, Junie boarded a flight going one way, and I took a different jet going back to Greece. I think I smiled all the way, believing that the world, except for a few nasty things here and there, was also relaxing. Maybe it would be a good autumn. Maybe no one would have to die in pain or suffer at the hands of madmen. Maybe those teenagers would recover from whatever drugs had been used on them and be normal and healthy afterward. Maybe Russo would cough up the information we needed to shut down a big part of what Boko Haram and ISIS had cooking.

Maybe, maybe, maybe.

As my flight climbed into the big blue sky, I think I believed that things were going to work out for a change.

I meant that with hope and optimism, with almost none of my usual cynicism.

The Universe, perverse as it ever is, took that hope as a challenge.

INTERLUDE 6
DR. CONTI'S LAB
PIRATE LAB
UNDISCLOSED LOCATION

THREE YEARS AGO

Jason Aydelotte stood on one side of a wheeled stainless-steel table. Facing him on the other side was Dr. Giada Conti. She was a middle-aged stick figure with a vibrancy that made her look as youthful and happy as a twelve-year-old girl.

Placed on the table was a large, reinforced covering box made of a kind of plastic used in BSL-4 biological research containment hot rooms. Inside that box was a smaller one about the size and dimensions of a hardcover book: her bug box—the one Shock used to collect the fungi and other biological specimens from the tomb of the Mad King. Special reactive tape was placed neatly along every seal; should the tape be pulled off or tampered with, it would undergo a color change warning of the seal breach.

The larger box had two openings with tear-resistant gloves inside. When Aydelotte had come into the lab, Conti had both her hands inside those gloves so she could take preliminary samples. He stood watching as she swabbed the outside of the bug box. Those swabs were numbered by a computer that fed adhesive tags that she attached to the swab sticks. Then she carefully removed the tape and placed that in a biohazard bag for later analysis.

She glanced at Aydelotte before opening the bug box, and he gave her a tight smile and nod. Conti took a steadying breath and then opened the box. When nothing actually leaped out, Aydelotte exhaled air he had been holding in his chest.

There were slots in the floor of the covering box, and as she gathered her samples on slides and adhesive test strips, she fitted each into a slot and then stepped on a pedal attached to the bottom of the wheeled table. This triggered the analytical computers built onto the table's bottom tray. Data began appearing on a row of medium-size screens on one wall of her lab. She glanced at them, frowned, nodded to herself, and continued working.

"What are you doing?" he asked. "Looking for a virus?"

Conti paused. "Looking for tetrads, actually."

"The hell is a tetrad?"

"Microbes. All sorts of fun little things like bacteria, fungi, algae, viruses, and protozoa."

"Are there a lot of those around?"

Conti gave him a pitying look. "You probably won't like my answer."

"Try me."

"Mr. Aydelotte," she said, "microbes are everywhere. Each square inch of skin has about a hundred thousand bacteria."

Aydelotte looked at his hands and shivered. "Okay, I suddenly need a shower."

"It would be very hard to find any surface that has no microbes. And some can live on ordinary household surfaces for hundreds of years. But . . . don't get too scared. Most don't survive very long. HIV, for example, lives only a few seconds on a surface."

"So . . . I can't catch the clap from a toilet seat?"

"Not unless you're having sex with an infected person on that toilet seat."

"Oh . . . yuck."

"And, not to be too pedantic, but AIDS isn't the clap," she said, then changed the subject. "Survival depends on several factors, though moisture is key," said Conti. "It's fair to say that humidity makes a big difference, because no virus or bacteria can survive on dry surfaces with a humidity of less than ten percent. They require moisture and nutrients that encourage breeding, like food particles, blood, skin cells, mucus. Here's a tip . . . throw out your kitchen sponge after a few days. Those things are breeding grounds for all sorts of little monsters. Temperature also matters, and there are bacteria that thrive at room temperature—and *Escherichia coli*—E. *coli*—comes immediately to mind—and some that like it a bit chilly."

"I will make a point of bathing in Purell." Aydelotte gestured to the big plastic box on the cart. "So, what do your gizmos tell you?"

"Well, right off the bat the sensors tell me that there are no active viruses—which is what I expected, given this box and its contents are a few thousand years old. Understand, most respiratory viruses can survive on surfaces for periods from roughly a half an hour to a few days. If you want to nitpick, then it comes down to the size and type of particle the virus is contained in, the temperature, the humidity, the characteristics of the surface, and so on. Most viruses of this type tend to survive better in low temperatures and in high humidity or wet conditions. Larger droplets with more liquid probably mean longer survival. The virus can be found in the air for up to three hours when aerosolized, on surfaces such as stainless steel and plastic for up to three days, though the median survival rate is about thirteen to sixteen hours; on cardboard it's a few hours; and on copper—which you and Shock found a lot of in that tomb—then it's just a few hours. So, there is really no way for there to be an active virus in any of what you found. Not unless someone handling it had a virus and inadvertently transferred it, but even then, it's been too long since you found it."

"That's comforting."

"Somewhat," said Conti. "We're changing our understanding of microbial survival all the time. A group of French scientists discovered a thirty-thousand-year-old virus recovered from Siberian permafrost that came back to life once thawed. Although that particular virus poses no threat, it opens the door to the possibility of other and more dangerous viruses that have been trapped in permafrost. Climate change is doing more than causing more intense hurricanes. As the planet warms, permafrost thaws, and anything trapped in it becomes exposed to the air, particularly when the ground is drilled or excavated. And that disturbance is happening more and more, because this newly exposed ground becomes potentially farmable land. We actually don't know the full potential because we don't know what has been frozen. The inventory of viruses grows at a fantastic rate constantly. I mean . . . that one virus—*Pithovirus sibericum*—is in a class of giant viruses that were discovered only about twenty years ago." She paused. "But I'm not finding any viable viruses in the bug box."

"Okay, so no super flu or any zombie virus?" he said, smiling.

"I think we're safe from the zombie apocalypse."

"Bacteria . . . ?"

"That's a whole different kettle of fish. Bacteria are hardy little bastards. Bacteria don't have what you'd called a fixed life span because they don't grow old. When bacteria reproduce, they split into two equal halves, and neither can be regarded as the parent or the child. You could say that so long as a single one of its descendants survives, the original bacterium does, too."

"That's scary."

"Oh, yes. There have been quite a few cases of bacteria surviving in permafrost. It gets even scarier when you realize that bacteria can turn themselves into spores with a tough coat to protect themselves from dry conditions. Bacterial spores have been successfully revived from two-hundred-fifty-million-year-old salt crystals found in New Mexico back in 2000."

"Jesus."

"I know. It's very exciting," she said, beaming. "Back in 1995, microbiologist Raul Cano and his team successfully revived twenty-five to thirty-five-million-year-old bacteria from ancient bees that were encased in amber."

"Jurassic bees," quipped Aydelotte.

"Well . . . no. You can't trust the science you see in blockbuster movies. Sorry."

Conti fed more swabs into the slots.

"I'm already finding some bacterium, but it'll take a bit to classify them," she said. "What I'm mostly finding a lot of are fungi. Now, generally speaking, fungi have a pretty short life span, though that does vary quite a bit from species to species. Some live as short as a day, while others can survive anywhere between a week to a month. You said that the tomb was unusually damp? Runoff from the Nile, or an underground river?"

"Yes. So, tell me . . . is anything in that bug box dangerous?"

"Depends on what you mean."

"As in alive and able to infect or whatever the right word is."

She studied him. "You're concerned because of the warnings on the tomb, the copper seals, and the additional warnings on this lead box?"

"Yes. The 'King Who Went Mad' or the 'King Who Saw Shadows.' Surely there's something to it. Shock told me that copper had natural antibiotic qualities."

"Oh, there's no mystery as to why the Egyptians who entombed that pharaoh sealed the doors and the lead box with copper. Bacteria, yeasts, and viruses die pretty quickly when on a copper surface. The ancients knew this as far back as the fifth and sixth millennia BCE. And the oldest *known* medical use of copper to sterilize chest wounds and drinking water was mentioned in an ancient Egyptian medical text called the Smith Papyrus, written between 2600 and 2200 BCE. Greeks, Romans, Aztecs, and others used copper or copper compounds to treat everything from headaches to intestinal worms. More recently, in the nineteenth century, there was a burst of new research about the medical potency of copper. For example, laborers working in copper mines were less likely to catch cholera. For a while, there were trace elements of copper in all kinds of treatments for things like eczema, impetigo, scrofulosis, tubercular infections, lupus, syphilis, anemia, chorea, and facial neuralgia . . . well, it's a long list."

Aydelotte nodded and gestured at the bug box. "I need to know what's in there. Everything. Even if it's all dead, I want to know, because maybe we can rebuild it or whatever you'd call it."

"Finding out should be easy enough," said Dr. Conti. "If I may ask, what do you hope to accomplish?"

He looked at her for a long time, his smile as merry as Scrooge on Christmas morning. "I need to know what kind of fun I can have with it."

Dr. Conti frowned. "Define 'fun.'"

MR. MIRACLE
PART 2

ONE WEEK AGO

The past is the beginning of the beginning and
all that is and has been is but the twilight of
the dawn.

—H. G. WELLS

CHAPTER 18

PHOENIX HOUSE
HEADQUARTERS OF ROGUE TEAM INTERNATIONAL

"What do you know about the Dead Sea Scrolls?"

I looked across an acre of desk at my boss, Mr. Church. I shrugged and said, "Just what I've seen on Nat Geo. Bunch of ratty old religious stuff found in some caves in Israel. Vatican has them locked up."

Church gave me one of *those* smiles. "Nearly every part of that is incorrect."

CHAPTER 19
PHOENIX HOUSE
HEADQUARTERS OF ROGUE TEAM INTERNATIONAL

Before we get to that, though . . .

Let's be real. It's been a rough couple of years. For the world, for my family, for me. For the people who are so damned unlucky that they seem bound to share some of my karma. People have died, wars have started, politicians on both sides of the aisles have stopped even pretending to care about the people who elected them, and I went a little crazy.

Okay, crazi-*er*.

In the military they call it "going off the reservation." Yeah. Something like that. I scaled the fences of my sanity and went romping through a surreal and dissociative landscape. I lit some fires and littered the ground with shell casings and spilled blood. The fact that they were all bad guys is very cold comfort. There were whole stretches where I didn't know who I was, where I was or, much worse, *what* I was.

But a year had passed since I came back to myself.

Signs of relapse are what Top was looking for back in Chad. He had every right to look, to ask, to be concerned. After all, it wasn't just my mental health that was in question. I was leading a team on a mission where people could die. If I made the wrong calls because my inner demons were wrestling for the steering wheel, then a lot of people could die. Top, always the sergeant, was concerned for the team. For me, too, but more for the others. As it should be.

Some people in Rogue Team did not think I was ready for a gig like that. Scott Wilson, the chief of operations, was dead set against it and had apparently said so to Mr. Church in unfiltered terms. More important, Rudy Sanchez did not like it one damn bit.

Trauma, PTSD, and related things are his specialty. That's why Church hired him, because Rudy understood how much violence gouges a mark in everyone. He was the one who put me back together after my girlfriend, Helen, committed suicide. When she and I were fifteen, we were jumped by a group of older teen boys. They beat me so savagely that all I could do was lie there, gasping, bleeding, screaming, as they raped and brutalized Helen. That incident fractured both of our psyches. She went deep, deep into herself and never really found her way out of the shadows. I became moody and violent but got involved in martial arts in the hope it would give me structure and focus. Then, when we were in our early twenties and no longer a couple, Helen's sister called me, worried because she was unable to reach Helen through phone or text. She asked me to go see if Helen was okay.

But she was not okay. I found her on the floor near the bottle of drain cleaner she'd swallowed. She had been there for days.

I lost myself right there and then. I could feel my mind breaking apart because this was too much to deal with. Far too much.

Both Helen and I had been under treatment by a brilliant young psychiatrist: Rudy Sanchez, newly moved to America from Mexico. He took it hard, too, because it was the first patient he'd ever lost to suicide. And I think that's one of the reasons Rudy focused so completely on me. He did not want to lose anyone else. For years, all through college, I had sessions with him. By then the fractures in my head had resolved into individual personalities. It was not the

JONATHAN MABERRY

textbook version of multiple personality disorder. It was a unique situation, and Rudy worked with me. He helped me find a way to address each fragmented personality, and over time we eliminated most of them, leaving only the Modern Man, the Cop, and the Warrior. They seemed permanent, and I was at peace with them.

He helped me use those personalities in ways that helped me when I joined the army and, after discharge, the Baltimore Police Department. I flourished in my strength and found purpose in my work. When new traumas moved like storms through my life, Rudy's wisdom and steady hand guided me through. I weathered my mom's death from cancer. I endured the death in combat of a new lover, Grace Courtland. And there were other black storms that tore through the landscape of my life, personally and professionally. By then I was part of the Department of Military Sciences and doing measurable good on a global scale. It was as if those three aspects created within me a set of abilities, coupled with understanding, that turned me into the kind of scalpel Mr. Church needed to perform surgery on terrorists who were using cutting-edge science to try to tear down the world.

Then Santoro delivered that goddamn bomb on Christmas Eve, killing everyone in my family. My dad, my older brother Sean; his pregnant wife, their two young kids. Even the family dog. All of them, gone in a flash and a bang.

The Darkness was my mind's response. Rudy tried to help, but I think the Darkness was afraid that he *could* help, and that it would prevent me from doing what I *wanted* to do. And so I went off the radar. I used every bit of spycraft I'd learned as an agent of the DMS and RTI. I went to war with Kuga's organization and did so under a very black flag.

Somehow, I managed to reclaim myself. And I even finished that mission as me, not as the Darkness.

Rudy was waiting for me when I got back. We did a full year with a lot of therapy, a lot of hard work, tough questions, difficult answers. He gave me every kind of test it is possible to give a human being.

I aced the tests and gave what I believe was good value on the therapy couch. I admitted to what I did and told the God's honest truth that no matter how deeply I looked inside the haunted house that is my head, I couldn't find a single trace of the Darkness. Whatever it was that owned me was gone. That's not wishful thinking. I truly believe it.

Then my boss asked if I was ready to go back to work.

The work I do is *not* typically handled by people whose psychological state is—to use the precise clinical terminology—equivalent to a bag of rabid mole rats. There is an understandable concern that psychic fractures leave a weak place, a stress point that can collapse under the right—or wrong—kind of weight or pressure.

Rudy went blue in the face yelling at the boss, Mr. Church, telling him I was in no shape to go to a live taping of *Family Feud*, let alone to a politically troubled foreign country on the trail of bad guys. Rudy swung back and forth between clinical analysis and impassioned pleading. I watched his swarthy face get redder and redder.

I did not tell him that I'd agreed to lead a mission. Like a coward, I slipped away with my team and went to Chad.

To say that he was not a happy camper is perhaps the grossest understatement in history. There's a vein in Rudy's forehead I'm afraid is going to pop any minute now. When I got back from Africa, he demanded that he and I meet with Mr. Church to discuss things.

Discuss. Yeah. Sure.

Rudy laid into Church hammer and tongs. Things got really loud. Church endured it all, nodding at every pointed Rudy made, being agreeable in every way but the way Rudy wanted.

Then, when Rudy paused to take a breath, Church said, "This decision to continue field work is ultimately Colonel Ledger's."

Rudy, who is a civilized and cultured man, a respected medical doctor, and perhaps the kindest human being I've ever known, fired back with four-, seven-, and ten-letter words that would have stripped the grain out of a hardwood floor. I mean, I've heard him curse before. Maybe . . . nine times in all the years I've known him, but this was new. I felt like I should be taking notes.

I sat in one of the two expensive leather visitor chairs in Church's private office, impressed and—I'll admit it—feeling a little scared of Rudy. On a different level, I was mildly annoyed that they were talking *about* me but not *to* me. I might as well have been a potted plant. And a plastic one at that.

"Take a breath, Doctor," said Church when Rudy wound down. "I have read your evaluation notes. There is nothing in there that indicates that Colonel Ledger is unfit for duty."

"Except the part where I say exactly that," growled Rudy.

"If you would read his after-action report from—"

"I read it. Load of horseshit."

"Have you read the report filed by Top Sims?"

"Yes," grudged Rudy, "but it changes nothing. Yes, I appreciate that they rescued a dozen teenage prisoners. I appreciate that they apprehended a criminal terrorist sympathizer, but at what cost? Things could just as easily have gone terribly wrong."

"That was an opinion, which of course I took into consideration," said Church. "But the substance of your psychological evaluation indicates that over the last several months Colonel Ledger had demonstrated remarkable resiliency in both his recovery and his attitude. Prior to my sending him into the field, he performed with top marks in every single combat drill, even live-fire drills that were specifically tailored to provoke negative emotional reactions. He has made so complete a recovery from what happened that I felt he was mentally and emotionally stable enough to return to work."

"Oh, *really*?" Rudy fired back icily. "And when did you get your medical degree?"

"Quite a few years before you did, Doctor," replied Church.

That should have been a conversation stopper. But Rudy brushed past it as if he already knew it and didn't much care. I found it endlessly fascinating, but now wasn't the time to start that conversation. I sat there, being the potted plant, keeping my mouth shut.

Rudy took a breath, regaining a thin slice of decorum, and said, "Joe has endured far more than his fair share of emotional trauma— setting aside for the moment all of the physical damage. We came to believe that his Warrior/Killer personality was his 'dark side.' But then the Darkness emerged, and he lost all perspective, all control over those three core parts of himself. He lost himself. That was born of the horrors when his family was murdered, and he held himself responsible, accountable. The Darkness consumed him, and we both know the extreme lengths to which he went seeking redress."

"We have agreed that there may have been outside influences amplifying that aspect," said Church.

"No," snapped Rudy, slapping his palm sharply on the desktop. "You don't get to blame it all on Nicodemus and say Joe's all better now because Nicodemus is not currently active."

Church reached for his plate of vanilla wafers, took one, tapped crumbs off it, and took a small bite. His hands were visibly scarred, but he no longer wore the black silk gloves. I wondered if they were healing or if he just stopped caring about how people might react to his scars. "If I thought Colonel Ledger was a danger to himself or to others, I would not have allowed him to return to active-duty status."

"Perhaps you need to blow the dust off of your medical degree," said Rudy in a tone as scathing and officious as a Broadway critic savaging a bad play. "After all Joe has been through, on all levels, he should consider retiring from *all* field work. He's done his part. More than his part. He has saved the world. It's incredible that I can say that without exaggeration or fear of contradiction. More than once."

Church is a big man. Blocky, powerful, somewhere in his sixties but looking like a fortysomething who could disassemble an Abrams tank and beat you to death with the pieces. Former field guy who is the kind of person you want running an organization like Rogue Team International. No red tape, no bullshit. Fighting the war. *The* War. Good guys fighting the kind of bad guys no one else can handle. I was half his age, and I wouldn't try him. I'm crazy, but I'm not stupid.

He leaned back in his chair and considered Rudy for a silent three count. "I will always appreciate your expertise and insights, Doctor," he said calmly. "However, I ask that you trust my judgment in how I run my teams and how I use those teams to fight this war. If he wishes to remain an active field team leader, then I will accept that and use him in any way that I see fit."

Rudy got to his feet. He is thicker around the middle than he used to be and has had some of his own physical trauma—glass eye and titanium knee earned from the bad luck of working with Church and me. He has a Mexican face that is an even split between his Spanish forebears and some obvious Mayan blood, and he sounds exactly like Gomez Addams from the Raul Julia movies. Very dignified. Usually the adult in any given room.

He bent forward and slapped the plate of cookies off the desk with such vicious speed that they flew twenty feet and shattered a little Chinese vase that probably cost more than my education.

"Fuck you, you heartless bastard," he said in the coldest voice in town.

He didn't even look at me as he left.

CHAPTER 20
MACHANEH YEHUDAH MARKET
JERUSALEM, ISRAEL

"Are you Mr. Miracle?"

The man in the white suit turned from examining a display of ornate and brightly colored Arabian lanterns. He was in his late forties, solidly built though with a comfortable belly. He had thick hair going gray and a lustrous white beard. His smile was affable, amused, interested.

The person who'd called him was a tall and very thin woman with a northern English accent, black hair in a tight bun, and a tailored suit that was perhaps not the best choice for Egypt in the summer. Her pale face was beaded with sweat.

"That's not actually my name," said the man. "It's Aydelotte. Jason Aydelotte. My company is called Miracle Acquisitions. And you are . . . ?"

Instead of offering a hand she produced a slightly wilted business card. "Rhona Sykes-Weller."

"Ah, I've heard of you," said Aydelotte, taking the card and studying it. "You're with the mission group? The New Presbyters?"

"Yes," she said, her smile quick to appear and vanish. Her default setting was that of guarded interest as a veneer over natural austerity. "I was told that you might be at the market today. They said that you like to browse markets like this all through the Middle East, looking for curios and lining up customers to buy your antiquities, and Thursdays were your common day to be here. And so, I came looking for you."

The Machaneh Yehudah Market was thick with a midafternoon crowd composed mostly of tourists from scores of nations. The hum of chatter, mingled with several strains of music from different shops, created a wall of sound that was as useful as a cone of silence.

Aydelotte beamed. "And now you've found me, Ms. Sykes-Weller. I am actually waiting for a business colleague, but I have a few minutes. How may I be of assistance?"

"Sir, if this is a bad time, I—"

"*Sir*? No, no, no, my dear. Please, call me Jason. Maybe I call you Rhona? Yes? Excellent. You were saying?"

She cleared her throat. "If you've heard of our organization, then you know that we are working to build a museum in Gateshead on the River Tyne."

"I thought I detected a bit of a Geordie accent. I'm familiar with the area. Lovely place," said Aydelotte. "Tell me, Rhona, what *kind* of museum are you building?"

"Why, a Christian one, of course."

"Of course."

"We want to collect and preserve proof of the Almighty and his blessed Son," she said, and there was in her cadence a suggestion that she was reciting, at least in part. "We want to collect objects from the Holy Land, of course, but also include within our collection artifacts that show the growth and expansion of Christianity, while also calling attention to its roots in Judaism."

"Seems reasonable."

In Aydelotte's ear, a woman's voice said, "She's legit, boss. Facial recognition confirms she's who she says she is. Looks like this is one of those instances of pure coincidence. Should we proceed or abort?"

"Tell me more, Rhona," said Aydelotte, which also alerted Sharon, the woman running overwatch for him, to know that he did not mind the casual interruption. There was still plenty of time before one or both potential bidders were due to meet him by the lantern shop. The phrase *tell me more* was the signal to Sharon.

"We have been fundraising for more than the building of the physical museum," said Rhona brightly, "which is nearly complete.

Some private donors have given us modest budgets with which to obtain items of great religious and historical interest."

"Something to draw in the tourists," said Aydelotte. "I understand."

The woman stiffened, and her mouth became pinched. It was clear she was offended by his comment, as he expected her to be. Sometimes it was entertaining to jab people like her with small needles. If she stormed off in a huff, then she wasn't serious in her need to talk to him. If she lingered and let the jab go, then she was in earnest. He watched her wrestle with what she *wanted* to say and finally squeeze out words of a more polite nature.

"Tourism is, of course, a necessary thing," Rhona conceded. "But we hope to attract scholars as well."

"Bully for you. Could not endorse such a course more fervently." He smiled, showing a lot of teeth and the crinkles at the corners of his eyes, a practiced expression from which he had gotten good value over the years. It worked with Rhona, too. Her expression softened, and small blooms of color appeared on her cheeks.

"We are following a clear call," she said brightly.

"Without a doubt—with. Out. A. Doubt. Now . . . how may I be of service to you and your organization?"

Rhona Sykes-Weller looked around with the kind of furtiveness that was so obvious it tended to draw attention to itself. The merchant who owned the lantern shop—Ali, an old acquaintance of Aydelotte's—laughed silently and rolled his eyes. Aydelotte gave him the quickest of amused winks.

"Well," she said in a confidential whisper, "rumor has it that you might be able to get hold of some fragments of some *Scrolls* found near the Dead Sea."

All she needed was a broad comic wink to qualify for vaudeville.

"Many things are possible," said Aydelotte quietly.

"And not like the ones the Americans bought for their museum in Washington."

"Heaven forfend."

"Real ones," she insisted. "It is important on so many levels that we are clear on that."

The fragments purchased by the Museum of the Bible looked

completely real, and they had passed muster with all of the standard examinations. However, deeper studies revealed that the items were made from very old pieces of leather, whereas the genuine Dead Sea Scrolls were written on tanned or lightly tanned parchment. It was even speculated that the leather came from the soles of shoes that had likely been recovered from other dig sites in the Middle East. Leather and parchment of that age—two thousand years old, give or take—look extraordinarily similar to the naked eye. Under a microscope, however, the truth became obvious. The leather was bumpier than parchment, and whoever had made the fakes had clearly had a difficult time with the forgery because of those irregularities.

Worse still, it became evident that the writing had been done without the care of a master forger. There was ink spillage and seepage in the cracked surface of the leather, which would not have been there if the material was new when it was written on. Additionally, the true Dead Sea Scrolls had a veneer that made them look like they had been washed with glue—a result of collagen breakdown over time. The fakes had a similar gloss, but it was of a different hue and source.

The result was a devastating loss of money and credibility for that museum, and this caused great embarrassment for the staff. It cast a pall over all such artifacts. Aydelotte was tickled pink, because when his merchandise was purchased and verified, a star in the heavens seemed to burn bright enough to lead customers to him.

Which is exactly why he had made sure the American museum got those fakes through a few carefully crafted removes. It was things of that nature that made him a truly happy man.

"Let me assure you, Rhona," said Aydelotte, "that we use three-D and scanning electron microscopes, and microchemical testing. I never deal in fakes, my dear. I go the extra mile to vet every item that comes through Miracle Acquisitions."

She looked greatly relieved. "That's very reassuring."

"Isn't it, though," he said, smiling like a happy barracuda. He dug in his pocket for a card, then he took both her hands, pressing the card into one palm. "My dear Rhona, this is my contact information. I need to meet my business contact, but I very much want to have a longer conversation with you, and perhaps in a more private place?

Call me and we'll set something up. I can assure you, dear lady, that Miracle Acquisitions can provide you with quality items at a fair price, and that those items are one hundred percent genuine. I stake my reputation on it."

Rhona looked at the card and then tucked it away.

"Thank you," she said, smiling and flushing. "Thank you very much."

Smiling and looking just a little bit glassy-eyed, she wandered away. Aydelotte watched her go.

"Stupid bitch," he muttered.

CHAPTER 21
PRIVATE LOUNGE
PIRATE LAB
UNDISCLOSED LOCATION

Dr. Giada Conti sat on the couch in a small lounge attached to her lab. The place was quiet. Jason Aydelotte and Shock were off doing whatever it was they did between visits. Her three lab technicians were busy in their own lab, working through the painstaking process of screening new clones—ergot hybrids—for the updated genes, and determining the differences in tryptamine profiles generated by these enhancements.

Creating the big scary weapon.

Conti got up, closed the lounge door, went to a small decorative cabinet, and opened the bottom drawer. Buried under old copies of *The Lancet*, *New England Journal of Medicine*, *Cell*, and *Nature Medicine* was her private stash: an antique pewter-wrapped glass flask of vodka—useful because it had no telltale aroma—and a small vial of very good cocaine.

She used the compact makeup mirror from her purse to draw two lines of the fine white powder and a tiny metal tube from a pen to inhale. One line per nostril. The rush hit her fast, though not nearly as quickly, nor as aggressively, as it used to. Even so, it flipped on all of her internal switches, brightening the day.

As that tingled its way through her system, she took two long pulls on the vodka. Neat like that it was merely alcohol and not a cocktail, but it hit all the places the coke did not.

Then Conti leaned back on the couch and stared up at the bland acoustic tiles on the ceiling, allowing the drugs to do their work. The immediate physical rush was nice, but it was her mood that she really wanted to modify. It amused her to think that, in terms of pure chemistry, alcohol was a depressant. Not in the way it hit her, though. And certainly not as a chaser to the coke.

It was also her armor. Without it—or even the thought that it was available and waiting for her whenever she needed it—there was no way she could continue doing this work. The more sober she was, the more easily she remembered being an optimistic and even altruistic medical student. She remembered the fun of working with research teams to build defenses against the biological monsters that Mother Nature threw at humanity.

Those memories used to be joyful. Now, in her most sober moments, they rose up like a chorus of silent judges, pointing accusing fingers at her.

The coke and the vodka—and sometimes some of what they used to call psychic energizers—kept those demons at bay.

And, as a research scientist, it amused her that the first of those energizers was discovered by accident. A drug—iproniazid—designed to kill the bacteria that causes tuberculosis turned out to have a secondary effect of improving mood and invoking joy. It was the world's first antidepressant, which had the additional benefit of moving the field of psychiatry away from treating depression with electroconvulsive therapy. Stranger still, that drug was a derivative of hydrazine compounds discovered in the late nineteenth century, and it was notably used as part of the fuel for the Nazi V2 rockets during World War II. Stockpiles of it left over after the war were sold to pharmaceutical and chemical companies.

What a long, strange trip, indeed, she mused. Of course the drugs she used were much more modern, safe, and readily accessible to researchers.

She needed those drugs. The coke, the booze, and the antidepressants, because without a doubt she was doing terrible things in her lab. There was not even a token nod to the Hippocratic oath. Or even to basic decency.

"I'm creating monsters," she said to the empty air of her lounge. The antidepressants kept her from crying. The coke kept her from screaming. The booze . . . it blunted the dagger points of guilt that her work jabbed into her.

In her most dangerously low moments, her memory—always sharper and more precise than she needed—would roll tape to show her the path from being that optimistic and empathetic medical student to . . .

To whatever the hell she was now. Jason joked about her being Dr. Frankenstein.

In her clearer moments, she knew that was exactly what she was —or, at least, a version with less hubris and more overt greed. And her bank account proved that crime paid very well indeed, thank you.

Today, she was caught somewhere in the middle. The coke was lifting her, but not as high as she needed. Not high enough for the air to be clearer and cleaner.

She lay on the couch and thought about the monster she had made for Mr. Miracle.

Even with the drugs pumping her up, she could not hold back the tears.

It took four more lines of coke to dry them.

CHAPTER 22
PHOENIX HOUSE

Church had not flinched or reacted.

At all.

He sat there, hands resting on the padded arms of his chair, one finger slowly drawing a small circle on the leather. His chubby gray Scottish Fold cat, Bastion, ran over and sniffed the cookies, took an experimental lick, flicked his fluffy tail, and walked away to find a patch of sunlight in which to bask.

"Well," I said, "that was fun."

There was a little twitch thing that happened with Church's mouth. I wouldn't want to go out on a limb and call it a smile.

"Dr. Sanchez is a good man," he said mildly. "What just happened is a measure of his concern for you."

"I've never seen him like that."

"I suspect few people have."

Church wore tinted glasses, more, I suspect, to hide his eyes than for any corrective purposes. He removed a pocket square from his Stefano Ricci suit coat and used it to clean his lenses, looking at a cubist painting on the opposite wall as he did so. My guess has always been that he recognized that his eyes were his tell, because when he took his glasses off, he never made eye contact. I've played enough high-stakes poker to know that everyone has a tell—that little thing they do on an unconscious level that betrays some thought or emotion.

I studied the side of his face, looking for anything to let me know how Rudy's outrage was really hitting him. I got nothing, though. When he spoke, his voice was that same calm, aware, vaguely New England Kennedy accent which gave nothing away.

"Many people have great respect and affection for you," he said, putting his glasses back on. "Some also feel that their trust in you was cast into question last year."

"Not entirely unfair," I said.

"Agreed," he said without a trace of either condescension or condemnation. "If you need or want more time, you know you have only to say so. I will never push you, and I will support any decision you care to make, even if it means watching you walk away. Dr. Sanchez is correct in that you have earned your rest."

"But . . . ?"

"No buts." He opened a drawer and removed a thick file folder with an MI classification stamped on the cover. Mission Intelligence. "This will always be your call, Colonel."

I looked at the file.

And that's how we got to the Dead Sea Scrolls.

JONATHAN MABERRY

INTERLUDE 7
THE BASEMENT ROOM
PIRATE LAB
UNDISCLOSED LOCATION

THREE YEARS AGO

"Dr. Conti," said Aydelotte as he breezed into her office.

The scientist looked up from her laptop, painted nails hovering for a moment above the keys.

"Mr. Aydelotte . . . I wasn't expecting you."

"I was in the building and thought I'd stop down to ask a question or two."

Conti pushed her chair back from the desk and stood. "Anything you need, sir."

He walked over to a wall that was covered with color printouts of fungi and other microorganisms. There were research notes thumbtacked to the boards, along with pages of chemical formulae.

Without turning, he asked, "Of all the stuff you recovered from Shock's bug box, are there any that could cause hallucinations?"

Her big eyes gave a slow, almost insectoid blink. "Yes, actually. We found traces of *Claviceps purpurea*, a fungus more commonly known as ergot, on rye and wheat that was stored in the tomb. Ergot has well-known perception-altering qualities."

"Tell me."

"Well, the Dancing Plague of 1518 comes to mind."

Aydelotte beamed. "Dancing? Seriously? Tell me about that."

"It's a phenomenon that has cropped up in various places throughout history," said Conti. "Choreomania is one of its names —and there are many. The term was coined by the Swiss physician and alchemist Paracelsus in the early sixteenth century. However, the earliest verifiable outbreak of choreomania dates back to the seventh century, and it kept popping up throughout Europe and elsewhere. You've probably heard of it by the more common names of St. John's dance or St. Vitus's dance."

"I'm not looking to start a new version of *So You Think You Can Dance*."

"'Dancing' is a relative term," said Conti, smiling faintly. "And it's really not that. It's a violent form of muscular spasming. Not like epilepsy, because the victims are often upright and mobile. I suppose labeling it as dancing is more romantic than scientific. And, to your point, no—we're not going to make them dance. Besides . . . not all ergot sufferers undergo that symptom. There are quite a few ways in which ergotism presents in humans."

"These are legitimate outbreaks?" asked Aydelotte.

"Oh, yes, but you have to understand that we know about most of the outbreaks because of historical or church records from hundreds of years ago. Those are hardly scientific studies. Very often there were not even reliable directions to graves where bodies could be exhumed and studied. Anyway . . . theories are all over the place."

"Are they all fungal?" he asked. "As far as you know?"

Conti leaned back in her chair and chewed for a moment or two on the cap of a Bic ballpoint. "Well, if you're only looking for cases where fungi are the likely culprit, we can probably eliminate the most famous of the dancing plagues, and that's St. Vitus's dance. We now believe that it's caused by an autoimmune response following infection by group A β-hemolytic streptococci. Two cross-reactive streptococcal antigens have been identified, the M protein and—"

"If it's not fungal then I don't want to know about it," said Aydelotte.

"Oookay, fair enough," said Conti patiently. "Well, one of the earliest-known suspected incidents of dancing sickness was in the 1020s in Bernberg, where eighteen people suddenly began singing and dancing around a church on Christmas Eve."

He cocked one eyebrow. "I hate to break this to you, Doc, but singing and dancing kind of goes with Christmas, at least in my experience."

"Not when those actions are beyond the control of the afflicted. The people were not having a good time, and it left them traumatized and exhausted. There was another outbreak in 1237, where a sizeable group of children going from Erfurt to Arnstadt began dancing and jumping uncontrollably. And a bit of an historical tidbit—the story of the Pied Piper of Hamelin was written around the same time, almost certainly taking inspiration from that incident."

Aydelotte took a chair and dragged it over close to the doctor. "Now you have me interested. Keep going."

"In 1278, two hundred people began dancing on a bridge over the River Meuse. Their weight and the impacts of them jumping and dancing caused the bridge to collapse. Another big outbreak happened in 1374, and so on. Some of the historical cases might be St. Vitus's dance, but many don't fit that profile closely enough," said Conti, warming to her topic. "Going to a darker place in the story, a monk danced himself to death in Schaffhausen in 1428. That same year, in Zurich, a group of women went into an uncontrollable dancing frenzy."

"And all they did was dance?"

"They called it dancing, but from what I gather it was more like an epileptic seizure but while standing. Twitching, jumping, moving. Not sure there was any sense of rhythm to it."

He dug into a dish of powdery buttermint candies on her desk and chewed loudly. "Imagine if that happened nowadays. Social media would explode."

"No doubt."

"So, this stuff's been happening for centuries. What causes it?"

"Well, first you have to look at the socioeconomic factors. Most of the documented cases occurred during times of hardship—war, crop failure, famine, things like that. People who could not afford—or did not have access to—top-quality crops sometimes relied on grain that was old or improperly stored. The outbreak in 1374 occurred only decades after the Black Death, and there are similar incidents. Unfortunately, many of the afflicted were either buried in mass graves, making individual identification virtually impossible, or they were cremated."

"Which means we have no idea?" asked Aydelotte.

"Not at all," said Conti brightly. "The leading theory is that the victims had ergot poisoning from bad grain, which takes us into the realm of mycotoxicosis, or poisoning caused by toxic molds. The big bad of that group is *Claviceps purpurea,* or rye ergot fungus. It grows on rye and similar plants and produces an alkaloid that causes ergotism. Now, this ergotism can cause all sorts of unpleasant symptoms, including convulsions and hallucinations. Now, think about the mindset of people in centuries past and you have to wonder if those symptoms, which are uncontrollable and pretty terrifying, might explain cases otherwise believed to be demonic possession."

Aydelotte nodded. "I can see it."

"This isn't anything new. Not even as new as the incidents I mentioned. There's an Assyrian tablet from 600 BCE that makes references to a 'noxious pustule in the ear of grain,' and we believe that is the oldest recorded mention of the disease."

Aydelotte nodded, and a gleam seemed to ignite in his blue eyes.

"In India, among the Parsees back in 350 BCE there was mention of 'noxious grasses that cause pregnant women to drop the womb and die in childbed.'" She looked at him. "Ergot again. Same goes for ancient Syria and elsewhere. Ergot, ergot, ergot. You see, this has been a problem all around the world where rye is grown. And it isn't just the spasms and convulsions. There are credible reports of something known as the 'holy fire' or ' St. Anthony's fire' that involves a gangrenous poisoning."

"Gangrene?" said Aydelotte.

"Oh, yes. The first mention of a plague of gangrenous ergotism in Europe dates back to 857 in Germany. And King Magnus II of Norway, nephew of King Olaf Haraldsson, that's Saint Olaf, died from ergotism right after the Battle of Hastings. And there are lots of other examples. And don't think this is all past tense. We're seeing it pop up in places like Ethiopia in the early 2000s, though that was barley and not rye. Whenever there is a combination of moist weather, cool temperatures, delayed harvest in lowland crops, and rye consumption, an outbreak is possible. There's even a theory that some of the 'devilish behavior' that resulted in women being accused of witchcraft in Salem might have its roots in ergotism."

Aydelotte digested this as he slowly ate one small buttermint after another. Conti noticed that he ate only the green and pink candies, leaving the white ones alone. Her inquisitive mind wanted to ask why, but she did not dare.

After a few long seconds of consideration, Aydelotte said, "I'm hearing about dancing and death and gangrene, but what I'm not hearing enough of is hallucinations."

"Any particular reason you want to focus on that symptom?" asked Conti.

"Yes," he said, but did not explain. "Just tell me."

"Well, we can stay in more or less recent history if you want science to prop this all up."

"Let's do that."

She nodded. "There are two forms of ergotism: convulsive and gangrenous. Ergot triggers the same neurotransmitters as serotonin, which are key for the efficient and proper functioning of our mood, digestive system, and sleep-wake cycle. But, in massive doses, serotonin produces something called serotonin syndrome, when the brain sends all kinds of erratic signals to the rest of the body. Muscles contract, which causes spasms, the skin gets sweaty, and mental faculties are confused and erratic. With me so far?"

He just looked at her.

Conti's face grew hot, and she plunged back in. "There is a serotonin syndrome called convulsive ergotism, and with that the alkaloids in the fungus begin harming the body by completely overwhelming the brain. People afflicted with this almost certainly believed they were possessed—or other people thought they were. God knows how many sick and afflicted people were tortured and executed for demonic possession. And how many innocents were subjected to the intense and often cruel procedures of exorcism."

She paused and brightened.

"Now we get to the fun part. Back in the 1930s, Albert Hofmann, a Swiss chemist, became fascinated by the fungus. Understand, his work with ergot would eventually result in treatments for infertility, Parkinson's disease, and hemorrhages. A bit later in his research process he focused on a molecule that would make a big splash in our shared culture—"

"Let me guess," said Aydelotte. "You're talking LSD, right?"

"Yes!" she cried. "Dr. Hofmann was trying to create a compound to stimulate the circulatory and respiratory systems when he formulated LSD-25. Drug companies were less than enthused about it and had given up on the substance. Rumor has it that Hofmann accidentally ingested some, but I rather think it was intentional. He tripped out and was astonished by the experience. Think of all the ways LSD influenced our expressive culture. From psychedelic rock to expressionist and surrealist painting, literature . . ."

"LSD trips can't be the same as those dancing people. Or whatever drove that pharaoh so nuts that his people buried him with warnings all over his tomb."

"Oh, of course it was different, but the root cause is the same. What Hofmann proved was the elastic nature of the ergot alkaloid. Different versions of it produce different effects, and we have a large body of research useful to us in exploring what might best be called 'designer ergotism.'"

Aydelotte seemed to come slowly to point. His smile became more rapacious, and there was a dangerous gleam in his eyes.

"Now let me tell you what I need you to do for me."

CHAPTER 23
PHOENIX HOUSE

"Scrolls? Not so much," I said. "But I can give you an inning-by-inning account of when the Baltimore Orioles beat the crap out of the Cincinnati Reds in the 1970 World Series. Stats and color commentary. All the way to the point where they named Brooks Robinson the MVP."

"Which, I'm sure," said Church, "would be utterly fascinating."

"You're lying."

"Of course I am."

We sat there. The afternoon sun had picked up water vapor from the blue Ionian Sea and kept whispering promises of rain. Seagulls floated lazily on the thermals, their bellies shining white. If they cared about the coming storm, they didn't show it. Although purple clouds were huddled on the horizon, bright beams of sunlight slanted in through the windows and turned everything to gold. Bastion lay in the middle of that light, apparently gone to heaven.

"So," I said, "Dead Sea Scrolls. Okay. What about them? Have they somehow come back to life?"

He ignored that. "There has been an unusual amount of interest in those artifacts in both the legal and black-market antiquities market."

"And . . . I should care about that why?"

"Because it is something I'd like you to look into."

I stared at him. "Oh, come *on*. Don't tell me you actually are caving to Rudy. I nail the Chad mission and now you're sending me on an *errand*? Bug could do a net search and get everything you need on this in ten minutes."

"He did," said Church, nodding to the folder.

"Then how in the hell is this something for me to handle? We have plenty of gophers, don't we?"

I was, perhaps, being unkind. Rogue Team International employed or contracted the services of a lot of specialists in countless fields. None of them were "number two guys." Church used top people at all times. And he seemed to have every useful expert on speed dial. Church always seemed to have a "friend in the industry"—a catchphrase I've heard so often I gave Church a coffee mug with that on it for Christmas a few years ago—who was well positioned to acquire useful information and provide cool toys. That level of work was what made RTI so efficient. Those friends—and our direct employees—were not gophers. They were skilled, talented, well educated, well informed, and brilliant. It was totally unfair of me to denigrate them.

But "gopher" is a funny word, so there we are.

"I gather you feel that this is beneath you?" mused Church, raising one eyebrow a millimeter.

In my best Liam Neeson, I said, "I have a very particular set of skills, skills I have acquired over a long career . . ."

He failed to be impressed.

"Under normal circumstances, Colonel, RTI would have little interest in the Scrolls. They are of personal interest to me and a few others, but never before in a way that touched on the work we do here."

"Now I *know* there's a 'but' coming."

"*However*," he said instead, "reports have found their way to me that suggest that interest is not only becoming more intense, but violently so."

I shrugged. "Struggling to give a shit, boss. Sounds, at most, like an Interpol thing. They *love* that kind of stuff. Smuggling, a bit of intrigue spilling across national lines . . . How much you want to bet the bad guys are a bunch of French art thieves with bad mustaches? Or Algerians with fezzes. I love a good fez."

In the silence I could hear Bastion quietly licking his ass.

"When you are quite finished, Colonel," said Church.

I sighed. "Okay, please enchant me with how I can help find two-thousand-year-old scraps of paper."

"Bullet points, then," he said. "The Scrolls have been found in—currently—twelve caves in the Qumran, near the Dead Sea. Original discovery was by three young bedouins. The value of the Scrolls was not immediately recognized. Once their nature was understood, their value increased dramatically, particularly with secular and religious scholars. Roughly nine hundred Scrolls were found, though many are badly damaged." He paused. "A full briefing on the subject will be made available to you by a couple of experts who are on their way here to Phoenix House."

"Gosh. Sounds exciting," I said, not meaning it. "Do go on."

"Over the last thirteen months there has been an uptick of interest in any privately owned fragments of the Dead Sea Scrolls."

"So, the Vatican *doesn't* have all of it in a vault?"

"The majority of the Scrolls are in the Shrine of the Book," said Church, "which is part of the Israel Museum in Jerusalem. Smaller collections of fragments are scattered around in public or private collections."

"Wait . . . didn't I read somewhere that some of those were fake?"

"Yes. That's been a problem with artifacts like these. A few years ago, a group of sixteen fragments on display at the Museum of the Bible, a privately owned gallery in Washington, DC, were discovered to be fakes."

"Ouch."

"Very much an ouch," he agreed. "It's the kind of revelation that calls all such displays into question because forgery for such items is big business, and verification is often prohibitively expensive. New and emerging technologies have begun to chip away at the forgery market, which ups the value of genuine items being sold on various markets. Legitimate and otherwise."

"Yeah, okay. And . . . ?"

"And there are many fragments of the Scrolls—and even the possibility of complete Scrolls—in private collections. Every now and then these items will show up in inventories of black-market antiquities."

"*Complete* Scrolls? How'd that happen? Someone loot the museum in Jerusalem?"

"No, actually," said Church, seeming to warm to his topic. "Before the full value of the Scrolls was understood, the bedouins who found them sold an unknown number of items to collectors. There is no real way of knowing how much was sold or even what those other Scrolls were. We do know that there are items missing from the overall find that are suggestive of theft or loss. For example, the Book of Esther is absent."

"Okay. Sucks for Esther."

"Colonel," he said with fading patience, "the importance of those Scrolls can hardly be understated. Prior to their discovery, the oldest known manuscripts of the Hebrew Bible dated only to the tenth century CE. However, the Scrolls include over two hundred twenty-five copies of biblical books that date to twelve hundred years earlier."

I whistled. "Okay, I'm getting a sense of the importance. But you're still not telling me why you want me—and I'm the first to admit that I'm no biblical scholar—to poke into it. It still sounds like we should be turfing this to Interpol."

"Because," he said, "there have been several deaths associated with this new interest in the Scrolls."

"Okay," I said, perking up a bit. "Who is shooting whom?"

"Oh," said Church, "it's not as easy as mere gunplay."

"How so?"

"Five days ago," he said, "two of the world's most renowned biblical scholars, working in a sealed room of the kind used for examining documents of that age and fragility, killed themselves."

"Killed . . . *themselves* . . . ? What do you mean? Some kind of suicide pact?"

"Unlikely. One stabbed his own eyes out with two ballpoint pens and then banged his face on his desk until the pens were driven into his brain case."

"Fucking hell."

"The other used a pair of tweezers to open arteries in his thighs and his throat."

"Jesus. *Why?*"

There was that lip twitch again, and I think he suspected that his hook was now set in my underlip.

"We don't know why. But if you open the file and look at the photos marked with a blue tab, you'll understand why I think this is a case for us."

I leaned forward, flipped open the cover, found the tab, and stared. It was an eight-by-ten glossy print of a color photograph of a section of glass wall, the inside of that a sanitized cubicle. A body was slumped at the base of the wall, and the fingers of one hand were bright with blood. Above him, written on the glass, were these words:

> *The bats*
> *The bats*
> *The bats from hell*
> *God save my soul.*

CHAPTER 24
PHOENIX HOUSE

I said, "I'm in."

Church nodded.

"I assumed as much. You'll have a briefing at noon, and then you'll be wheels-up in four hours."

JONATHAN MABERRY

INTERLUDE 8
DR. CONTI'S LAB
PIRATE LAB
UNDISCLOSED LOCATION

ELEVEN MONTHS AGO

They stood together—Jason Aydelotte, Dr. Conti, and Shock—watching the two subjects inside the glass observation cube.

On the other side of the tempered and shatter-resistant glass were two animals. On the left was a bonobo and on the right, separated by another sheet of tempered glass, was a chimpanzee.

"This is the quick-onset formula?" asked Shock.

"Yes. That was the most difficult and time-consuming part of this. Egotism typically takes days, weeks, or even months to present. And manipulating its DNA to change that required research and a lot of trial and error. I'd *love* to publish my findings."

"Now, now, Giada," said Aydelotte. "We've talked about that."

"I know," Conti replied. "I didn't say I would, just that I'd like to get that Nobel Prize."

"I'd like to lose fifty pounds and look like Chris Hemsworth," replied Aydelotte. "Life is full of little disappointments."

"Anyway," said Shock, leaning on the word in order to steer things back to the topic, "you were saying this is the quick-onset variant."

"Yes," said Conti, "it's the latest version. Series number eighty-one."

"We're calling it Shiva," said Aydelotte.

"Shiva?" mused Shock. "Why? No . . . wait, I get it. Shiva—or Śiva—is the 'Auspicious One,' and is one of the principal deities of Hinduism. But that aspect doesn't fit with a bioweapon. So . . . I'm guessing it's the other aspect, the one from the Trimurti, along with Brahma and Vishnu-Shiva the Destroyer. Am I close?"

"Partly. Keep going. There's a bit of nuance in the choice of name."

"Hmmm. Well, in the Shaivite tradition, Shiva protects, creates, and transforms the universe. He's also a demon slayer in some traditions. And he has a third eye that, when opened, turns everything that eye sees to ash. And there's an earlier, pre-Vedic aspect which includes that of storm god." She smiled. "Am I getting close?"

Aydelotte beamed and glanced at Conti. "You see why I love her to pieces?" To Shock he said, "It's a bit of all of that."

Shock stepped closer to the glass cubicles. Aydelotte came and stood next to her, his hands deep in his pockets, eyes nearly unblinking. The lab around them was silent as a crypt. The air smelled of chemicals and disinfectant and old coffee.

"The two test subjects were exposed at the same time," said Conti.

Shock nodded. "How long before it kicked in? I mean . . . how long before symptoms?"

Conti held a clipboard and leafed through until she found the page with a timetable. There were a series of handwritten entries, all in blue ballpoint, beginning at 8:07 a.m. and ending at 8:33 a.m. The handwriting was orderly at first and markedly less so as the entries went on. The last entry was a scrawl.

"Subject A," she said, gesturing to the chimpanzee, "began exhibiting symptoms after fifty-four seconds. Subject B at one minute and two seconds."

"Which symptoms at first?"

"These are animals, you understand, so there was no chance to interview the subjects about what they were feeling. We have what I witnessed and telemetric readings of blood pressure, heart rate, body temperature, oxygen intake, cerebral activity, and so on. All of those implants are set for continuous feed, from ordinary resting, eating, et cetera, so that we have a standard range of numbers before the formula was introduced via the vent."

Shock nodded. Aydelotte did nothing.

"In both cases the subjects appeared to react in a way consistent with hearing something. They paused what they were doing and cocked their heads, even turning their heads as if focusing on some perceived sound."

"But there was no sound?" asked Shock.

"None. We limited ambient stimulation beyond normal light and temperature so as not to influence actual reaction. So, to answer your question," said Conti, "there was no sound that could have caused the observed reaction."

JONATHAN MABERRY

"What happened after that?"

"That's where things get really interesting," said Conti, her face lighting up. "Subject A began prowling the interior perimeter of his cubicle, apparently looking for the source of the sound. He became increasingly agitated—possibly because he could not locate whatever it was he thought he heard—and at that point began throwing things around in frustration. His water bowl, the rind from a piece of fruit."

"And the other monkey?" asked Shock.

"Ape," corrected Conti. "They're both part of the great apes family and—"

"Whatever. What about the other one?"

Conti nodded. "Well, he sat for quite a while, still apparently listening. From facial tics and other observable actions, it was quite clear he was listening. EEG waveforms support this. He was in that listening state for nearly eleven minutes."

"And then?"

"Well," said the doctor, "you can see what happened after that."

Shock looked through the blood spatter on the inside of the cubicle.

"Did the other monkey . . . ape . . . whatever . . . get into Subject B's cube? Did he do that?"

"No. Even strong as they each are, they could not break the glass. It's designed to resist up to fifteen thousand PSI."

"Then how did Subject B lose both feet and his left hand?" demanded Shock.

"He . . . chewed them off."

"And did what with them? I don't see them anywhere."

Conti's smile was gone now. "Well . . . he . . . consumed them."

Shock stared at her. "Jesus Christ."

Aydelotte spoke for the first time. "Tell me about Subject A."

The chimpanzee in the first cubicle sat with his soft nose and muzzle pressed against the inside of the glass. His brown eyes stared at Aydelotte. He only blinked when the man did. Those eyes were filled with strange lights—they jumped and twitched as if he was seeing something that was both delightful and alarming.

"He has been like that since shortly after exposure," said Conti. "Nearly three hours."

"And you say they were both given the same formula?"

"Yes, sir."

"How many test subjects reacted like the bonobo?"

"Over the last few months . . . three."

Aydelotte walked over and stood face to face with Subject A. "And how many like the chimp?"

"Twenty-seven."

He nodded and placed his hand on the glass, fingers splayed. After half a minute the chimp did the same, his long fingers a mirror of Aydelotte's. Then slowly . . . very, very slowly, the ape's eyes drifted shut, and he slumped down, fell over, and passed out.

The EEG and EKG feeds on the screen above the cube showed readings consistent with deep REM sleep. Behind the closed lids, the animal's eyes moved rapidly side to side, and his limbs jerked and twitched.

"He's dreaming," said Shock.

"Yes," said Conti. "That seems to happen with the majority of animals who react like Subject A."

Aydelotte kept his hand on the glass.

"Will this work on people?" he asked.

"Yes," said Conti.

"With the same ratio? Twenty-seven like Subject A and only three like B?"

"We can't know until we do clinical trials."

Aydelotte lowered his hand.

"Then do it," he said. "Start tomorrow."

CHAPTER 25
MACHANEH YEHUDAH MARKET
JERUSALEM, ISRAEL

The young British man moved through the crowd in ways that were obvious and covert. He was like that.

He did not mind being seen and admired. He was slim, handsome in a David-Bowie-meets-Harry-Styles sort of way and worked it. Clothes were casual—naturally distressed jeans, sleeveless safari jacket with lots of pockets and unzipped to show a lot of chest through the open weave of a net undershirt. Doc Martens, Wayfarers pushed up on his short white-blond hair, eyes that missed nothing and promised everything. Surfer-braid bracelets on both wrists; rings on both thumbs. No necklace or earrings, though. Fighters aren't that careless.

He expected people to look at him, and even to paste labels over their assessments. That was fine. If they were doing that, then they weren't seeing what was beneath the veneer. His vibe was "look, don't touch." There was ice in his eyes and heat in his full-lipped half smile. Not anything as obvious as a Billy Idol sneer, or as frosty as a Paris runway model. Women looked at him, and so did a lot of men. Seeing what he projected, and only that.

What they didn't see—or, rather, what they saw and mistook for something else—was that he was a hunter. He moved with the indolent grace of one of the big hunting cats, and because he allowed a soupçon of carefully sculpted exaggeration, nearly everyone thought he was on the prowl for a playmate. Short or long term; singly or in small groups.

At other times, and in other places, that would be true enough. Now, he merely played to expectation without personal investment.

The truth was that he was on the hunt just now for sex.

The crowds filling the Shulk—the Machaneh Yehudah Market— were a living poster for the diversity of human appearance, style, culture, and intent. Skin tones ranging from Icelandic white to Papua New Guinea black, and every shade in between. Body types ranged from overfed American tourists to wasp-waisted French fashionistas. The variety pleased him greatly.

A voice in the Brit's ear said, "Anything . . . ?"

He had a cell phone earbud in one ear, nice and obvious so he did not look strange talking to himself. The speaker's voice, however, came through a tiny earbud affixed to the antihelix of his outer ear.

"If I had anything, Rugger," drawled the young man, "I would have told you. Or did you sleep *all* the way through the mission briefing?"

"Sorry."

"I already half believe you're dead from the neck up. Don't prove me right."

That was met with the right amount of silence from Rugger.

The young man kept strolling through the crowd, pausing now and then to pretend to look at something at a stall, but always in shops where they had mirrors hung in useful places. He was trying on a pair of godawful sunglasses when he spotted him.

Him.

A man of medium height, stocky, with a full white beard, a spotless white fedora. White on white on white.

"Bloody knob head," murmured the young man. Then to his team he said, "He's here."

He shifted position so the mirror reflected what was behind him and the ultra-high-def camera hidden in one of the snaps on his safari jacket caught and sent the image to the team.

"Looks harmless," said Armani, another of the team tuned into the team channel.

"So does an old lady poisoner, you wanker."

The bearded man seemed to be in a browsing mood and paused to look at some painted vases. The young Brit wasn't fooled. The actions were correct, but there was no corresponding expression, no sign of genuine interest.

"Okay, he's at the spot where he said to meet."

Another voice asked, "And you're sure this is Jason Aydelotte?"

"It's not sodding Father Christmas, Skiver." He tried on a different pair of bad sunglasses, which gave him a reason to study the mirror.

Skiver muttered, "I need a better combat call sign."

"Twat?" suggested the young man. "Pillock?"

"Fuck you."

The young man smiled.

Rugger said, "I don't like this at all. The mission briefing said Aydelotte was smart, subtle, and savvy enough to keep his over- and under-the-table business deals separate. He's been rumored to be a player in all kinds of hijinks, but he's never been his own field man. Why now and why here?"

"First," said the young man, "I'm debiting your pay for using 'hijinks' in an adult conversation."

"Blow me."

"Second, we don't know. Maybe he's gone 'round the twist. Maybe he has some reason that makes sense to him that we haven't considered. In either case, he's here."

"Has to be off his rocker," insisted Rugger. "Be careful."

"Okay," said the young man. "I'm going over and making contact." He was about to take a step, then paused. "Bloody hell. There's someone else. Hold tight."

He watched as a second man approached Aydelotte—a younger, taller, and very muscular man with a shaved head and Israeli features. He wore a dark blue sports jacket over a white shirt unbuttoned at the throat, loose-fitting trousers, and rubber-soled shoes. The newcomer stopped at the same table and nudged a few of the vases without really looking at any. His lips moved, but there was no mic in range.

"Is that the other bidder?" asked Rugger.

"Not a chance. That's muscle. He's here to take our boy to wherever this bloody auction is being held."

"Why not walk up and join them?" asked Skiver. "That's the plan, right?"

"The plan is flexible," said the young man. "And I currently don't like the way it feels. Going to tweak it in motion. Let's see if Aydelotte is playing straight or playing games."

Aydelotte and the big man stood with their heads bowed together in conversation. Aydelotte kept nodding as the other man spoke. Aydelotte paused, looked around, made no specific eye contact with anyone else, shrugged, tapped the big man on the shoulder, and they moved off together, heading toward the exit.

Rugger grunted. "I soooo don't like this whole thing. That prat's making it up as he goes and we're expected to just roll with it?"

"I'm sorry," said the young man, "is the master criminal being difficult?"

There were some chuckles on the line.

"Look, lads," said the Brit, "we know he gave this meet-up spot to multiple buyers, but instead of organizing a class trip, it looks like he's going off with the first bloke who made contact. Not sure why, but that's how he's playing it, so that's how we have to dance. We don't get to call in a ref to debate the sodding rules."

"Maybe it's some kind of test to see who wants it most," suggested Rugger.

"Mmm. You may be right for a change, mate."

The young man turned and very lightly and casually brushed Aydelotte's arm as he and the muscle passed by.

"Okay," said the young Brit after a moment, "I managed to put a bug on his sleeve. Dingo and Armani, pick them up at the exit. Stay in range but be careful. Skiver, you move ahead and wait for their hand-off. Don't crowd him, but don't lose him."

"Copy that," they all said.

"Where will you go, boss?" asked Rugger.

"I'm going to bloody well follow them to the meet site and tell him I got to the market in time to see them leave."

"What if he spots you tailing him?"

"Be your age. If he spots me, it's because I let him."

"We got your back, boss."

"You'd better," said Toys. "I don't like being out here waving my dick."

He moved off without haste, smiling very faintly to himself.

CHAPTER 26
INTEGRATED SCIENCES DEPARTMENT
PHOENIX HOUSE

Two men sat on stools in front of a complex set of computer screens. They were as different from one another as was possible, at least in appearance.

Isaac Breslau was barely above five feet tall and as thin as a blade of grass. When he was a kid, his uncle Murray used to say that if he stood sideways no one could even see him unless he stuck out his tongue, and even then he'd only look like a zipper. He was clean-shaven though with the blue shadows of a perpetual five o'clock shadow on his cheek and upper lip. Very little hair, and what there was clung to the fringes of his skull as if each strand were terrified of falling.

His companion, Ronald Coleman, was a few years younger, substantially taller, with a robust build and a comfortable belly. He had a full head of hair and a thick black beard and looked like a learned bear.

Breslau was a former professor of biological engineering from MIT, with a handful of master's degrees in chemistry, materials science, and health sciences. Coleman was a molecular biologist who received his doctorate from the Scripps Research Institute's Center for Regenerative Medicine for his work developing a stem-cell-based treatment for multiple sclerosis. Throughout his career he has used the tools of biotechnology to build novel antibodies to neutralize botulinum neurotoxin, worked to save the critically endangered northern white rhino, and better understand the fundamental mechanisms of neurodevelopment and immunology. Church had engaged each of them as part-time consultants under Doc Holliday's umbrella of experts, but on her recommendation, he had hired them as full-time staff.

On the main screen in front of them was a feed from the Oxford Nonopore PromethION-48 gene sequencer that dominated one corner of their shared lab.

"Ergot alkaloids," said Coleman.

"Duh. Obviously," said Breslau.

"Psilocybin, too."

"Yes."

"Weird."

"Very."

Coleman said, "Gives us the answer to why Bunny saw what he saw. And what those kids are going through."

"Glad Bunny got a tiny dose. Contact exposure of some kind," said Breslau. "We'll need to rewatch the video to see where and when. But the kids? Their symptoms are classic prolonged exposure. Some of them might never be right. Poor bastards."

They kept watching the data on the screen.

Coleman grunted. "Somebody's been screwing with the DNA."

Breslau pointed to him and then to himself. "Preaching. Choir."

"Yeah."

"Question is," said Breslau, "what are they doing? Why are they doing it? And how'd it get into those teens?"

"That's three questions."

"Okay, but the answer's going to be the same for all, don't you think?"

"Yeah, I really *do* think," said Coleman. "We need to tell Doc. And Church. And maybe Joe."

"Yes, we damn well do."

CHAPTER 27

INTERVIEW ROOM C
PHOENIX HOUSE

"Who *are* you?" begged Russo. Tears and snot clogged his nose and mouth. His fists were white-knuckled balls of swollen meat. He banged them on the tabletop.

The big man looked at him.

"Fucking *say* something," begged Russo.

After a long moment, the big man spoke. "What would you like me to say?"

Russo twitched and yelped at hearing his voice after the endless silence.

"Where am I? And who are you people?"

"You're nowhere, Mr. Russo," said the big man. "Who we are is not your concern."

"What do you *want*?"

For the first time an expression appeared on the big man's face. It was a smile. He said nothing.

And in a few minutes, he left the room with no further comment.

CHAPTER 28
INTEGRATED SCIENCES DEPARTMENT
PHOENIX HOUSE

Coleman gave the report via intra-office video messaging. Breslau stood behind him, leaning into shot.

"Genetically modified ergotism with a psilocybin booster just for shits and giggles," said Doc Holliday. She was smiling, which she typically did when there was very bad news.

"Weaponized ergotism," murmured Church.

"Weaponized hallucinogens," corrected Breslau.

"Now isn't that interesting."

"And there's more," said Coleman.

"Yes," said Breslau. "We ran gas chromatograph on the fluid in the syrettes."

"Oh, let me guess," said Doc. "It's going to be some version of ketanserin, isn't it?"

Breslau looked crestfallen. "You spoil all the fun."

She gave him a saucy wink.

"The dosage suggests that the guards at that facility would need to inject themselves every twelve hours," said Coleman.

Church nodded. "How quickly can we reproduce the same ketanserin formula and mass-produce syrettes?"

The two scientists looked at each other, then glanced at the vast array of the most advanced medical equipment that was currently available on the market, and the modified versions they—and Doc Holliday—had customized. When they looked back at the screen, they both gave identical shrugs and, as if rehearsed beforehand, said, "One to two days."

"Do it," said Church.

"Before we leap at that," said Doc, "we have to consider some of the potential side effects. Ketanserin can cause drowsiness, fatigue, headache, sleep disturbances, and dry mouth. And, less often . . . dizziness, light-headedness, lack of concentration, and dyspepsia."

"Can those symptoms be ameliorated?"

There was a pause, then Coleman said, "Could be done. But if you need this fast, then there won't be any chance of clinical trials."

"Do your best," said Church.

"Are we even sure we need it?" asked Breslau.

"Oh, honeybuns," said Doc, "that's like asking Joe Ledger if he needs extra bullets. There's a whole sermon he'll give you about how it's better to have it and not need than need it and not have it."

"Do it," repeated Church, and then his screen went black.

Coleman swiveled his chair around to face Breslau. "I guess we do it."

INTERLUDE 9
DR. CONTI'S LAB
PIRATE LAB
UNDISCLOSED LOCATION

SIX MONTHS AGO

They were safe behind the glass.

And that was a good thing.

Nothing on the other side of that glass was safe. Even without the blood spatter on the walls, Jason Aydelotte knew that. He wasn't blind.

He was, however, terrified.

The woman beside him, wearing a pristine lab coat and with no strand of hair awry on her expensively coiffed hair, was not terrified. She had not stopped smiling since he'd entered the lab.

"It's remarkable, isn't it?" she beamed.

"God . . ."

The glass was two inches thick, tempered and shatterproof. And also soundproof, which was a blessing. Aydelotte watched the man inside, saw his mouth moving, knew that he had to be shouting—screaming—but all in a kind of horrific pantomime. Like a horror movie with the sound turned down.

"We have been working with a number of variations on the compound," said Dr. Conti. "And you would be amazed at the variety with which symptoms present. With different subjects we have tracked auditory, visual, tactile, and olfactory hallucinations."

JONATHAN MABERRY

"How do you know?" asked Aydelotte, his voice a bit hoarse. "I mean, how can you tell when they're hearing things or feeling stuff that isn't there?"

"Oh, that isn't as difficult as it sounds," said Conti. "A lot of it is based on a great deal of published work on observation of persons experiencing hallucinations, with confirmations gotten through interviews once the effects have diminished. All manner of physical movements has been cataloged. Some, of course, are obvious. Someone sniffing and then reacting in some extreme way to a smell that we know—because of controlled conditions—is not present. We track eye movements, gestures including hand shaping and apparent interaction with objects that do not exist outside of the hallucination. Warming hands on a nonexistent fire, shivering as if there is a cold wind, or slapping at clothes and skin to extinguish flames that do not exist."

Aydelotte nodded.

"Subject One over there," said Conti, pointing past the standing figure to one who lay sprawled in a corner. "He kept cocking his head in a way suggestive of listening, then he would follow the sound he believed he heard, tracking it as if it were something behind the back wall. You can see from the condition of his fingernails that he tried to tear off the subway tiles."

"You had glass between the two apes," said Aydelotte. "Not here, though. Why?"

Conti shrugged. "We have all the individual data we really need. Or thought so, anyway. This was a test of both onset in a controlled group as well as interaction of subjects in a shared but contained environment."

"That one," said Aydelotte, pointing to the corpse. "How did he die?"

"You mean, was it suicide? No, sir," said Conti. "Subject Two kept yelling that there were scorpions on Subject One's skin. And, before you ask, we listened in and muted the sound when you got here. Anyway, Two held his hand in a way one might if holding a knife. He seemed to need to stab those scorpions, and he kept at it even after One was dead. As you can see, he used tremendous force and was committed to completing the task his delusion had set for him. Alas, the damage to One's head will make a useful dissection of the brain more of a challenge. The parietal bone is shattered and depressed into the tissues, with evident tearing of the dura mater."

Aydelotte turned away. "That's horrible."

Dr. Conti leaned her shoulder against the window and studied him. "Pardon me for speaking frankly, sir, but I feel like I'm getting mixed messages here. You do *want* this research, yes? I mean, when you had Shock provide the samples from the Luxor tomb, you seemed quite adamant that I follow the research in certain directions. What I've shown you today is just one of a dozen viable variations, ranging from mild hallucinations to . . . well . . . to this here." She gestured to the bloody mess behind the glass. "You provided the funding, gave instructions, and told us that you wanted the weapon. Or did I somehow misinterpret your intentions?"

Subject Two was pounding the side of his fist on the glass, trying to strike Conti. Or, maybe, to kill the scorpions he saw crawling out of her skin. Aydelotte watched the man's lips, trying to read the words he was shouting over and over.

I'll save you. I'll save us all.

"No," said Aydelotte.

Dr. Conti's eyebrows went up expectantly. "No . . . *what*, if I may ask?"

"No, you did not misinterpret anything."

He was aware that she was reassessing him, maybe factoring in his squeamishness and matching it against the other things she knew about this man. She had not expected Mr. Miracle—as so many called him—to have a weak stomach.

"If you prefer," she said, deliberately dropping the "sir" to see how he would react, "I can put it all in a coded report and upload it to your server. I can redact the more gruesome elements."

Aydelotte shook his head. "No," he said. "Keep going. Keep me posted. And . . . Doctor . . . ?"

"Yes?"

He gave her that wide, bright, beaming Santa Claus smile. "If you condescend to me again, I'll put you in there with one of your Frankensteins."

With that he walked away, without hurry or a backward glance.

JONATHAN MABERRY

CHAPTER 29
THE MESS HALL
PHOENIX HOUSE

Word went out to the members of Havoc Team to head back to Omfori Island. After Chad they'd scattered, believing that we all had a month of downtime.

Bunny was at his place in Corfu, where he and his wife, Lydia, had moved and settled in with their baby, Brad. Short for Bradley. They'd named the kid after Top Sims, who was Bunny's best friend. If that boy was lucky, he'd have Bunny's gentle nature, Lydia's strength, and Top's wisdom and empathy. Top was his godfather, too, and that was a very good call.

When Brad was born, I'd tried to tell Bunny to take six months off, but he opted for four, and shortened that for the Lake Chad operation. I had no doubt he'd be willing to come right back, too. My guess is that three months of sleepless nights and soiled diapers were enough. He'd rather be in the field and have people shooting at him.

Belle had gone off somewhere with Violin, my ex-lover and frequent colleague. Violin is the senior field operative and top sniper for Arklight, the militant arm of a group called the Mothers of the Fallen. They were a collective of tough women who had either escaped or been rescued from various kinds of sexual slavery, ranging from forced prostitution to inhumane breeding programs. The group was run by Violin's mother, Lilith. She was the single most frightening human being I've ever met. Not sure if she is actually tougher than Church, but I wouldn't want to live on the difference. Not surprisingly, Lilith and Church are lovers.

Oh, yeah, and Lilith is not my biggest fan. Long story, best saved for another time. Like when I'm halfway into a bottle of bourbon.

Andrea was back in Florence with his husband. It was their seventh annual "honeymoon." They're taking it in installments, which seems like a pretty decent plan.

As for Remy Neddo . . . he was in Germany, continuing his RTI training by doing some field combat simulations with my friend Oskar Freund. Oskar was the son of one of Church's old spy buddies from long ago. He was currently a captain in the GSG 9 der

Bundespolizei, a kickass police tactical unit of the German Federal Police. As far as the public knew, GSG 9 focused on hostage situations, kidnapping, terrorism, and similar threats; but like a lot of such organizations, there were off-the-books special divisions. His was known as Sturmfest. Means "stormproof," and is one of the top covert counterterrorism strike forces anywhere. Not surprisingly, Mr. Church was an advisor on its development, and it structurally resembles Rogue Team International.

Remy was in good hands. Oskar knew a trick or two. And he was one of the good guys—wise, optimistic with an underpinning of useful skepticism, stoic, and a humanist. We got along really well.

I was still getting to know Remy myself. Top had been on point as usual when he drafted the kid for Havoc. Remy had an easygoing way about him that was very Cajun; but at the same time, he was as devious and ruthless as he needed to be for this kind of work. Like all of us who work for Church, he is largely apolitical and an idealist willing to pull a trigger to protect the good guys. I had a feeling he was going to work out for the long haul.

That left me on my own for a bit. So I went down to the mess hall to read the file and have too many cups of coffee.

I half hoped, half feared that Rudy would be there, but he wasn't. Which is good because he and I had already had a dozen versions of the conversation between him and Church. There was some shouting but less collateral damage to decorative crockery.

I tried calling him, but every call went straight to voice mail. Sigh. There was a nut-cruncher of an argument waiting to happen there. Like Bunny, some juicy field work sounded pretty good to me about then.

The mess was quiet, with only a couple of techs huddled together over a chessboard and Dora from human resources reading a book titled—I shit you not—*Empathy Made Easy*.

Some kind of classical music was playing softly from concealed speakers, but I couldn't identify it. Moody piano and muted orchestral accompaniment. The RTI coffee wizard, Mustapha, brought me a cup of aromatic joy, and I sipped it in silence while I read the file.

It's always remarkable how something can skate past your social consciousness, leave a mark, but not really play into your understanding. The Dead Sea Scrolls were like that. I mean, I knew they were there. I *had* seen the TV documentaries, though I was likely either smooching with my lady, Junie Flynn, while they were on in the background; or, I was rolling around on the floor with my big goof of a combat dog, Ghost. So my level of comprehension of the details was, as Church pointed out, inaccurate.

The file included a timeline of the discovery of the Scrolls from November 1946 all the way to the present day. So far there had been Scrolls and fragments discovered in twelve caves, the last of which was a pretty recent find. There were notes on the wrestling match over ownership, with Israel, Jordan, and Palestine all making reasonable cases. There was a bit of intrigue with related items—both real and clever fakes—being bought and sold on the various levels of the antiquities markets. There was stuff about American evangelicals working in the Middle East somehow obtaining materials, mostly fragments, and sending them back to churches and museums in the States—which in turn kicked off more legal squabbles. There were a number of instances of complete embarrassment when treasured fragments and even complete Scrolls were determined to be phony.

The deaths of those two scholars, though . . . that was new. That had no precedent in the history of the Scrolls. And, frankly, I didn't know what to make of it.

What the file lacked were autopsy reports, specifically with toxicology results. I took a small notebook out of my pocket and began writing down things I needed, beginning with those tox screens.

It took me three cups of coffee to finish the report. It was heavy on details about the Dead Sea Scrolls, and I felt I had a solid sense of them and their importance. However, bizarre deaths of the doctors were the only thing that *might* make this an RTI case.

I closed the folder, leaned back, and stared at the ceiling. On one hand, this case didn't really seem like it was for us. I'd said as much before reading the file, wavered because of those deaths, but was back to thinking that this was 100 percent an Interpol matter.

So why had Church taken it on as something for Rogue Team?

My free-floating insecurities kept trying to tell me that it was

Church's way of indirectly catering to Rudy and easing back my involvement with anything likely to end in gunfire. Also, this kind of mystery played to my earlier career as a police detective back in Baltimore. For something like this, I probably didn't even need to pack a gun. Nothing would happen. I'd get to see the world a bit, meet some new people. No big.

At the same time, it wasn't like Church to either soft-soap me or waste time and resources. What, then, was he seeing that I was not?

CHAPTER 30
OUTSIDE OF INTERVIEW ROOM C
PHOENIX HOUSE

Bug stood outside of the soundproofed room, watching the inmate on a wall-mounted screen.

"I don't get it," he said. "Seems like he was ready to tell you anything you wanted."

Mr. Church brushed invisible lint from an immaculate lapel.

"He thinks he is ready to do or say anything that will get him answers," he said.

"Isn't that what you want?"

"He needs just a little more time."

With that Church walked away.

INTERLUDE 10
DR. CONTI'S LAB
PIRATE LAB
UNDISCLOSED LOCATION

NINE MONTHS AGO

"Who are they?" asked Shock.

"What does it matter?" said Aydelotte.

Behind the big wall of tempered glass was a long row of cubicles, each big enough for each test subject to lie down, sit, or stand. Every cubicle was filled by either an adult man or an adult woman, dressed in powder blue scrubs and paper slippers.

Dr. Conti was hunched over her desk, studying data that scrolled up from the telemetric units built into the floor of each of the fifteen cubes.

"They don't have electrodes and all that," said Shock.

"We are past that point," said Conti without looking up. "This is in preparation for field-testing."

They watched.

Aydelotte dug into a pocket for a shiny silver card of spearmint gum, popped two pieces out of the blister pack, put the gum in his mouth and crunched the candy coating. Then, without speaking, he offered the gum to Shock. She took it more by reflex than deliberate thought. Her hands went through the same actions her employer's just had, but then she stood, holding the card in one hand and a piece of gum in the other. She never put it in her mouth.

Behind the glass, only two of the figures were standing. Only those two seemed to be aware that there were people watching. Only one seemed to understand what was happening. He beat his fists on the inside of the glass and shouted with such force that bloody spittle flew from his lips. There was no sound except the faintest *thump*s of each blow. None of his words were audible.

The other test subjects knelt or crouched, lay or huddled. Some thrashed with agitated motion, some shivered, some writhed on the ground as if in the throes of slow-motion convulsions. Two lay unmoving, their eyes wide and sightless, the loss of blood pressure dulling the lenses.

"This all seems to be going well," said Aydelotte. "When can we start actual field tests?"

"Two to three weeks," said the doctor. "We'll need to do full workups on each of these subjects. For the survivors, we will want to do extensive interviews after the symptoms wear off."

"And the prophylactic shots? When will we have those?"

"The ketanserin cocktail? Oh, that's already done. I have one of my teams preparing them in single-dose syrettes."

"Very good, Doctor. You've earned your bonus. If you can be ready for field tests in *under* three weeks, I might even double it."

Shock cut him a sharp look but bit back anything she might have said.

Dr. Conti looked at her employer and beamed like a happy child on Christmas morning.

CHAPTER 31
ETZ HAYIM STREET
JERUSALEM, ISRAEL

Toys left the market and became someone else.

Just like that.

It was something he had learned to do back when he worked for Sebastian Gault. Animals like chameleons only change color. He considered himself closer to the leaf-tailed gecko, a small lizard that not only looked like a leaf, but could imitate the way a leaf moved in a breeze. Or the wrap-around spider—pliant, subtle, and patient, and virtually invisible even if you looked right at it. The wolf spider was another of his favorites, blending into gravel or sand so that the unwary prey never suspected it was right there.

He loved that about nature. And he loved those animals far more than he did most people he knew. Animals—even predatory spiders and lizards—were pure. There was no malice in them. Hunting wasn't pernicious, it was survival.

Toys wished he could change who and what he was and become one of them, able to hunt and kill and feed in a way that was in harmony with the cycle of life that defined the natural world. Maybe there would be a measure of peace in that kind of life, even if he was then consumed by something larger. No malice, no evil, no joy in pain inflicted.

No horror at the memories of having killed.

Yes, that would be wonderful.

He wished he believed in reincarnation. Toys would have been fine coming back as any insect or animal on any tier of the food chain. Not as a way of seeking some great karmic redemption. Hardly that. He knew that he deserved none. Not a whisper of compassion or a kind word. His sins were many, and they were cataloged with great

JONATHAN MABERRY

precision and detail in his head. Even when he eventually died—and he assumed it would be a violent death, because his life tended that way—he knew that peace would not be his reward. Punishment, damnation, torment . . . those were what he believed waited for him, and he had come to accept it. Even now, years after his old life with Gault, the Seven Kings, and Hugo Vox, Toys could still remember the name of every single person whose life he ended. Directly or indirectly, those lives were counted against him, and how could—or, indeed, *would*—God ever forgive his sins? Surely there were limits to celestial tolerance, and he had badly abused the privilege.

Those thoughts were always in his head. Always.

When Mr. Church and Joe Ledger destroyed Gault's plans and tore down the Seven Kings, there should have been one extra bullet for him. Dying, even at the hands of that total tosser Joe Ledger, would have been justice.

These were not thoughts he cared to share with the members of his new team. Not that it would matter to them. Every single person in the Wild Hunt had their own slate of crimes behind them. Murderers, spies, thieves, grifters, assholes.

Useful, though.

Especially for jobs like this. Setting up stings of this magnitude wasn't for choirboys.

When Toys stepped out of the market, he changed his body language—becoming less apparently fit, weaken his posture, hunching his shoulders to create a more introverted aspect, and swapping Wayfarers for eyeglasses with no lens correction despite the thick lenses, and fold-down sunglass clips. He altered his gait, removing the indolence and confidence and taking on, instead, a mousy, mincing pace. He dug his hands deep into his pockets to create an insecure and defensive appearance. Even without changing his clothes he became someone else.

Like a gecko or a wolf spider, he faded into the crowd, becoming just another tourist, but one either traveling alone or separated from the shelter of a group. Nothing overt, because it was the subtleties, the nuances that sold that kind of thing.

As he walked, he thought about what Rugger had said. The lad was not wrong about how weird this whole arrangement was. The brief on Aydelotte sold him as an incredibly careful man, one who had iron walls between his legal and illegal activities—so much so that the illegal stuff was just a rumor. Even now, all Toys had was a suspicion that Aydelotte was the bad guy here. This odd auction for some kind of high-tech arms deal was so strange that Church and Wilson thought it might either be a major player letting a convincing public mask slip, or a grandiose fool trying to elbow his way into a whole new league. Dangerous though interesting either way. So they had sent him and his new team, the Wild Hunt, to Israel to find out.

The other bidder was, according to Bug's intel, an Israeli national who went only by the name Lamech. And that name was weird to the point of being amusing. It was taken from an enigmatic character from the Old Testament who was either the father of Noah or the great-great-great grandson of Cain, who became a supreme warrior. Toys rather thought it was the latter that inspired the name's use for this kind of meeting. The biblical Lamech was a right bastard—treacherous and violent. Toys suspected that the implications of the name were meant as some kind of warning.

Note to bloody self, Toys mused as he walked.

He wondered how it would unfold. His revised plan was to accost Aydelotte once it was clear where the now one-sided auction would be held and flow in whichever way the encounter went. His team, with Rugger on overwatch, fed him details on the path Aydelotte and the muscle took. He went a more roundabout way, in case those two were under observation.

Toys's route took him down an alley between buildings, and he picked up his pace a little, skirting dumpsters and stacks of trash in boxes and bags waiting for pickup. The alley stank, but it was usefully placed to get him to where he would intercept his target.

The thing about planning, even superb planning that allowed for interaction and reaction to random events, is that all it takes is one little thing to cock it all up.

Like the two muggers who stepped into his path.

INTERLUDE 11
FIELD TEST 26
GARAJLAR POLIS NOKTASI
FEVZIPAŞA, TURHAN CEMAL BERIKER BOULEVARD
SEYHAN/ADANA, TURKEY

FOUR MONTHS AGO

"No," said Shock, "I'm in earnest. I will give you two hundred lira to deliver this to the police officer at the front desk."

The beggar stared at the mix of bills the woman waved at him. They looked new, and the zeroes had him spellbound.

"Will they arrest me?"

"No," said Shock with a comforting smile.

"But that is a doctor's bag."

"Yes, but you will be committing no crime. You hand the bag to the officer at the desk, tell them you found it on the street, and walk away."

"What if they ask for my name?" asked the beggar, eyes narrowed in suspicion.

"Tell them the truth. Show them your papers. All you are doing is being a good citizen and bringing in something that you found."

The man's eyes were glazed with malnutrition and confusion.

"Why do you want me to do this?"

"For two hundred you do not get to ask questions, my friend." She waggled the bills again and then held out the doctor's satchel with her other hand. Then she pulled the money back. "Unless you don't want the cash."

The beggar's eyes went wide in alarm, and he grabbed for the bag. "No!"

"Excellent," she said, beaming, then handed him a twenty-lira bill. "Here is a sign of my trust. As soon as you come out of the police station, I will give you the rest."

His eyes narrowed again. "How do I know I can trust you? What if you run off with the rest of the money?"

She handed him another twenty. "Would I give you this much if I was going to trick you?"

She watched him work that through. Although forty lira was little more than two dollars American, it was something. A token of good faith. The remaining hundred and sixty would buy very many meals if spent wisely.

"I will wait on that bench over there," she said, and turned away from him. Shock did not need to see him to know that he would do exactly as she asked. She crossed to the bench, sat, took out her phone, and waited. Her screen showed a jumpy picture of the front steps, front door, and then front desk of the police department. Shock put an earbud in and listened to the beggar talking with the desk officer, explaining the bag he found on the street.

The image abruptly changed as the spider drone that had clung unobtrusively to the side of the bag dropped off, scuttled across the lobby, and climbed the wall. It settled into a high corner, folded its telescoping legs back into its body, and became another spot on the busy wallpaper.

From there, Shock had an excellent view of the officer leaning over the desk to take the bag. After a lengthy conversation with the homeless man, the officer called a junior officer over to take a formal statement. While that was going on, the officer began removing items carefully, clearly looking for something that would identify the bag's owner. He removed a stethoscope, sphygmomanometer, infrared thermometer, pulse oximeter, glucometer including appropriate strips and lancets, alcohol wipes, gloves, lubricating jelly, reflex hammer, tongue depressors, and all of the standard equipment.

There was no identification and none of the various alarm devices many doctors carried. However, the instruments had serial numbers, and the officer peered closely at those.

"Where did you say you found this?" asked the officer.

Or at least that's what Shock thought he tried to say. The words that came out of his mouth were a tossed salad of nonsense. The officer frowned; head cocked to one side as if listening to an echo of what he'd said. He barked out a laugh, shook his head, and tried again.

This time he screamed it.

Nonsense words at first.

And then more specific, more striding as he began slapping at the instruments, swatting at huge centipedes that crawled over everything. The junior officer and the beggar turned sharply to see the desk officer pick up a heavy ledger and begin banging the contents of the bag, screaming at the top of his lungs as he did so.

"Sir, *sir*!" cried the junior officer, rushing over. "What are you doing?"

"What do you *think* I'm doing, damn you." *Swat! Swat!* "Get some bug spray."

The junior officer wavered in place, not understanding. Then he looked down at his left hand, frowned at it, recoiled from it, and then backpedaled as that hand began punching his own stomach and groin and chest and face. "That's not mine," he whispered between blows. "That's not mine."

The beggar gaped, cried to Allah, and ran from the station.

He did not run toward Shock, but instead turned and ran as far and as fast as he could from anything related to what was going on inside. He was a block away before the inside of the police station erupted in gunfire.

By then, Shock was in her car and driving away. Her feelings were completely divided. On one hand it was a successful test of the latest version of the designer ergot. On the other hand, her long-held atheism was beginning to crumble, and she was afraid for her own immortal soul.

CHAPTER 32
ALLEYWAY NEAR BEERBAZAAR BREWPUB
JERUSALEM, ISRAEL

They were both about twenty, with shaved heads, tanned faces, clothes that were inexpensive knockoffs of good brands, high-end trainers, and a complete lack of humor or compassion on their faces. One was taller than Toys, with a lot of beef in his chest and shoulders. The other was an inch or so shorter than he was, but heavier than Toys. The short one had a very nasty-looking knife that was probably modeled after something from an epic fantasy movie or a video game, all curves and serrations and a weirdly complex crossguard. The big one had no weapon, but his fists were balled into mallets.

Toys stared at the two of them, unsure whether to feel alarm or amusement. He chose the latter, seasoned with annoyance.

"Are you wankers literally out of your mind?"

"Let's be smart here, fuckhead," said the short one. "Wallet, phone, rings, the lot."

"Seriously? Is this an actual mugging?"

In his ear, Rugger said, "Do you need assistance, boss?"

"Not at this time."

"What?" asked the knifeman.

"Oh, just talking to myself. Where were we? Oh . . . right . . . mugging." He beamed at them. "You have no idea how novel this is. Truly entertaining . . . or would be if you sods picked a better time."

The big man took a threatening step forward. "Guy's fucking nuts."

"I know, I know . . . it's not a conversational moment," said Toys. "I get it. There's usually less banter in such circumstances. But it is really rather funny."

Which is when the big man grabbed him.

Tried to grab him.

Toys saw the weight shift and the movement of those big hands, and he simply walked into it and hit the man in the throat. His hands were a blur. His body gave nothing away—no telltale tension, no change of expression. Even the necessary shift of weight was hidden within the movement of that step. It allowed him to take the normal swing of an arm to hide the upward swing of the strike, the hand gaining speed and force backed by weight coming off his back foot and spilling onto his front one. The only challenge for Toys was to decide which kind of blow and the desired effect.

Killing the muscle-bound bastard would have been easy—two knuckles to the hyoid bone in the throat and Bob's your uncle. Maybe the asshole even deserved it. But murder, even in self-defense, created a raft of potential complications, and he was on the clock.

So he used a spread hand, fingers flat and angled one way, the thumb going the other, wrist angled to drive the side of the index finger knuckle into the side of the Adam's apple. Toys loathed imprecision, and so he put exactly the right amount of force and depth of penetration into the blow.

It felled the man.

His eyes bulged, his face darkened, he clutched his throat and dropped to his knees making thin, whistling, wheezing noises.

Toys's momentum did not stop or even pause; he finished the step that had powered the Y-hand blow, pivoted slightly as his foot landed, turned toward the smaller man and into the arc of the knife arm. He checked the arm's swing at the heaviest part of the forearm, not wanting to hit the inside of the wrist, which would have caused the man's wrist to bend and the knife to fly straight at Toys. Not that the blade would do much harm, but it was a new jacket.

As he blocked, he brought his rear leg up and flicked out with a sharp, snapping kick that buried the steel-reinforced toe of his Doc Martens deep into the knife wielder's scrotum. It folded him, and he made an almost identical sound to his colleague's, though a few octaves higher.

Toys took the knife away from him, kicked him again, this time in the pit of the stomach, and stepped to avoid the resulting spray of vomit. Both men knelt within reach of each other, so Toys cupped the backs of their heads and slammed them together. Very hard. They sagged down to the dirty pavement, blood welling from serious tears in the eyebrow, nose, mouth, and forehead.

"Fucking amateurs," he said with contempt.

There was a narrow gap in the wall where a line had zigzagged downward from the roof. Toys inserted the blade as deeply as it would go and gave it a sudden sideways wrench, snapping the steel an inch from the crossbar. Then he wiped his prints from the handle and dropped it in the puddle of puke.

He hurried along the alley to catch up to his prey.

Toys felt absolutely nothing about the confrontation beyond minor amusement. A mugging. Him? Of all things. Regret, anger, disgust . . . none of those emotions were even a flicker in his mind.

CHAPTER 33
INTERVIEW ROOM C
PHOENIX HOUSE

"Wake up," said the big man.

Marco Russo snapped awake. He saw the man in the folding chair. Different suit. Was it a different day? He scuttled backward into a corner. His body ached and felt oddly heavy. When he touched his face he nearly screamed. He expected stubble from the days spent here.

His beard was thick and long.

He looked at his hands. They were no longer bruised or swollen. Then he realized that he was not wearing the same kind of jumpsuit he'd worn before. That had been pale blue. This was dark orange.

"What . . . ?" he demanded. "What? How long . . . ?"

The question crashed through his mind, but he refused to ask how long he'd been there because no version of that answer was going to do anything but hurt. It was a time bomb of a question.

"Shall we have a conversation?" asked the big man.

"Wh-what . . . ?"

"Or would you prefer to have more time alone with your thoughts?"

Marco Russo began to cry.

"God! Fuck, just ask me . . . What do you want to know? Just *say* something."

The big man sat quietly, hands folded on the tabletop. After a forever time, he spoke.

"You know why you're here. You know what it is we want. What you don't know is how much you have already told us. You don't know how much we already know."

"T-t-told you . . . ?"

"Look at your arms."

Russo did. He shoved up his sleeve and saw the dozens of small marks—old and new—of needle punctures.

"I don't . . . I don't . . ."

"If you ever want to leave this room," said the big man, "you will need to tell it all to me again. No drugs this time. No tricks. As I

JONATHAN MABERRY

said, you don't know what you've already said. You can't know what I know. All you have is an opportunity to tell me everything again. In order. In detail."

"Will you . . . let me go . . . if I tell you?"

The big man stood up and began folding the chair.

"No!" screamed Russo. "Don't go. Please, for the love of Mother Mary and the saints, don't!"

"I will stay if you make it worth my while," said the big man, pausing. "If you ask me another question, then I will go away again. Perhaps it will be three months this time. Or six."

Russo's mouth hung open.

"Shall I stay?" asked the big man. "Or would you prefer to be alone?"

INTERLUDE 12
FIELD TEST 31
TRAVELER'S REST HOTEL
CAIRO AIRPORT ROAD
CAIRO, EGYPT

THREE MONTHS AGO

Shock did not look like herself. Kind of the point.

Her clothes were tailored to give her more hips, more bust, thicker thighs. The wig over her buzz-cut red hair was a confection of cotton candy blond with frosted highlights. She wore a thigh-length demitent of a dress that accentuated her fake curves in exactly the wrong way; beneath the dress were leggings of a deeply unappealing gray-green. Big sunglasses and a lanyard around her neck for passport, cards, and cash.

"What do you mean there's no reservation?" she said—loudly, repeatedly, with different pressures on inflection.

"Madam," said the assistant manager with fragmenting patience, "I can assure you that we have received no reservation in your name. I have checked our entire network."

"I booked it two months ago."

"As you have said. But see . . . ?" He turned his monitor so she could see the calendar of bookings. "There is the date you provided, and here are the confirmation numbers. Yours is not there. It is not in our system at all. And I apologize, but there are no rooms available. We are fully booked."

"That can't be. I *booked* it. And I'm an *American*!"

The argument went the way such arguments go. The more her voice crept up, the more the assistant manager lowered his, trying to coax things down to a discreet level. Finally, Shock threw up her hands and announced to—apparently—all of creation that she would never stay in such a dump of a hotel and would tell positively *everyone* she knew about the poor service.

And then she stormed out.

The assistant manager stood with his eyes closed for several moments, then opened them, hoping to see a happier world free of tourists like her. Then his eyes alit on a cell phone in a worn leather case that was crusted with fake diamonds. It rested on the counter and had to be hers.

"What was that all about?" asked the concierge, who had come back from his break but loitered at the edge of the lobby, not wanting to be drawn in. They spoke English because it was a tourist hotel where most of the trade was from America, Canada, and Great Britain, and it was easier to stick with that language until shift change.

"Another crazy American." The assistant manager told him about it. "And see? She left her phone. That means she'll be back."

"Now you understand why so many people drink," said the concierge, laughing.

The assistant manager nodded.

And nodded.

And kept nodding.

The concierge wore a half-frown/half-smile, waiting for the punch line to whatever bit of comedy the assistant manager was trying to convey.

But the man behind the desk kept nodding.

His head bobbed up and down. At first it was a small thing,

though oddly constant, but with each second the range of motion increased until with each forward movement his chin tapped the knot of his tie, and each lifting movement brought his face completely toward the ceiling.

The assistant manager's body did not move with it.

"What are you doing, Omar?" asked the concierge.

The head went up and down, up and down.

"Omar . . . are you quite all right?"

Up and down.

Up and down.

"Omar? Are you unwell?"

Up and down.

Concerned and alarmed, the concierge hurried around the desk but stopped a few inches from his friend, one hand reaching only to the halfway point between them.

Up and down, up and down, up and . . .

Stop.

The motion came to an abrupt halt.

"Omar, you are very funny . . ." said the concierge tentatively. "I don't . . ."

Without turning to him, Omar said, *"Wajhuk yahtariqu."*

The concierge froze. His friend had just told him that the concierge's face was on fire. Another joke?

"What . . . what are you saying?" he asked.

The concierge looked at the cell phone Omar still held.

"Wajhuk yahtariqu."

"Omar, you're scaring me. Should I call someone? A doctor . . . ?"

And the assistant manager struck him in the face with the cell phone. The leather case was thick and heavy, and the blow caught the concierge on the bridge of the nose. He staggered backward against the rear wall, grabbing his face with both hands, screaming in shock and pain.

"Wajhuk yahtariqu."

The assistant manager hit him again, this time smashing the backs of the hands clutching the shattered nose.

"Wajhuk yahtariqu."

The next blow was on the mouth.

"*Wajhuk yahtariqu.*"

The eyebrow.

"*Wajhuk yahtariqu.*"

Everywhere. The concierge sank to his knees, blood welling between the fingers of one hand as he tried—and failed—to fend off the series of fast, savage, relentless blows.

"*Wajhuk yahtariqu.*"

It took half a minute for those screams to bring the head of housekeeping and a porter running.

But by then the concierge was dead.

They had to tackle the assistant manager. He was not a big man, but every ounce of his body was committed to his task. He screamed the same comment over and over.

Your face is on fire.

Eventually it took five people to restrain him.

But by then the assistant manager had bitten off most of his own tongue.

CHAPTER 34
THE MESS HALL
PHOENIX HOUSE

Church sent me a text message that the scholars he was expecting had arrived and were setting up a briefing in mission briefing room seven. I responded with a gif of a dancing vanilla wafer. He did not reply. I sometimes wonder if I inspire him to bang his head on the wall when no one's looking.

I lingered over the last of my coffee while I sent two more text messages. One was to Junie, to tell her that I hoped she had a safe flight. She was taking a FreeTech team to Serbia, where droughts and the receding waters of the Danube River near the town of Prahovo had uncovered dozens of World War II–era German warships that had been scuttled in 1944 to hamper Soviet pursuit when the war was turning against the Third Reich. There was a multinational group in play because some of those ships still contained ammunition and explosives, which had to be removed, inventoried, and safely destroyed. However, Junie and FreeTech were there to assess some "anomalous Nazi tech," as she put it, that was found on two ships.

FreeTech is a company Church funds that takes the kinds of technology guys like me and my teams take away from the bad guys. Weird science, bad science, radical science. Junie, who is smarter than the average bear, works to analyze, reverse engineer, and then repurpose the stuff to use for humanitarian purposes. Some of the horrifying stuff we took from the Jakobys, Seven Kings, Red Knights, and other groups is now helping to reclaim farmed-out soil, provide medical care for people living in abject poverty, build houses powered by alternative energies, and more.

In a way, this is like some of the stuff DARPA developed for the Department of Defense making its way into everyday use— everything from the internet to GPS. Junie thinks bigger, though. One of about a zillion reasons I love her to pieces and, more importantly, respect the living hell out of her. If we, as a species, have any hope of surviving, she is the kind that we should encourage. She's on the right part of the bell curve. I, admittedly and without hesitation, accept that I am a more primitive and less productive member of society. I protect it, but I'm not sure that earns me a place in it going forward. Funny, that.

Junie was probably already on her flight, but I sent the happy travels message anyway. With lots of hearts and kissy face emojis. Yes. I use emojis. Big, strong, badass SpecOps goon. Sue me.

The second text was to Rudy.

I did not apologize, because that would have been conciliatory without being true. Instead, I said that I wanted to talk with him about it. Talk, not fight. I had zero doubts that once he calmed down, he would want to have that conversation. He is, as I've said a lot of times, one of the good ones. Civilized, moral, empathetic, insightful, ethical, and decent. The fact that he hadn't scraped me off his shoe long ago proved that.

I sent the text. No emojis. I'm not altogether weird.

Then I got up, tucked the file under my arm, and was about to leave when a large white bundle of fur, fangs, and slobber came bounding into the room, tail wagging furiously enough to give his ass some lift.

It charged at me, and if I hadn't had the reflexes to slap the folder down on the table the whole thing would have been confetti.

"Ghost, you silly bastard!" I yelled, trying to fend off what felt like eight wet noses and a dozen tongues.

"The correct phrase is 'son of a bitch,'" said a voice, and I turned to see a tall woman with thick brown hair standing apart, blue eyes filled with amusement, smile askew, hands shoved into the back pocket of her jeans. She wore a T-shirt with a logo that read:

I like my dog and **maybe** three people!
(Alas . . . you didn't make the cut)

"JM," I cried, "get this fool dog off of me. I thought you were trying to teach him some manners and decorum."

JM—Jessica McNerney—said, "'Sup?"

Ghost began prancing around between us, looking everywhere in case doggie treats materialized out of the blue. He cut some meaningful looks at Mustapha, too, who was known to smuggle Ghost's favorites—dried goat strips—in his apron pocket.

I patted my pockets, pretended that I had nothing, and saw Ghost's tail and ears begin to droop. Then I made the grand discovery of some treats and made him sit to take them with at least a pretense of manners.

JM watched me. She was the RTI animal trainer and was pretty much a dog whisperer. No matter how grouchy, moody, or aggressive any dog was, she could reach it and bring it back to balance. I'm pretty sure Ghost gave her higher placement in my own damn pack than he did me.

We sat at a table, and Mustapha appeared as if by magic with a fresh cup for me—a little milk, no sugar—and a sweet and light with half-and-half for JM. Ghost, apparently exhausted from ten seconds of foolish romping, flopped on his side and acted like he'd just run the Boston Marathon while carrying saddlebags of lead ingots. Dog really deserved an Oscar for Most Dramatic.

JM took an experimental sip. Sighed. Blew a kiss at Mustapha and sat back. "So, what did you do to piss off Rudy like that?"

"Like what?"

"I saw him heading to the helipad a bit ago. He looked like he was ready to bite the heads off live mice."

I shrugged. "He isn't a fan of me going back on the job."

She cocked her head at me. "Is he wrong, though?"

"Oh, don't you start."

"Just saying."

"Say something else." We drank coffee. "How's the pack?"

The pack in question was a bunch of young dogs she was training for field work. They were half white shepherd and half Irish wolfhound. Beautiful monsters, all seven of them. The mother, the full-bred wolfhound Banshee, had been a gift to Church's daughter, Circe O'Tree. Circe was married to Rudy. Circe and Church were rarely on speaking terms. Because I worked with Church and because Rudy had twice been hurt after I'd convinced him to join Mr. Church's war, Circe kind of hated me. It did not help that on a visit to their house, Ghost got jiggy with Banshee.

I am seldom invited to their house.

Those pups were now in the care and training of JM and would eventually get paired with members of the various RTI teams. The exceptions were two who, upon graduation, would be sent into private life. Siren, the largest of the females, and the one with more wolfhound genes expressing dominance, would be the new companion of my lover, Junie Flynn. The other, a husky male named Whisper, was a wedding present for Bunny and Lydia.

Part of that was for fun; part of it was protection, given what happened to my family. I also had Bug install all kinds of security systems in and around the homes of all the family members of the RTI staff. Church wrote that check without batting an eye.

JM, as sweet-natured as she appeared, was training Whisper and Siren to protect their new families. The parent dogs were friendly and playful to everyone who didn't try to harm their pack. Less so with bad guys. I can tell you stories, but you'd need a strong stomach.

"The kids are fine," said JM. "Smartest dogs I ever trained."

Ghost gave her a look that was half smug and half darkly amused.

"Yes, you, too, you crazy furball."

Ghost put his head back down and returned to his doggy dreams.

After a few small, thoughtful sips of her coffee, JM gave me an appraising look. There are chips of a vibrant green mixed in with the icy blue of her eyes. It gave her a somewhat ethereal quality, and her long nose and high cheekbones made her look like one of the high elves from *The Lord of the Rings*.

"Ghost went through a lot last year," she said. "With you."

"He did."

"I've been testing him in reactive drills to see how bad his PTSD is."

"You mean to see if he *has* PTSD . . . ?"

She looked at me over the rim of her cup. There was challenge there if I was dumb enough to walk down that alley.

"And . . . ?" she asked in exactly the way a cat might ask a question of a clueless mouse.

"And how's he doing?" I said quickly.

She smiled. Also catlike. "He's coming along nicely."

"Can I take him with me?"

We both turned and looked at Ghost. He has six titanium teeth—replacements for those lost in battle. He's had all kinds of upgrades in terms of hormone shots to repair muscle damage, steroid therapy for his hip joints, some spider silk–wrapped flex-metal reinforcements on his rib cage, and a daily cocktail of vitamins.

"Try not to get him hurt," she said.

"I'll be real careful."

"You better," she said in a way that was not a joke. I made a mental note to never get on her bad side.

"Scout's honor," I said.

We finished our coffee in companionable silence.

Then Church texted again. No written message. Just an emoji of a ticking clock. I smiled, gave JM a hug, and left with Ghost trotting happily beside me.

INTERLUDE 13
TRAVELER'S REST HOTEL
CAIRO AIRPORT ROAD
CAIRO, EGYPT

THREE MONTHS AGO

Shock sat in her car on the far side of the hotel parking lot. The wig and sunglasses were gone. The fat suit was in the trunk, and she wore modest clothes and a pale lavender hijab.

She waited until she saw the flashing lights in the distance, their glow seemingly lifted by the howling sirens.

"And . . . ?" asked Jason Aydelotte.

"Like a charm. Single person, full involvement, no cross-contamination."

"That's excellent," said Mr. Miracle. "Wish we had video."

Shock laughed. "You want me to bring a camera crew next time?"

"Ha! No," he said. "I need to know it works, but I don't need to actually *see* it."

He ended the call. Shock put her car in gear, and drove away at a sedate speed, though her boss's comments bugged her.

CHAPTER 35
OBSERVATION ROOM, ADJACENT TO INTERVIEW ROOM C
PHOENIX HOUSE

"God damn," said Bug, "he won't shut up."

He sat in one of the three chairs in the small, soundproofed room. Scott Wilson sat to his right, eyes narrowed, face intent. On the other side of the two-way mirror, Mr. Church sat with fingers laced on the tabletop as Marco Russo talked and talked and talked.

Wilson made a face of sour disapproval. "He's ranting. He keeps telling us the same thing over and over again."

"Sure, but each time there's a little more."

But the chief of operations shook his head. "I rather think he's stalling. Giving us more and more detail about one thing and trying to sell us on the idea that it's the only thing he has to sell."

"Okay, maybe," conceded Bug, "but this is literally why Joe and the guys nabbed him. This thing. A new kind of payload for an RPG and an updated version of the laser guidance system that ISIS has already been using. That's huge. I mean, granted, we have to figure out what the *new* thing is, but we have enough now to begin working on some kind of targeted jammer. I mean, come *on*, with what he's already given us I can start writing code right now to mess that whole guidance system up. This is big, Scott. This is a monster win for us."

"Yes, it's brilliant," said Wilson, but his tone was flat.

"You couldn't be less enthused. I don't get that. What else were you hoping for?"

"It's not what I'm hoping for, Bug. It's what Mr. Church wants."

"Which is . . . ?"

"That's just it . . . We don't know."

Bug blinked. "Um . . . you lost me."

"Church thinks there is something even bigger coming our way," explained Wilson. "This RPG guidance system is more or less yesterday's news. It's all about the new payload, and Russo knows it. Or maybe even something else. Bigger, badder, worse. Russo knows that the longer he can stall, the longer he figures it'll be before we ship him off to a black site prison where God won't even be able to find him."

"He's not wrong." Bug sniffed. "Okay, sure, Scott, but I got a bad feeling there's a big ol' clock ticking out there somewhere. Just the thought of a 'special payload' makes me want to hide under my bed."

"Learning what the payload is will get us only halfway there, Bug," said Wilson. "We know that he's developing it for ISIS, but to what end? What's the target? Where and when? We don't even know if Russo has those answers. Which is why Church is moving pieces around. Toys and the Wild Hunt working their way into one of Aydelotte's auctions in the hopes the materials he wants to sell *are* this thing. And he has a briefing scheduled with Ledger about some random oddities that Church thinks are somehow connected, though I don't yet see how. Nor, I suspect, does he. Not entirely. He's going on fragments of apparently unconnected intel, guesswork,

JONATHAN MABERRY

and—I think—his gut. Well, that and some of Church's personal contacts—"

"His friends in the industry?" suggested Bug.

"Just so. Some of them have whispered something about a *storm* coming."

"Should I assume 'storm' is a metaphor?"

"It could be that, or a group code name, or the name of a planned operation. Whatever it is, it's supposed to be big. More than big. Huge. Massive. Something that, according to whispers that have come down the lane, is the biggest terrorist action so far. Bigger than anything we've ever seen."

Bug's eyes bulged behind his glasses. "Bigger than 9/11?"

"If the rumors are at all accurate and can be believed, then yes. Many times bigger."

"What's bigger than that? Unless someone drops a nuke."

"Let's hope it's not *that* big," said Wilson with a bit of a nervous laugh. "But who knows? Rumors are just words on the wind. I pointed out to Mr. Church that this is hardly the first time we've had rumors of some huge ISIS event—an assassination of a head of state, some new way to knock down airliners, even a dirty bomb in the New York or London undergrounds. Lots of rumors that the sky is falling."

"To be fair, man," said Bug, "some of those things were real plans, and we kicked the dicks off the guys planning them. Like last February when Bedlam Team stopped that rogue Russian group from deploying that thermobaric weapon against Kyiv to try and turn the war back in favor of Putin. That would have pretty much blown the wheels off Ukraine's resistance."

"Point taken."

"Or maybe it's something like what happened in Beirut in 2020. There's been a lot of talk about how that whole 'accidental' detonation of stored explosives and chemicals and nitrates was actually done on purpose by an Israeli black-ops group."

"Which was disproven," said Wilson.

"Sure, but there's a crap-ton of people on the conspiracy theory network who say that the *proof* was really a cover-up. So . . . maybe Lebanon or their buddies in the terrorist fuck-head network want to pull a payback stunt in, say, Tel Aviv, Ashdod, or Haifa. Or New York, Philly, or Baltimore, for that matter."

"That's the kind of thing Mr. Church is hoping to find out." Wilson took a cigarette from a slim silver case, looked at it longingly, sighed, replaced it, and put the case back into his suit coat pocket. Then he fished a packet of gum from a desk drawer, popped a piece from the blister pack, and chewed for a few seconds as they watched the interview.

They sat for a moment, each digesting different parts of the conversation.

Bug said, "I think I'll put Nikki and her team on that 'storm' thing. If it's a code name of some kind, then it'll likely have been used more between players than an actual name, and we have a few zillion hours of wiretaps from all through the Middle East, and more emails and texts than I can count. Nikki has that new Polyglot software she wrote. It looks for words and colloquial phrases related to words and meanings, with a bias for metaphor, and includes all four thousand sixty-five written languages currently in use around the world, and a whole lot of dialects. Who knows, maybe we'll get a hit that helps us figure out what in the hell's going on. Or at least a direction to start looking. Something Toys or Joe can use."

Wilson brightened. "Yes, do that. When Mr. Church comes out for his next break, I'll let him know. Perhaps there are other keywords he can work into the next round of questions."

Bug nodded and stood up. "The storm is coming," he repeated. "Yeah, I really don't like the sound of that."

"Neither does the boss," said Wilson dryly. "That's why he's working Russo personally."

On the other side of the glass, Church looked at his watch and stood up, turned, and walked out in the middle of Russo's diatribe.

"Wait!" cried the prisoner. "I'm not done."

The door closed.

Wilson glanced at his watch, too. "You better make that conversation with Nikki a quick one. I think the big man is about to start the briefing for Colonel Ledger."

Bug's good humor leaked away. "Yeah, damn it. And between you and me, Scott, Joe's not going to like it one damn bit."

"Oh," said Wilson, "I expect that he'll absolutely hate it."

He wasn't smiling when he said it.

CHAPTER 36
THE BASEMENT ROOM
PIRATE LAB
UNDISCLOSED LOCATION

Jason Aydelotte took the vial from Dr. Conti and held it up to the light.

"It looks like water."

"That's a design feature," she said. "We don't want it too visible. In certain light it can look a little amber, but very faint."

"They'll still figure it out, though?"

"In time, sure. But that would happen days or, more likely, weeks after exposure. There won't be anything that alerts anyone that there is a bioweapon in play. Even while it's happening, there will be none of the usual telltale signs. No lesions, no coughing up blood or foaming at the mouth. No bleeding from anywhere. No skin changes. The liquid will keep Shiva viable, and the Gorgon warhead your Mr. Russo has developed will detonate with no bang, no fire, and no debris except for the cellulose casings and a light mist that will distribute it evenly. If there's anything alarming it will be the actual incoming rockets, if they see them, but he said he's field-tested the detonation of each Gorgon component, and the cellulose bursts apart very quietly."

"It'll probably look like either a failed attack or a prank," said Toombs, who stood looking at the row of empty cubicles. He was Aydelotte's latest field sales manager. A cold, reserved, intelligent man.

There was still old blood smeared on some of the inner walls. Toombs studied it for a moment.

"There'll be a lot of people running around trying to figure it out," he said. "But all they'll have to work with will be those pieces of the warhead."

"And by then the symptoms will be presenting," said Conti. She glanced from Toombs to Aydelotte, who was smiling from ear to ear. "And by then it won't matter at all."

That made Aydelotte's smile grow even brighter.

CHAPTER 37
MISSION BRIEFING ROOM 7
PHOENIX HOUSE

I came into the mission briefing room and saw that there were three people I knew in the room and one stranger.

Church was seated behind a conference table and damn if there wasn't a fresh plate of cookies in front of him. Mostly those ghastly vanilla wafers, but also some Oreos, a Noah's Ark of animal crackers, and some madeleines, which I'd never seen him offer before.

Sitting on the corner of the table, sneakered feet swinging, was Bug. Short, thin, nerdy-looking black man—he prefers the term "berd": black nerd. He had unkempt hair, glasses with bright red frames, and a *Wakanda Forever* sweatshirt. One of my favorite human beings. He grinned and gave me a Vulcan salute, which, of course, I returned.

"Hey, Joe," Bug said brightly. "Nice going in Chad."

"Thanks. Any word yet on those kids we brought out?"

"Doc has it mostly figured out," said Bug. "Some kind of fungus thing. I keep trying to get information directly, but every time I knock on her door, she threatens to have my organs removed and donated to science."

"She's joking."

"Would you call her on that?" he asked.

"Nope."

He made a *there you go* gesture.

Bug ran the joint divisions of computer support and information processing, which were two of the largest components of RTI. His understanding of computers, social media, cybersecurity, and hacking were second to none. Church hired him after Bug, using his own modified laptop, had hacked into the Department of Defense, the CIA, DARPA, and several branches of military intelligence as part of a well-intentioned but thoroughly illegal attempt to locate Osama bin Laden. It was jail or the DMS. And it wasn't long after that he actually located bin Laden and shared his intel with the Joint Chiefs, who then sent SEAL Team Six off to bag the bastard.

Bug also oversaw the functions, use, and upgrades for MindReader Q1, the bizarrely advanced computer system that had originally been built by some very bad guys. Church appropriated it, did some of his own tweaks, and then handed it off to Bug. Bug and Church co-wrote a super-intrusion software package that allowed MindReader to enter any other computer, rewriting the target's security software to eliminate all traces of the hack, and steal information. Most of the time the targets were the computers used by our enemies; sometimes they hacked our friends who were, for one reason or another, being stingy about sharing.

Ghost ran to Bug and began sniffing his pockets and wagging his bushy tail expectantly. The dog is not subtle. Like everyone else, Bug has been well trained by the fuzz-monster, and he dug into a pocket to produce some treats. Ghost licked his hand gently and then took the dried meat over to a corner, flopped down, and began eating them with the unusual delicacy that was his habit.

Church merely nodded to me. Man can't shut up. Total chatterbox.

The third person I knew was someone I hadn't expected to see there at Phoenix House. A woman, tall, thin, pale, freckly, with lots of frizzy brown-blond hair, piercing blue eyes filled with intelligence and knowledge, and an easy smile.

"Lizzie . . . ?" I said in surprise.

"Hey, Joe. Been a while."

She gave me a crushing hug.

Dr. Elizabeth Corbett was one of those multidisciplinary types who always make me feel stupid, but in a good way. Like being in an elevator with Neil deGrasse Tyson. Her former job had the wildly misinformative title of "obscure manuscript expert" for the Beinecke Rare Book & Manuscript Library at Yale. In truth she was a polyglot whose command of languages, current and dead, was astonishing. Even by my standards, and people think I'm a freak for being able to remember languages and dialects.

She was also a cryptologist who loved cracking codes, deciphering ancient texts, and making the inexplicable understandable. When I'd met her, she had signed on as some kind of super geek field agent for the Library of Ten Gurus, a group of Sikhs working to preserve works of art and literature from destruction by ISIS.

"Didn't expect to see you here, Lizzie."

"Well, I didn't expect to be needed. But . . ."

"Let me guess," I said, stepping back from her. "You're *also* an expert on the Dead Sea Scrolls."

She grinned. "I know one or two things."

"Of course you do."

"But the real expert is my friend Debra." She turned toward the stranger, a woman of medium height, brown eyes, and brown hair with vibrant purple streaks, wearing a University of Maine Black Bears hockey T-shirt under an open dress shirt with—god help me—an actual pocket protector sprouting too many pens. "Colonel Joe Ledger, meet Debra Getts, professor of archaeology from Harvard. Want to guess what her specialty is?"

"Not sure, but I suspect it rhymes with head tree rolls . . . ?"

Getts grinned and offered her hand. "Colonel Ledger," she said, giving my hand a hard one-two pump. "I've heard some pretty wild stories."

"I deny nearly everything."

"I'm told there's photographic evidence."

I liked her immediately.

Church said, "Colonel, in the absence of your team, you'll get the full briefing and Drs. Corbett and Getts will provide you with data you can share with the others en route."

"En route to . . . ?"

"Israel, but we'll get to that."

I took a seat on one side of the conference table with the two women across from me. Church and Bug sat at opposite ends. Monitor screens folded up from the tabletop in front of each of us.

Church cut me a quick look. "This may take a while, so try to listen without a glaze in the eyes."

"Sure," I said.

INTERLUDE 14
QUMRAN
THE WEST BANK, ISRAEL

NINETEEN MONTHS AGO

There were three of them left.

Eight members of the team had crossed from Jordan into Israel by a route so subtle and devious that it took ten days to make a journey of sixty-eight miles. Their destination was a nondescript-looking building whose website proclaimed that it was a field research clearinghouse for research into the dramatic drop in Israel's biodiversity. The center was currently involved in cataloging expansion of invasive species such as camphorweed, water hyacinth, sour grass, Indian myna, rose-necked parakeet, and burr ragweed.

That was all a front, according to intelligence acquired by Harith al-Wazir, the leader of the ISIS splinter group Al-zilal. Harith discovered that the so-called research center hid a factory making specialized military and espionage drones. Photos had been circulated to team leaders of the inside of the building, complete with cutting-edge 3-D printers, and long tables of artists painting and dressing the drones to resemble birds and insects. Machines that would help Israel hunt for Palestinian *fedayeen* and other dedicated resistance groups. Machines that would ultimately be used against the many cells and groups that were the freedom fighters for the Islamic State.

Harith seemed able to get information no one else could. None of the members of his group knew who he really was, but they all accepted him as a great leader. A visionary. Powerful, inflexible, dedicated to an interpretation of the Quran that did not allow for weakness or compromise.

His followers were known only as Al-zilal—the Shadow. Unlike many of the other Daesh groups following the Salafi jihadist path and fighting to establish and perpetuate the Islamic State, Al-zilal was always better equipped and possessed more reliable intelligence sources.

This sophistication allowed the eight members of the Shadow to obtain travel and ID documents that smoothed the way. But they could not travel in a pack. Each had a separate cover, except for two who looked enough like brothers to play those roles. Their equipment was sent in separately, and most of the time that passed was spent on watching, more watching, double-checking everything, and being sure.

The eight Shadows found their equipment where Harith had promised it would be. Long sand-colored canvas bags were buried at specific GPS points. They unearthed the bags and spent precious time checking each AK-47 and—more important—the four RPG-7s. The rocket-propelled grenade launchers were classics, the same basic model Somali militiamen used to down two US Army helicopters in Mogadishu in 1993, and all throughout the conflict in Afghanistan. They were lightweight, man-portable, and the perfect choice against vehicle convoys, checkpoints, and helicopters.

Or small research centers.

The downside was that the RPG-7 had a maximum effective range of about a thousand feet for a moving target and 1,600 feet for a stationary one. There were fences and foot patrols with dogs, and so the Shadows had to find positions that were within range but where they could not be seen until the weapons were fired. They split into teams of two, with one man each carrying an RPG and the other acting as spotter and ready to provide covering fire.

They waited all through a hot day, flattened into natural depressions on the ground, covered with canvas tarps that matched the ground cover. The men slept in shifts, with one always awake. They prayed very quietly. They talked very little.

As the sun set slowly in the west, they stirred. They ate some high-protein snacks, drank plenty of water, and stretched their aching muscles as best they could. Once darkness settled like a blanket over the area, they rose from their hiding places and moved into position near the four corners of the oblong Center for Biodiversity Research building.

Each of the spotters had wristwatches that had been precisely synchronized. When the shooters fired, it was like clockwork. Four streaks of gray exhaust; four bombs arching over the guards and the dogs and the fences. Four blows like the fists of God struck the building. Four massive explosions.

The spotters were ready to help them reload.

And fire.

Reload and fire.

Four rounds each. Eight explosions. Eight statements made in a way that everyone would understand.

And then the eight Shadows fled.

Two dogs, released by their masters, caught up with them, dragging two men down in screaming agony. Then the attack helicopters arrived. A pair of them, firing guns that tore the night to shreds.

Five of the Shadows made it to the first extraction point only to see it blown apart by rockets. One of the team was caught in the blast radius, and he vanished inside a fireball.

Four made it to the third extraction point. One lingered—the only one who had kept his RPG-7. He reloaded and drew fire from the closest helo, catching its rotor, knocking it out of the air, but then having no chance to run or even pray as the second bird opened up and tore him to rags.

The other three made it out of there.

It took days. They found one extraction point where they could change into civilian clothing and, pretending to be bedouins, vanish into the hills around the southern reach of the Dead Sea.

They were weary, frightened, grieving, and hunted. The hills of Qumran were rough, broken, difficult, and dangerous. That was to their benefit. By sunset of the third day since the completion of their mission, they found a cave in the hills that was deep enough to hide from air surveillance. They clambered inside and collapsed against the back wall.

There they prayed. And wept.

It was sometime in the middle of the night when one of them heard a faint cracking sound coming from one of the chinks in the rear wall. He risked a tiny, shielded light to see what it was. There were snakes and scorpions in those hills. There were also bedouin shepherds, and they did not want to have to deal with any surprises.

The Shadow moved his hand along the wall, listening intently for that cracking sound.

"What is it?" whispered one of his friends.

"I don't know," said the searcher. "The wall here is broken and the ground is—"

There was another, much louder *crack* and suddenly the rocky ground beneath his feet collapsed downward, and he fell screaming. Then there was a huge but muffled crashing sound, mingled with all sorts of strange interior noises, like newspaper and dishware breaking.

The others scrambled over and shone their flashlights down, expecting to see their companion in a shallow hole. But the beams reached much farther down and found the third man sprawled in an ugly and broken way in the midst of smashed debris. All around him, and stretching off beyond the limits of the flashlights' glow, were red-brown clay jars. Dozens of them. Scores. More.

The fallen Shadow groaned and whimpered in pain. He was alive, though with a badly broken leg. For a long moment the two others seemed oblivious to him. Their eyes were drawn to all those jars. And to the ones that had been shattered when the third man fell. Those broken jars had burst apart, spilling uncountable rolls of paper. No, not paper. Parchment or maybe vellum.

Old writings.

Very, very old.

They rigged a line and climbed down, and as one worked to lash a makeshift splint for their friend, the other began picking up and examining the scrolls. He saw that the papers were written in Hebrew. Some in other languages. One of the men thought it might be old Greek.

And others were written in a different kind of language. Pictures rather than words. Pictures they could not read but which all of them could recognize.

Egyptian. The old kind, but from the days of the pharaohs.

"What is all this?" gasped the injured man.

"You know where we are," said the second, the eldest of them.

"Jordan," said the third.

"No," said the eldest. "We are in one of the caves. One of *those* caves." He held up the scrolls. "These are Dead Sea Scrolls."

"Who cares what they are?" growled the third. "We need to get Ali out of here."

"Yes," said the eldest, "we do."

But he was thinking of other things they needed to do.

"We need to tell Harith al-Wazir about this."

"The Lion? Why tell him? This is Jewish trash."

The eldest shook his head. "No. This is not trash. I think this is important."

CHAPTER 38
MISSION BRIEFING ROOM 7
PHOENIX HOUSE

They dug in by giving me a history of the Dead Sea Scrolls. How bedouin teens found them. How an unknown quantity of them were sold before the real value was understood. How those items are still missing, and no one knows what was in them. Lots of post–World War II politics in the setting up of the state of Israel, and the resulting—and ongoing—conflict with Arabs who have lived in that area for centuries.

Nothing—not one single blessed thing—in the Holy Land is separate from politics. Not in, say, the last four thousand years. Probably never will be a time when that's not a factor. The Jews, Christians, and Muslims all feel they have a legitimate and religiously mandated right of ownership of the real estate and everyone found on it. No political philosopher I've ever heard of has ever concocted a solution that the individual parties would ever agree to. Which is both funny and sad. All three of those religions believe in the same god. But they will burn the world down in defense of their own interpretations of God.

This used to drive my mother nuts. She was a peacemaker and pragmatist. Very religious woman, though fiercely opposed to any kind of proselytizing. It offended her understanding of the peaceful teachings of Jesus that no one seems to have taken his "live and let live and along the way be nice to each other" teachings as an actual life plan.

I've lost my own religion over the years, and my view on the common goddamn sense of people has become quite cynical. Optimism in the face of that much enduring hatred is tough to maintain.

So, yeah, I could follow the politics, and that helped me grasp the importance of the Dead Sea Scrolls.

"The Scrolls have their roots in what we call the Second Temple Era," said Getts. "In 586 BCE King Nebuchadnezzar II of Babylon conquered the kingdom of Judah and captured Jerusalem in a violent attack that destroyed what we call the First Temple. The one built by Solomon. The Judeans were sent to Babylon as slaves. The level of brutality was shocking, with a kind of scorched-earth approach. The lands were emptied, and that entire culture teetered on the brink of extinction."

"First of many such disasters," said Lizzie grimly.

"Too many," agreed Church.

"Things got a bit better after the Persian conquest of Babylon. King Cyrus the Great issued an edict stating that the Judahites were allowed to return to their home. They began building a second temple in Jerusalem. But Persian tolerance was not actual freedom. It wasn't until the second century BCE that Judea regained its independence during the Maccabean Revolt. Things settled down a bit, but not for long. When Queen Regent Salome Alexandra, the very last of the independent rulers of Judea, died in 67 BCE, there was an ugly power struggle. This opened the door for Rome to step in, and in 63 BCE General Pompey captured Jerusalem, and that turned Judea into a tributary of Rome." She paused and cut me a look. "Are you following me?"

"I am," I said. "You have my complete attention."

"One of the side effects—and a rather understandable one," continued Getts, "was an abiding need among the religious class of Judea to protect their history, culture, and blessed writings. So many of these things, particularly the latter, had been lost to wars, oppression, enslavement, and a general hatred for their culture."

Lizzie nodded. "Monotheism likely played a big part in that. The Babylonians, Egyptians, and Romans were devoutly pantheistic, and were offended by the thought that there was one god. They wanted to squash that kind of thinking and were not gentle about it."

Getts nodded. "The Second Temple was originally a modest thing. Certainly nowhere near as grand as Solomon's. And that Second Temple stood for approximately five hundred eighty-five years before it, too, was destroyed. This time by the Romans in 70 CE as retaliation for a Jewish revolt. So much of Jewish history and writings had been deliberately destroyed by the various occupying forces that they had been forced into a practice of hiding things."

I snorted. "I would, too, if I was them."

"There's a lot of debate over who wrote the Scrolls, and why. One of the few definitive things we can say is that Jews wrote them. Beyond that we're into speculation, and there are a lot of experts with a lot of theories," said Lizzie.

"Whose theories are the most plausible?" I asked.

Getts gave me a nod of approval. "The conventional wisdom is that a group of religious ascetics called the Essenes wrote them. They are believed to have occupied Qumran during the first centuries BCE and CE. But new research suggests that a bunch of different Jewish sects wrote them. And the fact that they were all found in caves in the same region supports this in that Jews fleeing the Romans, knowing that destruction of religious writing was common to the legionnaires, grabbed what they could and simply hid it away in hope of returning it to a new temple in more peaceful times."

"'Peaceful times' in the Holy Land," I mused. "That sounds like an oxymoron."

"Sadly, history agrees."

I reached out and took a couple of Oreos from the plate and, just for fun, a handful of animal crackers. Tiger, rhinoceros, cow, and donkey. Shrugged. Fished around until I got the rest of the species. Bear, bison, camel, cat, elephant, hippopotamus, horse, lion, and mountain goat. Call me a completist. I debated going full Noah and taking two of each, but I was already getting looks.

"So, I get the ancient history," I said. "What's next? Oh, and when does this move into two scientists writing weird messages about bats and then killing themselves?"

Lizzie gave me a strange and enigmatic smile. It was a little creepy, truth to tell. "Oh," she said, "it's going to get a lot weirder than that. Buckle up."

INTERLUDE 15
QUMRAN
THE WEST BANK, ISRAEL

NINETEEN MONTHS AGO

The three Shadows escaped from the cave.

It took days, and it took effort.

Once the two uninjured men rigged a rope hoist and lifted Ali from the cave, they made a stretcher and carried him more than six miles north. Once they found a likely spot, one of them scrambled to the top of a steep slope, found some medium-size rocks, and tumbled them down. With a little set dressing the scene looked like the kind of place where even a young man like Ali could slip and fall. They placed him there, rehearsed their story, then left him with water and food. It took another few hours before they encountered local bedouins, told their sad tale, and brought help back.

It is the bedouin way to aid strangers and offer hospitality, and soon Ali was transported off to a local doctor. Only then did one of the other Shadows—Hakim—remove a burner phone from a concealed place in his clothes and make a call.

The person taking the call passed the message up the line. More than a day passed before a reply came. It was not Harith al-Wazir, of course. The Great Lion ran their group, but he never made direct contact. All messages and orders trickled down through a necessarily complex chain of command. The person who finally called used a false name, but Hakim recognized the voice. It was Ayoob Alazaki. That was a person of much greater importance than he expected to hear from. It both thrilled and frightened him.

"Are you somewhere you can speak freely?" asked Alazaki.

"I am. No one is around, and this burner was never used before. I have deleted the call I made and there are no numbers stored. Once we are done, I will destroy the phone and scatter the pieces."

"Very well. Now," said Alazaki, "tell me about what you found in that cave."

JONATHAN MABERRY

CHAPTER 39
CRAFT PIZZA
HATAPU'ACH STREET
JERUSALEM, ISRAEL

Jason Aydelotte stepped into the pizza shop, ordered a slice heavy with olives, chili pepper, Bulgarian cheese, onions, mushrooms, and tuna, and a Diet Coke. As he took his first experimental bite, he was surprised to find that it was a rich sourdough crust, and nearly did a happy dance. The big man accompanying him ordered a beer and then headed back to the toilet.

Alone, Aydelotte made a quick cell call.

"How's the weather?" asked Aydelotte when the call was answered.

"Clear skies and sunshine," said the woman. "How are things there?"

"Things are fine. Having a slice of rather astonishingly good pizza."

"Pizza?"

"Yes. Great pizza. Right here in Jerusalem."

"Not sure why you should find that so odd. We are actually part of the twenty-first century. We even have Wi-Fi."

"Oh, hush." He chuckled. "How are we doing *today*? Is everything ready, Sharon?"

Sharon was not her name but was used for the convenience of such calls. Aydelotte did not actually know her real name, nor what she looked like. As with other members of his logistics team, she was a friendly voice on the phone. There were other people—like Shock and a few others—who oversaw staffing and their management. He imagined that Sharon was middle-aged, short, plump, pretty, and a transplant from somewhere in North Jersey.

"It is, sir," said Sharon. "What about on your end? Did both buyers show up?"

"Lamech sent a big ape of a guy who is leading me to some hotel where we can discuss price. The other bidder was a no-show."

"And you're still comfortable letting the bidder dictate where you'll meet? That feels so . . . so . . ."

"So *what . . . ?* Foolish?"

"God, no, sir. I was going to say dangerous. I just don't understand why we're giving them that much control."

"Which is why you're doing the job you do, Sharon, and not the job *I* do." There was a moment of silence, and he smiled, imagining the wince on her face. "The rules were that the first bidder gets to choose the venue. But as I am not actually insane enough to have the actual product on me, there's a safety zone."

"Oh, of course," she said a little too quickly.

"Truth to tell, Sharon, I'd have preferred a good bidding war, but we can't be greedy. Well, not too greedy." He laughed. "So, anyway, the big lug and I came into this pizza place. He said he needed a pit stop, which means he needed to call in and explain the situation. All good. Will that give your team enough time?"

"Plenty of time, sir," Sharon replied. "We have people tracking you, so once we know which hotel he's taking you to, we can move assets into place lickety-split."

"Good."

"About the other bidder," said Sharon. "We pinged a man as a likely player before we lost him. Slim, young, handsome. Maybe too young to be the player, so maybe he was a gopher, too. Guessing he saw the big guy and got spooked?"

"Maybe."

"Given where you are, I think it's a safe bet the muscle is taking you to the Lady Stern Hotel. Which is where you guessed."

"Of course," said Aydelotte. "Our Israeli friend thinks he is being clever, but he's falling into cliché. *Everyone* does their business there. This kind of business. Anyway, my dear, my contact at Lady Stern is Misha Goldman. Have someone get on the phone with him. Do it quick so we can make sure that things are properly arranged. I want rooms and a lobby party."

"A lobby party? Got it. I'll have all necessary assets moved into place."

"Thank you, Sharon."

"Always a pleasure, sir."

He ended the call just as Lamech's man came out of the bathroom, picked up his waiting beer, and came over. Aydelotte hoped the lout had at least washed his hands.

CHAPTER 40
MISSION BRIEFING ROOM 7
PHOENIX HOUSE

"Before the Scrolls were found," said Getts, "and I mean all of the ones we know about, and in particular the books of the Hebrew Bible—the oldest known manuscripts of Scripture in Hebrew were the Aleppo Codex and the Leningrad Codex, both from the tenth century CE. The oldest versions in Greek of both the Old and New Testaments are in the Codex Sinaiticus, which most likely written in the fourth century CE. What was found in those caves, though lacking any books of the New Testament, are versions of the Hebrew Bible that are more than two thousand years old."

I whistled. Biblical Luddite that I am, even I could see the importance of all this.

"Now this is important. As scientists began exploring and inventorying Cave One, they found more Scrolls and Scroll fragments, along with linen cloth, jars, and other artifacts."

She paused with an expectant expression, waiting for my reaction.

"Other artifacts meaning what?"

"Well, that's the thing," said Lizzie. "There are five separate inventory sheets cataloging everything that was found. Four of them match. One does not."

"Ah," I said. "Was that fifth sheet longer or shorter than the other four?"

Getts glanced at Church. "You were right. He's not just pretty."

Bug did a spit-take. An actual one. Red Bull all over his end of the table. He grabbed for napkins and cleaned it up, his brown face turning brick red.

I pointed at him. "That will be reflected in the quality of your Christmas present."

He pretended to scratch his nose but used only his forefinger.

Church, as always, contrived not to notice the childish hijinks of two of his senior staff members.

"From an official standpoint," said Getts, "that fifth inventory is someone's mistake, and it was thrown out. Unofficially, it was never thrown out. And to answer your question, it was much longer, listing four additional Scrolls which have never been properly inventoried, and at least fifty fragments. These were mentioned on the list and have been referenced countless times since, but they've been *almost* universally discredited as conspiracy theories."

She leaned on the word "almost."

"More caves were found throughout the forties and fifties. Eleven in all. And it was thought that the eleven were all that would be found, but another, Cave Twelve, was discovered in 2017. That's suggestive of there being more. Perhaps many more."

"Cave Twelve is where things take another important turn," said Lizzie.

"When they entered Cave Twelve," continued Getts, "it was obvious that it had already been found and looted. All they found was a single blank parchment in a jar, but several other broken and empty Scroll jars and even a few pickaxes suggest that the cave was looted sometime in the 1950s."

"Is there a competing theory?" I asked.

Lizzie laughed. "There are lots of theories. Bedouins looking to cash in on what was, by then, a find of global importance. There was money to be made. But it could just as easily have been any group of opportunists looking to make a buck. The black market for antiquities has been around for a long, long, long time. Romans looted everywhere they went. So did other occupying forces. Look at what Napoleon did in Egypt, as did the British who chased Napoleon out of the area. The list of potential suspects is a mile long."

"Sigh," I said, actually saying the word.

Getts said, "Some of what has been found in other caves has *not* made it onto the public record. And, unlike the Dead Sea Scrolls—whose texts are now completely available—there are things from other caves that have been suppressed."

"Even destroyed," said Lizzie.

"Destroyed by who?" I asked.

"Gosh," said Lizzie, "everyone. Depending on when and where they were found. The Ten Gurus have been tracking this stuff for a very long time. ISIS destroys a lot of what's found on lands they occupy. But the Catholic Church has made a few bonfires over the centuries, and probably has more under lock and key where it will never be found."

I happened to cut a look at Church as she said this, and he looked amused. I filed that away.

"There are two noteworthy caves in the Nahal Hever by an intermittent stream in the Judean Desert that flows through the West Bank and Israel to the Dead Sea. Both are believed to be thoroughly documented and with nothing missing, no anomalous entries on inventories. One is the Cave of Letters, which had some interesting documents dating from 131 to 136 CE. The other—and you'll probably love this, Colonel Ledger—is called the Cave of Horrors."

"'Cave of Horrors?'" I grinned with cookie gunk on my teeth. "It feels like Christmas morning."

"Hush now," said Lizzie, shaking her head. "It gets its name because remains were found there. Jewish refugees fleeing the Bar Kokhba revolt. Same time as the stuff in the Cave of Letters."

"Given the date," I said, "should I assume this is another tussle with the Romans that ended badly?"

"Pretty much."

"I'm Scots-Irish," I said. "My ancestors weren't exactly BFFs with the Roman legionnaires, either."

"No doubt."

I picked up a bison and nibbled a foot. "Correct me if I'm wrong, but we've moved away from the standard Dead Sea Scrolls narrative."

"Actually," said Lizzie, her eyes darkening, "we haven't."

"Okay . . . and . . . ?"

Debra Getts looked troubled. Genuinely so, and I wondered what the other shoe was that she was going to drop.

"Tell me, Colonel," she said after a long pause, "do you believe in magic?"

INTERLUDE 16
AL-ZILAL SAFE HOUSE
FARSHUT, EGYPT

EIGHTEEN MONTHS AGO

"This is very dangerous," said the scientist.

"Being alive is dangerous," said Ayoob Alazaki.

"What if someone sees us?"

"What if they did? Dr. Hegazy, you are a well-respected scientist. You are on television. Your face is on the cover of books. You could walk down this street with a smoking gun in one hand and a bloody knife in the other and no one would blink. You are the Indiana Jones of the *real* world of archaeology."

Hegazy did not look convinced. "And you? Do you think no one might be curious who I am meeting?"

"That is paranoia, doctor. It is not a fair assessment. After all, what am I? A retired schoolteacher," said Alazaki. "I tutor mathematics to the children of well-to-do families. Like you, I enjoy a level of academic respect."

He leaned a little closer.

"Would you prefer that we meet in some clandestine place under cover of darkness?"

"That's not what I mean," said Hegazy, though he did not follow up with clarification of what he did mean.

"Ah," said Alazaki, "here is our lunch."

A waiter came and placed bowls of *hamam mahshi* in front of each of them—roasted pigeons stuffed with onions, rice, bulgur wheat, and spices. The Yemeni leaned into the rising aromatic steam. Hegazy stared at his food as if it were a plate of scorpions. But he eventually began to eat.

When they were done, Alazaki removed a cell phone from a pocket, pulled up a folder of images, and discreetly slid it across the table.

"What is this?" asked the Egyptian.

"Perhaps you will tell me."

Hegazy picked up the phone and stared at high-definition pictures of a lead box. There was a ruler placed alongside it for scale. Each of the subsequent images showed a different side. He studied all six and then looked up, confused.

"What *is* this?" he asked again.

Alazaki pushed away his plate. "Tell me what you see."

"It is a lead box. The seals look intact. The writing . . . the *phrasing* . . . is likely from the twenty-first dynasty. And there is a name. Wait . . ." He used two fingers to expand one section of the third image. Then he gasped. "No! That's impossible."

"Tell me."

"It says that this box was ordered and sealed by Netjerkheperre-Setepenamun Siamun, an important pharaoh. But it says on the other side that this . . . wait . . . let me pick through it."

Hegazy's lips moved as he translated, making small adjustments for subtle differences in writing style and phrasing from that era of ancient Egypt. He stopped mouthing the words, set the phone down, and stared at Alazaki.

"Is this *real*?"

"Oh, yes."

"How? I would have known about this. Is this a new find? But . . . no . . . it can't be. I would know if anyone had found something as significant as this. Also, it's strange. There are protection symbols on it that belong to other eras, older dynasties. It's literally covered in warnings. It implies curses on anyone who opens it."

"Does it say what is *inside* the box?"

"Not . . . directly . . . but there, see that? There are references to some kind of conflict between the magicians of Siamun's court and others referred to as Apiru. It means 'outsider' and is a general label that referenced many kinds of non-Egyptians who hired themselves out for different kinds of labor. But in this context, and given the apparent date, I think it is a reference to Hebrews."

Alazaki smiled. "A reference from the dynasty of Pharaoh Siamun that mentions a conflict between his court magicians and early Jews. Is that not suggestive?"

Hegazy was beginning to sweat. "If it is true, if this is real. Please, tell me where these photos were taken. Where . . . when? By whom?"

But Alazaki did not immediately answer those questions. Instead, he asked, "Does this not call to mind the Jewish stories of their captivity in Egypt?"

"It might, but really that is *biblical* rather than historical," insisted the professor. "There is actually very little evidence to prove anything related to the stories of Jewish captivity and subsequent exodus from Egypt, and what we know is mostly circumstantial. Actual mentions of the Israelites did not come until late in Egyptian history."

"You think that the story of Moses is fiction, then?"

"Metaphorical, perhaps. Or a parable told for so long that it became accepted as truth by the believers of that faith. Like the ark and the flood." He picked up the phone and studied the images again. "And yet . . . if that box can be dated to the time of Siamun . . ." His voice trailed off. He blinked and reached out to grab Alazaki's wrist. "Please . . . you must *tell* me."

"I will do much better than that, my friend. I will *show* you."

CHAPTER 41
OUTSIDE OF KATAIF MIDDLE EASTERN RESTAURANT
BEIT YA'AKOV STREET
JERUSALEM, ISRAEL

"You okay, boss?"

"I'm fine, Rugger," said Toys as he hurried along the street. "You're sweet for asking."

"Was that an ambush? Was it one of Aydelotte's men?"

"There were two of them, mate, and they were street trash. And not even moderately interesting street trash."

"Did you . . . ?" asked Rugger, leaving the rest hanging.

"Don't be daft," said Toys with a laugh. "Now, where's our boy? How far behind am I?"

"Boss," interrupted Armani, "you're actually ahead of him. Target stopped at a pizza shop on HaTapu'ach Street. He just left and is heading in your direction."

"Bloody hell. Any guess as to where he's heading?"

"Best guess, based on location and direction," said Rugger, "is the Lady Stern Hotel on Jaffa Street. It's—"

"It's posh and I know it," interrupted Toys. "Stayed there once before."

He did not explain that he'd spent a week at the hotel with Hugo Vox after the fall of the Seven Kings. It was there that Vox first made contact with a representative of the Red Order. Vox said it was such a fine and reputable hotel that it made an excellent spot for all manner of ghastly deals. Toys knew that Vox enjoyed that kind of juxtaposition.

"I'll head in that direction," he said, "and find someplace to loiter. Let me know when he's near."

INTERLUDE 17
MIRACLE ARTIFACTS AND ANTIQUITIES
CORPORATE OFFICE
THE AYDELOTTE BUILDING
HOUSTON, TEXAS

NINETEEN MONTHS AGO

"Boss," said Shock, "are you alone?"

"No," said Aydelotte. "I have some department heads with me."

"Send them away. I need to tell you something and you need to be alone and you need to be sitting down."

"That's a bit dramatic."

"Do you trust me?"

"Yes."

"Then do it. Please."

Aydelotte looked at the faces of the eleven people seated around the huge mahogany conference table. He rose, phone in hand, and smiled. "Folks, if you don't mind, this is a private call. Can you give me the room?"

They smiled back, nodded, rose, and shuffled out, with the last one closing the door behind her.

"Okay, I'm alone," he told Shock.

"Are you sitting down?"

"Stop with the drama, for god's sake. Just tell me."

"You know that hit Alazaki's guys did a few nights ago? The one in Jordan?"

"Of course. What about it?"

"After they got out of there they hid in Jordan, near the Dead Sea."

"So what?"

"They hid in a cave in Qumran."

Aydelotte paused. "Did they now?"

"Boss . . . they found something."

Aydelotte felt his mouth go dry. "Tell me," he said hoarsely.

Shock told him about the one man falling into a deeper and bigger cave, about the many clay jars they found and how they arranged to get everything out of the cave and onto a truck.

Aydelotte had a hard time forming words. He forced them out one at a time, choking on them. "How . . . much . . . did they find?"

"About a quarter ton of scrolls and other items," she said. "It's the biggest find ever. More than all of the previous twelve caves put together. It's incredible. Thousands of scrolls. Plus stuff from Rome and Egypt that may have been part of a trove rescued from the freaking Library of Alexandria. And, boss, there was another lead box."

"Egyptian?"

"No, that's the thing," she said. "The description I got tells me it's about the same size and weight, but instead of hieroglyphs, it's covered in a very old version of Hebrew."

"*What?*" he cried. "What's in it?"

"I don't know," admitted Shock. "My source only goes as far as the fact that ISIS has it. I don't even think they opened it yet. But . . . given what we found in the Siamun box, then maybe this is something similar. Something from the Jewish side of things. You know what I mean. Aaron and Moses. What do you think, boss? Boss . . . ?"

Jason Aydelotte did not remember sitting down. He barely remembered sliding out of that chair and onto the carpeted floor of the conference room.

JONATHAN MABERRY

CHAPTER 42
MISSION BRIEFING ROOM 7
PHOENIX HOUSE

I looked around and smiled. "Now . . . when you say *magic* . . ."

Getts's smile was different. Odd, bordering on unpleasant. "Straight-up question."

I munched my cookie, aware of Church and Bug watching me with real interest.

"I'll say this . . . I didn't used to. Maybe I still don't. But I say 'maybe' because I have seen a *lot* of very weird shit since I came to work for that guy." I pointed to Church with half a cookie. "I'm not entirely sure *he's* not some kind of magic."

Church laughed, a rarity for him. "Rest assured, Colonel, I am no kind of magic."

Bug looked down into the opening of his Red Bull can, clearly not willing to let anyone see his reaction to Church's comment.

To Getts I said, "I almost don't want to know why you'd even ask."

She and Lizzie exchanged a look the specific nature of which I could not begin to decode.

"Well," began Getts, "how well do you remember the Book of Exodus?"

"Old Testament?" I shrugged. "I probably read it, but mostly what I know is from *The Ten Commandments*. Like a lot of kids, I learned my Bible history from Charlton Heston and Cecil B. DeMille. And again, I ask . . . why?"

Getts turned to Lizzie. "You have a better memory. Can you re-cite?"

"Chapter and verse? Sure." She closed her eyes for a moment, then said, "Exodus chapter seven, verses eight to twelve. 'The Lord said to Moses and Aaron, "When Pharaoh says to you, 'Perform a mir-acle,' then say to Aaron, 'Take your staff and throw it down before Pharaoh,' and it will become a snake." So Moses and Aaron went to Pharaoh and did just as the Lord commanded. Aaron threw his staff down in front of Pharaoh and his officials, and it became a snake. Pharaoh then summoned wise men and sorcerers, and the Egyptian magicians also did the same things by their secret arts: each one threw down his staff and it became a snake. But Aaron's staff swallowed up their staffs.'"

Church pushed the plate of cookies in her direction, murmuring a faint, "Brava."

She took a vanilla wafer.

"Okay," I said. "And . . . ?"

"What if that *wasn't* just a religious parable?"

"What if bright blue pigs flew out of my ass?"

"I'm serious, Joe."

"I know, which is more than mildly disturbing. You're asking me to take a tale like that out of the Bible and accept it as literal truth. Hate to break it to you, but I'm in that group who thinks that a lot of what's in the Bible is *not* an actual historical account." I waggled a cookie monkey at her. "The whole ark thing. Adam and Eve. Walls of Jericho. Jonah and the whale. And don't get me started on all the shit that happened to Job. Now, before anyone clutches their pearls and is openly aghast at my heresy, I'm not throwing stones at anyone's faith. Hell, I'm Methodist if I'm anything. I even pray when things get weird, and they've gotten weird a lot lately."

"Just a bit," said Bug, holding two fingers a quarter-inch apart.

"Nor am I saying anyone is wrong for what they believe. I'm sure as shit no expert. All I'm saying is that I don't personally buy a lot of the miracle stuff."

"Fair enough," said Getts. "And I'm certainly not here to evangelize or proselytize."

"Which means we can still be friends."

"But . . . what if?"

"Yeah, yeah, what if," I said sourly. "Why are we going in that direction anyway? Last I recall, we were in Jordan, somewhere on the banks of the Dead Sea, with stuff that's two thousand years old, not five thousand. Or however far back Moses and all that was."

"I know a kickboxing rabbi—no joke," said Lizzie, "who would beat the piss out of you for saying that."

I laughed. "And I'd deserve it. Doesn't answer my question, though."

"Then let me connect the dots," said Getts. "Mr. Bug, can you bring up the pictures of the copper Scroll?"

"'Mr. Bug,'" he echoed, greatly amused. He tapped some keys, and the image popped onto all the screens. What it showed was pretty much what it sounded like. Two sections of a flattened-out Scroll made from hammered copper and written in Hebrew.

"The Copper Scroll was found in Cave Three," said Getts. "It's unlike all the other Scrolls, though, which were written on papyrus or parchment. The original Scroll was about eight feet in length. Also, unlike the others, it isn't any kind of literary work. Not any of the books of the Old Testament or some of the more mundane writings or commentary. What this is, is a list."

"A list of what?" I asked.

"Sixty-four places where various items of great value were hidden. Gold and silver. It was likely written—depending on which scholar you cleave to—anywhere from 25 to 135 CE."

"Nice. I like a treasure hunt."

"Well, that's one of the ways in which this gets frustrating. Although there are some directions on where to find what, no one has ever found anything. Theories range from it being a hoax—"

"Even I don't buy that," I said.

"—to the items having been recovered by the folks who hid them," continued Getts, "or others correctly following the clues. Or, even to the Romans, since one of the abiding theories is that all of these Scrolls, along with other items of real or spiritual value, have been secreted out of Jerusalem during the revolt and hidden from the Romans."

"Long history of people hiding stuff," I said. "My dad had an interest in that sort of thing in Scotland and northern England. People buried gold, family swords, silver plate, and all of that kind of stuff in fields to keep it from invading Vikings or Cromwell's troops."

"Exactly. Same idea," said Getts. "And just like those valuables, sometimes the knowledge of where they were hidden was lost, usually because the secret keeper died without passing along the knowledge. The challenge is that the clues or descriptions were often too specific. They required local knowledge of the landscape, orientation of rivers, placement of things like trees or large stones or wells that are now impossible to find. Here's an example. 'In the tomb that is in the riverine gulch of Ha-Kafa, as one goes from Jericho towards Sekhakha, there are buried talents at a depth of seven cubits.' Now, the riverine gulch mentioned here has never been identified with any certainty. The town, Sekhakha, though also mentioned in Joshua 15:61, has also never been identified. And so on. Each of the locations has its own issues. Until recently we had no way to make sense of the Copper Scroll. We had no key."

"Okay," I said. "But, guys, you're still talking in the past tense. I'm a field operator. By nature, guys like me are reactive to some unfolding crisis. I don't have a time machine, and I don't work in the past. So, unless something has happened *now*, why are we all here talking about this?"

"There are rumors that one, or possibly two, new copper scrolls have been found. One in a previously unknown Egyptian tomb and another that may have been found in a thirteenth Qumran cave. These scrolls are rumored to contain secrets of how to perform magic."

I stared at Getts and Lizzie. "Let me get this straight, I'm getting this briefing because of a rumor about how the ancients made balloon animals and pulled rabbits from their hats?"

Getts looked at Church. "Is he always like this?"

Church looked pained. Then he surprised me by picking up the narrative. "We will get to the part of this where magic becomes a more open question. This is all necessarily convoluted, Colonel. Please bear with us over the twists and turns."

"Sure," I said.

He nodded. "Over the last nineteen months, various intelligence agencies working throughout the Middle East have noticed a sharp uptick in a few areas that should be unrelated."

"'*Should be*' isn't a comforting preamble," I said.

"Nor was it meant to be." He folded his hands on the tabletop. "First, a surprisingly large number of items have come on to that part of the black market which deals with unusual antiquities from the Middle East. Items originally from Arabia, Asia Minor, East Thrace, Egypt, Iran, the Levant, Mesopotamia, and the Socotra Archipelago. What is remarkable about these items is that the sellers claim that they are legitimate Scrolls and fragments from Dead Sea caves. Materials that may account for items believed to have gone missing from Caves One through Twelve."

"Actual Dead Sea Scrolls?" I asked. "Have they been verified?"

Church spread his hands. "Yes."

"That's a bit more interesting," I said. "Who is the seller? Do we know?"

Church nodded. "We have some theories but nothing concrete. Leading candidate is a man who goes by the name of Harith al-Wazir. The name means the Great Lion Who Digs in the Earth."

I grunted. "If by 'digs in the earth,' can we assume an archaeologist?"

"It's possible," Church said. "As for the other, he's an American who is somewhat of the public face of Holy Land antiquities for the legitimate market: Jason Aydelotte."

I nearly choked on my cookie. "Mr. Miracle? That guy on TV?"

"That guy on TV."

"Since when is he a criminal?" I asked, amused.

"It's become apparent to us quite recently," Church said, gesturing to Bug, who saluted with his Red Bull. "However, we do not yet have actionable evidence. We recently opened a case involving him that is being looked into even as we speak."

"By whom?"

"We'll circle back to that later," said Church offhandedly. "It is possible, though not yet proven, that Aydelotte may be involved in a few different areas of criminal behavior. Illegally obtained antiquities was, until recently, the most serious of those alleged offenses, but in the power vacuum created by the death of the Turkish black marketer Ohan and the more recent death of Harcourt Bolton—or Kuga, as he called himself—the loss of top tier suppliers has opened the door for lower tier vendors to step up."

"Sure, but Ohan and Kuga were arms dealers. What's that have to do with magic scrolls?"

"Maybe nothing," said Bug. "But Nikki thinks there's a connection."

Nikki Bloom ran a division of Bug's computer sciences team that focused on patterns, and she used MindReader to acquire and collate information with an incredible degree of depth and sophistication.

"Her working theory," continued Bug, "is that the reason Aydelotte is able to get rarities no one else can is because he has deals with radical groups throughout the Middle East who procure items for him that might otherwise be destroyed by ISIS and Boko Haram and those cats."

"Why would they give that stuff to Mr. Miracle? He's like a Christian's Christian, and that's hardly going to play well with jihadists."

"That would depend on what he offers in trade," said Church. "There are always items of military significance that go missing from arsenals, bases, and depots. And there are pirate groups doing their own R and D in the field and selling the tech to the hungriest bidders. We've seen some radical new designs for man-portable weapons."

"First I heard of it."

"Dude," said Bug, "a lot of stuff happened over the last year."

It was the nicest way of saying the world continued to turn while I was having my head rewired.

"Actually, Colonel," interjected Church, "your recent op in Chad is a possible connection. The materials Havoc Team obtained in Chad indicate Russo has been working on guidance systems for a completely new man-portable rocket launcher. Not stolen from us or our allies, but a completely new design."

"Connected to Mr. Miracle?"

"As I mentioned—that connection is being actively investigated as we speak."

INTERLUDE 18
QAHWA, AL-JARAIB VILLAGE
HAJJAH PROVINCE, YEMEN

EIGHTEEN MONTHS AGO

The place had no real name. Only a sign that proclaimed "Qahwa." *Coffee.*

Ayoob Alazaki sat in a corner of the restaurant, far from any occupied table. Several of his people sat at other tables closer to the door and the curtained hall to the kitchen. The remaining patrons were old men hunched over their newspapers or games of chess or solitary cups of coffee. It was that kind of place.

Dogs barked outside as they pranced around ragged children, trying to understand the simple games, wagging their tails in hope of inclusion. Dusty cars lined the far side of the street. Old women draped in colorful shawls brooded on second-floor balconies. Vendors lifted their wares—figs and nuts, spices and sun-withered vegetables. The pace of the afternoon was slow, the sun hot, the sky utterly cloudless.

Alazaki took micro-sips of his coffee and tried not to fidget. He was never comfortable in such moments, though his outward appearance sold the opposite. His face was composed, his glasses perched on his nose, his beard falling to his chest.

When the man he was waiting for arrived, Alazaki felt his pulse jump. But he raised his head slowly, calmly. Out of his peripheral vision he saw his watchers slowly come to point. Some were subtle about it—the younger ones less so.

The newcomer—who went by the name Sadiq, meaning "friend"—looked around, spotted him, signaled the owner, and gave an order for coffee and a honey roll, then he came over.

"*As-salaam alaikum*," said Sadiq.

Alazaki looked up, gave a small nod, and replied, "*Wa alaikum salaam*. Please sit."

Sadiq took a chair and moved it around so that he, too, had a good view of both doors. Immediately two men at the table closest to the door got up and went out, each turning in a different direction, checking the street, looking for anyone either accompanying or following Sadiq.

The newcomer knew this and took no offense. Rather the reverse. Had Alazaki not exercised such caution Sadiq would have been disappointed. But he also expected it because Alazaki was a cautious man by nature.

"Thank you for meeting me on such short notice," said Sadiq. "I understand that you are a very busy man and that coming here is both difficult and not without risk."

Alazaki spread his hands and gave a small shrug. "You are my friend."

Sadiq smiled and leaned in a bit. "And I may become a better friend to you and your organization."

They never used certain names, not even in a place as secure as the café. Not in an age of the most sophisticated and subtle technology. He had his people sweep the place for electronics before the meeting, and then had one of the young ones, Ali, use a jammer. No one on that end of the seat was getting a cell signal or sending a text message.

Alazaki sipped his coffee. "In what way can you be a better friend to us? And before you answer, remember that we have already discussed the possibility of your being the exclusive vendor for what we need. My answer now will be no different than it was then."

"Oh, I quite understand," said Sadiq. "Eggs in one basket and all that. No, this is different."

"Does it affect the items we have already discussed?"

"Only in ways that will make you happy. I would like to talk about modifications to the product you want to buy from us. Actually, to be precise, to items that you have bought from us over the last two years."

Alazaki studied him for a moment, then gave a single slow nod. "When you asked for this meeting you said that there was a new product that would enhance the weapons we have already agreed to purchase."

"Yes. A guidance package that includes new software."

The schoolteacher pursed his lips for a moment, then nodded again. "Tell me about this guidance software."

"Oh, it's more than that," said Sadiq. "The thing that makes it so perfect for you is how it will change everything about your effectiveness in the field."

"You have said something like that before, which is why I agreed to meet you. But please, explain *how* it works. What will it do for us that the standard Russian RPG-7s will not?"

"First, don't misunderstand me, my friend. You can still buy all the RPG-7s you want. From us, from Russia, or Syria, or wherever. That is cheap hardware."

Alazaki waited for the pitch.

"What I am offering is an upgrade kit. Software *and* hardware to maximize the effectiveness of any RPG you buy. Any rocket system, in fact," said Sadiq. "The hardware is simple. There are small self-adjusting fins with tiny flaps. And there is a guidance piece that is fitted like a collar around the rocket. The installation on each projectile takes under two minutes to install. The software is pre-installed in that guidance collar. You attach it to any ordinary RPG and it will turn a rocket into a missile."

Alazaki's eyes widened and then narrowed to skeptical slits. "How would this happen?"

Sadiq smiled. "Easy. The software package comes with a laser system. You point it at the target like the laser guidance that advanced military groups use to—as they say—*paint* the target. That helicopter or plane or whatever you wish to destroy is assigned a unique GPS signature. The collar tracks the target and self-corrects the missile while it is in flight. Right now, you hit one helicopter out of every three hundred tries. And one jet out of every five thousand. At that rate our enemies can build new aircraft, tanks, and armored personnel carriers at a much faster rate than we can destroy them. We are not even close to the point where we are making a significant difference. We saw that when the SDF ripped through our forces in northeastern Syria. This new technology will give you odds of one hit out of every three shots on anything with a prop or rotor, and one in ten for anything with a jet engine. As for anything on tires or tread, the kill ratio is closer to a hundred percent, based on payload. An Abrams tank, of course, would require multiple hits with high-intensity explosives . . . but the new targeting system will guarantee that every rocket fired will hit."

Alazaki said nothing, but his eyes had grown larger again, rounder.

"And, on top of that," continued Sadiq, "the person using the targeting laser can operate from a different location than whomever is firing the RPG. That means any bloody fool can pull the trigger, but someone with a bit more smarts will aim it from a safe location that is not in the line of trajectory of the RPG. Return fire would go in the wrong direction."

"What about the man firing the RPG?"

"All he has to do is pull a trigger and run like hell. The guidance system can even reroute the projectile to confuse attempts at tracing the smoke trail back to the source. It's all in the training materials. We provide print and digital how-tos for you."

"This sounds like it will be expensive."

"A gun costs more than a knife," said Sadiq. He leaned in and dropped his voice. "But listen to me, my friend. Perhaps we can come to a different kind of arrangement. My employer knows that fundraising has become increasingly difficult for you, even using the dark web to thwart prying eyes. So, perhaps instead of picking your pockets for this new technology, we can discuss a barter."

"Barter?" repeated Alazaki, frowning. "How would such an arrangement ever be equitable to both sides? If you do not want our money, then what? Camels? Sand? You know that we have no other resources."

"Well, that is not entirely true, is it, my friend?" asked Sadiq.

"What do you mean by that?"

"My employer, as you know, has excellent sources of information. It's come to *his* attention that some of your fighters were hiding out in Jordan in the weeks following the rocket attack in Gaza. Now, now, don't look so surprised, my friend. It is *his* business to know such things, just as it is your business to know other things."

"In what way does this relate to our business?" said Alazaki.

"It relates in that my employer is aware that those fighters managed by accident to do something teams of archaeologists have been trying for decades to accomplish."

"And what might that be?"

Sadiq had to admire Alazaki's composure. His face displayed bored disinterest. He said, "In a happenstance so unlikely that it suggests the guidance of a divine hand, they found a thirteenth cave in the Qumran hills containing, among other things, quite a lot of previously undiscovered Dead Sea Scrolls."

Alazaki made a face of disapproval. "Even if such a thing happened, what of it? They are documents important only to the Jews."

"If that was even remotely true, my friend, we would not be having this conversation."

He sat back.

When Alazaki remained silent, Sadiq added, "My friend, I understand that it is of religious and political value to you that certain items be destroyed. You follow the precepts of Salafism, and it directs you to place deep importance on *tawhid*—monotheism as proclaimed in the Quran, and to refute in all ways *shirk*—the impious belief in polytheism. The writings of Muhammad speak this truth, and the teachings of Taqi al-Din Ibn Taymiyya, Muhammad Rashid Rida, and others support it. I understand that Al Assefa—the Storm—is all about clearing the path toward true righteousness. So, we can take it as read that I understand why your fighters destroy so many icons and artifacts."

Sadiq leaned forward.

"But I also know that some of those items are currency, and organizations of your kind do not finance themselves. It's not like you can launch a Kickstarter."

The schoolteacher shrugged. "And so . . . ?"

"And so, we both know that your people have not *actually* destroyed as many artifacts as has been reported in the world news. Just as we both know that the exaggerated version of these stories was fed to the press for effect. And for recruitment, of course."

"You seem very sure of these things," said Alazaki, his tone not entirely friendly.

Sadiq waved off the warning. "I would be a poor businessman *and* a fool if I came to this meeting without being sure. And, to be precise, I say these things because I want the air clear between us. It is important that we understand each other."

Alazaki considered the weight and value of Sadiq's words. Finally, he gave a small nod.

"How can you be so certain that those fighters—if any such existed in that place—did not discard them as trash, or burn them?"

Sadiq smiled. "Can we both accept that I *am* certain?"

"For the sake of argument?" suggested Alazaki.

"Certainly. Now, you must recognize the value of these items, too, or you would have simply burned them. Or allowed that field team to wipe their asses with them. I do not believe that you would allow such valuable trading commodities to be so crudely dispensed with. I have come to offer this expansion of our deal. You keep everything you've already purchased, and may Allah help you put them to their best use. *But*, if you would like to increase the effectiveness of them, then those Scrolls are the fee. A straight swap and a fair deal. Does this deal sound like something you could be comfortable with?"

Alazaki sat back and was silent for a very long time. Then he said, "As I have said, I know nothing of such items."

"Let us pretend that you do," said Sadiq quietly. "Let us further pretend that you can lay hands on the items in question."

"If this hypothetical Cave Thirteen existed," said Alazaki, "and if anyone I knew had discovered anything there, how would I know which items you feel are worthy of a trade?"

"My employer wants *all* of them. Every last scrap of parchment, vellum, or copper found within that cave."

"He must place a very high value on those items. How do I know this arrangement is not slanted in his favor?"

"Value varies. They are worth something to him, to be sure. He is aware that your group has sold many items that were supposedly destroyed. I will tell you now, in the spirit of full disclosure, that agents of his made some of those purchases from you. He did that to verify that the goods you were selling were worth the asking price. He trusts that you are dealing fairly, and in turn he will be fair. If you agree to this barter, he will give you five hundred pre-fitted collars on grenades that will fit the RPG-7s you recently bought from Russia. On *top* of that, he will give you an additional two hundred fifty rounds and another one hundred launchers. That package is worth seven-point-five times what you were willing to pay for the collars alone."

Ayoob Alazaki thought about it for a long moment, then said, "I have been sitting for too long. I will take a walk and refresh myself. Perhaps there is a breeze somewhere."

"Very well. I will wait right here while you do."

Before rising, Alazaki studied him for a moment. "You may have a long wait," said Alazaki. "If you are hungry, avoid the *fahsa*. The lamb may have been ill before it was cooked. I recommend the *shafut*."

With that he got up and walked out. Three of the men in the café followed; the rest remained. But that was fine with Sadiq. He ordered food and more coffee and ate without hurry or concern. He knew when he had a fish on the line, the hook set nicely in the underlip.

JONATHAN MABERRY

CHAPTER 43
LADY STERN HOTEL
JAFFA STREET
JERUSALEM, ISRAEL

"I have them in sight," murmured Toys.

"And we have you," said Armani. "I'm in a parked Toyota halfway down the street on your seven o'clock."

"And I'm around the near corner in a white panel truck," said Skiver. "If anything weird happens just give us a yell and we'll be right there."

"Good to know," said Toys. "Hold tight for now, lads. I'm going to attempt contact. See if I can ingratiate myself into the negotiations."

Toys spent a few moments loitering in the shadows of a doorway, watching Aydelotte and the Israeli muscle walk slowly along Jaffa Street toward the front door. They walked casually, but not companionably. No conversation. Toys reckoned that was just a decent way of checking for possible tails. So he decided to be seen openly. He stepped out of the doorway and crossed the street and walked straight toward Aydelotte. "What the bloody hell are you playing at?" he groused.

"Beg pardon?" asked Aydelotte, pausing in surprise. The muscle loomed, but Toys ignored him.

"I was at the effing market at the right effing time and then saw you go strolling off with this slice of effing beefcake. I thought *we* were going to have a little bit of a haggle over goods, but then you leave me back there holding my dick."

Aydelotte was only off balance for a split second, but he recovered quickly. He hoisted a concerned and placating smile on his bearded face. "My friend, *no* . . . this is just a misunderstanding. Some crossed signals. We were all supposed to meet there and then decide where to go for a drink and a chat. This fellow showed up and you didn't. But, let me assure you, son, everything is fine. I simply didn't see you at the market."

"I saw you," huffed Toys. "You were at the lantern shop as arranged, but then the Hulk here showed up and off you went. I nearly said fuck it but decided to give you the benefit of the doubt. Lost you on the street, but knew you were coming in this direction. There's nowhere else around here for . . . discussions . . . of this type, so it had to be the Lady Stern."

Aydelotte cocked an eyebrow. "You've been here before?"

And that's when Toys dropped a bomb, and from considerable height. He took a half step forward, lowered his voice, and said, "Yes, many times. With Hugo Vox."

The muscle clearly had no idea who that was, but Aydelotte's face brightened. "Ah! So you're *him*." And in an equally confidential voice, added, "You're *Toys*."

Toys contrived to look suspicious. "And if I am?"

"My boy, my *boy!*" Aydelotte thrust out a welcoming hand. "Had I known that *you* were the other bidder then of course I would have waited all day for you. Hugo was a dear friend. Very dear. He spoke glowingly of you. Spoke of you like you were his own son. And it explains how you knew how and where to contact me. Makes everything make sense."

Toys took the proffered hand, and they shook. He found the muscle's frown of consternation very tasty.

"Mr. Aydelotte," said the muscle gruffly, "I thought we had agreed that this would now be a one-to-one thing."

The American turned and looked up at him. His Santa Claus smile was there, but it was as cold as the North Pole in winter. "Oh? And when did I ever say that?"

"I mean, you came here with me and—"

"And let me guess," Aydelotte cut in. "While you were pretending to take a piss, you called your boss and said that he now had an exclusive. No, don't lie, I can see it in your face, son. I didn't get where I am by being unable to read people. Frankly I'm sorry we didn't have this discussion over poker because you'd be broke, naked, and in debt by now."

"But I—"

"Hush, son. There are grown folks talking." Aydelotte turned to Toys. "To give this one *some* credit, and maybe let him save face a bit, we'll go have a chat with his boss in the hotel bar. In public. And then we'll see if we can go somewhere more private for that *other* conversation."

"That suits me," said Toys.

Aydelotte didn't ask the big man's permission. Instead, he turned and headed toward the hotel entrance. Toys, amused and even a little impressed, was about to follow when a meaty hand landed heavily on his shoulder.

"This is bullshit and you know it," whispered the muscle. "You have no right to even be here."

Toys looked at the hand and then into the man's eyes. "You're rude, you're stupid, and you don't even have the basic decency to be pretty."

He made no threat, because it was all there in his eyes and his tone of voice. The big man hesitated and then removed his hand. He had enough dignity to mouth his own threat.

You're mine.

"Oh, don't you wish," said Toys airily, brushed away the hand, and walked off to catch up with Aydelotte. The day was turning out pretty well after all.

CHAPTER 44
MISSION BRIEFING ROOM 7
PHOENIX HOUSE

"So how does this Aydelotte bozo get away with selling them?" I asked.

"It comes down to provenance," said Lizzie. "We know that some Scrolls and fragments were sold prior to their full value and importance being discovered. One or more persons bought some from those bedouin kids. There's a very strong possibility that other members of their families or their tribe acquired and sold similar findings. Aydelotte's claim is that the stuff he's selling came from those. Sold in private exchanges prior to any country or organization making a formal claim of ownership."

"Let me guess," I said. "Every one of those groups are putting retroactive claims on Mr. Miracle's stuff."

"Of course. That's how this works in the antiquities world. At any given time there are scores, if not hundreds, of active lawsuits filed by governments against museums and private collectors. Egypt would *love* to get back all of the stuff looted from tombs by non-Egyptian archaeologists. And that includes Tutankhamun and all the others. The Greek government has sued Italy and Great Britain countless times to try to recover stuff from ancient Athens and elsewhere. It's a mess. And it's confusing, which gives Aydelotte the chance to slip through legal loopholes, or stall so long in the courts that continuing to sue him becomes very expensive."

"He has very good lawyers," said Lizzie.

"No doubt. But where is all this taking us because, truth to tell, I couldn't give less of a shit about any of this. Dead Sea Scrolls are hardly a threat that requires Havoc Team to go out guns a-blazing."

Getts turned to Lizzie. "You weren't joking when you said he has no patience."

"Hey," I said, but they ignored me.

"Here's the thing," said Getts. "Mr. Bug, would you mind showing the other thing?"

Bug, happy as a clam, put another image up on the screen. It showed a section of what was clearly one of the Copper Scrolls. "I lifted this from a dark web sales page."

"It's a fragment of what the black-market seller insists is a different and newly discovered Copper Scroll," said Getts. "You can see that he's used pixilation to redact sections of it. But what's there is more than intriguing. It's terrifying. With what we can read and translate, and with what's written on the dark web sales page, it *seems* that this second Copper Scroll contains the key to finding the treasures alluded to in the first Copper Scroll."

"Getting a little more interested, doc," I said. "Keep going."

"Moreover," she said, "it makes the claim that, apart from the gold and silver purportedly buried, there is—and I quote—a 'treasure of great and terrible power.' A treasure so feared that the legions of Rome hunted for it for many years, and that finding it was the real reason they burned the Second Temple. Not merely as punishment for an uprising, but to keep that treasure from ever being found and used against Rome."

"Whoa, whoa . . . you lost me . . . how could a treasure be a threat to Rome? It's not like the Jews back then had enough gold hidden to raise an army and overthrow the Empire. Rome was at the height of its power."

"It was," said Lizzie, "and yet they were so frightened that they sent the Tenth Legion to either find this thing of importance and bring it back to Rome, or to destroy any place where it could be hidden. They hunted Jewish scholars for decades and persecuted Jews for centuries to find what was hidden."

The room seemed to have gone very quiet.

"And you're going to tell me Rome believed that this scroll explained how to do magic, and that's why there was such persecution? Fear of a Jewish army capable of using ancient magic against the Empire?"

"Yes."

"Pretty much the plot of *Star Wars*," I said. "Just saying."

Debra Getts looked deeply irritated with me. Lizzie gave a small nod, seeing my point. "The other rumored Scroll is believed to have come from the lost tomb of Netjerkheperre-Setepenamun Siamun, the pharaoh of Egypt most likely to have been in power during the time of Moses. That scroll is believed to have been written by the chief priests and court magicians in the service of Siamun and describes in precise detail how the priests learned the magic they used when challenged by Moses and his brother, Aaron."

"Joe," said Lizzie, "the Sikh scholars of the Library of the Ten Gurus have been looking for those same Scrolls for nine hundred years, since long before the other Scrolls were found in Qumran. They believe those magic-themed Scrolls exist. And they believe that the sorcery described therein is real."

I ate an elephant. "People believe a lot of things."

Getts looked at me with fevered eyes. "As you can imagine, those Scrolls, if found, will have the effect of dropping a bomb into modern religion. Books of magic written thousands of years ago? Either it'll be seen as heresy, because it calls into question the nature of miracles, or it makes Aaron and Moses look like either morons or con men. Or . . . it proves that they were actual magicians and that their powers came from learnable sorcery and not from God."

Church said, "It would also give groups like ISIS a weapon that no mechanized army is equipped to deal with."

I held up a hand to silence everyone. Then I took a long breath and said, "Magic? You're talking jihadists with fucking magic? Oh, come on now," I protested, smiling at a joke that was going on too long and too far." Surely you guys can't believe any of that?"

No one else in the room was smiling.

"Do you . . . ?"

CHAPTER 45
MISSION BRIEFING ROOM 7
PHOENIX HOUSE

"I admit," I said, looking around, "that I'm having a hard time buying into this. ISIS waving wands and yelling *'avada kedavra.'*"

"Imagine how we feel," said Getts. "I'm an archaeologist. We're *not* Indiana Jones. We are professionally required to stay objective and to err on the side of what can be measured, dated, replicated, and peer reviewed. We chase religion and magic and all of that through history, but they are cultural abstractions to us."

"And yet," said Lizzie, and let the rest hang.

"Besides, Joe," said Bug, "it's not like we haven't seen some pretty weird shit. Zombies—"

"Wait," cried Getts, "zombies are real?"

"Bioweapons creating disease states approximating zombies," I said. "It's not *The Walking Dead.*"

"Might as well have been," said Bug. "And vampires? Remember those?"

Getts stared from one to the other of us with a kind of awe bordering on love.

"No crosses, no stakes through the heart, no sparkling," I growled. "The Red Knights were genetically engineered. Some assholes took an old genetic anomaly and enhanced it. Nobody turned into a bat, and none of them slept in coffins. No one sparkled."

"Aliens?" suggested Bug.

I shook my head. "Jury's out as to whether they were legit from outer space. More probably trans-dimensional, and that's string theory physics or quantum physics or something. Science, not magic."

"Just saying, Joe," persisted Bug. "We've dealt with some very weird stuff that is outside the bounds of what most people consider 'normal.'"

"Told you they were a fun bunch of guys," said Lizzie under her breath. Getts kept trying to say something, but although her lips formed words there was no sound other than a faint, high-pitched *yeep*.

"Okay," I said, "but I kind of want to draw a line in the sand at actual magic." I turned to Church. "I mean, are we talking Doctor Strange here? Is he one of your friends in the industry?"

"As entertaining as that would be, no," said Church. "He is not."

"So, what makes you four—two scientists, the world's biggest computer nerd, and whatever the hell you are, boss—suddenly go from historical oddities to magic? I heard what you said, but what I haven't heard is why you believe it. And, at the risk of sounding like a broken record, how in the wide blue fuck does any of this involve scientists killing themselves? I feel like I'm being pranked here. Someone make this make sense."

Getts turned to Bug. "Maybe now's a good time to show the video."

"So help me, Bug," I said, "if I see Dumbledore, I will do you considerable personal injury."

Bug shook his head and didn't smile. "I kind of wish that's what this was."

He dimmed the lights and sent a video to a big screen on the wall. We all turned to watch. The video showed a military base.

Church said, "This is Camp Lemonnier, a United States Naval Expeditionary Base, situated next to Djibouti–Ambouli International Airport in Djibouti City. It's home to the Combined Joint Task Force–Horn of Africa. It is the only permanent US base in Africa. This footage was taken by security cameras during an interrogation of a senior Boko Haram leader, Mesut Adebayor, who was apprehended by Delta Force during an operation in Nigeria."

"I read that report," I said. "But the report said that Adebayor was killed attempting to escape."

"If that were true, Colonel, we wouldn't be having this conversation."

The video changed from an aerial shot of the base to a grainier feed from inside an interrogation room. Bland walls, a table bolted to the floor; a single chair on one side, with Adebayor cuffed to a D-ring, and two men facing him. One big black guy with a shaved head and a big white guy with a receding hairline, both in desert camo fatigues with no unit patch or rank insignias.

"CIA?" I asked.

Church nodded. "Case officers Morris and Selkirk. This clip is lifted from a much longer file."

Adebayor was swaying back and forth, strung out with nerves, and maybe the CIA spooks had slipped him something. Before I could ask about that it stopped being important.

There was movement at the very edge of frame, and for a moment none of the men in the room seemed to notice. Until they did. The thing moved into shot, and the two interrogators yelled in sudden terror and flung themselves out of their chairs. The black case officer, Morris, jumped over his seat and backed all the way to the wall. The white guy, Selkirk, caught his foot in one leg and toppled backward. Adebayor stared in drugged semi-awareness, his eyes wide and mouth falling open as *it* glided into view.

A huge Egyptian cobra. Four and a half feet long, with a large head and a thick, scaly body as big around as a woman's forearm. It reared up as it approached the prisoner, and its long cervical ribs expanded out into a sinister hood. It opened its mouth to display wickedly sharp hollow teeth that dripped with venom.

Morris snatched up a chair and hurled it, but he was one second too late. The cobra lunged forward and buried its fangs in Adebayor's thigh. The man screamed in terror and agony as the blend of cytotoxins and neurotoxins shot into his bloodstream.

The chair struck the cobra, knocking it away, breaking its back.

But by then the prisoner was screaming as the venom began disrupting his nervous system, faulting out nerve conduction. He began twitching and thrashing.

The two CIA interrogators did not try to help him. They did nothing after that to attempt to save his life.

They were too busy trying to save their own.

Selkirk let out a piercing shriek of total terror as two more cobras

JONATHAN MABERRY

crawled out from under the table and sank fangs into his inner thigh and groin. Morris backed all the way into a corner as a half dozen more slithered toward him. He kept slapping at a holster clipped to his belt, but by the time he clawed it free he was already dying.

The screen went dark for a few seconds, leaving only the sound of screams to trouble the conference room. Then the video image resumed as soldiers banged open the door and rushed in, rifles ready to kill the snakes.

But there were no cobras in the interrogation room. Not anymore. Only three dying, screaming men.

Bug ended the video and brought the lights back up. I sat there, absolutely stunned. I could feel everyone staring at me. Waiting for me to say something. Anything.

But what could I say? What I'd just witnessed was impossible.

Absolutely impossible.

CHAPTER 46
LADY STERN HOTEL
JERUSALEM, ISRAEL

"My employer says he'll be down in a minute to have a drink," said the muscle.

Aydelotte smiled agreeably and ordered his own variation of a Mule—one ounce of limoncello, a generous knock of vodka, and lemon-lime ginger beer, all poured into a julep cup and mixed vigorously and garnished with a lemon wheel and mint sprig.

"A Limoncello Mule," he announced proudly.

The muscle, whose name, Toys learned, was Ari, had a Maccabee lager in a frosted glass.

Toys opted for something in the same area as Aydelotte's—a Limonana—a cocktail made from anise-based arak, lemonade, and mint. Not his usual, but he wanted a big drink he could nurse, but one with little alcohol.

"Will the other chap *actually* be joining us?" asked Toys after ten minutes.

Aydelotte sipped, used a cloth napkin to dab at droplets on his mustache, and then glanced at his watch. Toys noted that the watch was a Rolex Cosmograph Daytona eighteen-karat white gold men's watch. A quarter-million dollars' worth of mechanical confection. It was so absurdly expensive that no one ever wore it without intending the thing to be a "kiss my rich ass" to the world. Even Toys, who did not mind extravagance or excess when it came to fashion, thought it crossed the line from good taste into arrogant vulgarity.

Ari shrugged. "He said he'd be down."

"Would that be today or after the ice caps finish melting?" asked Toys.

The muscle gave him two seconds of hostility and punctuated it with a murmured, "Fuck you."

"Oh, god, sweetie, not even if I was very badly drunk."

Ari sneered. "Faggot."

"Ooooh, stinging comeback. Also, inaccurate. More pansexual than specifically gay, but thanks for playing. We can discuss your parting gifts later."

For a moment Toys saw the big man's muscles tense as if he were really foolish enough to make a move. But training overcame raw stupidity, and Ari turned away to look for his employer, grinding his teeth audibly.

Toys glanced at Aydelotte as he sipped his drink. The American looked amused. In that moment, the face of Hugo Vox overlaid that of Jason Aydelotte. Vox had also been an American, also a self-made billionaire. Also deeply corrupt, wildly talented, and diverse in his many plans and projects. It was hardly a surprise that this man knew Vox. Toys felt a wave of sentimentality about his former employer. Normally he would chase such feelings out of his head with a stick, but now he let it move through him like a spring breeze.

What would you think of me now? he wondered.

He had similarly poignant memories of Sebastian Gault, the pharmaceutical magnate and ruthless businessman who had lifted Toys out of poverty, educated him, trained him, and treated him like a younger brother.

Toys had betrayed them both, and that betrayal had brought Mr. Church and Joe Ledger into play in ways that left Gault a charred

corpse and Vox with a bullet in his brain. There was some guilt clinging like cobwebs inside Toys's head. He could have booked sessions
with Rudy Sanchez to try to exorcise both ghosts, but Toys did not
want to lose them. They reminded him of his sins.

But they also reminded him of his family.

He took another sip and realized the glass was empty, then signaled for the bartender.

"Here he is," said Ari, directing his comment to Aydelotte. They
all turned to see a man step out of an elevator.

The Israeli was tall, handsome, with a strong nose and jaw, lots
of thick black hair, and dark Einstein eyebrows. His suit was good
quality, but not a stunner.

What Bug and Wilson could not figure out was who the Israeli
represented. Not the government, because Israel bought a lot of its
arms directly from the United States and France. Or they designed
them themselves, and over the last few decades they had come up
with some bleeding-edge military tech. Who did that leave, though?
An even more radicalized version of Shin Bet? Hugo Vox had sold
them some arms once upon a time.

Shin Bet was a group of Jewish extremists who felt the Israeli
government—particular the courts—were too lenient on Palestinians violating the laws that enforced restraining orders distancing
them from the West Bank. They based their opposition on the *hala-
cha* religious laws, and many believed they were willing to tear down
the Israeli government with an aim toward putting a new and much
less flexible one in its place.

Or it could be a new group with similar views. Possibly even a
private group or family wanting more substantial revenge for deaths
from Palestinian rocket attacks.

The challenge, Toys knew, was no matter which side of the line
you stood, there was no shortage of hatred, intolerance, religious
outrage, grief, and malice. From his own point of view—being
Catholic—Toys knew he had no stones to throw when it came to
violence in the name of religion. None of that speculation helped put
a label on Lamech, though. Not yet, anyway.

The Israeli walked without haste, but Toys could see some tension lines in his face. Probably annoyance and a bit of apprehension that the second bidder was back in play.

Aydelotte slid off his chair and, smiling broadly, offered his hand. "Mr. Lamech, such a pleasure to finally meet you."

Lamech shook the hand and released it. After a moment of hesitation, he offered his hand to Toys, who shook it. Lamech had one of those utterly slack handshakes that always made Toys want to wash.

"We're on our second round," said Aydelotte. "You have to catch up."

"I don't drink," said Lamech. "Can't we just go on up and begin?"

"Or," said Aydelotte, "we can act like civilized people and get to know each other first. At least have a cup of coffee with us."

Toys wondered why Aydelotte was stalling. This was not how these kinds of business deals played out. Rather the opposite of sensible security protocol. But he played along, passively backing Mr. Miracle's preferences, ready to shift with the changes.

The Israeli ordered coffee, and the four of them moved to a conversational grouping of comfortable chairs in a far corner. As they were about to sit down, Aydelotte shifted slightly to get in Ari's way. "Why don't you wait for us at the bar, there's a good fellow."

Ari glanced at Lamech, who shrugged and nodded. The bodyguard gave Toys a lethal glower and stalked back to the bar and sat there, sulking like an overgrown child in a time-out corner.

When the coffee arrived and the waiter was gone, Aydelotte opened the conversation.

"Thank you both for meeting with me," he said affably. "I know this is all a bit unorthodox, but standard procedures are the easiest to predict, and none of us want that."

"And yet we are sitting here in public view," said Lamech.

"Oh, we're perfectly safe," said Aydelotte.

"There are two dozen people all around us. Two dozen witnesses to this meeting."

The American sipped his drink. "Not to be nitpicky, but there are twenty-six people here."

"That doesn't make it better," growled Lamech.

"Depends on your perspective," said Aydelotte. He raised his

JONATHAN MABERRY

right hand and snapped his fingers very loudly. All of the customers immediately stood up. The bartender and waiter and hostess stopped and stood in silent attention. Lamech goggled. Then Aydelotte snapped his fingers again and everyone resumed their seats and picked up their conversational threads as if nothing had ever happened.

"Bloody hell," said Toys, both impressed and deeply alarmed.

"I . . . don't understand," said Lamech. "You did not even know where we were going to meet until Ari brought you here."

Aydelotte settled back against the deep cushions. He offered no explanation, but merely smiled and took a small sip from his drink.

In Toys's ear, Rugger said, *"Jesus H. Christ."*

CHAPTER 47
MISSION BRIEFING ROOM 7
PHOENIX HOUSE

Long silence.

Real damn long.

Bug looked at Church. "I think Joe is broken."

None of us laughed. It wasn't really a laughing moment. Dr. Getts and Lizzie sat like a couple of actresses trying out for an adult version of Hermione Granger. Prim, aware of the impact of what they had just told me. Aware, too, of how I must be feeling about it. Even Ghost looked dazed. He couldn't know why we were all sitting around in various stages of shock, but he could feel it. Dogs know.

Church sipped his coffee and looked at nothing.

Finally, I said, "And are we going on the assumption that this is actual magic? Like Gandalf or Voldemort? Or are we leaning more in the direction of David Copperfield and my uncle Harry who used to find quarters behind my ears?"

The pause after that question was so long, I could have gone out and had my car detailed.

"Yes," said Lizzie.

"I don't know," said Getts.

Church said, "It'll be your job to find out."

I nodded.

"Just for the record, though?" I said. "I kind of hate all three of you."

We sat in silence.

Then I said. "Show me the cobra thing again."

Bug ran it once more. Then again in slow motion when I asked for that. I stood close to the big screen and studied everything.

"And they're all dead?"

"No," said Church. "The prisoner and Agent Selkirk were DOA. Morris is still alive, though in critical condition."

"Where is he?"

"In the hospital," said Church. "It's a bit of a miracle that he survived the bites, however."

"Do we actually *have* a diagnosis yet?"

"Apart from anaphylaxis from the cobra venom? No."

I went back to my chair and sat. Ghost put his head on my thigh.

"Okay, this is a lot to digest. Suicides, bats from hell, cobras out of nowhere, Dead Sea Scrolls, and magic. Now . . . going on the assumption that I'm not in a psych ward, warped out on drugs and imagining all this—which, I have to tell you, would easily qualify as the lesser evil—what *exactly* is my goddamn mission?"

Church almost laughed. "Colonel, your guess is as good as mine."

"Wait . . . what?"

"The only thing we can reasonably say is that Jerusalem seems to be the best place to start."

"Why there?"

"The largest collection of Dead Sea Scrolls—and experts on same—are there. Morris is there. We know that one of the two biggest hubs for black market religious antiquities is there."

"Okay. So I go to Jerusalem to do what, exactly? After all of this, I still don't see how this is an RTI case. Maybe Interpol, like I said earlier. Maybe Scully and frigging Mulder. But no one's blowing anything up at the moment. There's no big bad with a bioweapon threatening the free world. I hate to remind you, of all people, that we are a reactive group. Someone has to pick a fight first."

"Jason Aydelotte is also in Jerusalem," said Church. "Harith al-Wazir is believed to be in the region."

"Okay."

Church got up and walked over to where I sat. He lowered himself into the seat next to me. When he spoke, his voice was quiet, almost gentle. "We have been through a lot in the few years you've worked for me. *With* me."

"Yeah. A bit."

"Until now I've been able to provide you with considerable intelligence, leads, and motivation. As you say, Rogue Team is reactive. But this time it's something we have to go and take a closer look at. Too much of what's happened is either poorly documented or based on rumor, word of mouth, or assumption. I don't personally find that a comfortable place to be. Perhaps if we were busier, then I would pass this off to one of our sister organizations."

I shook my head. "No. You wouldn't."

He smiled. "No. I would not."

"Why not, though?" I asked. "What about this case has its hooks in you?"

"You won't like my answer."

"You want a detailed list of all the things about today I don't like? No? Then just tell me."

"It comes down to this, Colonel," he said. "I have a bad feeling. A very bad feeling. Twice before in my career I had similar feelings and did nothing because I trust in logic, answers, and details. Perhaps I trust too much in those things. Both of those times things played out in ways that showed me that I *should* have responded. I should have acted. This feels like that, and maybe a bit more. I don't know what this is. I cannot even say with any certainty that these disparate elements even belong to one case."

"But you feel that they do," I said. Making it a statement.

"Yes."

"On a scale of one to ten, how strong is that feeling?"

"I'm sending you and Havoc Team," he said.

And that was answer enough.

INTERLUDE 19
AL-JARAIB VILLAGE
HAJJAH PROVINCE, YEMEN

EIGHTEEN MONTHS AGO

Ayoob Alazaki walked for several blocks. His guards followed at a discreet distance because Alazaki had an important call to make.

When the call went through, he stopped in the shaded lee of a building that bore a sign saying it was closed for renovations. The sign was faded from years of brutal sunlight, and a coarse gray-green weed had crept up the wall.

He dialed a certain number and waited through a long series of soft clicks as the call was routed and rerouted across the hemisphere. When it was answered, the voice was soft, cultured, and deep. Greetings and praises to God were exchanged.

"The scrambler is active on my end," said the schoolteacher.

"As is mine," Harith al-Wazir assured him. "We may speak like brothers, Ayoob Alazaki. Is the deal complete?"

"Not yet," said Alazaki, and then he related the entire conversation that he'd just had with Sadiq.

"That is very interesting," murmured Harith. "Before we discuss that further, tell me if you believe that Sadiq or the American he works for is aware of what *else* was found in that cave."

"No, Harith al-Wazir, I do not believe so."

"You need to be quite certain."

"If he knew of the lead box, he would have mentioned it. His interest seemed wholly centered on the Scrolls. They are his currency, his gold."

"Very well. We are coming out on top of this arrangement. Ask him for another one hundred collars. If he wants to haggle, go no lower than fifty. If the American wants the Scrolls badly enough, he will agree."

"I will."

"And tell me, Ayoob Alazaki," said Harith, "do you think that Sadiq or the man he is working for have any idea about what our *true* goal is?"

"No."

"How certain are you?"

"As certain as I can be," Ayoob assured him. "I don't think Sadiq would meet with me if he had the slightest clue."

Harith nodded. "And when you deal with Sadiq—or any other of the American's agents—you must be very sure that we keep it that way."

CHAPTER 48
TRAINING HALL 2
PHOENIX HOUSE

I stood alone except for Ghost.

He couldn't, of course, understand what had gone on back in the mission briefing, and videos were nothing to him. But dogs are empathic, and on that level Ghost knows when I have been badly shaken. He sat next to me, leaning his body against my leg as I leaned against the doorframe, occasionally looking up to see my expression and to get some reassurance. When anyone else came by he shifted from companion to guard dog and sent more than one RTI staff member scurrying away with vivid memories of titanium teeth.

The training hall was in use, but it was big, and the group going through exercises was forty yards away. Bedlam Team, run by Major Munn, a former SpecOps badass from South Korea who was now one of our top agents. It was she, by the way, who handled some of the cases I would have led had I not been going through what I went through.

She saw me watching and gave a curt little nod. I nodded back. That was a long conversation for us. It's not that we had any issues between us. Rather the reverse. It's just that sometimes there are people, even respected work colleagues, where the chemistry is wrong for concocting a friendship. But I liked her and admired the quality of work she did.

Ghost whined softly, and I scratched his head.

"Fucking cobras," I said.

He looked at me, and if you know dogs you can tell when *they* wish they could talk, and when *they* want to tell *you* that things are going to be okay.

Except they weren't going to be okay.

The day was the same day, but the world had changed.

God almighty.

CHAPTER 49
LADY STERN HOTEL
JERUSALEM, ISRAEL

After the drinks were gone—and his bit of jaw-dropping showmanship completed—Jason Aydelotte took Toys and Lamech up to a room. Two of his own slabs of muscle joined them as they stepped into the elevator car. Both were very large, unsmiling, and exuded calm confidence.

When Lamech saw which floor number was pushed, he bridled. "No, that's wrong. I'm on seven."

"I know," said Aydelotte.

His people stood in the two far corners of the car, suit coats unbuttoned, hands folded in front, with the left on top. Which told Toys they were both right-handed and wore pistols in shoulder rigs under their left arms. At need, the left hands would peel back the coat flaps, allowing the right hand to reach the gun; and then the left would serve as a block in case someone tried to jam the draw or take their guns. Smart, professional, and smooth. Toys approved.

As the car moved, Toys thought about the drama downstairs and this current show of control. In theory, Aydelotte hadn't known which hotel he was being guided to. That meant he either had connections everywhere or had a large enough team in play to guess his destination and get things moving at top speed. Toys was impressed, and he did not impress easily.

The ride was completed in silence. They exited the car, and the guards conducted them to a high-end suite. As Toys stepped inside he heard Rugger's voice, but this time it was scratchy. "Boss, we just lost the feed from your button cam. And audio is cutting in and out."

Bloody hell, thought Toys, but he kept his expression bland.

"Make yourselves comfortable," said Aydelotte. Lamech sat in one of the armchairs. Toys took the other, leaving the couch to their host. The Israeli put his cell phone on the coffee table; Toys tossed his over as well, and it landed partly atop the other. Lamech tried not to look annoyed, but he was either too proud or not quite petty enough to reach over and move his. Toys hid a smile.

"So," said Aydelotte as he sat, "it's been a busy afternoon, hasn't it, boys?"

"I've rather enjoyed it," said Toys.

Lamech looked stiff. "Was that stunt downstairs necessary?"

"Why? Did it bother you?"

The Israeli took a moment to decide the best and safest answer. "It was . . . extravagant."

Aydelotte shrugged. "I suppose. I grew up in the theater, you know. Mostly church stuff. Choir, shoestring productions of *Godspell* and *Jesus Christ Superstar,* that sort of thing. Can't help myself for having a flair for the dramatic."

"I see it a bit differently," said Toys.

"Oh?"

"If you go to these lengths to protect yourself during a meeting, then I *believe* you're implying that there will be equal care when delivering the goods."

"Ooooh, top marks for Harry Potter." Aydelotte laughed. Toys managed not to wince.

"Yes, that is quite correct," agreed the American. "And, let's face it, I don't know either of you personally, and my father always said that trust is what you have after a check is in the bank and the money's cleared."

Lamech sighed with barely disguised disgust. "Can we get on with it?"

"I'm for that, boys," said the American. "First, show me your cell phones. I want to see that you are logged into your accounts and ready to transfer monies."

Toys and Lamech did as instructed.

"Very good," said Aydelotte. "Now, let me see you each put your phones in airplane mode. Ah. Excellent. Now we can all take a breath."

Toys thought Lamech looked like he was in physical pain. That was fine. The more discomfort, the more he was distracted.

"This is a lot of wasted time," complained Lamech. "You've been very cagey about what the product actually *is*. Do you expect us to bid blind?"

"Of course not," said Aydelotte. "Look, this merchandise is unique. It is exclusive and will remain so for three months after the sale is completed. After that there will be another auction. Got it?"

Toys and Lamech nodded.

Mr. Miracle looked at each of them for a moment. "First, cards on the table. You are *not* here to bid on a new kind of RPG, nor even a modified one. That is, shall we say, *last* year's model. The reason we don't have twenty bidders in the room is that I was deliberately vague with what I posted on the dark web."

Toys noted that Aydelotte tended to use *I* rather than *we*, particularly with anything of importance, anything worthy of praise. *Sociopathic*, he wondered.

"This new weapon is revolutionary," said Aydelotte. "It *is* fired from a shoulder-mounted launcher, but it isn't an explosive. Not in any conventional sense."

"What the hell does that mean? I'm not here to bid on something that doesn't get me the effect I need."

"And what effect would that be?"

Lamech hesitated before answering, clearly reviewing what was safe to say in front of strangers, even if those strangers were as criminal as he was.

"We want to make a statement," Lamech said eventually. "A series of statements. It is important that everyone involved take notice. The . . . *people* . . . on the ground, the government, the press, the world."

"Oh," said Aydelotte, "I can promise you that."

"Then what the fuck is it?"

"We call it the Gorgon."

"I like that," said Toys. "What's it do? Turn people to stone?"

"I wish. No," said Aydelotte. "Think less about the effect of looking at a Gorgon and think more about the hairstyle. All those snakes with fangs ready to bite."

"This makes no sense," said Lamech.

"Shhh, just listen. You are bidding on a set of ammunition—fifty rounds—that will fit any RPG launcher. Do you remember the so-called terrorist attack on the worshippers in Mecca this past April? The reports all said that ten RPGs were fired into the crowd?"

"Yes," said Lamech, looking more attentive now. "Very high body count. But what does that have to do with this? You promised something more efficient; now you're saying we'll need ten foot soldiers to deploy that many weapons?"

"Oh no, not at all. That strike was done deliberately so I could use it for this very discussion. There were not ten RPGs. There was only one."

"What?" asked Lamech.

"What?" asked Toys.

"One," Aydelotte said again. "That is my unique design. You see, each Gorgon has a slight oversize head—which, by the way, is compensated for by some new aerodynamic streamlining. The head itself is a delivery system that cracks open to deliver ten smaller warheads. They spiral outward and seek any target warmer than ninety-five degrees Fahrenheit. That's thirty-five for you fans of the metric system. Each one is packed with my own special mix of high explosives, approximating sixty-eight percent of the overall effect of a standard RPG. One man, one launcher, ten bombs. One person can walk into a sports arena, a concert hall, a mosque, a church, a government building, or onto a commercial airplane and . . . well . . . I think you can imagine the rest. "

The room was silent as both Lamech and Toys worked out the probabilities in their heads. Lamech's eyes were large as saucers. Toys felt his heart seizing up in his chest.

"This deal includes ten handheld launchers and forty mini-Gorgon warheads."

"God almighty," said Lamech.

CHAPTER 50
TRAINING HALL 2
PHOENIX HOUSE

Bug contacted me to say that Top and Bunny were on their way. The others had been notified that a partial Havoc Team was in play and they should continue to enjoy some time off.

"How'd they take that?"

"What, being told to have a longer vacation?" asked Bug. "They took it pretty well, on the whole. Belle grunted, but that's Belle. Remy yelled and said something very loud and very fast in Cajun, which I don't speak. And Andrea threatened to kiss me."

"So, no hurt feelings, then."

"Not as such, no."

I squatted down to pet Ghost, who immediately rolled over to get belly rubs. I obliged.

"Oh," said Bug, "and Bird Dog is wrangling gear. It's being sent ahead to our safe house in Jerusalem."

Brian "Bird Dog" Bird was the senior logistics supervisor for RTI.

"Who's on station at the house?"

"Helmut."

Helmut Deacon was a young man in his late teens who was one of dozens of illegally bred clones of one of history's most vile scientists—Josef Mengele. Grace Courtland and I helped tear down that whole thing during the Dragon Factory case. Since then, Helmut had been away at school. I get holiday cards from him and occasional Zoom calls. Helmut's growing up strong and smart and decent. The fact that he's a clone was shocking then, but let's face it, the only reason we aren't ass-deep in human clones is because of the backlash against it from every sensible human rights group. But it's science, not magic.

I grunted. "Since when is he doing field work?"

"Technically he's not," Bug said. "That safe house is the least used one we have in Israel. Helmut's working on his thesis."

"Wait, wait," I said, "I know I've been out of touch with the kid, but he's what? Eighteen? What's he writing a thesis for? Senior year of high school?"

"Dude, you *are* out of touch. Helmut tested out of high school a year after we rescued him. His IQ is somewhere in the one-sixties. Took the SATs and got eight hundreds on everything. Kid's a genius. He's working on his master's and is doing reading for his PhD."

"Holy crap."

Bug paused. "Say . . . Joe . . . about the briefing? Are you okay?"

I laughed. Short, harsh, bitter. "Bug, I am not okay on an epic level. I don't know if I'll ever be okay again."

"Yeah. I've watched that cobra video a million times. I don't think I'll ever sleep again. I think even Church was freaked out, though it's hard to tell."

"He didn't seem all that sure that this—magic trick or whatever—was done by ISIS," I said. "There are a lot of people who wouldn't want that Boko Haram clown talking to the CIA."

"Which is why he wants you, Joe." Bug paused, then added, "Church has a lot of faith in you."

I straightened. "Yeah, yeah. He's taking his number one psychologically compromised shooter and sending him into the field to look for wizards. Bug, I'm standing here wondering if this isn't all some kind of hallucination, and I'm in four-point restraints in a psych ward."

"If so," said Bug, "I'm in the padded cell next to yours."

We were silent for a moment.

"But those frigging cobras, Joe . . ."

"Those frigging cobras," I said.

"I don't want to sound like a wimp or anything," said Bug, "but this is scaring me on a whole new level. Especially thinking about what certain groups could do with that kind of thing if it's real. Spins the concepts of 'arms race' and 'global terrorism' into a whole new direction."

That suddenly called to mind one of the early conversations I had had with Mr. Church, before I signed on with him. When I was fishing around to try and determine what kind of work he was trying to hire me for, I asked if it involved terrorism. His response hit me hard then and now came back to haunt me.

"Terrorism is an interesting word. Terror . . . Mr. Ledger, we are very much in the business of stopping terror. There are threats against this country greater than anything that has so far made the papers."

"Christ, Bug, I don't even know how I'm going to explain this to the guys. I mean, you think you know how certain people will react, but then the rules of the game change, and it's all new territory for everyone."

"I don't envy you that conversation, Joe. Like I said, they'll be here in three hours. Look, I have to run. Yoda needs me to work on the . . . the . . . thing."

He ended the call. I leaned against the doorframe.

"God damn," I breathed. Ghost whined and pressed harder against me.

CHAPTER 51
LADY STERN HOTEL
JERUSALEM, ISRAEL

"That's bloody genius," said Toys. He said it for the ego-stroke effect, but he also felt it. It was genius. It was also terrifying.

"Here's a caveat," said Aydelotte. "The Gorgons are pre-filled ammunition. You are not bidding on mechanics of the weapon. That is proprietary. If you require more of it, you come to me. Is that understood?"

"Crystal clear," said Toys.

"Yes," said Lamech.

Aydelotte nodded. "And here's a really important kicker. You need to pay very—and I mean *very*—close attention to this. The pre-filled ammunition is sealed into special casings. If anyone uses *any* method to attempt to open those casings, they will explode. That detonation will trigger all of the other ammunition to explode. It's satellite uplinked, so don't think spreading them around the world will matter. Nor should you assume that if you take them to a hardened facility you'll be safe. If they lose my satellite's unique signature, they detonate."

"Bloody hell," said Toys, but with an admiring smile.

"Why all of this?" demanded Lamech. "We are buying a product. What is with all this jerking of chains?"

"You are buying the *effect* of that product, make no mistake," corrected Aydelotte patiently. "What we don't want is for you to get the damn-fool idea into your head that you can take one apart and reverse engineer the contents and make as much as you want. There is no way to do that."

Aydelotte leaned back into the cushions, crossed his legs, smoothed his tie, and then folded his hands in his lap. "Questions . . . ?"

Lamech bristled. "You are telling us how you are safeguarding *your* interests. How do I know that this is not a trick? How do we know that you won't simply detonate the weapons and sell the next batch to another buyer?"

Aydelotte looked pleased with the question. "You don't."

"And you expect us to trust you?"

"If you want my product . . . ? Yes."

"That is hardly fair."

"This may come as a surprise to you, my friend, but I don't really care." He gestured at Toys. "You already know there is a second bidder. There are quite a few more who would be willing to swap places with you. If you are troubled by my conditions, Lamech, then my people will show you out. No harm, no foul, and no hanky-panky."

"I'm good with those terms," Toys said quickly.

"Ahhhh, I had a feeling about you. Hugo taught you well. And, I believe, Sebastian Gault before that?"

Toys's heart jumped. "You knew Sebastian, too?"

"Oh, yes. Early on, though. Before that whole mess in Philadelphia. He cooked up some goodies for me back in the day."

"Such as?"

"Let's not be too explicit. How's this, though? DL-44."

Toys's heart thumped in his chest. DL-44 was a synthetic psychoactive compound that was the core of a street drug known as RawDog. It gave the user about ten hours of incredibly heightened sexual stamina while reducing awareness of pain. It was incredibly popular in a certain part of the porn industry, particularly with rape and snuff films. The downside of RawDog was easy habituation, and over time the effects diminished greatly. That made the drug a poor bet for a street product, but it became an enormous cash cow in Eastern Europe and Central Asian illegal porn markets. And if there was a high mortality rate after too many uses, it didn't matter, because there were always good-looking men from poverty-stricken areas who were willing to take those risks for big money.

Gault had sold the drugs *and* the formula to a buyer whose name Toys never learned. He wasn't as deeply embedded in Gault's trust at that time. All Toys knew was that the product had been made specially for a client, and it was a one-and-done deal.

"Sebastian was proud of that one," Toys said, only half lying.

"Sadly, the factory was taken down by somebody's special ops," said Aydelotte sadly. "You know, I never did find out who it was. Maybe DELTA, maybe SAS. Not sure."

Toys actually did know. It was Barrier, an above-top-secret group in the UK that Mr. Church had helped form and which he later used as a model for the Department of Military Sciences.

Aydelotte rubbed his hands together. "Toys, would you like to make an offer? Bidding starts at five million."

Toys grinned. "Dollars or euros?"

"Oh, I think euros, don't you? And, Lamech, if you'd like to join in, I'll be considering all reasonable offers."

INTERLUDE 20
QAHWA
AL-JARAIB VILLAGE
HAJJAH PROVINCE, YEMEN

EIGHTEEN MONTHS AGO

The man known as Sadiq took a discarded newspaper from a table after those patrons left. Over his fourth cup of coffee, he skipped over the local, international, and business news and beguiled the next hour with the sports page. The caffeine in his bloodstream was making his eyes feel jumpy, but he kept his hands from trembling by an effort of will.

JONATHAN MABERRY

When Ayoob Alazaki returned, Sadiq let the top half of the paper fall forward so he could see the man's face. It was the usual stone mask, and yet there was perhaps a flicker of light there in his eyes. As Alazaki sat, Sadiq folded the paper and tossed it onto the closest empty table.

"Did you enjoy your walk?"

The schoolteacher smiled warmly. "A good walk refreshes the mind and brings clarity."

"It usually does."

Sadiq waited. He knew that Alazaki had needed to get beyond the range of the jammer, check the list of items texted to him, then make some calls to verify if those items were still available—meaning that they were intact and had not been destroyed—and if the senior members of his group agreed to the swap. Those were probably long conversations, Sadiq judged.

"As it happens," said Alazaki, leaning in, "the items in question are available."

"That is excellent news. And the terms of the barter?"

Alazaki paused, and Sadiq thought, *Here it comes.*

"Is it an equitable trade, though?" mused Alazaki aloud.

"Is it not?"

"Perhaps you are getting the better camel, and in return I get a gelded donkey."

"Hardly that," Sadiq said and then laughed. "You give me a camel of good health and all of its teeth, and I give you a pride of lions."

The metaphor made sense to both of them, and they nodded.

"And yet we feel that there is room for more generosity on your part."

"What would make you feel that this barter is of equal weight on both sides of the scale?"

"One hundred additional collars seems fair to me."

Sadiq smiled as if a little child had made an adorable but senseless joke. "Twenty would be more than reasonable."

They settled into the routine of haggling, and it carried them through two fresh cups of coffee. They eventually settled on sixty additional collars.

"Then let us shake hands on this," said Alazaki.

They did and spent a few minutes settling small details about both sides of the deal. After that was done, they went to the small local mosque for *Asr*, afternoon prayers.

Much later, after he had returned to his hotel, and after his people assured him that he had not been tailed by any of Alazaki's goons, Sadiq poured himself a drink and settled onto the couch with a satisfied sigh. Then he made a call using a cell phone with a military-grade cyclic scrambler. The call was answered by a woman.

"How's the weather?" she asked.

"Clear skies," he said.

"What's the news?"

Sadiq took a breath, finally letting out the bottled tension. He did not even try to keep the bubbling excitement out of his voice.

"We will have everything in seventy-two hours."

"Wait . . . *all* of it?"

"Yes."

"The whole box? Every Scroll?"

"Every single one."

"Holy shit," said Shock. "The boss is going to be over the moon."

"I know."

And they both laughed like kids.

CHAPTER 52
LADY STERN HOTEL
JERUSALEM, ISRAEL

Toys lost the bidding war.

He gave it one hell of a try, but Lamech kept going higher and higher. Aydelotte was delighted because the bids weren't bumping in increments of only five thousand euros—Toys and Lamech were stacking it up fifty a throw. When the top bid reached eight million dollars, Toys threw up his hands and gave a disgusted shake of his head.

"Bloody fucking hell." He launched himself from the couch, stalked over to a corner, made a call, yelled a bit, listened for a while, ended the call and kicked a potted plant hard enough to send it skittering and rolling across the floor. Then he punctuated it with another and much louder, *"Fuck!"*

Lamech looked immensely pleased with himself.

Aydelotte tried to make conciliatory noises in Toys's direction, but his face was alight with Christmas morning joy. It increased the resemblance to Santa Claus. Or maybe Krampus, who, upon entering a house on Christmas Eve, found a whole bunch of naughty children he could stuff into his sack and whisk away to some unspeakable fate.

Toys's shoulders sagged in the acceptance of his defeat, and he was about to return to the couch, but Aydelotte held up a hand to stop him.

"Son, I know you're upset, and I can feel your pain, truly I can, but would you mind staying over there for a minute while we conclude the business end of things?"

Toys gave him a bleak, hate-the-world glare, and parked his rump on the windowsill. "Sure. Fine. Whatever. I'll just sit here and work out how to tell my client that I just got bent over a barrel and rogered by that bloody git."

He flapped an arm at Lamech who, having won, seemed suddenly affable and magnanimous. "It's just business."

"Bollocks."

Aydelotte and Lamech went through the process of transferring four million euros to a numbered account in the Seychelles.

"I would appreciate the balance being transferred upon receipt of goods," said Aydelotte.

"Where and when will that be?"

"The location will be texted to you. I'll have a team there to transfer the Gorgon and go over the basics. Okay?"

"Very well," said Lamech.

"It is a genuine pleasure doing business with you," said Aydelotte as they stood and shook hands. "You know how to reach me if you want to make any future purchases."

He walked the man to the door, handing him off to one of the guards, and stood in the doorway until the elevator began its descent. Then Aydelotte came back into the apartment. He made a pouty face and walked toward Toys with his arms wide, grabbed the young Brit, and pulled him into a fatherly embrace.

"I'm sorry things didn't work out, my boy," he said. "For what it's worth, you did very well. Hugo would be so proud of you."

"'Well' isn't the same as winning."

"No, but I like your heart, Toys. I like your spirit. Hell, I *love* your spirit."

"My client won't be quite as enthused."

"Who cares? He should have given you a higher limit." Aydelotte's smile changed into something more confidential and less charming. "Tell you what, son, give me a couple of days, a week at most, and maybe I'll have something even better."

Toys straightened. "Better . . . ?"

"Something I haven't yet shown to anyone. Something very special. It'll blow your mind, and I am being only semi-metaphorical when I say that."

"Are you taking the piss?"

"Ha! No. I told you before, I was very close with Hugo. He was a special man. A special friend. Without his support at some very critical points in my career, I might not be here right now. I'd either be behind bars, in an unmarked grave on prison grounds, or—worse still—poor and ordinary. He taught me how to have a public face and yet stay off the radar of law enforcement and the military. As you have probably worked out already, I took no real risks today. I had coverage every step of the way, and a dozen alibis all locked into place. I have done nothing anyone could ever prove in court." He chuckled. "Hugo was a force of nature, and I counted him as one of the very few people I trusted completely."

"He was that and more for me," said Toys.

"Dear boy, out of our shared love of Hugo Vox, I'm willing to bring you in on something else. I have a feeling that we can do some substantial business together."

Toys looked hopeful but wary. Aydelotte patted his arm.

"Don't fret over it. I know I'm being vague. Nature of the game. Just rest assured that you have my trust because you had Hugo's. And you can trust me for the same reasons."

Toys licked his lips, studied Aydelotte's face, and then nodded.

He offered his hand to shake, but the American pulled him in for another fierce hug. He held it for a long time and then gently pushed Toys to arm's length.

"Okay, son, so you probably know the drill. I'm going to leave, and you'll wait here for one hour. Order room service if you like. Get the lobster. Oh, wait, that's shellfish and this is Israel. Do they serve lobster here? I don't know. Whatever. Order what you want, live it up, don't fret over the deal that wasn't, but think happy thoughts about the deal that *will* be."

With that, he left.

CHAPTER 53
HANGAR A

Havoc Team trickled in over the next few hours. But only two of them.

First in was Top Sims.

He's the oldest active shooter I know. Solid as a rock, though, and you could use his washboard abs to play bluegrass. Smart, calm, dependable, and one of the very few people on this crazy planet that I trust completely. There are guys like him scattered throughout the world's better militaries—mostly sergeants, in my experience. The ones who keep their heads when things are going to shit and know how to provide subtle but critical on-the-job training for green officers.

He saw me in the hangar and came over, grinning with everything but his eyes. He offered a hard, callused hand, and we shook. Top's not a hugger. Then he stood back and gave me a thorough up-and-down appraisal, and I saw those eyes darken.

"You good?" he asked.

"Not really."

"Is it that other thing?" For some reason he never actually says the word "darkness." Not in context to last year.

"No," I said, "it's something else. The new mission."

Top studied me a moment longer. "I'm not going to like this, am I?"

"None of us are."

He nodded, saving his questions for the briefing I'd give in flight. "All right then."

There was a lot more to that conversation, but the rest of it was unspoken. I knew full well that he would be keeping an eye on me. And he knew I knew. We were okay with that.

"Yo, yo, *yo!*"

We turned to see Bunny striding across the hangar floor.

"I know it's only been a few days," he said, "but damn, I'm glad to see you guys."

"How's Lydia and the boy?" asked Top, in that deft way he has of making sure the focus isn't on me when I am in some kind of mood.

"Brad is either going to be an opera singer or a drill sergeant," said Bunny. "I never thought a kid that small could yell that loud."

"Small?" snorted Top. "He was nine pounds fourteen."

"But it's all lungs, though."

"And Lydia?"

"Lydia's great," said Bunny. "She's enjoying training the new nanny."

The nanny in question, Maria, is the niece of Rudy Sanchez, though I hadn't met her yet.

"Rumor has it that Maria takes zero shit from anyone," said Top.

With a crooked little smile and eyes that seemed unable to blink, Bunny said, "She's an apostate of hell."

We stared at him.

"So . . . when you said Lydia was 'enjoying'. . . ." mused Top.

"I mean that *they* get along great. *I*, on the other hand, seem unable to do anything right. I don't hold Brad the right way. I don't change him the right way. I don't heat his bottle to the right temperature. I can't do any-damn-thing right. Ever." He grabbed me by the front of my shirt. "For the love of baby Jesus, boss, take me somewhere people will be shooting at me."

I gently disengaged his hands. "More than happy to."

I might even have smiled.

CHAPTER 54

CAMP 1391, ROUTE 574
BETWEEN KIBBUTZ BARAI AND KIBBUTZ MA'ANIT
NORTHERN ISRAEL

TWO WEEKS AGO

"They tried so hard to make this place invisible," said Toombs as he handed the binoculars to the Yemeni schoolteacher.

The building was old, blockish, austere, and forbidding. That it had been built as a fort was obvious from the corner watchtowers, high, smooth-sided walls, and cleared ground on all sides to prevent covert approach. The two men were in a cleft of rocks nearly a mile from the camp. Well out of sight, deep in heavy shadows.

"It is out in the open where anyone can see it," said Ayoob Alazaki. "How is that 'hiding' it?"

"I mean, sure, it's there if you're sitting where we are. But up until a few years ago you couldn't find it on any map, and Israel's even found some way to scrub it off of Google Maps."

"Like the Americans did with—what was it called?—Area Fifty-one. That's where they are hiding the alien spacecraft."

"That's tabloid junk," said Toombs. "There was a lot going on at Area Fifty-one, but it wasn't UFOs they were hiding in the States. That was all to hide their stealth aircraft test flights from the Cold War era. And when doing early development of drones."

"I know," said Alazaki. "I was trying to make a joke."

Toombs was slow to smile, but the smile was genuine. "Well, damn."

The schoolteacher's smile was smaller and rueful. "It is fair to say that few people expect someone like me to make jokes. But we are human. We laugh and tell jokes. We play pranks and find many things amusing."

"No, I believe you, it's just that *I* haven't heard anyone from the Caliphate make a joke before. It's unique in my experience."

"Now I will be self-conscious," said Alazaki.

Toombs started to placate him and then paused. His grin was quicker this time. "You're a funny guy. I bet your students loved you."

The Yemeni looked away, but before he turned Toombs saw the shadow of pain in his eyes and wished he hadn't said that.

"I miss them, too," said Alazaki.

They took turns studying the fort.

"It is a bit daunting," conceded the schoolteacher. "There are no signs outside."

"They've been trying to close it down for years now," Toombs said, picking up the conversation from where it had tripped and fallen. "They kept it so secret that the minister of justice didn't even know about it. Netanyahu authorized it and funded it pretty well. A lot of Palestinians have vanished in there as completely as if they turned to dust."

"I probably knew some of them."

"No doubt, and I'm sorry if any of your friends went in there. Not a lot of people ever came out. They take the whole 'disappeared' thing to heart down there. Or they did. It's not a prison anymore, which is why I brought you here."

"You have been very reticent on that point," said Alazaki. "What *is* the purpose of that fort?"

"Storage."

"What is being stored?"

"Mostly military hardware and supplies. Lots and lots of weapons. Positioning it this close to the border isn't an accident. They have been quietly bringing in truckloads of weapons, tanks, drones, APCs, and that kind of stuff."

Alazaki studied him. "Why tell me this?"

"Call it a sales incentive," said Toombs. "We're working on something—a kind of biological weapon—that could, used correctly, incapacitate everyone in that place. Quick and simple. Then you could back a truck up and cram it full of whatever weapons and tech you need."

"Again I must ask, why tell me? If we buy your new bioweapon and use it to acquire a truckload of weapons from you, then isn't that contrary to your desire to continue selling the very same kind of weapons from your employer?"

Toombs turned to him and settled back against a rock. "I wondered that myself, and the boss told me that he will not be in the arms trade very much longer. Call this his thanks for being such dedicated customers over the last few years."

"This is true?" asked the schoolteacher.

"It's true. The boss likes you guys and supports what you're doing."

"He is a white Christian American."

"I know, but that just proves this is a funny old world." When Alazaki still looked skeptical, Toombs added, "Not sure if you know this, so I might be overstepping, but . . . my boss has been in contact with Harith. They are friends. Pretty sure that's why the guy before me, Sadiq, reached out to you in the first place. What the world thinks of Mr. Aydelotte and what he thinks of himself are pretty different. He has his own agenda for how the Middle East should be run. He may be Christian, but he speaks very highly of Harith al-Wazir and of the Caliphate itself."

"That is interesting."

"I thought so."

They watched the camp.

"Weapons stockpiled in there, you say?" murmured Alazaki.

"Enough for you and your people to make a considerable impact," said Toombs.

"Impact," echoed Alazaki faintly. "Yes."

INTERLUDE 21
KEMPINSKI NILE HOTEL, GARDEN CITY
12 AHMED RAGHEB, QASR EL NIL
CAIRO, EGYPT

EIGHTEEN MONTHS AGO

The man known as Sadiq lay soaking in a deep tub, a cold bottle of beer resting on the thick mat of chest hair.

The woman he picked up last night was gone. She had been lovely, but for the life of him he could not recall her name. Something French, which was good because as an Algerian, French was as comfortable to him as Arabic. More so, perhaps, since his Sadiq persona was a devout Muslim, but he was not. He'd left all traces of personal faith behind a very long time ago. So long ago that he no longer even felt weirdly guilty when praying in a mosque with various clients. Like Ayoob Alazaki.

Alazaki. He thought about the man.

According to the workup prepared for him by Shock, the fellow was clearly a true believer. Not only in terms of Islam, but in the deeper and more challenging belief systems of ISIS. He was a classic jihadist whose connection to politics had once been something for coffeehouse arguments. A Yemeni schoolteacher who got a call one day from his cousin, another teacher doing a multinational outreach program, to say that an American drone had fired a missile into a school in Iraq. Intelligence reports had rightly stated that ISIS was using the school—and its children—as armor against such attacks. Who would, after all, bomb a school? Who would dare in this age of cell phones and social media?

The United States president went on the news to say that the bombing was a tragic accident and threw blame like camel shit back at the Caliphate, saying that it was their fault for being cowardly and using children as shields.

Cowardly? That was the word that was pushed in every news story. Alazaki had been peaceful before that, but as soon as he voiced his outrage publicly, he was targeted by recruiters wanting to take that anger and passion and aim it like a gun. Ayoob Alazaki was radicalized over a period of five months. Within two years he had risen to a position of respect and authority. Four years later he was the person assigned to purchase weapons with which to fight back against the Great Satan.

Sadiq had lost his own faith from disuse and a natural cynicism. At heart he believed in nothing. No gods or devils, no saints or sinners. Nothing. And wasn't that such a pleasant place to be? He had no personal politics, either. He was what he aspired to be—an extremely clever chameleon who could be whatever his employer wanted him to be. He spoke Arabic, French, Farsi, English, and, at need, could infuse his Arabic with regional dialects.

He sipped his beer, added a little hot to the bathwater, and leaned back with a contented sigh. Life was good.

Well, good for some people. For the people in Mr. Miracle's extended family. Moderately good for Alazaki's ISIS splinter cell, too. Once the deal was closed, watching the twenty-four-hour news cycle was likely to become really interesting. *If* the deal went through down to the last penny being transferred to Jason Aydelotte's numbered account.

If Alazaki was able to somehow use those modified RPGs to bring down a bunch of US aircraft. Well, American and whoever else was hunting ISIS. SDF, the UN, Israel. ISIS was hardly short of enemies to shoot at.

Used judiciously, Sadiq mused, Alazaki and his men could do a considerable amount of damage. That, in turn, would escalate tensions throughout the region. One thing Sadiq knew from having worked with Aydelotte for all these years—in the presence of religious tension, everybody scrambled to buy more guns.

"Gods, guns, and glory," he said and saluted the heavens with his beer.

He soaked and wondered what value Mr. Miracle really placed on those dusty old scrolls. Even to that day, Sadiq had no idea if Aydelotte actually believed in the religion for which he had become an international spokesman. Sadiq and Shock had a hefty wager on that. She believed he was 100 percent devout, but in a literal fire-and-brimstone Old Testament way, while Sadiq thought it was simply a long con that Aydelotte played on everyone but himself.

The bet, he knew, would likely never be settled.

Those new Scrolls and the other stuff rescued by some daring ancient from the Library of Alexandria: the word "priceless" kept coming up in conversation, but everything—from the rarest stamps to newly discovered paintings by the old masters—had a price. As long as someone coveted it and the owner was willing to sell, there would be a dollar amount agreed upon.

How did one put a price on those Scrolls?

Alazaki reckoned that they were worth less to him than the guided-missile conversion kits. And that was likely true enough, since you couldn't knock down American Blackhawk helicopters with a handwritten copy of the Book of Exodus. Value, as always, was relative.

One thing that niggled at him, though, was the fact that Aydelotte seemed utterly convinced that those Scrolls—some of them, at least—might contain secrets of magic. Actual magic.

The first time Shock told him that, Sadiq had snorted beer out of both nostrils and laughed until he choked. Shock had smiled but not laughed; and that smile had been a bit plastic. Sadiq knew she had some faith left. Or perhaps it was that her scientific skepticism was crumbling the more she worked with Mr. Miracle. Hard to say. The point was that she *seemed* to believe that there was at least some chance that magic was real.

Sadiq shook his head and took another swig of beer.

"The world is fucked in the head, and I'm the last sane man standing," he told the steamy bathroom air. He toasted himself on that.

He soaked and sipped.

"Well," he mused after a while, "at least I'm out of it for now."

Saying that made him glance again to the closed toilet seat lid. His cell phone lay next to his watch. If Aydelotte called, he knew he would have to answer. Every call meant money, but Sadiq was beginning to wonder if it was maybe time to consider an extended vacation. Go away, spend some of that hard-earned cash to buy a top-quality set of new papers, become someone else, and vanish.

The thought had real appeal.

He took another sip, closed his eyes, and let the heat of his bath melt away the last of his work-related tensions.

He slipped into sleep and, deep in that sleep, comfortable in his tub, Sadiq had a myocardial infarction. On a deep level he realized that he was dying and was almost amused by it. Sadiq had always assumed he would die by some kind of violence. He never guessed that his heart would fail. No villainy, no betrayal, no murder.

His heart simply failed.

Sometimes life is like that.

Sometimes death is like that, too.

CHAPTER 55
OUTSIDE OF INTERVIEW ROOM C
PHOENIX HOUSE

Mr. Church came out of the interrogation room and saw Rudy Sanchez standing outside.

"Doctor," said Church as he pulled the door closed behind him, "if you're here to see Colonel Ledger, you just missed him."

"I'm here to see you. Do you have a moment?"

"For you? Of course. Shall we go up to your office?"

Rudy's smile was rueful. "I think I've done enough damage up there. We can talk here. We're alone, and this won't take long."

"Very well."

Rudy used his thumb and index finger to smooth his thick mustache. "I felt the need to say a few things. To clear the air between us."

Church nodded.

"First, I apologize for the bit of vandalism and I—"

"Doctor," interrupted Church, "I am going to head you off at the pass if I may. I neither want nor require your apology. I do not, in fact, accept it. You were completely within your rights to express your anger. If you were a different kind of person, you might have tried to knock my teeth in. I get it. Of *course* I get it."

Rudy blinked in surprise. "What?"

"You are entirely correct that Joe Ledger is compromised. You are entirely correct that he has PTSD from the deaths of his family and from other trauma. On this I will not dispute you."

Rudy studied him, trying to read that unreadable face.

"And you know a great deal about me," continued Church. "More than most. More than my own daughter. More, I dare say, than anyone currently working for Rogue Team International. You know as much about me as Aunt Sallie did."

Rudy nodded.

"With all of that knowledge, and with the insight you possess—which I respect greatly—you must also know that I am not ever going to put a weapon on the shelf that I feel still has use."

Church took a small step closer to Rudy.

"I am not a very nice person, Doctor. Some have called me a

monster, and they're not wrong. My motives may be less polluted than some other monsters, but make no mistake, I am a monster. If it were ever possible to win this war, I am acutely aware that I would have no place in the world that would exist after. That is a fact I have lived with for a very, *very* long time. And I make no apologies for the extremes that I feel compelled to go to in order to fight this war."

"Church, I . . ."

But the big man held up a hand. "Please. Let me finish. I once told Joe Ledger that I would burn down heaven to defeat the enemies I fight. At the time those enemies were Sebastian Gault, El Mujahid, and the *seif al din* pathogen. There is no person or group of people I would not have sacrificed to stop that threat. Why? Because to fail would not have resulted in a simple change in the political landscape, or the rise of a new regime, or some other occurrence that, when viewed through history's lens, would be another scar on the conscience of the human race. I meant what I said because to lose that fight would have seen the *end* of the human race. You know that. You were there. You knew the stakes. This is not a fight between ideologies. This war is about standing fast against a tsunami of destructive change. Unchecked, *seif al din* would have ended life on Earth. It appalls me—even me—to say that as literal truth and not hyperbole."

Rudy said nothing. He wasn't sure he could.

"With each new threat that comes to me—to the kind of person I am—there is always that level of threat. The weaponized rabies we fought, the Extinction Machine, the God Machine, the Rage bioweapon. I do not fight the fights other kinds of people *can* fight. I leave it to them, and I respect them for doing their part. Perhaps you think it's hubris that I feel that I am best equipped to fight the kinds of battles I take on. That the DMS took on, and the List before that, and fifty other groups I've started down the long corridor of years. The kinds of fights RTI encounters now. I fight this part of the war because no one else can. That is not ego. That is a cold assessment. I know what my skills are, I know the scope of my vision and the length of my reach. I also know that I am human and that this war will outlive me. I am not the field warrior I was once. My scars are many and they are deep. When I realized that I had become too damaged to fight, I stepped back and began scouting the world for soldiers who were *this* generation's champions. Joe Ledger is one such."

"Despite the weight of *his* scars?" snapped Rudy.

"*Because* of those scars," replied Church coldly. "You think he is too battered to keep fighting? You think he has seen too much already? You are rarely wrong, Doctor, but you are wrong about that. Colonel Ledger is, because of all he's seen and done and suffered and accomplished, at the very top of his game. He is my most fearsome weapon, and as long as *I* believe he is that kind of weapon I will continue to use him."

"Even if it kills him?"

"Yes, Doctor. Even then. If there is something out there so ferocious and powerful that it destroys Joe Ledger, then I can guarantee you that Ledger will drag it down with him."

"You really are a bastard."

"I am a *monster*," corrected Church. "I pretend to be nothing else."

Rudy turned and walked a few steps away. Then he stopped, head bowed between hunched shoulders. "God damn you."

"God damn those who bring this war to our doorsteps, Doctor. God damn the monsters out there who have no conscience, no vision of a better world beyond whatever last battle will end this. God damn those who think that they'll win because *they* won't stop and they can't believe that anyone is as committed, as fierce, as merciless as they are."

He walked over and around to stand in front of Rudy. He took off his glasses and let Rudy see him, see his eyes as he spoke. It was something Church had never done before.

"Doctor," Church said very softly, "I will tell you something I once told Joe. It was during the King of Plagues case, when he had been forced into a situation where there were no good solutions but merely a choice of bad ones. Of tragic ones. He made a choice that he felt was the only one he could make, but it was a terrible thing. He was right, but the cost was dreadful. Afterward, we spoke alone, as you and I are alone. He needed to understand what he was for having made such a choice, and what I was for putting him in the position where he *had* to make that choice. What I told him is this. I said, 'The darkness is all around us. Very few people have the courage to light a candle against it. We are of a kind, and neither of us is holding a candle against the darkness. Like the unknown and unseen enemy we fight, people like you and me—we are the darkness. In some ways we are more like the things we're fighting than the people we're protecting. We are part of the darkness. Granted, our motives are better—from our perspective—but we wait in the darkness for our unseen enemy to make a move against those innocents with the candles. And by that light, we take aim.'"

Rudy murmured, "*Dios mío.*"

"Tell me, Doctor . . . tell me, *Rudy* . . . am I wrong? Is Joe Ledger wrong?"

"In doing what you do? No, of course not. In how you do it? From any strategic perspective, I have no right to judge. But from the perspective of a human being and a humanist, and more so as Joe's psychiatrist . . . I'm surprised you even ask. That statement, though powerful and useful for you to say and for Joe to hear in that moment, is telling. You kept using the word 'darkness' as both a proxy for the kinds of global terrorists that the DMS fought and RTI continues to fight. And in the same speech you frame the darkness as a tactic. 'Waiting in the darkness.' Surely you of all people can't fail to see a likely connection between the overall mission you have brought Joe into and that toxic new personality that overwhelmed him last year."

Church looked troubled. "Surely you, of all people, must know that it was never my intention."

"Joe is my brother," said Rudy. "He is the best person I have ever known. This job will probably kill him."

"It will very likely kill us all," said Church. "That is the burden warriors face when they remain on the battlefield until the war has ended. I cannot and will not apologize for what I am asking of all the people with whom I work."

"Yes," said Rudy in a fractured voice. "Yes. I understand."

Tears rolled down Rudy's face, but he did not wipe them away.

Instead, Rudy took one of Church's hands and held it tightly in his own. He pressed that hand to his chest, to his heart, and held it there for a long moment. And then he released it and, without saying another word, walked away down the hall.

INTERLUDE 22
MONITORING SUITE
PIRATE LAB
UNDISCLOSED LOCATION

EIGHTEEN MONTHS AGO

"Boss . . . ?"

Jason Aydelotte turned to see Shock standing in the doorway. Her face was red and puffy, and her eyes were wet with tears.

"My dear girl," he said, rising from his chair and crossing to her. "Whatever is the matter?"

"It's Sadiq . . ." she began, and then her voice broke into a soft sob.

"What about him?"

"He's gone, boss," she said.

"Gone? What are you talking about? I spoke to him two hours ago. He's taking a long weekend in—"

"You're not listening to me," she said, tears running down her face. "He's dead."

"Dead . . . ?" Aydelotte repeated the word as if it belonged to another language entirely. "What do you mean? How could he be dead?" Then he stiffened. "Was it that motherfucker Alazaki? I swear to the living Christ that I will have his—"

Shock grabbed the front of his shirt and shook him. "*No.* They say he had a heart attack."

"What?"

"He was at his hotel in Cairo. His driver found him. Sadiq was supposed to go to the airport this morning, and the driver couldn't reach him by phone or text. So he went up and used his passkey to go inside. Sadiq was . . . was . . . in the tub. Like for days. Probably all weekend. Oh, god!"

She buried her face in Aydelotte's chest and began to cry. Very loudly, brokenly.

Aydelotte gathered her in his arms and held her tight. He knew that Shock and Sadiq had been sleeping together, but until that moment he hadn't realized that their relationship had gone to another level. Love.

He held her and rocked her and whispered soothing words.

All the time wondering what it must feel like to be in love.

Wondering what it must feel like to be able to love.

CHAPTER 56
IN FLIGHT
OVER THE AEGEAN SEA

The three of us flew to Israel.

Once we were in the air, Bunny said, "So what's the op?"

"Guys," I began, "I'll give it to you the way they gave it to me."

Bunny looked at Top. "Is it me or does this already feel weird?"

"Sit and pay attention, farm boy."

I gave them the story. All of it. Everything I'd heard. The background on the two potential sellers of antiquities, the stuff about the scientists committing suicide, the Dead Sea Scrolls, the Copper Scrolls, and then the video footage of the cobras. All of it.

They watched, and I saw the flow of emotions across their faces. Surprise, consternation, skepticism, amusement, doubt, shock, and then actual horror.

We flew a lot of air miles before either of them spoke.

"No," said Bunny.

I said nothing.

"I mean it, boss. No. I'm not buying fucking magic spells and Old Testament magicians or any of that shit. I'm sorry, but . . . no."

Top rubbed his eyes and looked at the calluses on his palms for a while, not sure what he was seeing. Then he reached over and squeezed Bunny's big shoulder.

"I'm having a hard time with it, too, farm boy," he said, and he'd never sounded old to me before. He did now. "But this is coming from the Big Man. It's coming from Lizzie Corbett, and you know her. It's coming from Bug, too."

"It *can't* be real," protested Bunny. I'd never heard him sound that scared.

"Look," I said, "I'm pretty far out on the edge of Freakoutsville, too. I think we can all agree that we don't *want* to believe it. We all want this to be somebody playing some kind of fucked-up game. Special effects, doctored videos, rubber snakes, whatever."

Top gave me a hard look. "But that ain't what it is."

"No, it's not."

Bunny shook his head. He tried to smile. It looked ghastly. "Does this bird have parachutes?"

"We're over the middle of the damned Aegean," said Top, willing to be his straight man.

"How's that matter?"

And then, for reasons that made no sense then and still don't make sense, we all burst out laughing. Ghost jumped up, alarmed. He began barking loudly. But his tail was wagging.

That made us laugh harder.

And if we laughed and cried at the same time, who cares?

CHAPTER 57
LADY STERN HOTEL
JERUSALEM, ISRAEL

Toys ordered his meal, ate heartily, retrieved his phone, and left.

Once he was down on the street level he checked his cell. It had been visibly placed in airplane mode, but Bug designed that phone so that it was never off or even idle. When Toys tapped the right keys the screen display read: *Transfer Completed*.

Got you, you fatuous git, he thought. He now had the account information for Lamech's private funds, and the destination account info for Mr. Miracle's numbered account. Bug was going to play merry hob with both.

Toys took a cab back to his own hotel, went to his room, turned on a small jammer, and took the stairs down to the street. He slipped out the back and walked several blocks before contacting his team.

"Rugger?"

"Here, boss."

"Where are we?"

"You want the good news or the bad?"

"Just tell me."

"Your button cam faulted out as soon as you entered the suite. We got bits and pieces of conversation, but not enough for us to know what's going on. I was listening with all my filters and distortion scrubbers on, and I couldn't say for sure we caught Aydelotte saying anything that would put cuffs on him. I'm not even sure there's anything worth sending to Bug."

"Oh, that's bloody brilliant."

"The good news is we got everything from Lamech's phone. We're picking through it now. Lamech probably thought he was being clever using a burner, but he's clearly used it ever since he arrived here in Jerusalem. Four days, thirty-two calls, fifty-nine text messages. Some fancy-ass signal bouncing, but nothing we couldn't dismantle. Fucking amateur."

"Don't look a gift horse in the bollocks," said Toys, though he was well pleased. "Did you see his face when Mr. Miracle pulled that stunt in the bar? Did we get that part?"

"Yup. Lamech turned fifty shades of pale. Kind of fun seeing him realize he was coming up short on the dick-measuring competition."

"Quite entertaining," said Toys. "Any idea where the meet will be for the Gorgon handoff?"

"That text was sent after we cloned the phone, so we don't have the address, but Armani picked Lamech up when he left Lady Stern, and Dingo got a tracker on the car when he stopped at a red light."

"Brilliant."

"Look, that stunt in the hotel bar was kind of crazy. Was he making a point or just showing off?"

"Bit of both, I'd say. Aydelotte's big on himself. Probably thinks he's the new Hugo Vox. And maybe he is. Maybe that's what all today's drama was—giving birth to a new legend. I remember some stunts Gault played that were nearly as dangerous, but he got more than jollies out of it. He impressed certain key people, and that put a lot of money in his accounts. Time will tell. But, yes, Aydelotte likes to be the big dog in the room. World's greatest businessman and world's greatest criminal mastermind, blah blah blah. He probably had pet names for each of his balls—profit and loss—and calls his dick Big Deal."

There was a sharp laugh followed by a wet noise and then a cough. "Sorry. Just spat Coke all over my laptop."

"Classy," laughed Toys. "Anyway, Aydelotte is dangerous as hell for all of that. This Gorgon is bloody terrifying. It's not time for us to make any rookie mistakes. Make sure everyone stays on point."

"We had that discussion while you were up there."

"Good."

"Not to kiss ass here," said Rugger, "but the way you played losing the bid . . . ? Academy Award stuff. You had me believing you were about to throw yourself out the window."

"Well, thanks. And you kiss ass very well. You should add that to your résumé."

"Sir . . . ?"

"What?"

"Fuck you."

Toys laughed and headed on his way to begin the next phase of this job.

CHAPTER 58
O'TREE-SANCHEZ HOUSE
CORFU, GREECE

"Hello . . . ?"

Her voice was soft, a bit weary.

"Junie," said Rudy, "I know you're traveling. Serbia? Well, I'm glad I caught you."

There was a short beat before she replied.

"I just finished listening to a bunch of voice mails and reading text messages from Joe."

Rudy Sanchez sat on a wicker porch swing on the back deck of his house in Corfu. He had just returned from Omfori Island and was considering everything Church said. It was a lot to process. Enlightening and painful in equal measures.

The Aegean was almost absurdly blue, and the sky above it but a shade lighter. Seabirds in their thousands were diving into a school of some kind of fish that had been unwise enough to cruise the shoal waters. There were dolphin fins out there, too. On any other day, he would have sat out there with Circe and the kids and shared what would have been a scrapbook day. One of those days that people bring up when they want to talk about how happy they are and what a wonderful place Earth is.

But this was not that kind of day.

The sun was rolling over the dome of the world, and in his yard the shadows were leaning backward from the ocean.

"Did he tell you about what happened in Mr. Church's office?" asked Rudy.

"He did," said Junie. She had a soft voice that reflected who she was: intelligent, calm, insightful. "It sounds like a painful encounter."

"It was not my finest moment."

"Joe didn't throw you under the bus, Rudy. You know he loves you. You're his best friend in the world, and he knows you would not have been so intense if you didn't also love him."

Rudy rubbed his eyes and was not surprised to see wetness on his fingertips.

"I told Church what you already know—Joe has earned his right to hang up his sword and shield."

"He has," said Junie, "but do you really ever see him doing that?"

Rudy watched a seagull coast across the horizon, high and slow, riding the thermals, his wings fixed as if he had no need to flap them.

"He should, though," said Rudy.

"I know," said Junie.

"I've tried to help him understand that. I've used logic, statistics, friendship. I've even tried emotional blackmail."

"Joe is Joe."

"I know that, sweetheart," said Rudy sadly. "And that's what scares me. It breaks my heart. He does so much good in this world.

The things he's seen and the terrible battles he's fought. The deep injuries he's endured and the losses . . . *ay, dios mío*, the losses."

"I know," she said. "I do. I get it. And I've had my own conversations with him about this. God, how many times? But we always get back to him needing to be fully what he is. And this *is* who and what he is."

"Church can change that with a stroke of a pen, with a word."

Junie laughed, but it sounded sad. "He could, but he won't. And you know why as well as I do."

"Yes. Because Church *is* Joe. From another era, another social background, another doorway into that damned war of theirs, but he is Joe. He won't ever leave the fight. I don't think he can."

"No," said Junie.

"No," said Rudy.

He told her about his conversation with Church, and he heard her sob very softly. All she said, though, was a quiet, "Damn."

They said nothing for a very long time, but the comfort was in knowing the other was there, not in the words said. They each knew this.

The sun pulled the last of the bright daylight around it and ghosted off the edge of the world.

TRAVELERS IN ANTIQUE LANDS
PART 3

There are things known and there are things unknown, and in between are the doors of perception.

—ALDOUS HUXLEY

CHAPTER 59

"Colonel," said the pilot via the intercom, "we're beginning our descent."

We all buckled up. I have a special harness for Ghost that attaches him in some comfort to the seat next to mine. He loves it. He sits with his head up like some kind of visiting dignitary. Grand Chancellor from the Isle of Dogs.

The three of us had moved on from pure shock through valleys of disbelief and over hills of acceptance. Conditional acceptance. Part of that process was for each of us to take a moment to allow ourselves to feel what we legitimately felt, and then to find a shelf to place it on. Then, each in our own way, we found our way back to some version of professional detachment. Along that crooked path I think we all began clinging to the idea that somehow the miracle stuff wasn't that at all. This is the twenty-first century. Deepfakes are common. There's CGI so real you can't tell. So maybe—*maybe*—this was that.

"So," said Bunny, "what do we think about those two researcher guys doing themselves ugly like that? And . . . bats from hell? That sounds like an Ozzy Osbourne CD that I would actually buy. How's it factor in?"

"To be determined," I said.

"There's no video of them killing themselves?"

"No. And no need for video surveillance of two men in a clean room looking at scraps of parchment," I said. "The only video cameras are in the parking lot and the hallways. But since some of the work they do in the clean rooms is sensitive, it isn't captured on video."

"They do autopsies on these guys?" asked Top.

"Piss-poor ones," I said. "And that's maybe a doorway in for us.

For RTI, I mean. Bug's team is trolling the computers belonging to each and to the organization. Doc Holliday is using her network of science geeks to see if she can suss out why they didn't do a tox screen. Scott Wilson has applied for temporary possession of the cell phones of both men."

Bunny frowned. "Seems like a full autopsy would have been top of the list, what with the guys going apeshit."

"You'd think," I agreed.

"Well," said Top, "even if they haven't, we can still order one, right? Worst case is Church has to finesse permission to exhume the bodies."

"Hard as hell to exhume ashes," I said.

They gave me identical looks.

"What about samples?" asked Top. "Surely the lab kept some."

"Again I say, *you'd think.*"

He was silent for a moment, slowly chewing the end of his pen. "I can see why the Big Man asked us to take a look."

"Uh huh."

"I know that this is weird, and the cobra thing is weird," said Bunny, "but I have to ask—how certain are we that these two things are connected?"

"We know exactly jack shit."

"God, it's fun to be us, isn't it?"

Top gave an extravagant sigh. "I don't want to burn up calories leaping to conclusions. There were bite marks left from the cobra thing, and there was venom in the bloodstream, right?"

"Yes."

"Any bat bites on the scientists?"

"Nothing that was noted in the autopsy."

"Sure," said Bunny, "but given that the autopsy was either done by the Three Stooges or it was deliberately short-sheeted, then we can't be sure, can we?"

"I asked Bug to see if there was any video from the morgue. Not the autopsy, because that wasn't actually recorded on video, but from when the bodies were being handled within the morgue. It's a slim chance, but maybe there's enough visual on the skin to see if there *were* bites. Very slim chance."

Top shrugged. "We've bet on slimmer."

"There's another thing twisting my nuts," said Bunny. "We got the Boko Haram asshole getting bitten by cobras. We have the scientists writing about bats. But there's another bit. That boy in the basement of the compound in Chad saying, 'That will feed the scorpions. The baby will like that.' Cobras, bats, and scorpions. And two out of the three of them have ties to ISIS."

"They are probably connected," I said. "Be weirder if they weren't."

"What's the plan, then?" asked Bunny. "Where do we start? Scrolls or psycho scholars?"

"I want to see the room where the scholars died," I said. "Let's start there."

They thought about that. Nodded.

I said, "We're all spooked by this. Fine. Spooked is a feeling, and we've spent our entire adult lives learning how to take emotions and put a leash on them while we were getting the actual job done. This feels bigger. If it actually is, then we go bigger."

"Hooah," said Top, and after a pause, Bunny echoed it.

I leaned forward as far as the seat belt would allow. "We *will* figure this out. You can count on that."

"Hooah," they said again, giving it some muscle this time.

CHAPTER 60
DR. CONTI'S LAB
PIRATE LAB
UNDISCLOSED LOCATION

FOUR YEARS AGO

They stood on opposite sides of a steel table on which the lead box from Pharaoh Siamun's tomb squatted. The table was in a small clean room built to the gold standard of modern biohazard safety. Both of them were dressed in white hazmat suits. Despite the safety of the suits and the internal air conditioning, they were sweating.

Aydelotte's eyes were bright as Christmas tree ornaments. "You do understand what this is, don't you?"

Shock used a gloved hand to trace the writing on one side. "This is Exodus chapter seven, verses ten through twelve. This is the first-ever proof that the Jews were in Egypt. It proves, at least to some degree, that Moses and Aaron had some kind of dispute with Siamun about freeing the Jews. This is it! This is going to change the course of religious history for the next hundred years."

"Shock," said Aydelotte gently, "I have been working toward this my whole life. This is more important than anything we have ever found, more important that anything we have ever done."

"Yeah?"

"Oh, yes."

"What do you think we should do with it?"

Aydelotte smiled. Not at her, and not even at the box. He seemed to be momentarily lost, staring at his own shadowy reflection in the darkened screen of a computer monitor that was turned off.

"Jason . . . ?" Shock prompted.

But he did not answer her.

INTERLUDE 23
THE VENETIAN RESORT
LAS VEGAS, NEVADA

FIVE MONTHS BEFORE CHAD

Jason Aydelotte looked up from the sheaf of papers. He was semi-sprawled on a pale gray couch in a suite at his favorite hotel in Vegas. Shock was at the writing desk wearing a set of noise-canceling headphones as she worked on a laptop, occasionally glancing at her boss and the man she had nominated to fill a key position in the organization.

"Your name is Toombs?"

"Yes, sir," said the tall man.

"Real name?"

"No, sir. Nickname because of how I look."

Toombs was rail thin, very pale, with a cadaverous face that looked as if his skin had gotten wet and shrunk as it dried. His eyes were half lost in shadowy sockets. On any other person the pallor and waxy texture of his flesh would scream illness. He looked emaciated and frail, but Aydelotte didn't think so.

"What *is* your real name?"

"Isaac Tomberland."

"I like Toombs better," said Aydelotte.

He found the man's appearance delightful. Toombs wore black clothes in a severe cut. His jacket was a fashionable take on a nineteenth-century frock coat in the style that was labeled "Pilgrim Chic" at New York Fashion Week. Straight-leg pants, white shirt, black tie with the top shirt button undone behind the knot.

"Shock speaks very highly of you," Aydelotte said affably. "And your references are rock solid. Everyone with whom she spoke said that you are exactly the kind of person I'm looking for. A mix of salesman, logistics facilitator, and fixer—is that right, Mr. Toombs?"

Toombs smiled. It was a horrifying smile that called to mind the Joker from the creepier Batman comics. Lots of big white teeth. Aydelotte swore there were more teeth there than was proper.

There was amused awareness in Toombs's eyes. "Yeah. The smile. I know."

"You use it, though," said Aydelotte. "You know you have a ghoulish, creepy look, and you do your best to sell it. That's smart. It's lemons from lemonade."

"People will fuck with you if you just look big and tough," said Toombs. "They are less anxious to mix it up with someone who looks like they'd fuck you up and eat what's left."

"Self-aware fiend." Aydelotte laughed. "I love it."

Toombs nodded. "Using it just like you use the jolly Santa thing. People would trust you even if they *knew* you were cheating them."

Aydelotte waved the papers. "I'm not seeing much of a criminal record in here."

"Why would there be? Only time I ever got picked up was for a gig I was lookout for when I was sixteen. They couldn't make me for it, and the other guys they busted didn't drop a dime."

"Honor among thieves?"

"Common sense, fear, and self-interest."

"Nice."

"So, as far as the law counts, I'm clean as Girl Scouts. Here and abroad."

Toombs sat in one of a pair of armchairs arranged in a conversational grouping with the couch. The fabric was a dusty rose, but Toombs's clothes darkened them, giving the color more pop. The effect was that the chair seemed real and in color, while Toombs looked like a sharp black-and-white photograph.

"Let's talk about your adventures abroad," said Aydelotte. "Shock said she met you in Cairo some years back, where you were working as field man for an arms deal between one of Putin's off-the-books group and a buyer for ABM."

Ansar Bayt al-Maqdis was another of the many names by which ISIL—the Islamic State of Iraq and the Levant Sinai Province—was known. They were the most active and capable terrorist group operating in Egypt and were dedicated to the destruction of Israel and the establishment of an Islamic emirate and implementation of sharia in the Sinai Peninsula.

"The deal went through?" asked Aydelotte.

"Without a hitch."

"And the materials which you helped the Russians sell were used to bomb the gas pipeline in the Sinai that supplies natural gas to Israel and Jordan."

"Yes."

"Why did you stop working for Putin?"

Toombs made a small dismissive gesture. "He lost his damned mind when he invaded Ukraine. And he reneged on what he owed to contractors like me. Actually expected us to either take a big cut in pay or to *donate* our time as a courtesy."

"Wow," laughed Aydelotte. "My own people would skin me alive if I ever did that."

"As they should." Toombs's dark eyes were intense. "Unless they're motivated by faith or politics, in which case you should fire them and maybe have them put down."

"You're not an idealist, I take it?"

"I believe in loyalty," said Toombs, "not in causes."

"What if someone were to try and lure you away from me with a promise of better money?"

Toombs shrugged. "If I thought it was a legit offer, I'd come and tell you about it."

"To see if I would match it?"

"No. To see if you wanted me to put a bullet in them because it meant they knew you were my boss and had some idea what you were paying me. Which could only happen if they had an inside track. That's a dangerous thing. Look, here's how I work. If you hire me on and pay me a fair wage, then you buy my skills and my loyalty. I don't shit where I eat. I don't go looking for a better gig. I expect you to show me the same loyalty. Shock says you play it straight with the people in your inner circle. I trust her because we've known each other for a long time. I trust you because she trusts you."

"You're remarkably frank."

"I don't get the impression you needed your ass kissed by the people on your payroll."

Aydelotte considered that. "Works for me." He picked up a folded piece of paper that was on a side table, opened and looked at it, then set it down again. "Shock says that you have advanced skills in armed and unarmed combat. Obviously well versed in a wide range of military weapons and equipment. But she also says you're a computer guy. Tell me about that."

"For a while I was working the dark web sales floor for a vendor in Kosovo. He knew jack shit about the net, cell phones, and how computers work. I've always been a quick study, so I brushed up and handled it for him, set up his online catalog, built his e-commerce, wrote code for firewalls. Like that."

"What were you selling for him?"

"Mostly surveillance drones, some medium-to-small tactical drones, grab-and-go surveillance camera systems."

"For a Kosovo criminal?"

"Sure. He had a good sideline in blackmail and extortion, so I helped him set up the network to capture useful political players with their dicks in the wrong holes. And worked out how to make contact and follow through all the way to payment using some useful rerouting and email-shielding software. But that's all past tense. I prefer face-to-face sales. I like being in the field because I dislike doing deals with people unless I can look them in the face, watch their eyes, listen to their inflection. That's where it gets real, and that's where it gets fun. For me, at least."

"Ah, you would have liked Sadiq," said Aydelotte. "Cut from the same cloth."

"Shock said the same thing."

After a few seconds Aydelotte stood and offered his hand. "I think we'll make a lot of money and have some fun together."

Toombs stood and they shook. Toombs's hand was large, white, dry, and hard as bone.

CHAPTER 61
BEN GURION AIRPORT
JERUSALEM, ISRAEL

The man looked like a weary business traveler. Slightly rumpled suit, five o'clock shadow, haggard and yet patient expression, scuffed middling-quality briefcase that looked like it had been handled by every customs agent from Israel to Brazil and back, shoes that were good for walking. There were scores just like him in every airport in the world, and no one gave him a second look.

Which was entirely the point.

He watched the three big men go through the formalities of customs. One of them had dark glasses and held on to the handle of a large guide dog. The dog was a white shepherd, and there was a printed service animal sign asking people not to pet him. The second man was a tall, somewhat older black man with a shaved head and salt-and-pepper goatee; and their companion was a towering blue-eyed blond wearing a volleyball T-shirt and a nondescript sport coat.

Unlike the business traveler, they did draw the eye, but their stern faces in no way invited chitchat. They got their passports stamped, collected their carry-on bags, nodded to the agents and headed out to the street.

The business traveler followed at a discreet distance. He stopped inside the terminal and watched the men climb into a black SUV. He took photos of them and the license plate of the car.

When they were gone, he made a call.

"You called it, Mr. October," he said. "Joe Ledger, Bradley Sims, Harvey Rabbit, and that dog. Ghost. Sending you images right now. Got them? Good."

CHAPTER 62
RTI SAFE HOUSE
HEBRON ROAD
JERUSALEM, ISRAEL

We drove to a safe house in a quiet part of Jerusalem.

I have no actual idea how many such places there are around the world, but I have rarely been to a city where Church could not provide that kind of resource. In the few instances where it wasn't actually something he owned, then it was on loan from Britain's Barrier and MI6, the CIA, India's Marine Commandos, Arklight, Pakistan's SSG, Chess Team, Sigma Force, France's GIGN, and Israel's own Mossad and Sayeret Matkal . . . plus scads of others. Sometimes I wonder if there are any *un*affiliated residences anywhere. Bunny thinks there should be weekly meetups, with the team from the host city buying the drinks.

Naturally, I'm always most comfortable on home turf, meaning something Church put in place, with all of Bug's electronics in the walls, and lots of toys hidden where we'd need them. Those houses usually have shatterproof and bullet-resistant windows and steel-core doors with tamper-proof locks. I sleep better.

The place had a small, protected entry shell, ostensibly to keep rain off you while you sort out your key. Considering the paucity of rain in Jerusalem, it's kind of funny. But it's a useful thing, because hidden inside, behind a certain section of aluminum siding, is a hand-geography scanner, a retina scan, and a voiceprint scanner.

The door opened before I could grab the handle, and there he was. Helmut Deacon. Tall, slender, with dark hair dyed a milk-blond. He wore jeans and a Nine Inch Nails T-shirt that looked old enough to be vintage. Rope sandals and a lot of visible tattoos. More than I remembered from the last time I saw him.

He smiled, and I walked into his embrace. He is generally not a hugger and doesn't do the whole manly back-slappy stuff. But he hugged me like a brother would. Or maybe a nephew. Then he stepped back and welcomed me inside. He shook hands with Top and Bunny. There were odd smiles and knowing looks going around, and all of us knew why. Top, Bunny, and I had rescued him from the Dogfish Cay, where he had been in lifelong captivity by his maniac father. I'd bagged his father at the end of that gig, and I had not been nice about it. Not even a little bit. Last I heard, Mengele—known as Cyrus Jakoby then—had been taken by Church to one of *his* black sites. I don't expect that anyone will ever hear of him again. I also hope Church fucked him up even worse than I did, and maybe killed him in some ugly and cosmically just way. But it's not something we ever talk about.

In my own personal lexicon, I have a nickname for people who have been through terrible personal trauma and come out, scarred but on their feet. People who don't hide their scars, people who aren't ashamed of being who they are because they chose to own their whole history rather than whine about being victims. I call them Children of the Storm Lands. I'm one. Junie is another.

Helmut was *born* in the Storm Lands.

I know that Helmut talked about a lot of it with Church, and also with Rudy. And Rudy was the one who convinced him that he was not evil just because he was a clone of one of history's most vile monsters. Rudy explained that the nature versus nurture equation was fundamentally flawed in the way most people view it. It wasn't only those two factors, because that suggests human actions are trapped in an absolutist imperative, and they aren't. Rudy explained that it was nature versus nurture versus *choice*. And boy, if that doesn't make the world make a lot more sense.

The dyed hair, the grunge clothes, the tats—all of that was Helmut evolving into someone else entirely different from the kid we rescued. The kid who was known as SAM. One of many SAMs on the island. All Mengele's genetically identical *children*. SAM was his acronym for "Same as Me."

God almighty.

Ghost got his turn, and Helmut knelt and caught the dog's face between two gentle palms. They looked into each other's eyes for maybe ten seconds. Then he kissed Ghost's head, and the fur-monster licked Helmut's fingers.

Once inside, we dropped our bags. I saw a backpack set near the door. Helmut picked it up.

"I know you guys have work to do," he said as he slung it over one shoulder. "I'm going to bug out and go to the other place to work. Deadline looming."

Top said, "I heard about your thesis. Like to read it when it's done."

"Sure," said Helmut. He doesn't smile much, but there was a hint of it in his eyes. "You need me to show you around before I go?"

"Nah," said Bunny. "Scott sent us the basics."

"There's fresh coffee, and the fridge is full."

And he left. Helmut isn't a chatty kid, but he's a good one, and I wished him well.

He closed the door behind him and was gone. I made a mental promise not to let that much time pass before I saw him again.

Maybe I'd even tell him about the Darkness. The real story. The things I'd only ever told Rudy and Junie. I think he'd understand.

I *know* he would.

INTERLUDE 24
DR. CONTI'S LAB
PIRATE LAB
UNDISCLOSED LOCATION

FIVE MONTHS BEFORE CHAD

Aydelotte gave Toombs the full tour of his facility.

"I like the name," said Toombs. "Pirate Lab. Kind of dashing."

"Ha! Yes, I suppose. But that's my nickname for this whole facility."

"Really? Why lab, though?"

"Glad you asked, because here we are," said Aydelotte as they approached a nondescript door at the end of a long hall in the second sub-basement. As they passed through, Toombs gave a soft whistle. The lab was larger than he expected and was crammed with gleaming machines, racks of instruments, a dissecting table, and more. There was a row of glass-enclosed cubicles lining one entire side of the room. Each cubicle was empty except for the last, where a man wearing coveralls and a plastic safety mask was scrubbing something off the inside of the wall that looked suspiciously like dried blood. Across the room a woman sat peering at the screen of a large desktop computer.

"Dr. Conti," called Aydelotte. "If you have a moment, I'd like to introduce you to our new field sales agent."

Giada Conti looked up from her screen, pushed her glasses up her nose, sighed with visible irritation, but got up and came over. Aydelotte introduced them both.

"So, again I have to ask," said Toombs. "Lab? To study what? And what's this have to do with the stuff you want me to sell?"

"Dr. Conti is working on a special project. Go on, Giada, tell Mr. Toombs what you're developing for us. Tell him about Shiva."

Conti looked profoundly uninterested in doing any such thing, but she said, "It's an ergot-based mycotoxicosis bioweapon. We're blending it with genetically engineered psilocybin and naturally occurring psychedelic prodrug compounds that can be fitted into a non-incendiary warhead for low-altitude detonation and dispersal."

Her look was challenging and condescending, as if she expected him to be flummoxed.

Toombs smiled and said, "Convulsive ergotism or gangrenous?"

Conti grunted in surprise and then gave him a reappraising look. "Convulsive."

"And the psilocybin is to increase the intensity of hallucinations?"

She paused. "Yes."

"How will you keep the fungi viable?" asked Toombs. "If it's in powder form, won't it be inert?"

"We'll suspend it in a liquid medium that will keep the fungi active, and the detonation of the warhead will vaporize the liquid into a mist."

"Okay, but if the warhead is non-incendiary, how will you manage a broad-area dispersal?"

Aydelotte beamed with approval. "That's where the Gorgon comes into things," he said. "Different department. Giada here is a molecular biologist and biochemist. Gorgon is being designed by a very bright lad named Russo. You'll meet him next."

"Got it," said Toombs, "but what's the purpose of the weapon?"

"You seem like an exceptionally bright lad, maybe you can tell me."

Toombs shrugged. "I can tell you how *I'd* use it. If I wanted to hit a target in a location with any kind of containment to maximize effect, and—I guess more to the point—if I wanted to avoid a gunfight, then something like this would be ideal. Deploy the weapon, wait for it to take effect, and then go in wearing some kind of protective overgarments—hazmat, HAMMER suit, whatever—and take what I wanted. A soft hit for a quiet steal."

Aydelotte let out a belly-shaking laugh and clapped Toombs on the back. "Clever lad."

"It brings up a question, though," said Toombs. "I don't ever remember hearing that these kinds of fungi took effect fast, and you'd need it to be really fast or there will be alarms ringing and calls made. Now, I can assume you know this, so how are you solving it?"

Conti looked visibly surprised. "Are you a scientist?"

"Me? No, doc. I just like to know something about a lot of this."

Aydelotte said, "The short answer is genetic manipulation. I don't fully understand the hows and whys of it, but the good doctor is something of a sorceress when it comes to that sort of thing."

"It's a new process," she said. "Something I'd love to patent, but that's hardly possible."

There was some bite to her tone, and Toombs could tell this was part of some long-standing feud. He found that very interesting and filed it away.

"Well, I don't need to know all of the details," he said, shoving his pale hands deep into his trouser pockets. He cocked his head. "I will say that I'm impressed as all hell, doc. This can't have been easy and its potential as an off-market weapon makes it ideal for small, mobile groups to use so they don't have to try and slug it out with bigger and tougher players. Brava."

He saw the gratitude in her eyes, and filed that away, too.

Aydelotte clapped Toombs on the shoulder. "Come on, my boy. There's much more to see."

They turned, but then something in a glass-fronted case caught Toombs's eye. He stepped closer and saw rows of glass or plastic darts filled with a dark amber fluid. On the shelf below were what looked like prototypes for a modified dart gun, similar to the old Snellig models. "And what are these little pop guns?"

Aydelotte came and stood beside him. "Something brand-new, still in development. The dart casings are cellulose. A slightly stronger version that would be used in the Gorgon because it has to penetrate clothing and skin. The loads are a much higher concentration of Shiva. Giada calls them 'God's Arrows,' and I have to say that they are quite something. The intensity of the hallucinations is something to see. Makes the infected highly aggressive and very dangerous. So, they would have to be used with the greatest care."

"Nasty."

"You have no idea. Now, let's go. Lots and lots still to see, including your own office, which is on this floor. This is sub-four, as you may have seen on the elevator panel. There's a level below, which is all machinery, so we can skip that. We'll finish this floor and work our way up."

As they were heading toward the door, Toombs contrived to step his right foot down on the heel of his left loafer, pulling it partway off. He took his hands from his pockets, steadied himself against the wall with one hand and used the other to pull the shoe back on. The natural reaction of Aydelotte was to glance at the mishap and the fix, and not at the edge of the doorframe molding. The tiny video bug was one of the Chinese Chameleon models with a photosensitive coating that quickly turned the dull gray bug into a perfect match with the off-white of the frame.

It was the eighth such bug he had planted since the tour began, and he had another dozen in his pockets.

CHAPTER 63
RTI SAFE HOUSE
HEBRON ROAD
JERUSALEM, ISRAEL

There's this old saying we have in the military: "No plan ever survives contact with the enemy." It's been true so often in my life I ought to have it tattooed on my goddamn head. In reverse, so I can read it clearly in the mirror every morning while I brush my teeth.

We locked the place up and went on a prowl to match the details we'd been sent with the actual location. It was designed along certain lines that Aunt Sallie had put together. Practical, comfortable, and safe. It would take a hefty dose of explosives to beat that security, which meant we could relax for a bit and get oriented.

Top went around tapping sections of the inside wall, which slid open to reveal rows of pistol butts, trays of grenades, long guns, electronics, and all the rest.

"Wonder what all this shit costs," mused Bunny.

"A lot," said Top. "The Big Man doesn't shop in the bargain basement."

Top and I took the bags upstairs while Bunny went to see what was yummy in the fridge. When I came into the kitchen, Bunny gestured to a mug on the table.

"Somebody must have figured you'd be here eventually."

It was a black mug with this in white letters:

How do I take my coffee?
Very seriously.

I smiled. The coffee was awesome.

Even Bunny, who only half-ass liked coffee, sighed deeply after a sip. "If the college thing doesn't work out, the kid's got a future as a barista."

Top joined us a few minutes later, carrying two canvas gear bags he had filled with items from various caches around the place. He set them on the big table in the kitchen.

"Party favors," he said. He unzipped one bag and began placing items on the table—comms units, portable Anteaters, and a whole bunch of James Bond stuff hidden inside wristwatches, sunglasses, and wallets. Micro-gadgets that pushed the edge of miniaturization, battery duration and power, and overall effect. Toylike, but in no way toys. Bunny began rooting through the other bag and brought out firearms, empty magazines held together with rubber bands, and boxes of ammunition.

First thing we did was put the earbuds in place and the lighter-size combination battery pack signal-boosters into our pants pockets. And, just because he likes to show off, Bug designed the booster *as* a functional lighter. Then we set about filling magazines for the guns we each preferred.

"We going to wait for the rest of the team?" asked Top. "Or jump right in?"

It was said offhand, but it darkened the mood fast as a finger snap.

"Let's *do* something," said Bunny. "If we have to sit here and wait instead of trying to get some answers, I will literally go out of my goddamn mind."

"Without a doubt," I said.

Ghost said, *Whuff.*

"Like I said on the plane, I want to see the lab where those scholars died."

"It's been a couple of weeks," said Top. "You think there'll be anything left to see?"

"Won't know until we're on site."

"Fair enough."

"And after that?" asked Bunny.

"Been thinking about that cobra thing," I said. "And before either of you say anything, I mean thinking about how to poke at it. I don't want to have only the video to go on and the word of whoever at Camp Lemonnier provided it."

"What then?" asked Top.

Instead of directly answering I tapped into the command channel.

"Outlaw to Grendel," I said, and Scott Wilson was right there.

"Grendel here. Status report."

"Home and dry," I said. "I have a request."

I explained about the video equipment from the base where the cobras appeared out of thin goddamn air. "We're all taking that video as gospel, but I don't want to play that. I want Bug and Yoda to tear that shit apart down to its last molecule."

"You're reading my mind, Outlaw. I put that request in already, and a friend of a friend on that base has promised that a courier is already on his way."

"Glad to hear it."

"None of us want to believe it," said Wilson. "Currently I fall into the agnostic column. Don't want to believe it but will accept it if it's an actual fact."

"Fair enough," I said. "Anything you need to catch me up on?"

"I have something, and then Huckleberry and Merlin each have things to share."

Huckleberry was the combat call sign for Doc Holliday, and Merlin was Church's current call sign. He changes his as often as I change socks.

"We're all three on the channel," I said. "Go."

"First," said Wilson crisply, "a packet of surveillance photos and accompanying data has been uploaded to your tactical computer."

As he said this, Bunny removed the wrist-mounted units from the second tabletop panel and handed them around. I used my ring-finger print—one less often used—and when the little screen lit up, I saw that there were several new folders. One was from Grendel.

"Got it. What is it?"

"A list of names of people you might want to interview in Jerusalem. Associates of the two dead scholars, family, and other employees at the facility. Likewise, names and contact info for everyone from the janitor on shift that day to staff where the body was taken. Oh, and if for any reason you need to cross Jordan, use your D-level passports."

"Copy that."

Because of the political instability of the region, we had different passports that had visa stamps from different groups of countries. If your passport showed a lot of trips to the United States, Great Britain, and Israel the border guards look at you differently than if you have visited Egypt, Saudi Arabia, Yemen, Lebanon, and other countries that do not recognize Israel as a legitimate nation. Since our cover story was that of two businessmen and a retired athlete in the sporting goods industry looking to establish new markets, we wanted to be seen as friendlies and not immediately added to the top of this week's watch list.

"Switching to Huckleberry," said Wilson.

A moment later I heard the rich contralto of Doc Holliday. Amused, superior, relentlessly and unapologetically flirtatious.

"Hey, boys," she said. "How's it hanging?"

She says that sort of thing because even though guys say it to one another, men are typically disconcerted when a woman says it to them. Top just smiled and shook his head. Bunny blushed even though this was an audio-only chat.

"Behave," I told her.

"Haven't ever. Why should I start now?"

"Because the kids are listening."

"Spoilsport."

"What have you got for us? And please tell me that you have more on the autopsy reports of those scholars."

"I do, as a matter of fact," she said, some of the humor dropping from her voice. "But it's passive. You asked Bug to check on the morgue video. He did, and you earned yourself a foot massage and a big fat kiss. He did some kind of wizardry with the pixels and all that nerd stuff and managed to get me fifteen bad and two good pics of anomalous marks."

"You going to tell me they're bat bites?" I asked, and my blood was already starting to run cold.

"Yes," she said. "That's exactly what I—"

And the whole front wall of the safe house blew up.

CHAPTER 64
RTI SAFE HOUSE
HEBRON ROAD
JERUSALEM, ISRAEL

It was a massive blast that exploded the shatter-proof glass into ten thousand jagged splinters that shredded the couch and chair and ripped the rear of the living room wall back to the studs. It tore the steel door out of the frame and sent it whomping into a tall wooden cabinet and knocked that to kindling. The door pirouetted on one corner and then slammed down onto the floor.

Smoke billowed inward, whipping through the open kitchen door. There were flashes of fire inside that cloud, and a dozen small blazes started on curtains and tattered wallpaper and the rug.

The force of the explosion picked the three of us up, along with two chairs and the table, and threw us against the stove, dishwasher, and fridge.

We hit hard.

I felt something punch me in the back, just below the left shoulder blade and upper buttock. Two points of sudden, intense agony. I dropped onto hands and knees, coughing and blinking, trying to shake off enough of the shock to make sense of the moment.

Everyone can be blindsided. Anyone can be taken off guard. The difference between John Q. Public and guys like us is that we don't sit there and allow ourselves to be shocked. That's a luxury for civilians. People like Top, Bunny, and me either shake it off and react, or we die. There's no middle ground.

I rolled over onto hands and knees and saw the others doing the same. I couldn't see Ghost, but I heard him whimpering, and the whimper turned into a growl almost at once as figures moved through the smoke. They were only silhouettes, telling me nothing about who they were. Thin crimson targeting laser beams crisscrossed the room, and bullets followed in three-shot bursts.

"Ghost *hit, hit, hit!*" I yelled as I launched myself toward the closest gear bag, caught it by one corner, hugged it to my chest as I rolled lumpity-bump across the floor, tore down the zipper, and grabbed the first gun I could find. A Sig Sauer M17 with an extended twenty-one-round magazine. I racked the slide.

In the other room, Ghost went silent, but a split second later I heard a terrible high-pitched scream.

Good dog.

I yelled into the smoke. "Pappy, on me." He came over in a fast duck-walk, keeping low. I slapped the Sig Sauer into his hand. "One up."

He rose and fired through the doorway.

"Outlaw," croaked Bunny, and I felt his big hands pulling at me. I pivoted on my knees, and we both grabbed weapons and magazines.

He had a Daewoo USAS-12 twelve-gauge combat shotgun loaded with a twenty-round drum magazine. A real crowd pleaser. He immediately opened up while still kneeling. The smoke turned red.

The gun I had was an IWI Tavor TAR-21—an Israeli bullpup assault rifle chambered for NATO rounds. I slapped the magazine in place, got to my feet, and ran in a tight crouch, aiming into the smoke at chest level—high above Ghost's height.

"Who are these assholes?" growled Bunny.

"They're bad guys," snapped Top. "Shoot their damn asses off."

The three of us sent enough ordnance downrange to clear the doorway, and then Top went through first, breaking right; I followed and broke left, which left Bunny plowing the road straight ahead with the shotgun.

Chaos ruled the moment. Smoke and fire, flying lead and exploding debris, shadow figures and a snarling dog. As I moved, my combat-trained mind assembled details even while my reflexes found targets and pulled the trigger.

The sound of my shot was lost in the sudden and massive bang as the rear door blew inward. There was a large combination mudroom and laundry room behind the kitchen, and suddenly the interconnecting door began to splinter as automatic gunfire tore it to pieces.

I dug into the bag and fished desperately for a grenade, found two, pulled the pins but didn't let the arming spoons fall until the barrage ripped a big enough gap.

"Frag out," I roared and tossed the grenades.

We all dove out of the way as the bombs exploded. What was left of the door turned into burning matchwood that swept between us. I threw myself across the shattered doorway and hosed the room. Through the smoke I saw bodies and parts of bodies. To my relief, those parts were not wearing anything that looked like official uniforms. Not local police, not Israeli army, not any domestic special forces. Top said it—bad guys. I kept shooting. Two men in the outside doorway were caught by my fire, and they danced a terminal jig and vanished into the alley. I dropped the mag and swapped in another. In the movies the stalwart action hero seems to have magazines that are apparently filled with ten thousand rounds. In the real world, full auto burns through a full mag real damn fast.

But just for the hell of it, I grabbed a third fragmentation grenade and did a sidearm pitch that sent it into that alley. It blew, and the screams were terrible. But they were punctuated by more gunfire from out back.

One of the corpses lay in a patch of flickering firelight. I expected him to be obviously Arab because ISIS seemed to be the bad guys in most scenarios I could imagine. He had the AK-47 and even had a turban and scarf, but the dead face I looked down at was no kind of Arab. Not an Israeli face, either. Call it generic white guy. I hoped my body cam was picking up the image.

I heard a voice behind me say, *"Joe, move!"*

I moved and actually felt a bullet punch through the air where my head had been a microsecond before. I ducked, dodged, twisted, and swung around with my gun to see another of the hostiles crouching in the doorway with a pistol held in both hands. He looked surprised that his bullet hadn't taken me. I was, too. And for a whole different reason. There was no one behind him to whisper that warning.

Half of my mind tried to process that. The other half pulled the trigger and blew the shooter's face off.

Joe, move.

I'd heard the words very distinctly. A man's voice. A familiar voice.

My father's voice.

But my father was in the ground in a Maryland cemetery, along with my brother Sean, my sister-in-law, and their kids.

It could not have been Top because he was to my right, and his voice had a completely different pitch and timbre than Dad's. Bunny was in the other room blasting away with his shotgun.

Joe, move.

"Jesus Christ," I breathed. Top shot me a look. Maybe his face was registering surprise at my close call. Maybe he was reading the expression on my face.

Through sheer force of will I shoved myself back into the here-and-now.

But . . . god damn.

I glanced around very quickly and saw other corpses—some with the scarf still in place, but two more uncovered. Neither looked even remotely Arab or Jewish.

"We're in a box," Top yelled. "Car's out front. That's our exfil."

"Move!" I bellowed.

"Rock and roll," roared Bunny, sounding like he was actually enjoying this. I'm not the only member of Havoc Team who has some mental issues.

I stuffed more grenades into my pockets, swapped in a new magazine for the rifle, and began crabbing my way into the living room. There was a lot going on. Bodies in motion, muzzle flashes beyond counting, smoke and fire everywhere. I kept shifting position, dodging down and around, shooting from every good angle. Whoever these fuckers were, they brought the textbook definition of overwhelming force, and used a very smart two-point breach. Every oddsmaker in Vegas would have given them good numbers.

And no one would have bet a wooden nickel on Havoc Team.

The Warrior—the Killer—in my head woke up with a feral growl of bloodlust. That part of me *lives* for this shit. Absolutely hungers for it. He also loved charging into the Valley of the Shadow with fellow warriors like Top and Bunny and Ghost.

Speaking of Ghost, he lived up to his name, fading in and out of the gray smoke, his white fur giving him a chameleon edge; his titanium teeth tore through Kevlar, muscle, and bone.

"No, you don't," roared Bunny, and out of the corner of my eye I saw that a shooter was taking aim at Ghost. Bunny hit him side-on at five feet with a blast from the shotgun. It shredded the man and threw a screaming ruin against another of the hostiles.

Top moved past my right side, the Sig in two hands, his eyes streaming tears from the smoke but that grip rock-steady. His shots and resulting screams overlapped in the madness.

"Frag out," I shouted again and tossed another grenade back into the kitchen, which was filling with new shooters. Blood and debris showered me all the way into the living room.

"These fuckers ain't no goddamn ISIS," Bunny said as he reloaded.

"I know."

I bumped up against the wall and slid along it, aiming past the red laser sights and shooting center mass. Then I switched from semi-auto to full and sprayed the doorway. As I dropped the magazine and reached for the replacement, a figure came at me fast, swinging the barrel of an AK-47 toward my chest.

I stepped, using the barrel of my rifle to swat his wide and high, and then—the magazine still in my right hand—struck him in the face, shattering his goggles and knocking his head back. I checked my follow-through, changed direction, and hammered the magazine onto his Adam's apple. He reeled back, firing wildly at the ceiling, dying as he fell, guns tumbling unaired.

I rammed the mag in hard and blew a hole through the center of another hostile who was directly behind the one I had just killed. Bunny's shotgun was thunder and lightning to my right. Top fired his gun dry, kicked a wounded man in the knee so hard his leg snapped backward into a bone-crunching reverse forty-degree angle.

"My fucking leg, you fucking fucker," he wailed. The accent, despite all sense and logic, was straight out of the Bronx.

Top swapped mags and shot the crippled guy through the right eyebrow.

Three more figures were phantoms in the ruined front wall, but even as I turned toward them, their heads snapped sideways at sharp, weird angles, and they crumpled down.

"Havoc, Havoc, Havoc," came a voice from outside. Then Andrea dove inside, rolled up into a shooter's kneel, and ripped upward with three rounds through some poor bastard's crotch.

"Friendlies," I yelled, but Top and Bunny had heard the cry. The same shout came from behind me, and Remy materialized in the smoky kitchen doorway, a Glock in his gloved hands and Scout glasses on his head. I couldn't see Belle, but suddenly two of the shadowy figures stepping through the charred hole in the living room toppled and fell, their heads blown to red garbage.

All at once silence, huge and loud, crash-landed around us.

"Havoc Team, count off," I barked, crouching low to look under the pall of smoke that had started rising toward the ceiling.

"Clear," growled Top.

"Clear," said Bunny.

Belle's voice floated to us. "Clear outside."

"Cajun, Mother Mercy," I roared, "check the perimeter."

Remy melted away.

Bunny said, "Outlaw, I got one with a pulse."

"Bring him," I snapped. "Jackpot, rig a cleanup charge."

"Hooah."

There were no sirens yet, but then again this had all taken seconds—perhaps a full minute, but I didn't think so.

"Anyone hurt?"

"Negative, Outlaw," said Top. "Ghost's good, too."

The fur-monster came wagging out of the smoke, looking happy as a puppy who'd just chewed up my entire sock drawer.

"Grab and go," I said. "Thirty seconds. No traces."

They moved and moved well.

In less time than it takes to tell it we were hustling outside, each carrying a heavy gear bag. Bunny trailed behind, dragging a semiconscious man by the back collar.

"This guy's no ISIS shooter," he said, dumping him in front of me.

He wasn't wrong. The man had hair as blond as Bunny's and between groans was cursing in a thick Tennessee accent.

I knelt and put the hot barrel of my rifle against his crotch.

"Who are you?" I demanded. "Who are you working for?"

Suddenly Bug's voice was in my ear. "Outlaw, facial recognition pinged this guy. Lyle Hardee, thirty-two, Lynchburg, Tennessee. Former US Army. Discharged six years ago. Worked two years for Blue Diamond Security. Now he's with Tenth Legion, based out of Johannesburg."

"PMC," said Top.

All Hardee heard was Top's comment. He sneered, showing bloody teeth. "Fuck you, nigger."

Top smiled. His smiles range from those of a kindly uncle to something you never want to see in moments like these. The one he wore now was the latter.

"Say the word," murmured Bunny as he rapped Hardee on the top of the head. Not a hard hit, but hard enough to make a point. "Do we take this cocksucker or leave him to burn?"

Hardee's eyes were bright, filled with a strange kind of light. He looked at the barrel I had screwed into his nutsack and then up at me. A smile blossomed as bright as those eyes.

"Go ahead. Pull the trigger," he dared. "And God will raise me up as one of his angels. I will stand on his right hand on Judgment Day when you and all these fuckers are on your knees at the gates of Heaven."

"Giving you one chance to make it out of here alive," I said. "Who sent you?"

"God sent me, and I am his righteous wrath. Me and my brothers."

Then he bit down hard, and immediately there was a thick white foam bubbling on his lips. His eyes glazed, but before the cyanide took him, he tried to spit the poison at me. I slipped it but felt it spatter on my shoulder and the side of my neck. The brightness in Hardee's eyes dulled and went flat, and he sagged down.

Bunny let him go and recoiled a little. "What the hell?"

"Gotta go," called Remy. "Gotta go now."

Top did a quick pat-down but found nothing. No ID, no personal papers, not even a stick of gum. We backed away from the dead man, turned and fled.

As we ran for the car, ten thousand questions crowded into my head, elbowing one another for my attention even though they knew I had no goddamn answers. But what kept pulling my attention, my inner thoughts, wasn't the shooters, the trauma of the attack, the near misses. None of that. It was my dead father's voice.

Joe, move.

Warning me. It wasn't something I could have conjured because I don't have eyes in the back of my head or that tingly spider-sense. I could not have known there was that specific danger at that specific moment and in that specific direction. It's the specifics that made the voice I heard just hang there.

It was my dad's voice.

There was no doubt at all about that. None.

So . . . what the actual hell?

INTERLUDE 25
MONITORING SUITE
PIRATE LAB
UNDISCLOSED LOCATION

FIVE MONTHS BEFORE CHAD

Toombs looked at Aydelotte across the width of the conference table.

"Just so I have it straight, boss . . . you don't care what they'll use this stuff for?"

Aydelotte took a long sip of coffee before he replied. They were in one of the smaller conference rooms that lined a hallway in the building that served as a research lab, testing facility, and planning center for his Middle East operations.

"Why?" he countered. "Do you?"

"To a degree, sure."

"Oh?" said Aydelotte, his eyebrows climbing up his forehead. "Then tell me, Toombs, what's your personal line in the sand?"

"If they're going to disperse it in a public setting," said Toombs, "I want to know about it so I can be anywhere but there."

"So, it's self-interest?"

"What else would it be?"

They both thought about that.

"Would it bother you, for example," said Aydelotte, "if they used it on a school? Or on a plane in flight?"

The tall, pale salesman smiled his Joker smile. "If you're fishing to see if I have a soft spot, boss, you're wasting your time. If I had that kind of a conscience, I'd have washed out of this trade a long time ago. Being self-aware in any meaningful way means that you have to accept who and what you are."

"And what are you, Toombs?"

"I already told you. I don't want to be in the blast radius or dispersal field of anything we sell. Not Shiva or Gorgon or any of it. And, since I care a great deal about where my bread is buttered, I wouldn't want you or Shock in the zone, either."

"And that's not sentimentality," said Aydelotte, not really making it a question. "It's *shared* self-interest."

"It's good business," said Toombs. "If I was an arsonist, I wouldn't set fire to the clothes I was wearing. I asked if *you* cared because I know you have all kinds of business interests throughout this region. So, maybe a better way to ask it would be to know if you had restrictions or conditions I need to pass along to the buyer."

"Ah. That's better." Aydelotte got up and walked over to the wet bar. He tossed his tepid coffee down the drain, rinsed the cup, and poured some fresh. He added a dollop of 2 percent milk and returned to the table. "My answer is also conditional."

Toombs was amused. "On . . . ?"

"On the weapon in question. If this was a transaction for a dirty bomb or something that would significantly destroy certain real estate, then of course I'd impose conditions. I'll give you an example. When and if we sell any K-144 fuel-air bombs, I'd have to know that no jackass would detonate one anywhere near the Qumran area."

"Because you're still looking for more Dead Sea Scrolls?"

"Always. I have to continue to feed my legitimate businesses to keep certain agencies from wondering how I make my money. With all that's going on in the world, particularly in parts of Europe and the United States, items of legitimate and unique religious nature are worth considerably more than their weight in gold. Oh, and the same condition goes for the Valley of the Kings or the city of Jerusalem. If any bloody fool were to bomb it then there would be a world war right there in the Middle East. Some of the interested parties have nukes, and I couldn't sell the fucking nails from Jesus's crucifixion if they were radioactive. Let alone the other stuff I've been collecting."

"Ah. Got it."

"Just about anywhere else, though," said Aydelotte, "would be fair game."

"As long as nobody you care about is in the neighborhood at boom time," suggested Toombs.

"Yes, but there are very few people on my hands-off list."

"Mine, too," said Toombs.

"Then, by all means, go ahead and make that deal for me. And when you're done with that, I have something really special for you."

CHAPTER 66
RTI SAFE HOUSE
HEBRON ROAD
JERUSALEM, ISRAEL

Our SUV sat on four flats.

Three nearly identical cars were parked haphazardly out there, but behind those was the SUV the rest of Havoc Team had rolled up in. We crammed inside. Andrea was the last out. He had a small trigger in one hand and a wicked grin on his face.

Remy beat Top to the driver's seat, and he had the car in gear before Andrea was even inside. Bunny reached out, grabbed Andrea by the front of the shirt, and hauled him in.

Then we were gone.

As we turned the fifth random corner, we heard the wail of sirens. A moment later that sound was erased by a massive *ka-whummmmph* as the entire safe house leaped off the ground and collapsed back into a pile of burning rubble.

CHAPTER 67
IN MOTION
JERUSALEM, ISRAEL

As we drove, I tapped into the command channel and told Scott Wilson what happened.

"Want to tell me how in the wide blue fuck anyone knew we were going to be at that safe house?"

"Calm down, Outlaw," he began, but I cut him off.

"Calm down, my left nut. We barely got in and settled before a full team hit us. Fifteen shooters. Possibly more. Well armed, well trained, and wearing body armor but also head scarves meant to look like kaffiyeh. But these jokers weren't Arabs."

"Yes, we are aware of that. Bug lifted six useful images from your body cams. Hardee was one of three Americans. The others he pinged are Canadian, French, and Australian."

"You heard what Hardee said. Some twisted kind of Christian propaganda. Thought it was just trash talk, but then he suicided out. We didn't get much of use."

"We got enough for a good start," said Wilson. "So far we've verified four from Tenth Legion out of Johannesburg."

"Yeah, Bug mentioned them. Never heard of them. Who are they?"

"Private military contractors based in South Africa but working globally. The company is three years old. Small and unimportant, but now it seems as if they've swept up the leavings of Blue Diamond."

"Going out on a limb here and saying these clowns are working with or for Mr. Miracle. If you disagree, Grendel, give me a better reason for Christian religious extremists shooting at me and mine in Israel."

"Everyone here at the TOC is working on it."

"Work faster," I said.

"On it," he promised. "Are any of your team hurt?"

"Negative. The only damage is my faith in you, buddy boy. This was on your watch, and I want to know how, who, why, and what's coming next."

There was a beat, and despite not liking Wilson very much, I had to give him props for what he said next.

"Yes, Outlaw, this is on me. I take responsibility, and you can be assured that I will find out how it happened. I'll reach out to contacts in Jerusalem city police as well as their intelligence community. When they know, I'll know, and you'll hear it from me ASAP."

"Damn right," I growled ungenerously. Then I caught a look from Top. All he did was raise a single questioning eyebrow. Message received. I took a breath and gave him a micro-nod. In a more even tone, I said, "Okay, Grendel, you run that down. They probably picked us up at the airport, though we need to know how they knew to look for us, so you may need to backtrack home."

"Too right," he agreed. There was a pause, then, "Switching you to a private line."

There was only one person who ever used that channel with me.

Mr. Church said, "Was Nomad on site?"

Took me a moment on that because I hadn't heard Helmut's call sign in years, and never in a real crisis situation.

"No. He's probably with Arklight, but have someone check on him."

"I will. Now, Outlaw, listen to me," he said gravely, "I add my own culpability to this. It not only shouldn't have happened, but it also shouldn't have been *able* to happen."

"Copy that."

Church seldom apologizes. Instead, his tone promised action, and I could hear some anger in his voice. Never a good thing for whomever he outs as the bad guy. That was fine with me. I wasn't arrogant enough to need to spank that person myself. If Church got there first, then appropriate spankage would be administered.

Yes, I know spankage isn't a word, but it should be.

"You have a recommendation for where we can regroup?" I asked. "Still need to bring the rest of the team up to speed."

"Head to the Arklight house. There is a two-person team in residence, not counting Nomad, who is not—I repeat *not*—a combatant."

"Copy that."

"A good friend of the family is at that house. She'll help you with anything you might need."

"A *musical* friend?"

That was a personal code for Violin.

"Yes."

"Okay."

"In the meantime," said Church, "I have been interviewing our Italian friend from Chad."

"That's something, at least. You're saying he's actually talking?"

"He is. Useful information, though he tends to ramble. From what we've already gotten, though, a few pieces are falling into place. The challenge is that he's not on the policy level, so much of what he knows is hearsay and inference. What's germane to this conversation is that we are beginning to see some moderately formed connections between your current case, the op in Chad, the cobras, and another operation that is underway in Jerusalem. It is entirely possible that our enemies in one case may have somehow conflated that with yours. That's guesswork, only because we have no proof that our other team has been made. Nor do we know how the other side has managed to gather intel on your actions. So far it *appears* as if the other field team there in Jerusalem still has an intact cover."

"Whoa, I know where the other RTI teams are. Who are we talking about that's running an op here in Israel?"

He told me about Toys. It felt about like it would feel to stand there while the entire Manchester United football club lines up to take enthusiastic kicks to the nuts.

"Hold the fuck on," I growled. "You let that psycho freak go into the field?"

"You know that he has already been deployed in recent operations."

I did know, but I didn't like it and didn't feel generous about it. He had helped save my ass—and a big chunk of the US of A—last year when we were tearing down an arms deal that culminated in an attempt to execute every American governor at a convention in LaBorde, Texas. Toys was a key player in the big blowout brawl at the end of that gig.

Church was giving the guy a second chance for reasons that make sense only to Church. What I couldn't figure out was why Toys was doing this. He'd made it clear on a number of occasions that he did not want thanks, forgiveness, or even a pat on the back. He wasn't looking for, or expecting to receive, any form of redemption. That said, even I had to admit that he was a useful little prick. Lethal, well connected, and willing to cut throats when the Big Man needed him to.

What made the math even trickier for me was that Junie loved him. He was like a brother to her. They worked together at FreeTech for quite a while, with Junie overseeing the R and D, and Toys managing the money. Funny thing was, the money in question was something Church pilfered from Hugo Vox after that ass-clown was too dead to need it.

The real takeaway here was that I did not like Toys. At all. Not even a little bit. Reformed or not, he was still knee-deep in the blood he spilled. People I knew and cared about died because of things the people he worked for had been doing. There wasn't going to be a Hallmark moment for us. No Christmas TV movie special where, caught up in the spirit of the holidays, we'd come to the realization that all was forgiven and everyone was, at heart, a nice guy.

Excuse me while I vomit.

So, now . . . driving away from a serious goddamn attempt on my life and the lives of my two most trusted fellow soldiers, I had to hear that Toys was not only in the field, he had a goddamn son-of-a-bitching *team*.

"Tell me that last part again," I said. "The Wild Bunch?"

"Wild *Hunt*," corrected Church. "Named for the folkloric characters. Wild Hunts are groups of mythological or supernatural characters who—"

"I know who the Wild Hunt is," I snapped. "Correct me if I'm wrong, but they are not typically the good guys of those stories."

"Your combat call sign is Outlaw," he said dryly. "Our three main teams are Havoc, Chaos, and Bedlam."

"Cute, but that's different than having an actual criminal leading a team of criminals. Who the hell are the others? Hitler, Stalin, and Mussolini?"

Church sighed very faintly. "Each member of the Wild Hunt is working on doing measurable good in the world to balance some questionable things in his or her past."

"Questionable . . . ? Jesus. First you build a base in a hollowed-out volcano on your own private island, and now you have your own Suicide Squad. Does that qualify me and my guys as henchmen now?"

"Outlaw . . ."

"It's a hell of a risk, boss."

The silence from his end was crushing.

"You still there?" I asked.

"I will say this only once, Outlaw," he said. "There are quite a few people—colleagues and mutual friends—who believe I made a grave error in judgment by allowing you to return to active field work. Are you saying that you alone deserve a second chance?"

Now it was my turn to be silent. I was damn glad we were on a private call. The others in the car could hear me, but none of them had heard that from Church. We drove several blocks before I trusted myself to reply. Fifty bad things fought to make it out of my mouth. Things that I couldn't walk back, so I bit down on them.

"Okay," I said, and I said it very carefully.

"Okay," he said.

"Grendel will send you a coded file that will bring you up to speed on the Wild Hunt's operation. What I can tell you right now is that two operations that appeared to be separate may be threads dangling from the same tapestry. Religion is the connection, but that's true of nearly every operation in that part of the world. PMCs are a new factor, and as our body of information grows so, too, will our understanding. We will all need to keep open minds and avoid leaping to judgment. We don't want to cleave to any specific belief because it is a convenient answer to a set of difficult questions. Coordinate with Toys, share intel, and proceed as you both see fit."

"I'm not taking orders from him."

"I never said that was a requirement."

The line went dead.

We drove. I stared hot electric death out the window.

Remy said, "Um . . . Suicide Squad . . . ?"

"Just fucking drive."

He drove. But I saw his eyes flick back and forth between the rearview and side-view mirrors.

"What?" I asked.

"We're being followed."

CHAPTER 68
IN MOTION
JERUSALEM, ISRAEL

I turned around and peered past heads and shoulders and gear bags to see headlights behind us.

"Should I try to lose him?" asked Remy.

"We need answers," I said. "Andrea, what goodies have you got?"

He was already rooting around in a bag and produced a pair of pigeon drones. Belle lowered the window for him and leaned back to give Andrea room to toss the little machines out into the night. Their wings deployed, and after the briefest wobble they corrected and took off, arching high to come down behind the pursuit car.

Andrea tapped the keys on the small tactical computer strapped to his forearm, and a holographic screen appeared in the air above his wrist. The screen split to show the camera views from each drone.

"License plate," said Top.

"Got it." A moment later the plate number appeared on an inset box, but it belonged to a different make and model of car. "Stolen plates, stolen car."

"Thermals," I ordered.

One of the birds changed course to fly over the vehicle, which was a dark late-model SUV. The screen image changed to show the roof and glowing red lumps inside.

"Six," said Andrea. "Looks like four men, two women."

I tapped Remy's arm. "Get us onto an empty street. Andrea, tell me you have a hop-toad."

"*Sì, colonnello.* Say the word."

"Do it."

Andrea produced another little robot monster. It didn't really look like a toad, but once he threw it onto the street it did hop. The driver of the pursuing car must have seen the thing land, and he swerved to avoid it. Well, *tried* to avoid it. As the car raced by, the hop-toad leaped at the front passenger-side wheel. Powerful magnets clamped it to the hubcap, and then there was a sharp *crack*, and suddenly that driver had a lot of things to do all at once. He had been on our tail, clocking around fifty miles per hour. The hop-toad blew up and turned the wheel to melted rubber and twisted metal. The SUV tilted down, and the driver did everything he could to keep it from tumbling.

Again, *tried*.

The ruined wheel hit the edge of a curb, and that was all she wrote. The front corner of the SUV bowed down, and the ass jumped up, and then it was tumbling *rump-a-bumpity-chunk*. It clipped a fire hydrant and a parking meter and kept tumbling.

Remy hit the brakes and went into the kind of sliding, slewing,

JONATHAN MABERRY

screeching turn only the very drunk or the very best stunt drivers can manage. Our vehicle burned rubber at close to a right angle, and if we hadn't been buckled up for safety, we'd have been one big pile of jelly. Top grunted in pain as Bunny's elbow chunked him way too high on the inner thigh. Andrea made a kind of *yeep*ing sound. Ghost shrieked. Belle was laughing the whole time.

Our car stopped and squatted in the center of the street, the body oscillating, smoke rising from the abused tires.

The pursuit car wasn't going to follow anyone anywhere. The driver and whoever was in the front passenger seat were on the hood, having gone through the windshield during one of the tumbles. Part of another man hung out of the rear driver's-side window, but everything from mid-chest up was red jelly. A fourth person—I think it had once been female—lay in the middle of the street. She was missing one arm, and the ragged wound wasn't bleeding, proof she had died instantly.

We piled out, guns up and out. Belle remained behind; her rifle lay atop the frame of an open door. We swarmed around the car, looking in through misshapen windows. The two in the back seat, one man and the second woman, did not look injured. Not at first. And then I realized that what I thought was them hunching down was worse than that. The roof of the car had bowed sharply inward and hit them both on the tops of their heads. Their necks were crushed downward so that their chins rested on chests in which no hearts beat. They stared with sightless eyes filled with terminal surprise.

"*Madonna santa*," cried Andrea. "I . . . I . . . did not mean to . . ."

"Save it, son," Top said. "What's done is done. Can't unring that bell."

"Search them," I said. "Take everything we can carry. Thirty seconds and we're gone."

Remy ran back and turned our car around. In twenty-five seconds, we were out of there.

INTERLUDE 26
PRIVATE APARTMENT
PIRATE LAB
UNDISCLOSED LOCATION

FOUR MONTHS BEFORE CHAD

Toombs sat on his couch, bare feet up on the coffee table, his laptop open on his lap, and let his eyes flick back and forth from Shock to Conti to Aydelotte. The feeds from the mini Chameleon bugs were good, though some resolution had to be sacrificed because of the small size.

Shock was in her lab, bent over a trove of documents recently received in the ongoing barter arrangement with Ayoob Alazaki. Toombs was not skilled in ancient languages, but he could at least tell that the scroll she had open was written in Greek. That told him it was part of the document cache found by the ISIS clowns who'd fallen into Cave 13 at Qumran. Something, Shock told him, that had been rescued from the Library of Alexandria. Interesting.

In another lab, Dr. Conti was *tap-tap-tapping* away at her computer, adjusting the graphic of a 3-D model of a section of ergot DNA.

"Dr. Frankenstein," he murmured.

As for Aydelotte, he was talking to Harith al-Wazir on a video call, but unfortunately the Chameleon was in the wrong place to allow Toombs to see the ISIS leader's face. Aydelotte was animated and talking fast in English, but his desk was too far from the bug's tiny mic. Toombs knew he would have to get into Aydelotte's monitoring room again and place another mic closer to that desk.

He twisted the cap off a beer, took a small sip, and continued to watch.

There was always something new to learn.

CHAPTER 69
IN MOTION
NEAR ASHDOD, ISRAEL

"Get in, boss," yelled a man with a thick Australian accent.

A car had angled to a curb to intercept him, and Toys slipped quickly into the passenger seat.

"Isn't your license revoked?" asked Toys as the car pulled away and slipped into the flow of early evening traffic.

"I'm not allowed to drive in most civilized countries," said Dingo. "And for good reason."

Dingo looked like the kind of person who would play a second-rate supporting villain in a low-budget western. Shoulders a yard wide, chest and stomach as flat and hard as plate steel, curly red hair that was thinning on top, and an attempt at a beard so thin and weedy as to look like an ironic statement about all stylized facial hair. No lips, a crooked nose, spit-colored eyes, and a perpetual peeling sunburn.

But Toys hadn't hired him for looks. Dingo was a fighter. Hands, feet, knives, clubs, broken bottles, whatever. If it could inflict harm, then Dingo knew how to use it. He also had deep skills in *hadaka korosu*, the Japanese art of using commonplace objects as weapons. He could—and had—killed people with a McDonald's drinking straw, a shoelace, a cell phone, a bikini top, a paperback copy of the Bible, and a cup of Starbucks coffee.

Toys had known him during the Sebastian Gault era, when Dingo was muscle for a Chechen arms smuggler. One of Church's former team leaders, Samson Riggs, had been the one to tear down the smuggling operation, and in the weeks leading up to it had cultivated Dingo as an asset, turning him, using him, but then arresting him. Like many of the people swept up in the old Department of Military Sciences operations, Dingo—real name Marcus Halley—had simply vanished.

Toys knew that some of those people were—like him—offered opportunities to pick another path. Church worked with them. Dr. Rudy Sanchez, too. And all of this was so far off the record Toys believed that even Joe Ledger was unaware of it.

Now Dingo was part of the Wild Hunt.

Dingo wasn't suave or subtle enough to do infiltration work except in extremist groups or bands of mercenaries. But he had his talents, and Toys preferred having him along for situations where things could get rough. Toys often categorized people, and their potential in such circumstances as these, as different kinds of animals. He likened himself to a viper—quick and dangerous when provoked. Dingo was more like a pit bull. Big, ugly, covered in scars, and more than willing to bite pieces off.

"Rugger thinks he has the info on the meet," said Dingo. "Maybe a warehouse in or near Ashdod."

"Hardly precise."

"We're working on it. Ashdod seems certain, though, so the whole team's in motion. Armani, Zombie, Inky . . . the lot." Dingo cut him a look. "Where the hell did you come up with these stupid code names?"

"Combat call signs," corrected Toys.

"Whatever."

"They amuse me," said Toys. "And I can change them whenever I want."

Dingo shot him a look. "Mr. Church lets you do that?"

"He lets me do quite a lot of things."

"Cool. But the nicknames—*call signs*, whatever. Really? Skiver pretty much hates the nickname and would be okay if you were eaten by rabid weasels."

"Fair enough. If he asks nicely, I may reconsider."

"As for me . . . 'Dingo' is okay, but it's a bit cliché. For an Aussie, I mean."

"Mr. Church needed us in the field quickly," said Toys. "There wasn't time to take a bloody poll."

"No, I get it," said Dingo. "It's just a bit on the nose, mate."

Dingo paused at a corner, then made a turn as the light changed. "I'm open to suggestions."

"I rather fancy Dreamtime."

"And that's *not* too cliché for an Australian?"

"It is. A bit, I guess," agreed Dingo. "But since I'm not even one percent Aboriginal, who would connect it with me?"

Toys thought about it and thought of a dozen reasons why someone would assume he was Australian even if they didn't know his

JONATHAN MABERRY

call sign. "We can come back to this before the next gig. Right now, let's focus."

"Fair."

They drove in silence. After a considerable distance, Rugger *bing-bong*ed on the comms to give them an address.

"This is it for sure," he said. "We picked up some chatter from Lamech. He ditched his car and met a full team. He gave them the address and time. Eight p.m. Aydelotte's team leader is the woman called Shock. Good chance she's already in place."

"Brilliant," said Toys.

"Our team's in play, boss," said Rugger. "We'll meet you there."

Dingo found the location—a book warehouse—and slowed to a stop, angling over into a dense patch of shadow. The dashboard clock said that it was seven-thirty local time.

"Crikey," said Dingo. "Imagine us getting the scoop on this Gorgon thing before Bug or that pelican, Scott Wilson."

"Yes, we'll all get gold stars on our homework," said Toys lazily.

Dingo looked at him. "You think this Lamech cunt is going to use those Gorgons to massacre some Palestinians?"

"Probably."

"So he's daft enough to want to start a war *and* become an outlaw in his own country?"

"We can assume he'd put some layers of protection between him and whoever pulls the trigger. He's management, not a field man."

"Still a cunt."

"Did you hear me argue?"

Toys checked the clock: 7:37. Less than half an hour to go.

CHAPTER 70
ARKLIGHT SAFE HOUSE
KIRYAT MALAKHI, ISRAEL

I had Remy drive us to another part of the suburbs and pull into the rear part of an industrial parking lot. Then we went out and ran Anteaters over everything. The stolen car, the gear we stole from the dead crew in the SUV, and even our own gear.

"All clean, Outlaw," said Top.

We got back in and, at a very sedate pace, drove to a pleasant little residential area and a charming house with yellow lights glimmering with welcome. As we pulled up onto the asphalt driveway, the metal garage door opened, and a figure stepped out of shadows and waved us inside.

The door closed, and only then did she turn on the garage light. The woman was tall, slender, and very fit, with lustrous auburn hair pulled back into a tail. She wore jeans and a cardigan loose enough to hide the pistol I knew she carried.

"Hello, Joseph," she said as I climbed out.

"Hello, Violin," I said.

INTERLUDE 27
SCHOOL OF CLASSICS
ASBAHI NEIGHBORHOOD, BEYNOUN STREET
SANA'A, YEMEN

FOUR MONTHS AGO

"The deal is the deal," said Toombs. "Not going to hurt my feelings either way, so if you walk away, that's cool. If you want the product, also cool. But let's be clear . . . I don't haggle."

He sat on one side of a battered old wooden desk in a room that was once used for teaching mathematics. Now the room was nearly bare except for a few sticks of furniture, bullet holes pocked across some of the walls, and windows covered with obscuring rugs. On the other side of the desk was a man who once taught in a room very much like this one.

"What you ask is too much," insisted Ayoob Alazaki, managing to sound both surprised and affronted by a number that had been agreed to before the meeting even took place. "An agreement was already made with the man I believed I would be meeting here."

"You mean Sadiq," said Toombs. "Yeah, he couldn't make it."

Alazaki sat in thoughtful silence. "And why is that?"

"Because he's dead."

Alazaki tensed, and as he did that the two guards he had brought with him tensed as well. The barrels of their rifles began to rise and turn in Toombs's direction.

"How did he die?" demanded the schoolteacher. "Who killed him?"

"Nobody killed him. He had a heart attack while soaking in a tub in his Cairo hotel room. And before you ask, it was an actual heart problem. Poor guy had a bad ticker. Who knew?"

"This is very sad news," said Alazaki. "Sadiq was a good man. We often prayed together."

"Never met him," said Toombs. "Before my time. But I heard good things. Good head for business. A guy you can trust, and we both know how much trust matters."

"I hope we do."

Toombs did not take that bait.

"We were counting on a software package that man was preparing," said Alazaki. "Without it some of the weapons purchased from your employer are worthless."

"Hardly worthless," countered Toombs. "Let's maintain perspective here. The RPGs and LAW rockets you bought work fine, and you got them for a good price."

"We were promised more. We were promised the upgraded software and guidance collars. Without those you can have your RPGs back."

"Yeah," said Toombs. "No. We don't do returns and refunds. You haven't been cheated. Sadiq died and that's that. Blame God if you want to."

"I would advise you to tread very carefully," warned Alazaki.

"And maybe you should listen to what I have to say before you get pissed off." Toombs took a breath. "Okay, so Sadiq was the finesse guy. From what I heard he was a smooth talker, and I admire that, but it's not how I do things. I'm more of what you could call a straight talker. I don't play little games of subtlety. I don't run business deals as if we were haggling over spices at a market stall."

"You are not even of the faith."

"And if we were going to the mosque that would matter a lot," said Toombs. "But we're not. And let's not put on airs. You want to buy weapons to blow people up. I want to sell those to you. You're buying on behalf of your boss, Harith al-Wazir. I'm here to sell my goods to you on behalf of Mr. Aydelotte. We are both middlemen, so we don't need drama now, do we?"

Alazaki studied him for several moments. He smiled slowly. "Very well. Tell me what it is you have to say."

"Ah, now there we go," said Toombs, nodding happily. "My boss recognizes that you fellows need to make some serious statements. And I think we can both agree that RPGs, fun as they are, are *soooo* last week. They are a very long way from cutting edge, and every year your enemies get new toys, new weapons, new software, new surveillance equipment. You may be fighting on your own turf—what we in the States call the home court advantage—but you're not winning. You're losing ground, and neither of us have to pretend you're not."

"You are speaking a lot but not saying much."

"Ouch," said Toombs. "Okay, that point goes to you. So, I'll cut to it. We'll still sell the software and guidance collars to you. No problem. That will give you a leg up. But . . ."

He paused, and Alazaki even leaned in a bit. "But . . . what?"

"We could change the nature of the deal so that you get an even better set of toys. Hell, we'll throw in a bunch of extras just to put a happy smile on your face."

"Why would you do this?"

"You and Sadiq were working out barter arrangements," Toombs reminded him.

"Yes. He already told us what he wanted in exchange for the guidance system."

"Yeah," said Toombs, stretching out the word, "but that was before we got wind of some other items that your smash-and-grab field teams supposedly destroyed."

"You mean antiquities. Sacrilegious garbage."

"I do. When you and Sadiq spoke, my boss thought you had a certain group of items. But it's come to our attention that you actually have a bit more. Some stuff that matters more to him than it ever will to you as some kind of statement."

"How is it of value?" asked Alazaki. "The world believes these things have been destroyed. He cannot then profit from trying to sell them. No museum or government would ever purchase them. At best they would demand their return; at worst he would be arrested for trafficking in stolen goods."

"That's only true if his customers wanted them for, as you say, museums. But there are a lot of other people out there who want them for private collections."

"That is covetousness."

"Sure it is. Who cares? And don't quote scripture at me, because we both know that you sell some of these things on the black market already."

"So your employer wants to do the same?" asked the schoolteacher.

Toombs gave him a skeletal leer. "Trust me when I say that he has better contacts for moving that merchandise. There's levels to the black market. He's a shark, not a bottom feeder."

"If these things are so valuable to him, then surely they must be worth more in trade."

"Which is why I said we'd sweeten the deal. You could get money from your sales, but we can give you weapons of such sophistication that your next statement will be heard around the world."

"That is a bold statement."

Toombs, still grinning like a ghoul, folded his bone-white hands in his lap. "Yes," he said, "it damn well is."

CHAPTER 71
PIRATE LAB
UNDISCLOSED LOCATION

Toombs and Conti sat together on the floor of her lab. Eight beer bottles stood or lay between them. Conti had her pewter-encased flask in her lap, with her fingers laced around it. The air smelled of beer, alcohol, and very good Jamaican grass.

"He's crazy," said Conti. "You know that, right?"

Toombs took a very deep hit off the joint, held it for as long as he could, and then exhaled blue smoke above his head.

"Aren't we all a little crazy, though?" he asked.

"Not like him."

He turned and studied the side of her face. She had delicate features that seemed accentuated when she was drunk. It made her look young, like a medical student instead of a seasoned professional research physician.

"Um," he said, half smiling, "not to be mean here, sweets, but you are literally making a bioweapon for him that mindfucks everyone exposed, up to and including encouraging murder and suicide."

Conti took the joint from him, hit it hard, and handed it back. "It was his idea."

"Even so."

"Every time I had a variant that—to me—was more than dangerous enough, he told me to amp it up."

"Again I say . . . even so."

She looked at him. "Yes, yes, okay, sure, that makes me complicit. It makes me a monster. But he's still worse."

They thought about that. Smoking. Drinking. Chewing on it.

"Yeah," he said after about five minutes.

Conti elbowed him lightly. "And you sell weapons to terrorists."

"I do. But I already said we were all crazy."

"Jason is worse," she insisted.

"Okay, but why?"

"I'm a fuckup in every way possible outside the lab. You have no moral compass at all. We're both in this for the money," she said. "Jason, though . . . ? He does it because he loves it. Because it makes him feel . . ."

"Powerful?" suggested Toombs, but she shook her head.

"No. It makes him feel like God."

Toombs snorted. "That's a funny thing to say."

"It was something Shock told me," said Conti, waving off the joint he held out. "She had this weird conversation with him the other day. We got interrupted, so she didn't tell me all of it, but she was really freaked out. She said she'd tell me the whole conversation after the thing tonight. We're supposed to have lunch tomorrow."

"Yeah, but what *did* she say?"

"She said that Jason thinks he's either the instrument of God on Earth, or maybe God himself."

"Bullshit. Jason was fucking with her."

Conti shrugged. "Maybe, but Shock didn't think so. She was really upset."

Toombs took the last long hit and crushed the roach out on the floor. "I mean, I know he's weird, but it sounds like she was talking more about Alazaki or maybe that Harith dude, whoever he is. Those guys are bugfuck nuts and no mistake. Maybe you heard it wrong."

"Maybe," said Conti, but Toombs could tell she did not think so.

CHAPTER 72
BEERBAZAAR
REHOV ETS KHAYIM 3
MAHANE YEHUDA COVERED MARKET
JERUSALEM, ISRAEL

The man sat nursing a beer and trying to summon the courage to make the call. The restaurant was open late, and they had a lot of good beer choices. He was on his third, but stress was keeping a comforting buzz from any chance of sanding off the sharp ends of his nerves.

His name—for this gig, at least—was David White. But it was a name of convenience. Something to be shed like a snakeskin for each new job.

Though, after tonight, David wasn't sure there would *be* another job.

He had made one call already, but that was to his longtime friend and fellow mercenary, Kevin. Also not a real name.

"I saw something on the news," said Kevin when he'd answered the call. "Was that you?"

"That was Alpha Team," said David.

"What's wrong? You should be celebrating."

"They're gone."

"Who? The targets? I should damn well think so. You blew that place halfway to heaven."

"No," said David. "The targets did that."

A beat. "Wait . . . what?"

And David White told him about what had happened when Alpha Team hit the DTI safe house.

"*All* of them?" gasped Kevin.

"Every single one. Total loss."

They were silent for a moment.

"What about Beta Team? They were supposed to pick up anyone who slipped the hit."

David's answer was a long and telling silence.

"Oh, jeez, man," said Kevin. "How the hell did they take out both teams? There was only six of them and a flea-bitten dog. Please tell me that the teams got *some* of them. If they got Ledger at least, then the boss will just see everything else as collateral damage."

"The only things that makes sense," said David, "is that they either had someone on overwatch who alerted them to the hit, or someone called in and tipped them off."

Now it was Kevin's turn to be silent.

He finally said, "Have you called this in yet? Have you told Mr. October?"

"No," admitted David wearily. He looked around at the other customers. Happy people, talking and eating and laughing like the world was a wonderful place and all was right in God's paradise. He loathed them all for it, for every smile, every relaxed posture, every happy moment. "I've been sitting here trying to figure out what to say."

"The truth? You were coordinating the teams, but it was on them to eliminate the hostiles."

"The truth? Really? Fuck, man, I'm thinking of going dark and getting myself into the wind."

"Don't," said Kevin quickly. "You know he'll find you."

"I can run pretty far. I have cash here and there. Equipment, too. I'll go off the grid and wait it out."

"And what? Look guilty? Shit, listen to me," said Kevin. "If you bail and run, then Mr. October will think that you're involved. That you tipped Ledger off, or that you didn't verify some detail and let things go off half-cocked. The boss will never stop hunting you. I'm telling you now, friend to friend, brother to brother, just make the call and own this shit. I mean . . . hell, there's a reason the boss wants Ledger dead. He's been a pain in the ass for too long."

"I want the chance to make this right," said David, staring down into the amber depths of his IPA.

"Then *tell* him that," urged Kevin. "That's what he'll want to hear. And I bet he'll give you another chance, especially if you speak straight. Don't sugarcoat it, don't throw anyone under the bus. Take the hit and tell him what you just told me."

David took a long sip. "Thanks, brother."

That call was half an hour ago, and he still hadn't made the next call. The call that mattered. Each minute that passed made it harder to justify why he hadn't already called in. His hands were shaking badly.

But he picked up the burner phone and found the coded contact name in his recent calls. He stared at the nickname he had been given to use for Mr. October while on this assignment.

Trickster.

David White finished the beer, took a few steadying breaths, and punched the button.

CHAPTER 73
ARKLIGHT SAFE HOUSE
KIRYAT MALAKHI, ISRAEL

It occurred to me that Remy had not met Violin and, despite his affectation of Cajun cool, he stood there staring at her transfixed. She has that kind of effect on people, and it's hard to pin down exactly why.

Violin is beautiful, yes, but there are women in the world more beautiful than her. There are women with better curves, better hair, more classically lovely faces. Sure. But how many does the average person actually know? Plus, she has a presence. When you meet her, you know you are with someone unlike anyone you've ever met. Her brown eyes look at you and into you, and there is a sense she knows things about you that she shouldn't, and things maybe you don't know. There is a tendency for grown men to want to check to see if their fingernails are clean. It isn't a sexual thing, though there is that component as well. Not porn star sexy or movie star sexy; something older in a way that even after years I doubt I could put into words. Mostly it's the power she exudes, and the confidence. You could not look at her and imagine anyone overpowering her in any meaningful way.

She earns all of that, too. Not by trying but by living her power. By using it in ways other people can't. Or wouldn't dare try.

I'm not entirely sure how old she is. She looks thirtysomething. But I've seen photos of her from a long time ago, and she looked thirtysomething then, too. Rudy said once that if even half the stories we heard about her were true, then she would have to be somewhere between fifty-five and sixty-five.

Her mother, Lilith—who was Church's lover—looked twenty years older. Every bit as beautiful and maybe twice as powerful. God only knows how old she is. And more than once I've wondered who is actually older—Lilith or Church. Most of the time I don't really want an answer to that question. Life is already weird enough.

"Hey," I said, "where's your puppy?"

"I wish you wouldn't call him that," said Violin.

Her puppy was a young, deeply inept but otherwise harmless former CIA field guy named Harry Bolt. His father was the late and not at all missed Harcourt Bolton Sr. Harry had split off from his dad when it was clear that Harcourt was not the noble, upstanding American James Bond everyone thought he was. In reality he was a master criminal who formed the Kuga network, a mass murderer, and an all-around piece of shit.

"Okay," I said, "where's Harry?"

"At the moment? I have no idea. Probably on a beach somewhere with his girlfriend."

"Girlfriend? So it's like that?"

She shook her head. "You never understood what I saw in Harry. And you persisted in thinking he was my lover."

"You're saying he wasn't?"

"Not in any meaningful way. He was . . . uncomplicated."

"Ah. Or, should I say 'ouch'?"

"And, as far as I am concerned," said Violin, "he is past tense. After what happened in Texas last year, Harry decided that the life of an international adventurer was not for him."

"Wise choice."

"Safe choice," she said and shrugged.

"Is Helmut here?" I asked.

"Oh, yes. Safe and sound."

"That's something."

"Yeah," said Bunny. "We could use a little safe and sound our own selves."

"There's hot food inside," said Violin, looking faintly amused by Remy's goggle-eyed stare.

The others went into the house, but I lingered in the garage with Violin. When we were alone, Violin pulled me into a fierce hug. I did not yield, but at the same time for me it was just that: a hug.

Once upon a time, fairly early on in my DMS tenure, she and I had become lovers. It was hot, too. Very intense. But it also did not last. I almost fell in love with her but didn't. She did fall in love with me but managed to detach herself from the fullest part of that emotion once she realized that I was not a keeper. Not hers, anyway. Not all that long after that I met Junie Flynn, and I fell hard. I keep falling farther every year. At first Violin resented Junie, but then she moved past her personal hurt and got to *know* Junie. Now they're friends, and quite often Violin will show up unannounced at one of Junie's field operations in whatever part of the world it happens to be. She also saved Junie's life once, and that means that I will always owe Violin a debt that can never be repaid. Not that she'd ever call that marker in. She's not that kind of person. Nor, for that matter, am I.

"The Deacon called to read me in on this," she said, using one of Church's many former aliases. None of us knew his real name. "All of it."

"And?"

"It's not your kind of case."

"That's what I keep telling everyone."

"Unless it is," she said, and there was a hint of a wicked smile.

"Gosh, thanks."

She studied me. "And how are you doing?"

"If that is another indirect question about whether I'm about to sing another chorus of 'Hello Darkness, my old friend,' then . . ."

"It's not. But I can see a shadow in your eyes."

Some people say that, and it's New Age woo-woo claptrap. A few people actually say what they see, and I believe they see it. Violin is in that smaller, latter group.

So I told her about hearing Grace's voice in the basement in Chad and my dad's voice at the RTI safe house. The first was a creepy yet heartbreaking echo from my emotional past. The second actually saved my life.

"Who else have you told about this?"

"Junie knows about hearing Grace. I haven't told anyone about my dad. Does any of it make any sense to you?"

She did not ask me if I was sure I'd heard those voices. Violin's world is different from mine in more ways than it's similar. A question like that would never occur to her.

"I will ask this," she said. "Do you feel like those voices are connected to the Darkness? You told me months ago that you heard and even saw your family back then. When you infiltrated the black site prison in Germany, you saw them. You spoke with Sean. Is this like that?"

I chewed my lower lip for a minute. "I've been asking myself that question ever since Chad."

"And . . . ?"

"No," I said. "I think this is something else."

Her dark eyes glittered as she assessed me. "So do I," she said.

CHAPTER 74
EDUCATIONAL BOOK WAREHOUSE
ASHDOD, ISRAEL

The warehouses in that part of Ashdod were mostly occupied. The city's industry thrived, and during the day there was a constant parade of trucks in and out. However, in one corner stood five warehouses that were all owned by a family whose patriarch had died and left no will. The members of his family had been waging a war in the courts for so long—with no end in sight—that the companies leasing the buildings moved on. Now the book warehouse, the clothing warehouse, and three others that were mixed use stood empty, wasted opportunities and huge amounts of wasted revenue for a family who were squabbling over the potential. Toys found that equal parts irritating and amusing.

The former book repository was ideal for meets like the one about to happen. No active security, either electronic or foot surveillance.

Toys and Dingo got out of their car and put on Scout glasses, careful to not let the night vision fool them into thinking they themselves could not be seen.

"Everyone report in," ordered Toys, feeling just slightly like a horse's ass because this was almost too much of a Joe Ledger thing, and Toys loathed all the macho running around, asking for sitreps, using combat call signs, and grown-ups playing at silly buggers. When he'd asked Church to send him into the field, he hoped that it would be straight espionage. Diving back into the world of Vox and Gault, renewing old contacts who didn't know he was now on the side of the angels.

Not this.

But *this* was what Church needed, because Joe Ledger was not batting on a full wicket at the best of times, and much less so since that whole Darkness thing.

Head in the game, you twit, he told himself. *Head in the game.*

He chased Joe Ledger out of his thoughts and ran through the darkness there at hand.

CHAPTER 75
THE TOC
PHOENIX HOUSE

"Sir," said Scott Wilson, "there's a call for you."

Church glanced up from a monitor showing countless police, fire, rescue, and military clustered around the smoking ruins of the Jerusalem safe house.

"Is it Outlaw or Toys?"

"No, sir. It's the lady. Do you want to take it in your office?"

The lady. Church almost smiled. "No. Patch it through to this desk."

He was at the rear of the TOC and gestured to an empty workstation. Two techs at nearby stations got up and moved away to give him privacy.

"Coming through now."

Church sat and lowered the volume on the speaker. A woman's face appeared on the screen. She was strikingly lovely in a cold and regal way. Her age was impossible to determine with any certainty— thirty-five, fifty-five, or older. She had that flawless skin that some rare women have as they age, unmarked by crow's feet or laugh lines. Only her throat hinted that she was likely older than any first guess. Her hair was intensely black except for threads of silver at the temple. Brown eyes so dark they might as well have been black, but the sclera were the blue-white of peak health. Her mouth was full-lipped but generally held in compressed lines, suggesting an anger kept in check by iron control.

"Lilith," said Church, and as he spoke his fingers brushed his tie right over his heart.

"St. Germaine," she said, and the stern mouth softened for the briefest of moments. "I have some information about the team that hit your safe house in Jerusalem."

"Tenth Legion?"

"Yes. As you likely guessed, they're named after the Roman legion sent to Jerusalem to put down Jewish rebellion. We've brushed past them a few times but have not been in direct conflict. They're on our list, though, because they provide security for a number of arms dealers who work with multinational corporations who run sweatshops and sex camps."

"Understood."

And Church did understand. For many years Lilith and a number of other women had been prisoners of a group known as the Red Knights, a subdivision of an old religious order created as a more militant offshoot of the Knights Templar and Knights Hospitallers. The Red Knights themselves were men inflicted with a rare genetic disorder whose symptoms were the basis for the belief in vampires—pale skin, unusual longevity, enhanced physical strength, and a hunger for human blood. They were not, however, supernatural monsters, though over the centuries their former masters in the Red Order deliberately cast themselves in that light to heighten fear of them. The Knights were the crusaders' response to the cult of assassins created by Hassan Ibn Sabbah in the early twelfth century. The rumor was that the word "assassin" was based on the belief that those killers were high on hashish. But it was closer to the truth that the word comes from *asasiyyin*, an Arabic word meaning "people who are faithful to the foundation of Islam."

The Red Order was a radical splinter group of the Knights Hospitaller, and they endure even to this day. Creepy bastards who think using genetically mutated bloodsuckers as their troops is somehow a good idea. Not sure which is worse, the humans in the Order or the freaky Knights.

The women held captive by the Red Knights were forced to bear children for them, and endured years of humiliation and torture. Then Lilith led a particularly brutal revolt, and the women—known as the Mothers of the Fallen—escaped. They formed a group of women dedicated to the fight against sexual slavery and human trafficking. Arklight was the Special Ops arm of that group.

"Is it your feeling that the Tenth Legion is working on behalf of the Red Order?"

"Yes, but it's literally that—a feeling. We know that the Red Order still exists. It is greatly reduced in scope and power, but it is not, sadly, extinct. This may be a step toward them reasserting themselves as a power in the Middle East."

"And the Red Knights?"

"They are still out there," said Lilith. "Baba Yaga and her team eliminated a number of them a month ago on the Romanian side of the Carpathians."

Baba Yaga was one of the most seasoned Arklight team leaders. She was entirely humorless, ferocious as a piranha, and possessed no trace of mercy. All four of her own children were murdered by the Red Knights in the years leading up to the revolt.

"Another piece of the puzzle," said Church. "And another militant religious group casting a shadow across the chessboard. Tell me, Lilith, has this intel been forwarded to Violin?"

"Of course, and by now she'll have told your pet dog."

Church did not rise to the bait to defend Ledger.

"There's something else," she said. "Do you know about the cobras?"

"Yes. We are trying to make sense of it."

"What is there to understand?"

"How it was done. We are certain that there was no manipulation of the video, and the one surviving person from that interrogation passed a polygraph."

"Of course he did. Why should he not?"

"If you know something, Lilith, please don't be coy."

"You are always such a pragmatist, St. Germaine. You think Occam's razor is the only possible lens through which to view events."

"That's a bit unfair," said Church.

"But not entirely untrue."

"Make your point. What am I missing?"

"That this is exactly what it seems."

Church paused. "You mean that it cannot be explained away by any practical means?"

"Unless your personal worldview is flexible enough to accept that magic is real. Or, perhaps more precisely, my love, that what you define as science should be open to expansion and inclusion."

"You think me so inflexible?"

Amusement twinkled in her dark eyes. "I am recommending keeping a very open mind."

"I said as much to Colonel Ledger during his mission briefing."

"And . . . ?"

"He is struggling with 'magic' as a possibility."

"Are you?"

"Despite your assessment, Lilith, my mind is always open. I cannot fight this war and be close-minded."

She studied his eyes, then nodded. "I have my people looking into that as well."

"I am reachable whenever you want to share."

"Does that go both ways?"

"On this? It would have to. We are treading on ice of uncertain thickness."

"What will you do if it turns out that ISIS has cracked the secrets of ancient magic?"

"Oh, I rather enjoy the old motto of the British Empire—adopt, adapt, and improve."

She nodded and hesitated once more. "I was surprised to find that you sent Ledger into the field on *this* case."

"Why? Because he is also a pragmatist?"

"No. Because he is literally insane."

"He and I are both aware of the nature and extent of his psychological damage and how it may be affected by cases of unusual—even radical—dimensions."

"Oh, goddess," laughed Lilith. "You are so rarely naïve, my love. But when you are, you do not go with half measures."

And with that she ended the call.

CHAPTER 76
O'TREE-SANCHEZ HOUSE
CORFU, GREECE

"You still out here?" asked Circe, and she stepped out onto the deck. "You must be freezing." She'd brought a richly patterned Greek blanket with her and draped it around her husband's shoulders. Then she went inside and came out almost immediately with two big ceramic mugs of spicy tea.

"*Gracias, mi amor*," he murmured.

Circe sat down next to him. Her wildly curly black hair was pinned up in a sloppy bun, and she wore no makeup. There were some small paint smudges on her hands and one cheek. The colors matched a seascape she had been working on in her studio on the third floor. Circe was not a very skilled painter, unschooled and self-taught, but her sense of color was superb. She understood the emotional subtleties of color and relied on those rather than on formal techniques of composition. Her work was in an undefined valley between abstract impressionism and primitivism.

"I heard you talking earlier," she said as she settled down onto the swing next to him. There was no moon, and the sky had exploded with millions of glittering stars. There was a faint wash of paleness from the Milky Way, something neither of them had seen in the

United States. Rudy had seen it in the most rural parts of Mexico as a boy, and far out to sea on a sailing trip he'd taken with Joe and Sean Ledger. For Circe, that celestial vista belonged to their life in Corfu.

"I spoke to Junie," he said.

"Yes."

"She didn't tell me I was wrong for what I said to your father."

Circe smiled, barely visible in the darkness of the deck. "I can't believe you knocked his cookies to the floor."

"That was childish of me."

"There are grown men—seasoned combat veterans—who would never have dared do that. If it ever got out, honey, you'd be a legend."

"Let's pray it never gets out. I'm so embarrassed by that."

Circe turned to him. "Why? You love that big blond Neanderthal. Joe is closer to you than a brother. Dad knows that, and he knows you're right. He should never have sent Joe back into the field."

"And yet . . ."

Circe made a small growly noise in her throat.

A shooting star ignited and burned its way across the sky.

"Make a wish," said Circe.

But Rudy already had.

CHAPTER 77
ARKLIGHT SAFE HOUSE
KIRYAT MALAKHI, ISRAEL

We gathered in the living room and compared notes, covering every aspect of what was going on.

"Is it me, or is this just plain weird?" asked Remy.

"It's not you," said Bunny.

"Okay, let's sum up," said Top. "We have ISIS buying advanced weapons—*possibly* from Santa Claus's evil twin. We have an Israeli extremist group also buying some pretty damned dangerous toys—and maybe from the same cat—in a deal involving Toys and his new team. And now we have *another* group that, by definition, has to be an extremist Christian gang sending PMCs after us. Do I have it all now?"

Bunny snorted. "All we need now are some Hindu Thuggee and

a handful of cranky Buddhists and we have our terrorist bingo card complete." He glanced at me. "Going into the field with you is never boring, boss."

"Hey," I said.

Violin gave me a tolerant, amused look. "To be fair, you are a magnet for weirdness, Joseph, do you know this?"

Top laughed. "Hell, sister, *everyone* knows that."

Ghost literally *whuff*ed at that moment.

"You can keep your opinions to yourself, fuzz-bucket." He sat there wagging his fluffy tail. "And as for the rest of you," I said, "feel free to line up and kiss my ass."

"Thanks, but I'm married," said Andrea. "And he has a cuter ass."

Belle punched him on the arm. I guess that was her version of laughing out loud. I saw Andrea discreetly massaging that spot.

Remy said, "If there are three groups that hate each other that much, can't we just sit back and let them duke it out? Could be entertaining."

"Sure," I said. "Just as soon as we personally escort to safety all four hundred million noncombatants here in the Middle East. Remember, we're at war with the few, not the many."

"I know we all keep asking this," said Top, "but where does this leave us? What's our next move?"

"Do we go help that Toys fellow with his thing?" asked Remy.

"No, we damn well do not," I said. "We stay on mission. We came here to make sense of things, and first thing in the morning we tackle that. Top and I are going to see where those scholars died. The rest of you will partner up—Andrea and Belle, Remy and Bunny. You'll watch to see if anyone is watching us. It's been a long day, so everyone grab some rack time. We're up at first light. I want every weapon cleaned, every magazine filled, all electronics checked. Violin, can you provide vehicles? Late-model sedan for Top and me. Whatever's fast but low-key for the team."

"Of course," she said.

"I'll take first watch," I said. "And wait for fresh intel from Phoenix House."

They all nodded and tramped off to find their beds. I noticed that none of them took their coffee cups.

When we were alone, Violin came and stood near my chair. "Do you want some company, Joseph?"

I smiled and shook my head. "Thanks, but I have a couple of calls to make."

She nodded and left.

Ghost came over and laid his head on my lap, looking up at me with big puppy dog eyes until I began to scratch his ears. I removed my cell from my pocket and checked to see if Rudy was still ignoring my messages.

He wasn't, but there was only one text from him.

> *Call me.*

And one from Junie.

> *I love you.*
> *Call Rudy.*

So, yeah. I called Rudy.

CHAPTER 78
ARKLIGHT SAFE HOUSE
KIRYAT MALAKHI, ISRAEL

He picked up on the second ring.

"Outlaw . . . ?" he asked tentatively.

"It's me, Rudy."

"This is a safe line?"

"No, I completely forgot the rules and am calling from the middle of a firefight," I said. I meant it as a joke, but there was an edge of bitterness in my voice that even I could hear. "Sorry, brother."

"No," he said in his rich baritone. "How *are* you?"

"Relatively speaking, peachy."

"Is that sarcasm?"

"A bit."

"Will you try again and maybe answer the question?"

"I'm as okay as circumstances allow," I said. "At an Arklight safe house in Kiryat Malakhi. Ten kinds of scramblers and signal filters. We can talk."

"I asked you to call because I want to apologize about what happened earlier," said Rudy.

"I really wish you wouldn't."

He laughed softly. "Mr. Church wouldn't let me, either."

"I know you'll always have my back, man."

"Yes."

"And I know that you believe what you said."

"Mr. Church and I had a meaningful discussion about all that," said Rudy. "And I also spoke with Junie. I told her everything."

"Is she okay?"

"She's well," he said, "but she's concerned."

"Look, we both knew I was coming back to the job. But I will tell you one thing and I hope you *hear* me."

"Okay, to use your own phrase—hit me."

"I know that guys like me have a sell-by date stamped somewhere on body and soul. Last year I thought my time was up. But the Darkness went away. It's gone. I'm not just saying that, but I *know* it. I feel it."

He said nothing, knowing in his wisdom that there would be more.

"If—no, *when*—I feel like I've lost more than a step getting to first base, I'll hang up my glove and call it a game. I'm still in my thirties, Rude. I've never been faster or stronger, and maybe that means that soon I'll be past that mark. When that happens, it will have to come down to a moment when I think that I'm a danger to the people I am trying to save, and to the people in the trenches with me. I won't let hubris put bull's-eyes on Top and Bunny or the rest. I won't do that. And I do not believe I'm at that point now. I give you my word, Rudy. As your patient, your friend, and your brother."

There were a few long moments of silence, and then he said, "Then I will take you at your word and stop pushing."

"Thanks," I said. "That matters."

"As does your honesty."

We talked for another half hour. About his family, about Junie, about life. We even laughed a little. If it sounded a bit forced, what of it? We were moving through uncertain territory looking for common ground and finding it a bit at a time.

When we hung up, I sat there and scratched Ghost and wondered why I hadn't told him about the voices. Grace and my Dad.

Was it cowardice?

Or was it the faintest, distant, sly whisper of the Darkness?

CHAPTER 79
EDUCATIONAL BOOK WAREHOUSE
ASHDOD, ISRAEL

There was a faint *bing-bong* in his ear, and Rugger said, "Armani, Inky, Skiver, and Zombie are on deck."

"Brilliant," said Toys. "Rugger, you're on overwatch."

"Already in position," came the reply. "Top floor of the paper warehouse to the east."

"Zombie here," said another voice. "We're approaching on foot to cover west and north."

"Skiver is outside behind a dumpster," said Armani. "I'm at the back entrance. There's one guard on the loading bay here. Looks pro from the way he's doing things."

"Be ready to scratch him off the card," said Toys. "Rugger, who's inside?"

"Caucasian woman with red hair," said Rugger very quietly. "Dressed in civvies but she's strapped. I can see a nine in a shoulder rig."

"Sounds like Shock," said Toys. "Who else?"

"Six others scattered out. Five men and one more woman. All of them with long guns kitted out with suppressors. I have bat drones hanging on the rafters. Sending the feed now."

Toys and Dingo bent over the feed that was sent to their tactical computers. The aerial view from a pair of bat drones showed the interior of the warehouse. There were three vehicles inside—two midsize SUVs and a small commercial panel truck. The woman—and Toys presumed this was Aydelotte's throat-slitting archaeologist, Shock—was pacing slowly along a ten-foot stretch of greasy concrete floor, using two of her guards as turning points. The other four guards were positioned around the medium-size warehouse floor.

"Where's our way in?" he asked.

"There's a small personnel door next to the big truck bay in back. It's closed, but I taped the spring bolt back. No lights back there, so you should be able to get in easy. And Shock turned the big ceiling fans on, so there's noise cover."

"Moving," said Toys. He tapped Dingo, and they went running along the way, slipping like a night breeze through the shadows. They found the door but waited a few seconds until one of Aydelotte's guards did a patrol pass. Then they reached the door, opened it with infinite care, and slipped inside. The place was big and nearly completely empty except for Shock's cars at the far end, and some stacks of old pinewood skids. Toys chose those as cover because it allowed them to get close enough to hear her talking to her men, but far enough back so that no light touched them.

"Lamech is ten minutes out," said Skiver. "Small convoy. Three black SUVs. No other local traffic."

"Lovely," said Toys very quietly. "Okay, kids, everyone hold position. We need intel for the Big Man. We return fire if it comes to it, but our job is to watch, record, transmit, and wait for orders. This is *not* the OK Corral."

CHAPTER 80
INTEGRATED SCIENCES DIVISION
PHOENIX HOUSE

She sat like a queen in her big leather swivel chair, glasses perched halfway down her nose, eyes bright, a half-smile on her lips.

"Tell me you have something," she said.

Isaac Breslau and Ronald Coleman sat on lesser chairs—comfortable but not grand—and looked at her like attentive schoolboys rather than world-class scientists. Coleman, who was the newest member of the ISD, often tried to understand how the pecking order was implanted in their shared consciousness. He was used to being the big dog in any medical research group to which he had ever been associated. His degrees, certifications, and awards filled a whole wall of his office. Isaac was similarly celebrated by his peers. Either of them could have run this shop. Both had been scouted by Dr. William Hu as potential replacements should he ever step down. When he died a few years ago, Church had reached past—or perhaps over—them to bring Dr. Joan Holliday in as the new boss.

Under virtually any other circumstance Coleman might have been miffed, and deservedly so. And yet . . .

There was something about Doc Holliday. She was, like Church himself, on a different level. Her outward and deliberate outrageousness was as much a deception as was Church's cool and perpetual calm. He supposed that it was the fact that Doc—and even the other medical doctors and PhDs called her that—was so thoroughly talented. A true multidisciplinary genius. Possibly, and even probably, a super genius. There were few of those.

He wondered if physicists working with Einstein felt like he did. There was only the merest flicker of jealousy. Closer to envy, really.

"We have a lot," said Isaac, "but it doesn't yet add up to answers."

"Yeah," said Coleman. "We did a full tox screening on all of the kids. We drew blood from all of them and did ultra-high-performance liquid chromatography–tandem mass spectroscopy. That's how we found the ergot alkaloids in the blood. The gene sequencers have been running twenty-four seven. Quick answer is that there's clear evidence of ergotism. Three of them had lesions, and we took scrapings and cultured them, and that let us know there was ergot in play. Have to say, it wasn't what we expected to find."

Doc smiled. "I suspect there is a 'but' poised and ready to drop."

"*But*," said Coleman, smiling, "it's unusual."

"A new form," said Isaac. "It has characteristics of both the gangrenous and convulsive forms of ergotism, but modified."

"Significantly modified," Coleman said. "I'd even go out on a limb and say weaponized."

Isaac nodded. "Given the circumstances I think that's a safe word."

"Weaponized in order to accomplish what, in your opinion?" asked Doc.

"Not really sure," said Coleman. "Those kids have suffered repeated exposure to the point where they are largely unresponsive. They're traumatized. Rudy says they will need weeks if not months of therapy. But that has its own challenges."

"These are village kids," said Isaac. "Poor bastards. Only two of them speak Arabic, though it's clear it's not their mother tongue. Nor is French, before you ask. Three of them speak only the Runga dialect of Aiki, which is one of the Maban languages of rural Chad. Another speaks only Maba. The others are all over the place. The Koniéré dialect of Karanga, Surbakhal, Amdang, and so on. These are kids from tiny villages with little or no previous contact with the outside world."

"You're saying kids whose families lack the resources to locate them or protest their absence," suggested Doc.

"Yes."

"Perfect test subjects if you want to see physical reactions but don't require verbal feedback," said Coleman. "Though it's possible that the guards at that facility could act as interpreters."

"Shame they're all getting ass-raped in hell," muttered Isaac.

"Oooo, biblical *and* medieval," cooed Doc. "I like it."

"I mean, not a shame that they're actually being ass-raped by fiery demons part, but the fact that we can't force them to help us."

"I caught your meaning, Ike honey," said Doc.

"Not that I'm a fan of ass-raping and—"

"Please stop while you're ahead."

"Um. Right. Sorry."

"Okay," said Doc. "We can't interrogate the guards, and we can't easily interrogate the kids to get information about what happened to them. That's quite a pickle. Got it. Let's move on. What can we infer from the form of the weaponized ergot?"

"Even that's tricky," said Coleman. "We've logged four separate variations of that bioweapon: three based entirely on the convulsive form, and the fourth using the gangrenous ergot as its centerpiece. Whoever was overseeing the science here was testing variants."

"That kind of science is expensive," said Isaac.

"Ish," said Doc. "The new portable sequencers and grab-and-go chem labs are all the rage, and since they can be set up in a private home, basement, even the back of a decent-size van, we can assume a lower overhead. You boys have been spoiled."

The two men nodded. Each of them had always worked in heavily funded organizations, and neither had paid much attention to the newest trend in high-end portable equipment of that kind. They knew it existed, but that was about it.

"One thing that confuses me a bit," said Isaac, "is that ergot doesn't make for a good bioweapon. I mean, sure, the effect is awful, but it's hardly quick-onset, which is a desired design element in every bioweapon I've heard of."

"Yeah, and it needs moisture to keep it viable," added Coleman. "They would need to solve both of those problems to make it practical for field use. And nothing we've seen from the materials Joe brought back from Chad indicate they're anywhere close to cracking either of those."

"Which means," mused Isaac, "that either this is something Havoc stumbled on early in the overall development of the weapon . . ."

"Or there's a bigger, better, badder lab doing the hard work somewhere else," Doc finished for him.

"That's scary," said Coleman.

"Tell me, cuddle-bear," she said, "which part of working for Rogue Team *hasn't* been scary so far?"

He flushed. "You know what I mean."

"Changing direction a bit," said Doc. "Where are we with the analysis of the syrettes? My guess is that it's some kind of prophylaxis for the guards?"

"Sure," said Coleman. "I've taken point on that. Isaac's working more with sequencing the genes from each kid to see if there's been any other kind of manipulation done with them."

"And to see the impact on their DNA of the modified ergotism," added Isaac.

"As to the syrettes," Coleman continued, "we ran that through a mass spectrometer and found it was loaded with ketanserin."

Doc leaned forward and her eyes lit up. "Ketanserin blocks the serotonin receptor that gets overloaded by LSD. That's very dang interesting."

"We're drilling down into what this is," said Coleman.

Doc nodded and sat back. "I can see it. An ergot-based weapon that is predominantly nonlethal unless the final version relies heavily on the gangrenous ergot, and the weapon is enhanced with LSD."

"Right," said Coleman, "but why would freaking ISIS want a non-lethal bioweapon?"

"I can think of several reasons," said Doc. "Reducing combat effectiveness of enemy combatants in an area where civilians are present. Those Daesh guys have gotten some bad press by hiding behind schoolkids, in mosques, and all that . . . This new cell might want to be seen being careful and respectful of other Muslims. Bear in mind that Islam as a whole is *not* aligned with ISIS. There are a lot of Muslims who wouldn't mind seeing ISIS fall into a black hole. And every time the bad guys strap a suicide vest on some sixteen-year-old, or destroy a historical treasure, or set up a hideout in the back room of a grade school, they are doing great harm to the global perception of what it means to be Muslim. If you want the full rant on that, go down to the café and talk with Mustapha. He has quite a lot to say on the point, but make sure you have a comfortable seat, because when it comes to ISIS he doesn't summarize. You get the full lecture on why they're scum."

"Point taken," said Coleman. "That still leaves us with a bunch of unanswered questions. Who is funding this? Where did they get the science team? What's their purpose for an ergot bioweapon?"

Doc got up and walked across the room and stared at the long row of technicians huddled over their work. She shoved her hands into her back pockets and hummed a few bars of a George Strait song. Then she turned slowly.

"I can think of a whole bunch of reasons somebody might want a bioweapon like that. None of them are *good* reasons. And all of them are scaring me right out of my overpriced cowgirl boots." She wasn't smiling anymore. "You boys keep at it. I need to have a very long and unpleasant conversation with Mr. Church."

CHAPTER 81
IMURA SECURITY SERVICES
BELVEDERE EXECUTIVE CENTER
1 EAST CHASE STREET
BALTIMORE, MARYLAND

"Sir," said the executive assistant, "there's a call for you on line two."

Sam Imura looked up from the papers he had been reviewing all morning.

"Who is it?"

The assistant was a woman in her forties with a few facial scars and a prosthetic left arm, a souvenir from her days as a helicopter pilot in Afghanistan. "He said his name was Ledger. He said you'd know him."

Sam winced and considered telling her to tell Ledger to go jump off the nearest cliff. He looked at the budget report papers spread like a plague across his desk.

"Fine," he said sourly. "I'll take the call. And Jeannie? No interruptions, okay?"

She nodded and left, pulling the office door closed behind her.

Sam Imura slumped back in his chair and glared at the small yellow blinking light on his desktop phone. Once upon a time he had worked as a sniper for Echo Team, a covert Special Ops team under the Department of Military Sciences umbrella. Joe Ledger had been the team leader, and—for a while—a friend. But their relationship had soured over time. Ledger, though effective in the field, seemed to be a magnet for bad luck and trouble. Sam had too many scars from too many bizarre field ops, and blamed Ledger for his lack of caution and the fact that he went on gut more than specific and verifiable intel. They had tried to remain civil, but a visible and lasting bitterness had crept into Sam's heart, and he eventually left the DMS. He had gone to the funeral of Ledger's family after they had been murdered by a terrorist bomb, but that had been more out of courtesy than any lasting bond.

"Shit," he said as he lifted the receiver and punched the button. Into the handset he said, "Yes?"

He heard the brusque intolerance in his voice even in that single word.

"Sam," said the old, familiar voice.

"Joe."

There was a beat, and he knew that Ledger was savvy enough to read his tone.

"Look, brother," said Ledger, "I know things are a bit strained between us. Not really sure why, but for whatever I've done to deserve it, I apologize."

"We don't need to do any of that," said Sam. "And I hope this isn't some kind of AA make-amends thing. What is it, step eight or nine?"

"Okay, let's not fuck around. This isn't a personal call, and I'm not looking for some kind of Hallmark moment between us. This is a business call."

"What kind of business?" asked Sam guardedly.

"Two things. I know that your ISS group does some PMC contracting and some field investigation work."

"We do."

"First part is a favor," said Ledger. "What do you know about a PMC group in South Africa—Tenth Legion?"

"Why do you ask?"

"How secure's this line?"

"You know me."

"Okay, good." Ledger quickly explained about the hit on the RTI safe house. "They were wearing kaffiyehs, but I think that was just to fool us in case we slipped their punch."

"And the one you interrogated gave you some militant Christian rant right before he killed himself?"

"Yeah. Have you run into these clowns?"

"Not directly," said Sam. "But I've been hearing noises that they are sweeping up all of the former Blue Diamond shooters they can find. My guess is that someone from the Blue Diamond management is using Tenth Legion to rebuild under a new name."

"That's what I thought. Look," said Ledger, "you have better contacts in the PMC world than I do. Can you poke around and see what you can find? Very much on the down-low?"

Sam thought about it, gave a mental shrug, and said, "I can see what there is to see. What was the other thing you wanted?"

"ISS does investigations. I want to hire you—and I actually mean you, not a flunky—to do a deep background check on someone."

"Bug and MindReader can do that in two seconds."

"We already know the facts, Sam. We need something else. Personal takes on the guy, going back before he was famous."

"Famous? Who are we talking about?"

"Jason Aydelotte."

Sam almost smiled. "Is this a joke? You're calling me all the way from Israel to run a background check on Mr. Miracle?"

"Yes."

"For god's sake *why*? There are actual books written about him. Christ, Joe, he hosts the annual Christmas movie marathon on the Peacock streaming service."

"I need the truth, not the hype."

"Again . . . why?"

"Because, old buddy, I think Mr. Miracle is one scary, dangerous son of a bitch."

"Dangerous? To *whom*?"

"Maybe to a hell of a lot of people. Look, will you do this? You don't have to like me. But I need someone with the right skills and someone who I can trust."

"And you thought of me?"

"Of course I did. Just because there's some kind of weird bad blood between us, it doesn't change what I know about you, Sam."

Sam looked down at the budget reports. The numbers seemed to swirl and swim. He swiveled his chair and looked out at the bright sunlight and the puffy white clouds.

"Sure," he said. "Send me what you have so far."

"Thanks, Sam, I—"

But Sam hung up and ended the call.

CHAPTER 82
MONITORING SUITE
PIRATE LAB
UNDISCLOSED LOCATION

Jason Aydelotte was alone in his suite. A stale cup of coffee sat cooling on a side table next to the remains of a large plate of garlic knots. There were a few small coffee stains on his shirt and clumps of parmesan clinging to his tie.

"You are being reckless," said the voice of the man on the large computer screen on the desk.

"Reckless? First off, Harith al-Wazir, that's rich coming from you," said Aydelotte. "Second, sometimes you have to take some risks to make sure things move along."

Harith, leader of Al-zilal, gave a derisive snort. "Risks? Is that what you call the stunt you pulled at the Jewish hotel?"

"Lady Stern is an *Israeli* hotel. Not a Jewish one."

"They are one and the same. It is a place of sin and excess, as are all such places in *al-kiyān al-Sihyawniyy.*"

"Christ, I wish you would talk like a normal person instead of throwing around nicknames. And can't you call Israel by its name rather than the 'Zionist entity'?"

"It is an abomination in the eyes of God."

"They did own the territory long before you Arabs did, you know."

"And were rightfully chased off like the vermin they are. Cockroaches. They live there now because the United States and England bullied their way in and stole the land from people who have been living there for countless generations."

"Okay, stop the speeches," growled Aydelotte. "You go off on these rants every time we talk, and I have to tell you, they're getting old. Yes, I *get* it. You hate the Jews and feel aggrieved because they wanted to live on their own sacred lands. But that's the whole problem. No one who ever lived there has ever done so with any real peace. You Arabs, the Jews, the Christians during the Crusades. I swear to Christ there must be something in the water. It's the *Holy* Land. For all of us. Muslims, Jews, Christians."

Harith sneered. "And now who is making a speech?"

They sat and glared at each other for a few moments.

"I don't want to fight, Harith. I wish no one would."

"A peculiar thing for an arms dealer to say."

"Yeah. Sure. Maybe. Or maybe you just don't understand why I sell arms."

"Perhaps you would care to explain," said Harith.

Aydelotte sipped the tepid coffee and winced. Then he popped one of the garlic knots into his mouth and chewed noisily. He swallowed and smiled.

"Maybe I will," he said.

And he did.

CHAPTER 83
BEERBAZAAR
REHOV ETS KHAYIM 3
MAHANE YEHUDA COVERED MARKET
JERUSALEM, ISRAEL

"I appreciate your candor, David," said Mr. October.

David White was on his sixth beer now. There was a faint tingling around his eyes, and his fingertips had gone cold. He wasn't sure how much of that was the alcohol and how much was fear.

He guessed that most of it was fear.

Though was *fear* even the right word? Just talking to the boss was a few degrees hotter than terrifying. There were a lot of stories told off the record by other Tenth Legion fighters who used to work for Blue Diamond. Bad stories. Crazy, wild, fucked-up, scary stories.

David believed all of them. Every single one. Most of the guys who were in his level of Tenth Legion believed them. After all, belief was part of the job. Faith.

"Thank you, sir," said David, trying to keep his voice free of any nervous tremolo. "I'm sorry that things turned out this way. I thought we had them bagged."

"Well," said the boss airily, "to be fair, others have thought that about Ledger before. Oh, believe me when I say that I could tell you stories."

"I'd like another shot," said David, acting immediately on the lightness he perceived. "Let me handpick a team and—"

"Shhh," soothed Mr. October. His voice was soft and oily, and always with a lift as if he was smiling all the time. Or ready to laugh. David had seen those smiles and heard that laugh, and there was nothing about them that offered even a tiny bit of comfort. But then the boss said, "Don't fret. Of *course* you'll have another chance."

He almost slid off his chair. "God, *thank* you. I promise I won't drop the ball."

"David . . . ?" said Mr. October.

"Yes, sir?"

"I already have some work for you to do."

"Anything."

There was the faintest little laugh on the other end of the call. "'Anything' is a very dangerous word, David."

"I . . . I mean . . ."

"Hush now. Listen," said Mr. October. "Your work here in Israel is done. Travel information and documents will be sent to your server. You will go to your hotel, pack only clothes and toiletries. Leave behind your weapons and anything else that could connect you to what happened tonight. Keep the name 'David.' You'll have a new last name and history. Fly to America, to Georgia, where you will be met by Karen, another of our team members. She will be your number two for this operation. There is a research facility in Fort Gaines. Very small, very discreet. It will look like a Gulf service station. Karen will have the exact address."

"Georgia, sir . . . ? Don't you need me here?"

"Not at the moment, David. The hit on Ledger was a whim, an amusement. It can wait, or I can hand it off to someone else. There is a lot going on in the Holy Land right now, and it's not our game."

"I understand, sir."

"No, you don't," said Mr. October. "But that's fine. That is all yesterday's news. This other matter has come up, and it is of great importance. Very great importance to me."

"What do you want me to do?"

Mr. October said, "You will go to the facility. It is beneath the gas station. It is code-named Inferno."

"Inferno. Yes, sir."

"In that facility there is a cold-storage room. Room seventeen. You will secure the contents of that room and bring them to me. Karen will provide you with all of the weapons and equipment needed."

"Rules of engagement, sir?"

"Oh, my dear boy . . . everyone at the Inferno is a hostile and a witness. Surely you know what needs to be done."

David swallowed. "Yes, sir. I do."

"Good."

"How will I know what exactly to bring you? What does it look like?"

"It will be the only thing in that room, David. It will look like a coffin, but it is not. It will have equipment attached to it. That equipment cannot be damaged. Do you hear me on this? No damage. Not a scratch."

"I understand, sir."

"Be sure you do."

"May I ask what's inside the, um, casket?"

"David," said Mr. October, "pray to God that you never find out."

David felt his guts turn to ice water.

"And one more thing, David," said Mr. October. "And it's more of an aphorism than an explanation. It will also be the code phrase you will use when you interact with Karen and the others on the team there."

"Of course, sir," said David. "What is the code phrase?"

There was a strange hissing on the line that sounded much less like static and more like steam escaping a cracked vent. Or the warning sound a snake might make.

Mr. October said, "*Sometimes you have to burn to shine.*"

And the line went dead.

CHAPTER 84
1517 SYCAMORE AVE,
WILLOW GROVE, PENNSYLVANIA 19090

Sam Imura parked his car, got out, and stood looking at the row of homes.

There was a vacant space that made the homes look like a mouth with one missing tooth. He crossed to it because that was the address his GPS had brought him to, but the lot was odd. According to the records provided by Joe Ledger, this was where Jason Aydelotte grew up. The house had been thoroughly demolished and the lot graded flat and covered in coarse gray gravel. No weeds poked through, though, and that was odd. Who would bother to tend to weeds in a vacant lot?

The houses on that block were clean but most showed wear. A poor neighborhood clinging to its dignity. It was happening all over as housing prices soared and the recession wobbled.

He turned and walked to the closest house, the one on the left, and knocked on the door. He sensed more than heard someone behind the door and made sure he stood where someone looking through the peephole could see him. He was dressed for this, in a quiet gray wool suit, modest tie, and a briefcase. No sunglasses, despite the glare. And a smile.

Sam was not typically a genial person, and he was aware of it. The smile was deliberate so that he didn't look in any way imposing. Not too happy a smile, though—he did not want to give the impression he was there to talk about salvation or to serve papers. Just mildly happy. That was a safe zone.

There was a scrape as someone slid a security chain into place, and then the door opened one full inch. A rheumy eye peered suspiciously out at him.

"Yes . . . ?" A woman's voice. Older, suspicious, afraid.

Sam produced a business card, holding it up so she could see it.

"Good morning, ma'am," he said. "My name is Sam Imura, and I'm with *Philadelphia* magazine."

"I don't subscribe to anything."

"I'm not here for that," he said quickly. "I'm a writer."

"A writer? Here for what?"

"I'm doing background research for a feature on Jason Aydelotte, who used to live next door."

"And . . . ?"

"If you are Mrs. Harper, then I believe you were living here at the same time as the Aydelottes. I'd like to sit down and ask you a few questions."

"About him now or about what happened when his folks were here? About the fire?"

Sam gave her a very small but encouraging smile.

"The fire," he said. "Let's start there."

She thought about it and then closed the door, removed the chain, and pushed it open wider. "I had some coffee. There's still plenty left."

INTERLUDE 28

MR. MIRACLE
WILLOW GROVE, PENNSYLVANIA

FORTY-FIVE YEARS AGO

When he was nine, Jason Aydelotte thought he was an arsonist.

He'd heard the word on TV. One of those cop shows from the seventies, *Kojak, Columbo, Starsky and Hutch*, or maybe *McCloud*. Looking back, Jason Aydelotte could not remember which.

What he remembered was his love of fire. The phrase "naked flame" had intrigued him even before his body matured into a sexual awakening.

There had been a huge fireplace at his grandfather's house. Heavy oak mantle with a flowing live edge. Deep hearth with soot-smudged Italian tiles. An antique set of well-used tools, each with a distinctive hand-carved animal head—a poker with a tiger's snarling face, a cobra curling down onto the shaft of the shovel, a glaring gorilla topping the tongs, and a smiling crocodile crowning the brush. Four predators, each with rapacious hunger carved into every line.

He loved those tools, but what really drew him and held him, sitting cross-legged in front of the fire for hours on end, were those tiles. Each was unique, though clearly painted by the same artist. The Twelve Apostles, each given his own separate tile. Grandpa had told young Jason which was which. Judas was on the tile closest to the ground, only visible through the flames. Even to a nine-year-old that was a bit on the nose.

And yet . . . seeing the saints burn fascinated him.

The smiling—well, *eleven* smiling and one looking sneaky and guilty—seemed to whisper to him through the fire and smoke. He leaned in, wanting and needing to hear the secrets they told. All twelve of them.

Sometimes he would sit there with one of Grandpa's dusty old Bibles, picking a specific saint and reading his words or about his actions while cutting looks up to the flames.

He wished he had more of those tiles, but the hearth had those twelve, and everything else was some kind of decorative filigree but no other faces, no other players from the Bible. No other martyrs.

He felt bad for Judas. During his many re-readings of that story, told from various perspectives, even as a kid Jason felt the man had been given a raw deal. If the betrayal was ordained by God because the plan was to save the world through Jesus's trial and crucifixion, then how was Judas really to blame? And in movies, like that rock 'n' roll *Jesus Christ Superstar*, they showed Judas as a pretty decent guy. Just confused, misled. Desperate to force Jesus to show his power and kick Rome's ass. Then the man's horror at how that all turned out wrong because God had other plans.

Judas hanged himself.

Judas went to hell, according to his Sunday school teacher, his grandpa, and everyone else in the family. Judas, burning for all time just because he made a mistake. Just because he wanted Jesus to stop being hesitant and kick a lot of Roman ass.

It made Jason angry. The anger burned in him. Day and night. Awake and in dreams.

It made him think about doing something—anything—to release that fiery anger.

When he sat in front of the fireplace, brooding over it, he wished the flames would leap higher and burn the Apostles. He wished they would set fire to Heaven, because payback is only fair.

He dwelled on the fire. And on something Grandpa once said about how fire cleanses.

Cleanses.

Yes.

That was how it was in his dreams. Fires cleansing things that needed to be purified.

He thought about that at school—which he liked for the classes and hated for the drama of recess. Fire for schoolyard bullies, and there were always bullies. In every schoolyard, he was sure of it. The two in his school were a brother and sister: Tommy and Angie. She would always say something—about Jason's clothes, his hair, his glasses, his weight, his face. If his pants were baggy, she'd tell everyone it was to hide a diaper because he wasn't toilet-trained yet. Stupid, but it got laughs. If his cuffs were too high, then she said he was a geek, a nerd, a sissy, or too poor to buy proper clothes.

If Jason complained or yelled back; if he said something about her clothes or face . . . then Tommy would be there. Tommy wasn't a talker. Not much. He was a hitter. A shover and a kicker.

One evening after a very bad autumn day at school, Jason watched the flames and instead of Apostles he saw Tommy and Angie. Burning.

It took a week—a really bad week where Angie's tongue was as relentless as Tommy's fists—before the flames began speaking to Jason. Whispering to him. Confiding in him. Making promises.

He snuck out at two in the morning and walked the seven blocks to their house. It was no different from the one where he lived with Grandpa. No different from the house he'd lived in with Mom and Dad before the car accident took them home to Jesus.

The fire was easy to start. That autumn had been cool and dry. He'd brought a can of lighter fluid and splashed it up the wall beneath a bedroom window. It wasn't until after that he knew whose window it was. Angie's, according to the papers.

One simple strike of a match and then he was off, running as hard as he could while the night behind him transformed from black to yellow and then to a wild Halloween orange.

He was almost home before he heard the sirens.

That night, as he stood by his own bedroom window and watched the glow paint the sky and billowing smoke smother the stars, he tried to decide how he felt.

This was hours and hours before he found out that Angie and Tommy both died, burned so completely that dental records were needed to verify which was which. Their parents died, too. Smoke.

None of that truly rocked him.

But when he read in the paper that the family dog and two cats also died, and the heat boiled everything in Tommy's fish tank, that ripped him apart. He cried his eyes out.

Grandpa held him and rocked him and told him that things would be all right, told him that it was proof of his good heart that he wept for that family, even though those kids had been unkind.

But Jason didn't care about Tommy or Angie, or their parents.

It was the dog, the cats, the tropical fish. The smoke and fire had killed them, too.

He knew he would never forgive himself for that.

Never.

And Jason never set another fire.

CHAPTER 85
THE TOC

Church looked at the phone, sighed briefly, and answered.

"Unless this is crucial, Lilith," he said, "can it wait? There is a lot happening right now."

"I do not yet know how crucial this is," said Lilith, "but I feel it needed to be said, and said sooner rather than later. I will be brief."

"Very well."

"I know you have limits of what you allow yourself to believe, my love," she said, "but I have seen things with my own eyes. I will tell you this . . . watch the video of the cobras again. Watch it with an open mind. Remember the old stories. And then tell me what you believe."

"I will," he said.

"Good, and there is something else. There is a name my sisters and I have been hearing on the wind. A player whose name appears more often in conjunction with matters of importance. He calls himself Mr. October. He is feared by people who aren't easily scared. He is moving behind the scenes and may be behind the attack on Ledger and his people."

"That's useful to know."

"There's more. The latest intel—and by that I mean information that has come my way in the last hour—is that October and his Tenth Legion are no longer an immediate threat to your team."

"He is standing down? Why?"

"Not standing down," said Lilith. "From what little information I have, it's more likely he is shifting to a different project entirely."

"Are you saying that he is not the main force behind all that's going on here?"

"I never thought he was. More like a bit of friction between two unrelated cases that happen to be unfolding at the same time. The hit on your safe house might have been a miscalculation—eliminating Havoc Team because of an erroneous assumption he is here to hunt October or his people."

"Hm. So he's either learned differently, or doesn't want to draw any more attention to whatever he *is* doing."

"Or maybe a bit of both."

"Very interesting. I'll hand it over to Bug to do some deep dives. He's already intruding into some of Tenth Legion's computer networks, which may allow us to determine what October is up to. That could give us a chance to get out in front of him."

"Yes. That's the wise play."

"Thank you for this information, my love."

"There is another thing, St. Germaine," said Lilith, and he could hear some unease in her voice. "I have had terrible dreams lately. About a storm that is coming that will change the face of the world."

Church paused. "Yes. I've had the same dream."

INTERLUDE 29
PHONE CALL

EIGHTEEN MONTHS AGO

The people who knew him did not know him.

Even within Al-zilal, no one could credibly attest to having seen his face. None of them felt that was wrong or even strange. Harith al-Wazir, the Great Lion Who Digs in the Earth, did not need to be the face of the group. He was the brains and the heart; he was the voice and the fist. It was his vision and his courage that gathered up Daesh fighters whose cells had been hunted to extinction by the West, or by sympathizers like the Jews and the Syrian government. Hunted by people who had become deaf to the voice of God, whose minds had closed out all of the wisdom recorded in the Quran by the prophet Muhammad.

Harith, they all said, turned his thoughts toward heaven every moment of every day.

And yet . . .

He was a voice on a telephone, a face behind a mask, and fist in a glove.

This made the fighters of Al-zilal happy; it gave them a measure of security because the West—particularly the merciless and godless Americans—had made it a game to hunt down the leaders. Abu Bakr al-Baghdadi, Abu Ali al-Anbari, Abu Mu'Ad al-Qahtani, Abu Ibrahim al Hashimi al-Quraishi, Rakkan Wahid al Shamman, Maher al-Agal, and so many others. Heroes of the faith, martyrs of the Caliphate. They put their faces on playing cards so any soldier could win praise for having murdered one.

Harith knew that it was more important to be the heart and mind of ISIS, and not its face. When he formed Al-zilal, it was as its symbol, but he did not foolishly challenge the West to come and find him. Instead, quietly, cleverly, Harith build his new cell. Some called it a splinter, but he considered it to be a drawn sword that did not need to be inside the protective sheath of ISIS. Smaller, more easily able to pivot, stronger for its ability to react and respond at once rather than to hide and wait.

This was Harith al-Wazir. This was the Great Lion Who Digs in the Earth.

Digs, indeed.

Digs for secrets hidden by the wise long ago.

And if some of those wise men who buried those items were not of the faith, it could be overlooked because they lived and died before the prophet Muhammad ibn Abdullah was born in Mecca nearly fifteen hundred years ago. Perhaps, as so many suggested, they were guided by Allah to bury their secrets where only the Great Lion could find them.

Then Ayoob Alazaki, who *was* a more public face for Al-zilal, informed Harith that a small group of fighters, fleeing from a successful action, found a cave in Qumran containing ancient documents. Old Jewish texts, some of which were worth protecting because the Quran contained some of the same history, most notably from the Torah—the first five books of the Hebrew Bible. The scrolls were important to Islam because they contained the earliest known text of part of their history. And, since only Hebrew texts were found in the first twelve Qumran caves, with no trace at all of Christian texts, it reinforced the truth that Christianity was a false religion.

But there was so much more in Cave 13. In it, the ISIS fighters found thousands of scrolls written not in Hebrew, but in Greek and even Egyptian. Scrolls from the Library of Alexandria and elsewhere, preserved from destruction.

Harith, who was more pragmatic than most of his peers within the caliphate, knew that these documents could be sold to raise hundreds of millions of dollars to better arm and equip the fighters, and to rebuild mosques and schools and other key places in nations where the oppressed and disenfranchised needed to know that their faith would be rewarded. That their lives mattered. And that a clear path existed to holiness.

But Alazaki told Harith something else. Something he told no other.

In that thirteenth cave was a lead box, carved all over with dire warnings in Egyptian hieroglyphs. A box sealed with copper.

Upon hearing this, Harith said, "All praise Allah. What you and

JONATHAN MABERRY

your soldiers of the faith have discovered may give us our greatest weapon against the enemies of God."

"But what is it?" asked Alazaki. "How could an old box from thousands of years ago be of any value to us?"

"When the time is right, my brother," said Harith, "I will tell you."

"But—"

"Be patient. That time is coming soon. Very soon. And the Storm that comes will change the face of this world forever. I have seen this in a dream, and I know it to be true."

CHAPTER 86
INTEGRATED SCIENCES DIVISION
PHOENIX HOUSE

Doc Holliday gave Church a piercing up-and-down look. "You look like you're going to fall down."

"I'll manage," he said.

"If you say so," she said. She'd changed her clothes since earlier that day and was wearing a western shirt embroidered with cowboys roping dinosaurs, skinny jeans, and high-heeled boots with hand-tooled sunflowers. Her masses of curly blond hair were piled high and pinned in place with bright Ticonderoga pencils. Her lipstick was the only understated element of her ensemble, and that was a shade of pink a little paler than her natural lip color.

They were in her lab, with Bug sitting on a table swinging his sneakered feet. He looked like a precocious twelve-year-old. "She's right, boss," he said. "Maybe a nap?"

"Not quite yet."

"Red Bull?" Bug suggested. His eyes were red-rimmed, and his pupils were barely dots. "I have some mixed with espresso. It's awesome."

"As tempting as that is, I'll pass for now."

"Well," said Doc, "then while you're still conscious, let's take some stock and see if we have any real perspective. There's a lot of confusing and overlapping intel," she said. "Still not sure if we are doing the three-blind-men-trying-to-describe-an-elephant thing or if these cases are legitimately separate."

"Tell me as you see it," he said. "I won't hold you to anything."

She opened her mouth, lunging at that opening, but Church held up a finger.

"Don't."

"Spoilsport."

Bug looked like he was going to have a stroke trying to stifle his laughter.

"Okay," she began, "and, Buggie-baby, feel free to throw your two cents in if I miss something."

"Sure."

In a marginally more serious tone, Doc said, "We know that there's a big weapons buy going down today. Thanks to Toys we now know that Jason Aydelotte is the seller. That confirms a suspicion, though I personally find it amusing that Mr. Miracle has gone all Doctor Doom on us. Absolutely did not see that coming."

"He might not be that big a threat," suggested Bug. "Personally, I mean. We know he wants all that Scroll stuff and anything else ISIS might have looked at and only pretended they destroyed. Maybe since Aydelotte is trying to save all that stuff, either because he thinks it's really that valuable culturally or—and let's be real here—he wants to make a lot of money off it, maybe he got desperate and cooked up something huge. His version of *Breaking Bad*. From what I've read about him online, he'd do just about anything to get his hands on the most important old stuff. Who knows, maybe he's even able to justify it to himself because it's preserving history, blah, blah, blah."

"Entirely possible," said Church, though his tone wasn't convincing.

"Or," said Bug, "he might have something nasty in his backstory. Videos of him screwing church ladies, whatever. And someone found out and is turning dials on him. Using him to do crimes."

"Colonel Ledger seems to be of the same mind," said Church, and told them about Sam Imura's investigation in Pennsylvania. "With luck he'll turn up something that will provide insight."

Doc said, "We don't yet know where Aydelotte even got the items he's selling. We know that the Boko Haram ISIS subgroup in Chad hired Russo to design the guidance system for the RPGs. That's one thing, and except for what's already been sold, we have a good line on shutting that down in the future."

Church nodded. "So it would seem."

"Next time you're in with Russo," she continued, "ask him about what *else* he designed. The stuff Toys bid on wasn't the laser guidance system."

"The question has come up," said Church. "Despite being frightened and disoriented, Russo has managed to talk around that issue. He covers the evasion by giving us enormous details on other matters. Some we knew about and others that are new, but so far there are no clues as to what project he was working on most recently."

Bug nodded. "I have Yoda working on decrypting his hardware."

"What's the delay?" asked Doc. "I thought MindReader just breezed past that stuff."

"MindReader is getting old now," Bug said and sighed. "Even with the new quantum structure it's hit a few walls here and there. Russo's is by far the most sophisticated, and I think I know why."

"Pray enlighten us mere mortals," said Doc.

"Okay, so a few years ago, after the Deep Silence gig—the last DMS case before we shut down in the States and opened RTI here in Greece—we . . . um . . . *looted* the private bank accounts of a certain Vladimir Putin."

Doc beamed. "You didn't!"

"We did, and there was a lot. I bet this whole lab was underwritten by Uncle Vlad."

"It's possible," said Church quietly.

"So, after all that," said Bug, "suddenly Russia got a serious upgrade on all aspects of its computer security. Not yet sure who they hired to do it, but whoever it was knew his shit. Yoda and I have been chipping away at it, but it's top of the line. And Russo's encryption has the same kind of fingerprints that Putin has. So there's a new hotshot—or team of hotshots—out there who are pissing me off."

Doc Holliday's eyes went wide, and she pretended to be in a near-faint. "Lord-a-mercy, Big Bad Bug is admitting defeat?"

He gave her a withering look. "Defeat is not an option. Putin won one round, but I'm still me and Yoda is still Yoda, and MindReader does not like to be fucked with."

"Profound," said Church.

"Given time," continued Bug, "we'll crack it. I won't bore you with how, but I'll say this much—Putin's security is massive, complicated, and keeps getting tweaked. They anticipated counterattacks, and they probably know something about MindReader. Russo's encryption—because we actually took possession of his hardware and it's stored in a clean room with no external Wi-Fi—is static. It can't adjust to what Yoda's trying, so he'll break it."

"Before or after the sun burns down to a cinder?"

Bug looked at Church. "Will I get in trouble with HR if I call her a bitch?"

"No, sweetie, but I might put you over my knee," said Doc.

"Getting back to Aydelotte," said Church. "So far the only connection between him and Russo appears to be the laser-guidance system for RPGs. We don't yet know if his latest project in Chad is directly related. There's also the possibility that Russo designed the Gorgon weapon. I'll focus on that during our next session. Russo may not have worked directly with Aydelotte, but instead through a third party such as Boko Haram or another group within ISIS. There are a lot of rumors lately about a new and very clever, forward-thinking splinter cell known as Al-zilal."

"The Storm. Yeah," said Bug, "Nikki's seen that name pop up all over the place, but so much of it is hype and rumor. There's even a catchphrase. 'The storm is coming.'"

"What kind of storm are we talking?" asked Doc.

"No idea," said Bug. "Could be a person, an op, or a metaphor."

"We are rich in leads but poor in substantive intel," said Church. "And Aydelotte keeps popping up in unexpected places."

"Hey," said Bug with a lopsided grin, "maybe Mr. Miracle is just out of his mind. Like really crazy."

"Oh, little one," said Doc in a placating voice, "it's adorable when people who don't understand abnormal psychology try to diagnose."

"Or, maybe someone capable of objectivity is seeing a bigger picture," said Bug.

"Ouch. Stinging comeback." Doc thought about it for a moment.

"Look, I don't agree even a little about that theory, but I promise to keep it in mind, 'kay? And if it turns out this is all Mr. Miracle being crazy as a soup sandwich, then I will personally give you a foot massage."

"Um . . . sure."

"Another possibility," said Church, "is that Aydelotte came into possession of a large quantity of weapons from some source as yet unknown and is selling them to different buyers, along with some new tech that makes them more effective. That kind of product might encourage the higher echelon members of ISIS—the ones who are likely less legitimately fundamentalist and more actually political—to agree to the antiquities-for-weapons deal. One of Ohan's rivals tried that in the early 2000s. Selling former Soviet missile tech as an exclusive to three separate buyers."

"Wasn't he found crucified upside down against a wall in Istanbul?" asked Bug.

"Biblical," said Doc, "but effective."

"It sent the right message." Church took another sip of coffee. "Others have done it more successfully. Kuga in the United States a year ago leading up to the attack on the conference of governors in LaBorde. Various parties selling to Ukraine and Russia. It's been a successful business strategy in the past. Ohan was not only selling weapons to all parties in several different conflicts, he was pulling strings to keep those wars going. Kuga as well, and a dozen other arms dealers, including nations that sell arms, do it as a matter of course. Now, with Ohan dead and the Kuga organization at least temporarily gone quiet, perhaps Aydelotte—or associates of his— have decided to exploit the sales opportunities."

"Nature abhors a vacuum," said Doc. "Larceny doubly so. Bad boys like that would have sold six-guns to the Earps *and* the Clantons. Making money coming and going."

"If Aydelotte's being a bit clumsy about it," mused Church, "we might be seeing either a learning curve, or some level of incompetence. Because he's made billions in his antiquities trade does not automatically translate to being successful at something as subtle and complex as international arms sales."

Bug nodded. "That, at least, makes a little sense."

"A little," agreed Church. "But not complete sense. As I said, we are missing a lot of pieces to this puzzle. We'll keep it in the mix, though."

"Tell you what, though," said Bug. "I'd love to see the software from the Gorgon buy that's happening tonight."

"I'll pass that along to Toys."

"Yeah, about that," said Bug. "I know you're giving Toys a real shot here, what with the Wild Hunt and an actual field op, but how sure are you that he can pull this off?"

"If I had serious doubts he wouldn't be in the field."

"That is you dodging Bug's question," said Doc.

Church gave a weary half-smile. "I put Toys and his team into play because Toys knows more about that part of the black market than anyone currently working for RTI, and that includes everyone in this room. He knows it on a deeper and more personal level. Call it a practical level. We saw already how Aydelotte responded to him once he realized who Toys was. That's not the first time that's happened on this op. That part of the international terrorist network and the criminal organizations that fund and supply them *know* Toys. They still think he's one of them. That is likely to prove very useful in this and future operations."

"And if it gets him killed?" asked Doc.

Church looked at her over the rim of his cup as he finished it. "In war," he said quietly, "people die."

That plunged the room into silence. Church tossed his coffee cup into the trash and stood. "Keep on this," he said, and went out.

CHAPTER 87
MONITORING SUITE
PIRATE LAB
UNDISCLOSED LOCATION

A red light began flashing on a console, and Jason made excuses and ended his conversation with Harith. It was dangerous talking with him anyway. That kind of thing could lead to trouble.

He tapped a key, and the light went dark.

JONATHAN MABERRY

"Shock?" he said.

"I'm on site, boss. Lamech will be here in a couple of minutes."

"That's excellent. I'll stay on the line, so don't be flustered if I whisper in your ear."

She laughed. "Last time I was flustered was when my professor back in college put his hand on my thigh during a meeting in his office."

"You never told me about that. What happened?"

"I let him feel me up," she said. "Then he got a little rough and made me blow him. I did. Then after I got the grade I wanted I went to his house. He lived alone just off campus."

"Why'd you go there?"

"To kick his ass."

Aydelotte laughed. "And did you?"

"The police report said he fell down a flight of steps and broke his neck."

"Serves him right."

"That's what I told him at the top of the stairs."

"I adore you, Shock," said Aydelotte. "You know that, right? Like an uncle. Not like that professor."

"Boss," she said, "if I thought otherwise, they'd have found you at the bottom of a set of steps, too."

"And I would expect nothing less."

There was a pause. "I guess I adore you, too, Mr. Aydelotte."

"We're family," he said.

"We are."

"Now, go close the deal and then tell me what you'd like as a bonus. I have that condo in Aruba that no one's using all next month."

"Now that's how you win a girl's heart."

He ended the call and switched over to the comms system. The garlic knots were cold, so he threw them into a trash can, went and made fresh coffee, and settled down to enjoy Shock's little show.

CHAPTER 88
PRIVATE APARTMENT
PHOENIX HOUSE

"St. Germaine," Lilith said, and he thought he could hear a smile in her voice. "I knew you would call back."

"Did you," he said, not really making it a question. "Is this about Mr. October? Many things are happening," said Church. "The Middle East is in motion in ways I haven't seen before. While there are always threats, many seem to be trying to weave themselves into a single tapestry. But if that is the case, the purpose—the pattern—eludes me."

"Even with all of your resources?"

"You enjoy mocking me for my reliance on technology, my love, and sometimes you are quite correct. But other times your gentle condemnation misses the mark."

"Gentle condemnation," she repeated, then laughed softly. "You are a killer with the soul of a poet."

"Please."

"And you are calling me to accomplish what? To see if I have something corroborative?"

"In part, yes."

"Or as a sounding board?"

"Always that. As you say, I tend to view the world through one lens, and you through another. What's happening here seems to cross both of our worlds."

"Very well," said Lilith, "tell me."

He sat on a chair in his apartment. Bastion lay purring on his lap as Church used the fingertips of one hand to scratch little swirls in the cat's smoky fur. Every now and then, and not wholly on a conscious level, he traced some very old alchemical symbols. The cat did not seem to notice or care as long as he did not stop.

He told Lilith about what was happening, even the things they had already discussed, but framed with new information and revised theories. Aydelotte, the weapons deals, rumors that he might have financed or even been part of a venture to unearth the tomb of the Pharaoh Siamun, the threat of the ISIS splinter group Al-zilal, the question of who their leader Harith al-Wazir might be, the teens rescued from Chad, the ergot poisoning used on them, the strange bidder war in Aydelotte's hotel room, the cobras, and the suicides of the two scholars.

Lilith listened with patience, rarely interrupting because Church provided great detail and summed up with theories. When he was finished, Bastion was asleep, and Lilith was silent for nearly thirty seconds. He waited her out, knowing how she preferred to process things.

"What is your question?" she asked. "Are you wondering if any of these are connected?"

"I'm wondering if all of them are."

"Ah."

"Yes."

"Let me start with Harith al-Wazir."

"Why him?"

"Because my sisters who are Muslim and who we've seeded into the various communities of Islam have been hearing whispers about him for more than four years. Now, before you ask, whispers are all there are so far. What we know is that Harith has taken control of Daesh fighters who have become frustrated with constant defeats. Very dedicated fighters of the kind who *would* strap on a vest if they thought it would do some measurable good, but who don't want their lives thrown away merely to make a political statement. They would rather engage their enemies with weapons that would give them some kind of edge, which would level the playing field. *As yet*, such weapons are not in the hands of ISIS."

"As yet," murmured Church. "You leaned on those words a bit. We know, but cannot yet prove, that Aydelotte is selling high-tech versions of low-tech weapons."

"Yes, the modified RPGs. We've heard about that."

Church told her about the Gorgon warheads.

"That is one of the rumors my sisters have whispered to me," she said. "But there is more, and this is more troubling. There is talk among Daesh extremists that a lead box was found that contains secrets set aside by Allah and is to be used when the time is ripe for his warriors."

"A lead box with Egyptian hieroglyphs?"

"What? No. Inscribed with writings in Hebrew."

"Hebrew? Are you certain?"

"Of the writing? Yes. Why would you ask about Egyptian writings?"

"Because we have been hearing rumors about such a box, but with hieroglyphs, found in the tomb of Pharaoh Siamun."

"That is strange. I heard rumors of an Egyptian lead box two or three years ago and from contacts within those parts of the community that deals with antiquities. Nothing that I've heard connects that one to the Hebrew box. Nor do I think anyone would confuse Hebrew with Egyptian hieroglyphics."

"Which means there may be two lead boxes," said Church. "Now isn't that interesting."

"I will have my sisters look into it," said Lilith. "Into both."

"Do any of the rumors say what *kind* of weapon?"

"No. Just 'a weapon of great and terrible power,' which is ominous but not useful."

"Agreed."

"But . . . wait," she said, "give me a moment to think. There was something about the Egyptian box, and something else you said about it tickling that memory. Ah! Yes, I remember. The story told to someone who told it to one of my sisters is that anyone who touches the box falls under a curse."

"What kind of curse?"

"Again, no specifics except that they go mad and see the demons of air and fire."

Church looked across the room at a painting by the Egyptian surrealist Mayo. It was an original that he had bought from the artist many years ago, an early study for his masterpiece *Coups de Bâtons*. He felt something in his mind go *click*.

"Ergot," he said. "Lilith . . . I need to go. I think I will be needed in Israel."

INTERLUDE 30
MR. MIRACLE
WILLOW GROVE, PENNSYLVANIA

FORTY-ONE YEARS AGO

When he was thirteen, Jason Aydelotte thought he was a serial killer.

In the years since the fiery deaths of his grade school bullies and their family, he marveled at the fact that no one ever connected him with that arson. He was never asked, nor—he was positive—even suspected. Even after all those schoolyard bullying encounters. Which was strange to him, because the newspapers all said that the fire inspectors found clear traces of accelerant and a spent match outside. No connection between the bullying and the burning, as if cause and effect didn't matter.

But nothing.

He watched the news a lot. He read novels and true crime books about arson investigations. There was even an episode of *T. J. Hooker* back in 1983 where a former cop friend of Hooker's died in a suspicious fire. On TV and in books, the cops always figured it out.

And yet no one ever suspected him.

He knew that he wasn't an arsonist. After that fire he even stopped spending as much time staring dreamily into the fireplace. He also knew that he had absolutely no remorse about the four people who died. Not a flicker, not a trace.

It occurred to him, somewhere around his thirteenth birthday, that his lack of remorse was balanced by his lack of joy. They died. He didn't dance about it. He didn't hide under his blankets and jerk off about it.

Which meant what?

In church—and Jason was at the church a lot for sermons, community service, choir, Bible study, fellowship clubs, and more—he expected to feel the weight of divine judgment. He looked for accusation and recrimination in the eyes of Jesus and the saints, but every statue and painting and stained-glass window seemed to look at him with approval.

Meaning *what*, damn it?

That year, he bought every book he could find. A bunch of Ann Rule books—*The Want-Ad Killer, The Stranger Beside Me*—an old copy of *Helter Skelter*, Daniel Keyes's *The Minds of Billy Milligan, Son* by Jack Olsen, Truman Capote's riveting *In Cold Blood*, and Terry Sullivan and Peter T. Maiken's *Killer Clown: The John Wayne Gacy Murders*.

Looking for meaning. Looking for himself.

But none of those stories was *his* story.

He had to experiment, though, because Jason always needed to know things firsthand. He picked someone at random. A bag boy at the local A&P. Josh Fender, seventeen. A stranger to him because Fender did not go to the same junior high, was not involved in the church, had no friends in common with Jason. He was just a person. Random in every useful way.

Which made him a perfect choice.

Jason spent weeks studying him. Going into the store to make random purchases even though there was a ShopRite a few blocks closer. Loitering in the shadows thrown by trees to establish Fender's work schedule. Following him on several occasions to see where he went—home, to the park to hang out and drink beers with some buddies, to a girl's house, to the movies, to a parking lot to buy weed.

The surveillance was kind of fun, and Jason wondered if maybe he should apply to the police department when he was older. Or maybe the FBI after college.

When he decided to make his move, Jason reread sections of several of the true crime books. Learning. Always learning.

Then on a blustery March evening, when the cold wind and the threat of snow kept every sensible person off the streets, Jason began ghosting along behind Fender as the kid walked home. There was one spot—near the shell of a hardware store that had been abandoned after the owner died and the heirs hadn't yet solved their legal wrangling—where Jason made his move.

The street was dark because it was a Sunday night and everything was closed. The wind was noisy, rustling through the trees lining the far side of the street and whapping loose tin signs. Fender had headphones on and was listening to metal so loud that as Jason came up behind him, even he could hear Mötley Crüe blasting out "Shout at the Devil."

Jason swung the ball-peen hammer as Fender stepped into a puddle of shadows. His timing was good, and he had the shoulders and arm strength to do it right. The ball struck Fender above the left ear, and it felled him. He went down without a word and with no attempt to use his hands to break his fall. Down, out.

Nearly dead.

He lay there, nearly invisible in the shadows, twitching. The toes of his sneakers made a dull *thumpity-thump-thump* on the dirty concrete.

Jason was prepared. He pulled a plastic bag from his pocket and slid the bloody hammer inside. Next, he removed a roll of duct tape and made quick turns around ankles, wrists, and mouth.

He crouched there, letting his night vision blossom in the pool of shadows. Listening to the night. There was nothing except the wind.

He grabbed Fender by the ankles and dragged him over to the empty hardware store. The door had been jimmied open the previous evening and held closed by a strip of tape placed below where the eye of any passerby would naturally fall. A hip-check broke the tape, and he pulled Fender inside. A plastic tarp was spread out—laid while Jason wore gloves and a pair of shoes he got from a Salvation Army thrift store. The same shoes he currently wore. Jason rolled Fender onto the plastic, went and checked the street, then closed the door.

The young man made a soft moaning gurgle but did not wake. Jason changed quickly out of his clothes and into a set of coveralls that were also bought at the Salvation Army. Rubber gloves and a ski mask completed the ensemble. And, of course, the knives. It amazed him how one thrift store could be so convenient a one-stop shopping experience.

It took an hour to desecrate the body. The killing part was quick, but making sure the incisions and placement of internal organs matched drawings from one of the true crime books took time. Precision always does.

When he was done, Jason stripped naked and put everything into a black plastic trash bag. He put on jeans and a sweatshirt, changed into the second of two pairs of thrift store shoes, and made sure not to step on any drops of blood. The hammer, roll of tape, knives, and the photocopy of the page from the book went into the bag. He wore a second pair of rubber gloves—Playtex sold them in boxes of three—and left through the back, leaving the front door ever so slightly ajar but closing the back firmly.

He went home.

The bag of evidence was in the shed by the pool. No one would need to go in there in March. Two days later he took the stuff down to an overpass where the homeless slept, found a fifty-five-gallon drum they used for fires, poured in two cans of lighter fluid, doused the clothes and tools with a third can, tossed them in, stuffed in newspaper for kindling, lit a match, and fled.

The news story broke after five days. As it turned out, it wasn't the slightly open door that drew attention, but the smell. Even in winter things rot. Note to self.

The story was big, huge. It went regional, though, sadly, not national.

If the police ever found the stuff he'd burned and managed to connect it to a murder forty-two blocks away, that detail never hit the news. But Jason knew from the books that police and the FBI sometimes withheld details in order to weed out cranks taking credit.

As far as Jason knew, the crime went unsolved. Not even incorrectly solved.

But as the weeks passed, he felt no urge—and certainly no driving compulsion—to kill again. Not in that way, at least.

After much reflection and soul searching, he decided that he was not, after all, a serial killer. He wasn't even much of a killer, despite having ended five lives. Their deaths meant nothing, and that was telling. There was no profit in it.

Profit mattered more to him than the power of ending a life. Unless, he mused, there was some profit in that he did not yet see.

"Yet" being a word he enjoyed very, very much.

CHAPTER 89
INTERVIEW ROOM C
PHOENIX HOUSE

Russo looked up as Scott Wilson entered the room. He recoiled, crouching down on the far side of the room, wary of tricks and traps.

"Who are you?" he demanded. "Where's the other man?"

Wilson pulled out the chair and sat down at the table. He folded his hands primly and stared at the Italian electrical engineer.

"You will be talking to me today, Mr. Russo. Have a seat."

Russo hesitated, convinced there was a trick, but the stranger did not move. Finally, the younger man climbed onto his chair.

"We have been very patient with you," said Wilson. "We've been allowing you time for contemplation, for thinking it all through. You know that you belong to us now. This room is your world, though it won't be forever."

"What . . . what do you mean?"

"I mean that you have a choice, Mr. Russo. Option one is that you tell me everything I want to know, and do that today. Here, now. No stalling, no giving us great detail on some side topic as a way of preventing us from learning about other and more important things."

Russo's eyes were big and filled with anxiety.

"If you do that, then you will eventually be transferred to a minimum-security prison in Greece. You will have good food, a chance to exercise in the open air, and have access to books and cable TV."

"Greece?"

"On the other hand," said Wilson, "option two is a great deal less appealing. If you stall any longer, or if I think you're either lying to me or giving half-answers, then things will go another way." He leaned back and smiled. "I am not as friendly or as agreeable as the man who has been interviewing you. I am, in fact, not a very nice person at all. Would you like to find out the ways in which I am disagreeable?"

Russo stared at him, searching Wilson's face for clues as to what that might mean. What he saw was a bland smile and eyes that were as cold and lifeless as a mannequin's.

"Understand, Mr. Russo," said Wilson, "that nobody knows where you are. Nobody. You are dead to the world at large. You are here with us, and you belong to us. Body and soul. We can do . . . well . . . *anything* at all we want. And we are quite good at being dreadful."

Russo licked his lips like a nervous lizard. "What do you want me to say?"

"That's a start," said Wilson. "We know about the guidance package upgrades you developed for RPGs. We know about the Gorgon weapon with its multiple warheads. We know many things, Mr. Russo. Many things. You do not know what we know, so if you lie to me, or if I think you are playing some kind of game, then I will give you a little taste of what option two is like. You currently have ten fingers, ten toes, two testicles, a nose, two ears, two eyes, and a penis. In the *early* stages of option two I'll even let you decide which of those things you can live without."

The younger man's eyes went so big and round that it looked like his eyeballs would pop free of their sockets.

Wilson looked at his watch. "You have exactly five seconds to begin telling me what you were working on. I want information on the teenagers in Chad. And on anything you might feel will prevent me from calling in the two guards outside who have the tin snips and the bone saw. Four seconds. Three . . ."

"Okay!" cried Russo. "God, please, I'll tell you everything."

"You haven't yet. Two, one . . ."

"Shiva!" cried Russo. "I'll tell you about Shiva. And Blind Eye. I'll tell you all about that, too."

"Start now or tell me between screams, Mr. Russo."

CHAPTER 90
ARKLIGHT SAFE HOUSE
KIRYAT MALAKHI, ISRAEL

I couldn't sleep. The voices in my head kept nagging me, so I gave it up and went downstairs. Violin was in the kitchen, but I settled in the living room to make a couple of calls.

"Bug," I said when he answered, "what are the chances of us getting the original video camera and files from the cobra attack?"

"You psychic?" he said with a laugh. "I made that request right away, and it's already here. Yoda is working on it."

"Awesome. Find anything yet?"

"Too soon. We just got it a couple of hours ago, and we've been busy with that thing Toys is doing. There's a deal going down."

"Yeah, yeah, bully for him. Make sure Yoda stays with it."

"Sure. You have anything in particular you want him to look for?"

"I do. It's a digital recorder, right? Not tape?"

"Tape? What century are you living in?"

"Okay, not sure how to phrase this in technical terms, but I want to know if there's a hard drive on it."

He rattled off the brand name and model of a military video recorder and told me more about how they worked than I needed or wanted to know. When he paused for a breath, I said, "That's great. Is there some way to see if the file sent to us matches the one on the hard drive in every measurable way?"

"Easy."

"Okay, then let me ask . . . can someone hack into that hard drive and somehow replace that file?"

"We don't use 'hack' anymore."

"I don't care, Bug. Really. Not even a little bit. Can it be done?"

"Joe, we use MindReader to do that every day."

"Okay, that's what I mean. Can anyone *else* do it? Could someone have hacked into the video system at the base and either revised the original feed or replaced it?"

"Other than us?" I heard him making little *hmmm*ing noises. "Sure. It can be done. But the process isn't easy. They'd need to have a prerecorded file ready to upload, which would be impossible given that this was a CIA op and it went bad in a locked room."

"Impossible literally? Or just improbable?"

"Right in between those two."

"Could you do it?"

"If I knew that interrogation was about to happen? If I knew who all was going to be in the room? And if I had really good, ultra-high-res three-D, three-sixty-view video files of all three men?"

"Yes."

"Sure."

"Now don't take this the wrong way, Bug, but if you can do it, isn't it possible that there is someone else who can do it?"

He was silent for a moment. "All of the top visual effects people in Hollywood could do it. We're talking companies like Industrial Light and Magic, WETA Digital, Animal Logic, Blue Sky Studios, DreamWorks Animation . . . places like that. And there are some pirate code monkeys out there working with off-book FX labs to do deepfake stuff for political groups. There are definitely some guys at DARPA who might be able to do it. And maybe five or six cats like me who could do it."

"Then maybe we should start looking at that."

"No, you're missing the point . . . the actual manipulation of the video is one thing. That's deepfake, like I said. Remember when they put Princess Leia at the end of *Star Wars: Rogue One*? That was rudimentary compared to what they can do now. *Doing* it isn't the issue, it's the timing. The only real way to do it would be to have the video file with the effects already done and ready to upload so it can overwrite the actual video being recorded in the moment. That all happened unexpectedly, and people were watching from another room."

"Watching through a two-way mirror or on a monitor?"

There was silence. "Monitor."

"That's what I thought."

"No, no, you're going down the wrong street here. There was a third guy in the room. He was an eyewitness to it. And there were the snakebites."

"Who's interviewed that third man?"

"Supervisors from the Agency."

I said nothing and let Bug work it out.

"Shit," he said, and hung up.

INTERLUDE 31
MR. MIRACLE
WILLOW GROVE, PENNSYLVANIA

THIRTY-NINE YEARS AGO

When he was fifteen, Jason Aydelotte thought he wanted to be a preacher.

Church had always been an important part of his life. Even before he spent all those hours staring at Apostles through the flames. Like a lot of kids, he was raised in the church. His parents had taken him there since he was a baby, and encouraged him to participate in Sunday school, Bible study, and other things when he was little. After they died, Grandpa kept it up. Grandpa had been a devoted member of the church since he was a kid, too.

Grandpa and both his parents had visited other countries as part of evangelical outreach, building churches and teaching from the Bible for villagers throughout Africa, Central Asia, and South America. It was an easy equation for them—come to church, accept Jesus as savior, and in return reap the benefits of food, fellowship, and even some healthcare.

Jason felt pretty cynical about a lot of that, but he did believe in God. His favorite stuff, though, was in the Old Testament. Jesus was great and all, and Jason said his prayers, but God was a badass. The God of the Old Testament kicked ass and took names. He was unforgiving, inventive, murderous, and demanding. Jason could appreciate all of those qualities. He loved the fundamentalist preachers, really digging the fire and brimstone, the thunder and sheer power of sermons. He loved the variations—from snake handlers to revival tent healers to mega-church crowd-pleasers. It was grand. It was entertaining.

He wanted that kind of power.

To walk up to a pulpit or onto a stage or even the front of a tent and know that every eye was on him, that every ear was straining to hear whatever he said. To know that the hearts of the people there were beating fast because they knew they were in the presence of a shepherd, a guide, a voice that spoke with thunder.

He wanted that very, very much.

When he told his grandpa, the old man sank to his knees, clasped his hands together, and praised God even as tears choked his voice. The preacher at their church hugged him. If the hug was a little too close and lingered a little too long, that was fine. Jason did not think it was any kind of come-on. No. He reckoned that the crushing force of the hug was an expression of resentment and even a little fear. Like an old lion pretending to tolerate the upstart who had just gone through one hell of a growth spurt.

Even so, the preacher—Brother Michael—did not try to dissuade him. Rather the reverse, he encouraged Jason to think big, not to become merely another preacher in the neighborhood, but to go out into the field, to other countries, to build a church where there wasn't one. In other words, anywhere but in that city.

Brother Michael arranged for a fundraiser to allow Jason to go to a summer Bible camp that was designed to prepare teens for the heavy responsibilities of ministry. And there, Jason flourished. That first summer was about him making sure he knew the name of everyone of importance, from the camp director down to the newest camper.

The second summer, between tenth and eleventh grade, was about practicing his showmanship. He went to every sermon by every minister who visited the camp up there in the Poconos. Jason took copious notes, spent hours reliving the sermons, and in the privacy of his tiny cabin, he practiced the postures and movements, using well-placed mirrors to watch himself, drawing faces on paper plates and positioning them so he could turn and practice the techniques of inclusion. When he was sure no one could hear him, he recorded himself repeating key phrases from the Bible and from those sermons, and then played them back, re-recorded many times, until he knew where to lean on words or syllables, where to put dramatic pauses in the middle of key points, when to match words and eye contact.

He gave his first trial sermon as part of that second summer's farewell festival. The crowd went crazy. Four weeks later the letters started arriving from tent revival promoters who wanted to interview him. Within five months he was doing weekend sermons, first as a kind of opening act for bigger ministers; and then—before senior year—he was filling tents and halls all by himself. And getting a cut of the take from the believers.

He was three days shy of seventeen when he made his first million.

By the time he was thirty he had that many millions in the bank, and that was just the liquid cash. In college he'd worked on a split major of world religion and business, with minors in marketing and sales.

God had been very good to Jason Aydelotte.

It was kind of a shame that along the way he had very personally and very quietly stopped believing in the Almighty.

CHAPTER 91
EDUCATIONAL BOOK WAREHOUSE
ASHDOD, ISRAEL

Lamech opened the door of his vehicle and stepped out, holding his hands away from his body and moving with the exaggerated care of a professional who has done this sort of thing before. He opened the flaps of his sport coat to show the holstered Glock snugged into a nylon shoulder holster.

The warehouse was medium-size and smelled of moldy old paper and rat droppings. Although the lights were off, Shock made sure that the overhead fans were running. They helped with the stink and also provided enough background noise to foil any long-range microphones. It was a standard tactic in her profession, like talking in a hotel bathroom with the shower turned on or walking along the beach as a noisy tide thundered in. Unless one of the parties was wearing a wire, ordinary conversation was unlikely to be recorded or even monitored.

She stood waiting in front of one of her vehicles. Its headlights were off, but two other cars were parked at angles so that their lights created an obvious meeting place. On either side of her were big, unsmiling men, each of whom had an automatic rifle slung from the shoulder, the barrels turned vaguely in Lamech's direction. Two of Lamech's men likewise flanked their boss. They had rifles, too. Like the others, their guns made eloquent statements without starting arguments. There was an air of tension in the air but not of actual hostility.

"Mr. Lamech," she said brightly. "Pleasure to finally meet you."

Lamech gave her a terse nod. "You're Shock, yes?"

"I am."

The Israeli glanced around, looking at the other men Shock had waiting at the edge of the pool of light. "Where is Aydelotte?"

"*Mr.* Aydelotte doesn't run his own errands," said Shock.

"He did earlier."

"Oh, please, let's not confuse sales with shipping."

"You're saying he's not coming?"

"He sent me instead. Is that going to be a problem?"

"I don't like this," said Lamech.

Shock gave him her most charming smile. "I don't really care, though. If you don't want what I brought, then we can all go home and call it a night."

"This is irregular."

Shock took a few steps forward. "Is this because you have to deal with a woman? If so, then that's on you. I'm Mr. Aydelotte's voice for this exchange. Take it or leave it."

"Please get your employer on the phone. I want to hear this from him."

In Shock's ear, Aydelotte said, "You can tell him where to stick that."

Shock smiled. "To be clear, Mr. Lamech, I don't need my boss's permission to close this deal. And you don't need his reassurance. Either you want to make this deal, or you don't. The deposit is non-refundable, as you well know."

"What if I decided to simply take what I paid for?"

Shock's smile grew. "Then we'd all have a bad night. Your people wouldn't get the weapons. Maybe my boss would have to train someone to replace me. Your crew would definitely have to replace you, because if you fuck with me, you'll be the first to drop. Or don't you think that little red dot on your chest means anything?"

Lamech did not look down at the pinprick of red laser light that trembled above his heart. He had too much personal dignity for that, and Shock had to give him points for it. Not that it would change the outcome. If he twitched, her man up in the rafters, the one wrapped in a canvas shroud that made him blend into the dark gray-black shadows, would punch his ticket. Probably get both of the guards, too. The sniper, who had the genuine but unfortunate last name of Boop, did not miss.

She waited to see how the Israeli would play it. There was a curl of annoyance and contempt on his mouth, but he did not act on it. Instead, he said, "I will need to inspect the merchandise."

"Sure thing," said Shock. "You want it on the truck or on the floor?"

"On the floor, if you please. No offense, but I prefer to inspect everything out in the open so there are no misunderstandings about what is being bought and paid for."

"No offense taken." Shock snapped her fingers, and six of her men broke ranks, slung their rifles, and began off-loading long metal boxes. They brought them to the halfway mark between Shock and Lamech and laid them in a neat row. One of them went from box to box to flip up the latches and open the lids. The whole process took about four minutes. No one relaxed at all during that time. Shock waved her men back.

"Go ahead and check them out."

Lamech gave her another small sneer, but he came and looked. He spent five minutes checking that everything promised was there. When he was done, he straightened.

"And the technical specifications?"

"They will be sent as soon as the balance of the deposit is transferred," said Shock. "They work exactly like an RPG with two exceptions. See this thing here? That little gizmo attached to the housing? That's a receiver hardwired to the GPS built in each shell. You can operate it from any cell phone as long as you input the sending phone number on that little keypad. That way the person directing the shot doesn't actually have to be the person handling the weapon. It's not point-and-shoot like an RPG, and it isn't heat-seeking like infrared stuff like Stingers. It's easier. You can get GPS coordinates from any source from a text message to Google Maps. Doesn't matter. Once the coordinates are on your phone, you punch in the code for the individual weapon. See there? Each one has its own seven-digit code. Once fired, the missile will find the target as long as the range is not greater than two miles. The only danger is to the guy firing the device, because he has to get out of that two-mile range to avoid electronic detection. But the person sending the signal could be anywhere in the world as long as there's cell service."

She paused for questions. Lamech had a few, but it looked like asking them of a woman not only hurt his mouth but his whole face. Shock was amused but made sure she didn't show it.

"Very well," said Lamech. "This is acceptable."

"Delighted to hear it." Shock produced her cell phone and opened the page for Aydelotte's numbered account. "We're ready when you are."

Lamech removed his own cell from his jacket pocket and began punching in numbers. Shock waited patiently, and then her own phone pinged to tell her that the transfer went through.

"Mr. Lamech," she said, "it's been a pleasure."

The Israeli smiled thinly as he tucked his phone into an inner pocket of his jacket. When he withdrew his hand, he held a small leather ID case. He flipped it open and held it up in front of Shock's face.

"On behalf of Mossad Merkazi le-Modiin ule-Tafkidim Meyuhadim," he announced loudly, "I am arresting you for illegal weapons trafficking."

The backs of all three of his vehicles sprang open, and armed agents poured out. Many more than Shock expected. Many more than Toys expected. They had badges hung around their necks on lanyards and automatic weapons snugged into their shoulders. Shock's men brought their own guns up, but they were outnumbered three to one. The Mossad team spread out in a ring of gun barrels and hard eyes.

Shock gaped. She fought for something to say and only managed a single word: "What?"

Outside, sirens suddenly tore the night air to shreds.

In her ear, Jason Aydelotte said, "What?"

Far above, crouched over his sniper rifle, Rugger said, "What?"

In the shadows inside and to the right of the side door, Dingo and Toys both said, "What?"

Hundreds of miles away, in the TOC, Scott Wilson choked on a mouthful of tea, dropped his cup, and yelled, "*What?*"

And it was at that precise moment that one of the mullioned windows high up on the east wall exploded inward, spraying glass and bits of metal as something punched through. Everyone cried out and crouched, with many of the guards on each side diving for cover.

There was a soft *crump* but no fireball. No shrapnel. Just a fall of delicate pieces of plastic and a spray of moisture whose droplets were caught by the overhead fans and whipped throughout the warehouse.

Toys stared up at it.

"What the bloody hell . . . ?" he breathed.

And then everything went to hell.

CHAPTER 92
EDUCATIONAL BOOK WAREHOUSE
ASHDOD, ISRAEL

Shock and Lamech both looked up. The look of complete surprise was identical on both of their faces.

Their men looked up. The broken window glass and pieces of plastic rained down, but everyone was able to move out of the way. Everyone in the warehouse was spattered with the mist. Shock wiped at her face and looked at her fingers. They were wet, and there was the faintest tint of amber.

Lamech regained his composure very quickly. "Weapons down. Right now. Hands on your heads, fingers laced."

That, at least, was what he intended to say. It's what his mind told his mouth to say. His lips and tongue even began forming those words.

What he actually said was, "It's early spring when the horses do that."

For a moment those words echoed throughout the empty old warehouse. Shock turned slowly to stare up at him, her face a mask of comprehensive confusion. Lamech heard his own words. His face took on a puzzled expression. He tried it again.

"It's never summer when the horses *do* that."

Shock said, "What?"

It came out wrong. It came out as, "Eleven . . . ?"

"God damn it, Mother," roared Lamech, "your face is full of ants. Do you know that? It's not normal."

Shock wiped the moisture off on her shirtfront. With the other she drew her pistol.

"Well," she said boldly, "there's no coffee in the freezer. Here's a goldfish."

Then she shot Lamech in the throat. The bullet punched through the softness of skin and cartilage and then burrowed a trench between the fourth and fifth cervical vertebra. His eyes went wide and dark; his mouth opened to say something profound about the nature of life, law enforcement, criminality, and God. He said none of those things and instead fell backward, striking the back of his skull on the concrete, splashing blood around him in a wide halo that painted Shock's shoes in shades of dark crimson and scarlet.

One of the Mossad agents yelled something, but it wasn't in any language Shock knew. He ran at her, his rifle held above him like a club. She did not move her body, but her head turned to watch as he raced past and began wailing on the hood of one of the cars.

"*Narish eyzl!*" he roared, saying it over and over again.

Shock looked down at her hand and blinked in surprise to see that she no longer held a gun. Instead, there was a mutilated fetus resting in her palm, its destroyed little body gleaming with mucus and blood. She shrieked and flung it from her. Or tried to. It was dead, but its small, twisted hands gripped the base of her thumb. As she watched in total horror, the malformed mouth opened and tiny teeth—fangs— curved downward from the gums and sank into her thumb. The pain was so intense, so exquisite that it made her scream. A moment later she had an orgasm so overwhelmingly powerful that it dropped her to her knees.

There was gunfire everywhere, but the bullets whanged and banged off cars and concrete walls and missed everyone who could bleed.

Toys, watching, stared at the scene as if the world had gone suddenly and completely mad.

"The fuck's going on in there, boss?" gasped Dingo.

"I . . . I don't . . ." began Toys and then to his horror realized that he could not construct the rest of that sentence. He gagged and touched his face but jerked his hand away when he could not find his mouth. Not teeth or tongue or lips or anything. He tried to scream but all he made was a pointless muffled groan.

He whirled toward Dingo, but the Australian wasn't there. Instead, Toys squatted next to a seething, writhing, twisting, and roiling pile of maggots. Huge ones. Each was two or three inches in length. Mushroom-colored, with snapping little mandibles.

He wanted to scream so badly—he *needed* to—but he had no mouth at all.

Ari, Lamech's second in command, stood exactly where he had been when things went crazy. He held his rifle in both hands, but he was terrified to use it. All around him the air kept flashing with white-hot lights as moths swirled and swirled and then exploded into tiny fireballs. Ari knew that if he took a step in any direction the moths would see him. He was only safe while he stood where he was. His bladder failed him first, but he endured the warm run of urine down the inside of his left trouser leg. Even when his bowels began to empty in a fierce fire-hose discharge of diarrhea he kept stock still.

All the time he recited prayers. Or at least he thought they were prayers. They felt like prayers in his mouth. They felt like prayers on his lips. He heard someone nearby singing and did not for a moment believe it was his own voice. He heard the voice sing the lyrics in Yiddish and then English. The same refrains.

"*Patshe, patshe kikhelekh, mame 'et koyfn shikhelekh, tate 'et koyfn ze-kelekh, un Ari 'et hubn hobn royte bekelekh.*"

Then . . .

"Clap, clap little cookies; Mother will buy shoes, Father will buy socks, and Ari will have rosy cheeks."

Switching back and forth.

As the moths swirled around him and died in balls of brightly colored flame.

Shock crawled along the floor, feeling her insides turn to greasy sludge.

She looked back only once and saw that she was leaving a glistening trail behind her, but not the clear and silvery trails made by snails, but a wavering, too-red line of blood. Her body shuddered over and over again with one intense orgasm after another. They were not in any way pleasant, but rocked her, tore through her, exhausted her. She kept falling over, and each time it took more of what little strength she had left to get back onto her knees.

Dingo saw Toys clawing at his face, and he dropped to his knees and tried to help him.

He grabbed Toys by the front of his shirt and began laughing in his face. In his mind he was asking what was wrong and how he could help. But the laughter filled his mouth and the air and the moment. The laughter rose and rose until it was a piercing shriek. Dingo could not understand why Toys wouldn't answer him. After all, his team leader had a dozen mouths. They kept appearing all over his skin. Even on his clothes. Long, forked snake's tongues lolled out—fighting and wrestling with one another as Toys screamed.

Dingo begged him to explain what was going on, but someone was laughing too loud for him to be heard.

Skiver and Armani heard shrieks and laughter coming through on the comms.

"Christ," breathed Armani, "what's going on in there?"

Skiver touched his earbud. "Skiver to Grendel, there's something wrong. Hearing gunfire. We're going in."

"Proceed with caution," advised Grendel. "Lamech is hereby designated as a friendly. He's with Mossad."

"Mossad?" gasped Armani. "What the hell?"

They ran toward the building.

The group of Mossad agents and the rest of Shock's men were wandering around the warehouse. Those who were not already dead. The injured ones—and that was the majority of each team—dealt with their pain and confusion in uniquely different ways.

One of the agents stood facing the side of an SUV. He did not move at all. He held his breath for as long as he could, until his face flushed a dangerous red and veins stood out on the side of his neck.

JONATHAN MABERRY

When he could no longer hold the stale air in, he exhaled until his lungs were completely empty, then dragged in another huge double lungful of air and held it in. Blood vessels began bursting in his eyes.

Two of Shock's men faced each other in a terrible gun battle, though neither had a weapon in their hands. They each screamed, however, as they felt the agony of rounds tearing into them.

An agent had stripped down to his skin and ran back and forth, pausing now and then to punch himself in the face. Then he would run a long lap. Punch. Lap. Punch. After the fifth blow his hand was puffed so thoroughly it looked like an overinflated balloon. And he left pieces of teeth behind him as he ran.

One of the women on Shock's team was on her knees, trying to bite through the metal cover of one of the cases in which the Gorgon rockets were stored.

Nearby, a longtime employee of Jason Aydelotte who acted as foreman for the team of guards sat cross-legged on the ground. He had removed all of the bullets and was slowly, methodically swallowing each one. They tasted like honey. When he was out of bullets, he looked around for more . . . saw a fallen AK-47, crawled to it, and removed the banana clip. His fingers trembled with nervous tension fueled by hunger as he popped all thirty rounds out. When he had them all in his palms, he began swallowing those. He appreciated the subtle differences in taste and wondered if the honey on those bullets was from bees from another part of Eden.

Rugger, high in his perch among the shadowy rafters, saw the orcs of Mordor closing in around Toys and Dingo. He did not for one moment question the sanity or reality of this. The orcs were there, and they wanted the One Ring.

And so he said, "No, you damn well don't!"

He began firing.

His first round hit one of Shock's men—one of the bigger orcs, one of Saruman's new breed, the Uruk-Hai of Isengard—and the high-velocity round blew its head apart. The orc fell and exploded into bats. Rugger thought that was wonderful. He fired again. And again.

He saw Toys crawling, but he was glowing from within, which meant he probably had the Phial of Galadriel inside his shirt.

Awesome. But there was an orc about to bite him, so Rugger shot it in the chest.

Dingo never felt the bullet that killed him. His last thought was a simple one. He was thinking about Jennifer Hoffer, the first girl he'd ever kissed, back when he was thirteen, back home in Adelaide.

All he felt was a push that made him sit down. He could taste Jennifer's sweet, tentative kiss. Her strawberry-flavored lip gloss. The Coca Cola on her breath. He was acutely aware of her small breasts pressed against his chest. It was such a sweet memory, and as he fell backward the memory became his only reality. He died with a smile on his lips.

Toys fished for a knife to cut himself a new mouth, but something wet slapped him across the face. He pawed it out of his eyes. Red? Red paint? Tomato sauce? Something like that. Odd, though, because it smelled like copper.

He turned and saw a man sprawled on the ground. Smiling, but dead.

"Sebastian?" he cried, only vaguely aware that he now had a mouth again. He crawled toward Sebastian Gault. "I'm here, Sebastian. I have you. I'll take care of you."

Bullets struck the ground, but none of them hit him. Not that he cared. He thought it was rain.

Armani and the other members of the Wild Bunch slipped into the warehouse quietly and quickly. Zombie, who had met them at the door, took point and rushed inside, his rifle up and out.

The inside of the warehouse was not a slaughterhouse. Or not only that. It was a madhouse, and that was its most defining aspect. People were staggering or crawling, screaming or laughing, beating at themselves or biting each other, crumpled in pools of blood or slowly undressing. Some of them still held their guns, but most seemed to have forgotten how to use them.

"Grendel," cried Armani, "something's wrong. Are you seeing this?"

"Get the rest of the team out of there," ordered Wilson. "Do it *now!*"

"Copy that," breathed Armani. He turned to the others. "Find Toys and—"

But Zombie drove a knife into Armani's mouth as he spoke.

"Don't *even* try and tell me that it's not Tuesday, you pig fucker," said Zombie as he twisted the blade this way and that. "I wasn't born in a manger."

As Armani sagged back, Skiver leaped at Zombie and began biting him on the thighs, the hips, the groin, the arms.

Zombie looked down at him, nodding with each bite. "That's Tuesday right there. That's Tuesday for sure."

Several of the Mossad agents were dancing.

Each of them was unaware that anyone else danced alongside them. The individual agents were lost in dreams of their own construction. One of them was back in high school, dancing with Ruth, his first crush. He held her and they turned slowly as Snow Patrol sang "Chasing Cars."

Nearby but in another universe, an agent was twisting and jumping with a frenetic dance that followed no rhythm or pattern, but which engaged every single muscle to its limits. Sweat poured down his body, soaking his clothes, pooling in his shoes. The dance was all. The dance was everything. And he was terrified to even try to stop.

Two others danced facing each other, though they did not see their fellow agents. One jumped and moved, pulling bits of moves from Michael Jackson, Netta Barzilai, Bruno Mars, and Sarit Hadad. The other was waltzing the way he learned in ballroom classes he took back when he thought he would marry Esther Cohen. It was going to be *their* dance at the wedding. Did he ever marry her? Were the kids at home theirs? He could not quite remember.

Once Shock realized that she no longer had the fetus and that her hands were free, she reached for the open door of one of the cars and used it to pull herself up. She caught sight of herself in the side-view mirror, and for one fragment of a second her mind was clear. Insight was sharper than any knife. She knew what this was. She knew what was happening.

She crouched there in total terror as awareness drew its scalpels and began to cut. This was the weapon. This was what Dr. Conti had been working on these last couple of years. This was what Shock herself had been field-testing all through the Middle East.

This was ergot. This was Shiva.

But how?

She had not brought any of that weapon with her. Not her nor any of her team. Why would they? Even though all of the field tests were completed and Conti had declared the effects a success, Jason said that he had not yet decided where or when to use it.

When she had pressed him on it, he'd admitted that he meant to sell it to select buyers but that it would take weeks or even months to make any decisions on whom he could trust with it.

In a flash of horrible clarity Shock realized that Jason had lied to her. About this and possibly about many things. He never planned on selling it. And he had decided to use it on . . .

"No," she said out loud. That made no sense; the logic of it collapsed immediately under the weight of its own implausibility. This was Jason's deal. Her team was more than enough security. Why would Jason send the weapon here without telling her? Had he suspected Lamech was Mossad? Maybe, but so what? That didn't solve it, either. He could have canceled the whole buy. He could have called Shock to warn her.

Jason hadn't done any of those things.

And yet no one else had the weapon.

Did they?

The room was beginning to lose substance. And she felt ants begin to crawl out of her pores. They scuttled all over her face, over her eyelashes, into her nostrils, in her ears.

"No," she said, as the last insight crumbled once more into unreality. "Jason, no . . ."

Her voice was so soft, so faint, that no one else heard her. And every time she said "Jason" it came out as "Daddy."

She struggled to keep her grip on that clarity as she pulled herself into the car and started the engine. There was a man crawling on the floor in front of her. A stranger. Young, handsome, slim. She had no idea who he was, but he hadn't been party to this shit show of a business deal. Had *he* brought Conti's weapon here? Was he the one?

"I'll bake you some goddamn bread," she yelled at the top of her voice as she put the car in gear. With the last fading fragment of clarity, she knew—absolutely knew—that her mind was tumbling off its perch. Tears filled her eyes and rolled down her cheeks.

Then she stamped down on the gas.

Toys held Dingo in his arms and rocked him back and forth, heartbroken that Sebastian Gault had left him yet again. First time was when the geothermal venting blew Amirah's lab apart in the Helmand Province of Afghanistan as the *seif al din* project burned down to nothing, thanks to Joe Ledger and Mr. Church. Then Sebastian had fallen in love with Hugo Vox's insane mother—the Goddess, as she called herself—and the two of them were blown to pieces aboard a yacht. What was left of Sebastian orchestrated the Predator One gambit that nearly killed the president of the United States, but this time Joe Ledger killed him. Burned him alive.

And yet here he was. *His* Sebastian. Dying in his arms.

"I'll take care of you," promised Toys. "I won't let anyone hurt you this time. I love you, Sebastian. You know that. I always have. Please stay with me. Don't leave me again. God, please don't leave me again."

He only looked up when he saw the headlights of the car rushing toward him.

CHAPTER 93
THE TOC
PHOENIX HOUSE

The TOC did not pause for astonishment. No one sat and stared. No one gaped as images of madness filled the screens. They were not those kinds of people.

Instead, they were working with furious efficiency.

Scott Wilson was on the phone with Mossad, telling the section chief that they knew that Lamech was one of their senior agents and that his entire crew was in terrible danger.

"No, sir," he said crisply, "I do not know the precise nature of the bioweapon, but my science chief believes it is a weaponized form of ergotism. Yes, of course, let me put her on the phone."

Doc Holliday snatched the phone from him and laid into an explanation of what ergotism was and what could be done. Meanwhile,

Wilson was using long-established contacts within the Israeli government to request emergency services.

Bug had his entire team working on controlling any messaging as it happened so that Toys and his people would be treated as friendlies under the influence of a toxic substance. MindReader Q1 smashed through layers of security around social media so that it was positioned to intercept and reframe any posts. He used pre-written tapeworm scrubbers to look for and modify any graphics that would show the faces of the team members.

Mr. Church, still in the back of the room, had given up trying to contact anyone on the Wild Hunt. It was clear they were compromised. His next call was to the Arklight safe house in Kiryat Malakhi.

CHAPTER 94
EDUCATIONAL BOOK WAREHOUSE
ASHDOD, ISRAEL

The car very nearly hit Toys.

Shock tried. But there were so many giraffes in the way, and she couldn't bear to kill them, or even hurt any. So she veered and slewed and spun out, fishtailing with such force that the rear fender caught a Mossad agent on the hip and hurled him through the air. The agent slammed into Toys with such force that they both slid a dozen feet across the concrete. The agent was dead meat and felt like he weighed a thousand pounds.

Toys found that very comforting. It was nice to be back at Sebastian's chalet in Switzerland, in his usual bed, with a pile of nice quilts over him as snow fell outside. Maybe later he could talk Sebastian into making a snowman with him.

He smiled at that thought.

Then he heard a commotion and peered out from under the very heavy blanket of cooling flesh and saw a group of beekeepers running across the floor. At least he thought they were beekeepers. They each wore white coveralls and had oversize hats with broad visors that showed their faces. Toys wondered if all beekeepers had such luxuriant beards.

The beekeepers clustered around the row of metal cases. What had been in them, Toys wondered? Games? Food? Extra skin so Sebastian could cover up his burns? All of that seemed likely.

He watched the beekeepers lock up the cases and carry them away out of sight. He thought they were going outside. That made sense. Bees lived outside.

One of them paused by the door and looked around. Toys thought the man was smiling. Well, why shouldn't he be? Everything was so lovely here in Switzerland. All the snow. The healthy skiers. The cheerful fire crackling in the hearth.

"I love this place," said Toys. Then, much louder, hoping the last beekeeper would hear him, "I love you! You're as yummy as choc ice!"

The beekeeper studied him for a very long time. Days, at least. Then, still smiling, the beekeeper turned and left.

CHAPTER 95
ARKLIGHT SAFE HOUSE
KIRYAT MALAKHI

We stood around like people turned to statues as we listened to Church tell us about what was happening to the Wild Hunt.

To their credit, not one of them made a joke. No one threw jabs at Toys or his team. They, like I, were acutely aware that it could have been us. And, had I not been off campus after the Darkness thing, it probably *would* have been us.

"Tell us what you need," I told Church.

"Ashdod is close, Outlaw. I need you on-site."

Before I could say anything, I saw Remy running for the door that connected the house to the garage.

"We don't have HAMMER suits," I said.

Violin interrupted. "We have hazmats. Plenty of them."

Without waiting for me to ask, she hurried off down into the cellar. Bunny and Belle went with her.

"Grendel is on with Mossad," said Church. "He's negotiating with them to contain the scene and allow us to extract our people."

"Mossad *agrees* to that?"

"They will," said Church. "Ashdod is seventeen minutes from your location. Be there in ten."

I was already running for the car.

Ten minutes?

"Remy," I roared as we piled in, "run lights. Break laws. Get us the fuck to Ashdod."

We blasted out of the garage and into the night.

CHAPTER 96
STAGING AREA OFF ROUTE 574
BETWEEN KIBBUTZ BARAI AND KIBBUTZ MA'ANIT
NORTHERN ISRAEL

Ayoob Alazaki waited for the call. Every ten minutes he looked at his watch and was disturbed to see that only one minute had passed. He wanted to fidget, to complain, but he did not allow himself that luxury.

They will call any minute now, he told himself.

The men of his team—two dozen of the best, brightest, and most reliable fighters of Al-zilal—were demonstrably calmer. They stood or sat. They nibbled at their rations or drank coffee from thermoses, or even napped. Their weapons were cleaned and loaded and ready. Each of them had participated in prayers, and some continued to pray within their own envelopes of privacy.

When the call came through, Alazaki nearly screamed. He snatched up his cell phone, engaged the scrambler, and answered.

"The weapon is perfect," said Harith al-Wazir.

"It worked?" cried Alazaki and then, realizing his men had all turned to him, he added, "Praise God."

"Praise God indeed," agreed Harith. "And with the blessings of Allah, you may proceed. As we hoped, all eyes are now turned toward Ashdod. The police and military are focused there. Mossad is there, and some other group. I believe they are the Alchemist's people."

"The Alchemist? I thought he was long dead."

"No," snarled Harith. "He endures while those who are righteous fall. He is a plague who wears the disguise of a man. He has revealed himself and has aligned his goals with those of our enemies. He is Satan's fist on Earth."

"Then may he and all those who stand in his shadow wither and die," said Alazaki.

"Indeed." He paused. "The Storm is coming, my friend. It is almost here."

Alazaki rose, and his men rose with him. Everyone was smiling. They had trained for this, prepared for this, and now the moment was here.

"Let us pray," said the schoolteacher.

And they did—praying for God's mercy and guidance, praying for strength and the courage to change the world forever.

CHAPTER 97

EDUCATIONAL BOOK WAREHOUSE
ASHDOD, ISRAEL

Shock found herself standing beside the car.

She didn't remember getting out of it.

She wasn't sure she was ever really in it. Was it even her car? She looked down at her hand and saw that there were no keys. Then she wondered what a car was. She was sure she knew. Or kind of knew. Or thought she knew.

"Car?" she asked. The word didn't sound right. "Rat?" she tried. "Bar? Bat?"

Only small words made sense and then tumbled out as she stood swaying.

Then a sound made her turn, and she saw him. Jason. Standing behind her. He was fifteen feet tall and his white beard was made of icicles.

"Is it time to come in?" she asked.

"Yes, sweetie," said the giant who towered over her. "It's bedtime. Time for all good little girls to say their prayers and have sweet dreams."

He bent to reach for her. Took her in his massive arms. Cuddled her close and began rocking her. For the first time in thirty years, Shock was happy, safe, at peace.

That was where Shock's mind was when Rugger's bullet took her in the back of the head.

Toys kept having brief moments of clarity.

"This isn't happening," he said, though the first three times he said it, his audience were very fat green rabbits.

Then the rabbits flickered and were gone as abruptly as if he had changed a TV channel. Suddenly Toys was on his back with a dead man sprawled atop him. His body hurt in ten thousand places. His mind hurt worse.

"This isn't happening."

Clarity brought perspective. It *was* happening. At least that part. He lay still, afraid to move.

Something's wrong, he thought. It was a hard truth, and he clung to it like a drowning man holding on to a sea buoy. He looked around and saw impossible things and ordinary things, with each state of perception altering one blink of the eyes to the next. He fought for understanding even as he fought to crawl out from under the dead man.

"What is this?" he asked. Then he recoiled as his words appeared in midair, floating and burning and falling like ash. "No," he snarled, and that anger made everything worse. Fingers of bone dozens of meters long erupted from the concrete floor. He yelled at them, denying their existence, but the more he ranted, the more real they became.

He passed out.

Then he woke seconds later, aware of some profound truth. Something important. He lay, passive, looking at the madness around him, but for the moment it was an ordinary madness. If that made sense. People *acting* mad. People being driven mad.

Yes.

There was something there.

He yielded to thought instead of emotion, to seeing more than looking.

Reality seemed to firm up.

"Be calm," he told himself. "Just chill the fuck out."

Those first two words kept things as they were. The second sentence made reality flicker.

"Calm," he murmured. "Peace. Calm. Everything is good."

And the madness became ordinary again.

That was his weapon, and he knew it. Passivity rather than resistance; observation without reaction.

People were dead all around him. Toys thought he understood why, even if "how" was an impossible concept. He began to crawl toward the shelter of another car. Slowly at first, and then more quickly when he saw someone walking toward him. There were sirens all around, but . . . outside? Yes. Not in here.

He looked for police. Saw none.

He looked for the beekeepers, but they were gone. It occurred to him that his mind assigned more substance to them than to the other things he had seen.

Beekeepers?

Or . . . hazmat suits?

He lunged at that thought, and the intensity of his need spun him away again. A second. A month. He had no idea.

When his mind cleared again there was a monster standing above him. Hideous, its mouth and hands smeared with blood. Pieces of meat swung pendulously from his teeth, the flesh caught there.

"Boss," said the monster, "I . . . I don't feel so good."

Toys recognized the voice. Zombie. Looking like his nickname. What was real, though? Was it really Zombie, or was it delusion?

"My stomach hurts," said Zombie. He was trembling, weeping. "My stomach feels . . . feels . . . feels . . ." He got stuck on the word and could go no further. Repeating it with rising panic, Zombie turned and shambled away, sobbing, pawing at the meat scraps caught between his teeth.

"God save my soul," begged Toys. Meaning it. But even the intensity of his prayer, of his need, brought the monsters back.

Spiders the size of dogs scampered across the floor. When one got close, Toys could see that its face was human. Familiar.

"Hugo . . . ?"

"You let me die, Toys," said Hugo Vox. "You betrayed me and let me die."

It was then that Toys understood what was happening to him. This was not the warehouse in Ashdod. It was not even Israel.

This was hell.

He was in hell.

He would be in hell forever and ever and ever.

It was where he deserved to be. There was no redemption for someone with that much blood on his hands. He saw the ghosts of Sebastian Gault and Amirah wandering around, lost and damned. Beyond them, standing in clusters like witnesses at a trial, or patrons at a freak show, were many people. Men, women, and children.

The faces of everyone who had died because of him.

His victims.

His accusers.

They looked at him with eyes of fire.

"I'm sorry," mumbled Toys, his voice nearly buried beneath sobs.

"God doesn't love you," said Mr. Church, who towered above him. He was dressed in old-fashioned clothes from the early eighteenth century. Vibrant colors, gorgeous embroidery, and expensive lace used in jabots and cuffs, with hand-carved silver buttons. The coat had large cuffs and deep pleats from both sides of the waist to the hem at the rear. A waistcoat of gray silk was richly embroidered with gold and silver thread. The breeches were exquisitely tailored. One of his coat flaps was pulled back to accommodate a beautiful *épée de cour* slung from his belt, the pommel and knuckle guard reminiscent of a rapier.

"Church . . . ?" whispered Toys.

"You know that's not my name, you piece of shit," replied Church. He was ten feet tall, and smoke rose from his clothes as if internal fires were burning through. "I gave you every chance. I trusted you. I thought you had a chance and hope of redemption. But look at you." Church spat on the ground, and the spittle hissed with steam. "I should have let you burn."

"No, please," begged Toys. "I'm trying. Give me one more chance. Don't let me burn. God, please don't let me burn."

But Toys was already burning. He felt it first on his shoes, as if that part of him was descending into hellfire first. The pain was immediate, intense. Unbearable. The flames raced along his trousers and shirt. He could feel its kiss on his skin, and the agony was worse than anything he had ever felt. Toys felt himself burn. He felt his flesh melt. But he knew this was not death. Those flames would burn him forever. The nerve endings would burn but not die. There was no escape into damage. Hell was not that kind. He would feel each moment of the fire as acutely as every other moment. He would burn this way forever.

"I'm sorry!" he screamed. "God in heaven, I'm sorry, I'm sorry, I'm sorry."

Church stared down at him with bottomless contempt, and then he turned away.

"Please don't leave me," Toys pleaded. "I'm sorry. God, please . . . I'm so sorry."

Then he felt hands on him. Not Church. Not the spider or the other monsters. Strong hands. Gentle hands.

"I'm sorry," cried Toys as tears blinded him. "I'm so sorry . . ."

Toys felt himself fading, falling, dying forever. His eyes could not see. All he could feel were the flames and those strong hands. A voice close to his ear spoke to him.

"It's okay," said the voice. "I got you, brother. I got you."

And Joe Ledger lifted Toys from the ground and carried him out of hell.

THE DAYS OF
THE STORM
PART 4

It is not light that we need, but fire;
it is not the gentle shower, but thunder.
We need the storm, the whirlwind, and the
  earthquake.

—FREDERICK DOUGLASS

CHAPTER 98

TOOMBS'S OFFICE
PIRATE LAB
UNDISCLOSED LOCATION

Toombs sat in a comfortable chair, but there was no comfort to be had. Not there. Not for them.

Body cams on Shock and the members of her team filled the screens with images from the Ashdod book warehouse that looked like the madness of Hieronymus Bosch brought to life and forced into reality. Forced into *their* world.

"This can't be happening," he said aloud. "There's no goddamn way this is happening."

And suddenly he was out of his office and running for Aydelotte's monitoring room.

CHAPTER 99

CAMP 1391, ROUTE 574
BETWEEN KIBBUTZ BARAI AND KIBBUTZ MA'ANIT
NORTHERN ISRAEL

Lieutenant Sarah Zohar walked silently along the side of the parked semi. It was a brute. Big, new, sturdily built, and painted in nondescript white with signs on both sides and across the rear doors proclaiming it as belonging to the Hasharon Catering Limited fleet.

Armed soldiers stood at clock-points around the truck, each of them in the green police uniforms and powder blue berets of Medei alef ground troops, each with American M16 rifles slung. Their eyes were alert, and every man and woman on that detail was a seasoned combat veteran. Lieutenant Zohar was young for her position of authority, but it had been earned in several small, dirty actions. She was smart, un-compromising, fiercely loyal, and knew her trade.

A sergeant walked beside her as they made a full inspection around the truck.

"Granted," said Zohar, picking up the thread of their conversation, "it's a bit bigger than your average catering delivery truck, but it's all a matter of the crew selling it."

The drivers were not present and were probably asleep. They had driven to the camp from the Shimon Peres Negev Nuclear Research Center and off-loaded their cargo of four of the new L-51 Maccabee weapons. Before dawn tomorrow the same crew would set out with older bombs that were being sent back to Negev for dismantling. The Maccabees would remain at the camp for at least three months, and then be moved again to an air base. Which air base was not the concern of Zohar or anyone at the camp. Safe transport and storage were what mattered, and they had done this sort of thing several times. It was Zohar's eighth trip handling weapons of this kind.

"The new signs are good," said the sergeant. They were old friends, and conversation was always casual between them except when they needed it to be formal. "The last ones *looked* like we were carrying something important."

"If I had a shekel for every time I put some version of that in a memo I could buy an island and retire."

"If you ever do, let me know. I'd make a pretty good butler."

"Ha! You don't even make a very good sergeant."

The sergeant leaned close and in a very quiet voice said, "Bitch."

They chuckled as they walked.

The night was calm, though overcast. No stars to see, but there was a pleasant breeze out of the south. Zohar was thinking about a beer or two after her shift was over, and then a few hours' rest before she had to get up, get dressed, and load the four old Popeye missiles onto the truck.

"Does it ever freak you out?" asked the sergeant. His name was Laviy but everyone, even his own brother, called him Lava because he had unusually intense red hair.

"Does what freak me out?"

"What we do? Carrying this stuff back and forth."

Zohar snorted. "Of *course* it does." Then she considered and added, "Though not like it used to. First trip, it was a single weapon, and I was sweating bullets. But that settled down after a while. What about you?"

"I was at the crash test in Sandia, New Mexico. First time I was ever in America. I was still a corporal and was part of an escort for Colonel Ganaim, and we were doing that technology exchange thing. They had a semi on rails and strapped a rocket onto it and slammed it full speed into a brick wall. I nearly shit my pants because there was a nuke inside. I think even the colonel needed to change his clothes afterward. And don't get me wrong, there were a lot of Americans looking scared, too. But all those techs on the Mobile Guardian Transporter program were grinning like jackals because the nuke casing was just a shell. Sneaky bastards. They were having the time of their life watching all the officers and enlisted men—their own and ours—freaking out."

She cut him a look. "You do know they tested it a lot of times *without* a weapon inside, right? I mean, even the Americans aren't that crazy."

Lava raised a flat hand and waggled it back and forth. "You ever been to America?"

"No."

"They're all literally crazy. So, yeah, we all thought it was a real bomb."

They walked.

There was a soft *crump* sound, and they looked up but could not see anything.

"Did you hear that?" asked Lava.

"Something . . ."

The guards were all looking up, too.

The sound came again. *Crump.*

And again.

Six noises.

"What the hell is that?" asked Lava.

"Lieutenant," called a guard sharply. "There's something over there. Debris falling."

She turned to where he was pointing and saw some pieces of plastic. It was starting to mist, and she wondered if it was going to rain.

"Is that a drone or something?" she asked.

One of the guards had run over to it and was squatting down. He pivoted on the balls of his feet. "Sir, it's some kind of casing."

"From a drone or . . . ?"

That was as far as she got. Her total attention was suddenly pulled away by the roar of the tiger. She frowned, unsure in that moment if tigers were supposed to be there. The tiger was very big. Heavy, muscular, and . . . green?

"I don't—" she began to say, but Sergeant Lava kicked her in the mouth.

"That's for the dry cleaning," he said. And he kicked her again, again, and again. "That's for the god damned dry cleaning, you antelope."

She fell, bleeding, her jaw shattered, teeth snapped at the gum line, the bones around her left eye smashed to pieces. Zohar fell on her side as the sergeant kept kicking her. Even with all that damage she never stopped smiling.

By the time the soldiers of Al-zilal blew open the gate and swarmed inside, each of them in white hazmat suits and gas masks, Lieutenant Zohar was dying. She did not see any of what happened after that. She saw things that did not look like men. She saw monsters and ghouls, dybbukim and djinn. She saw the creatures that had haunted her dreams as a little girl. The things that her *bubbee* had told her weren't real. That had been a promise her grandmother swore to.

There were no such things as monsters.

As Lieutenant Zohar lay dying, she saw the monsters come in and take away the big bad things from the trucks. Part of her mind knew this was bad; worse even than the monsters themselves. She knew it, but that part of who she was could not do anything about it. She sank deeper and deeper into herself until her own darkness swallowed her whole.

CHAPTER 100
MONITORING SUITE
PIRATE LAB
UNDISCLOSED LOCATION

Toombs knocked on the door to Aydelotte's private office and entered without waiting for a reply. He saw his employer seated in his big leather chair, surrounded by all of his screens, each of which was filled with static images, dark web sales pages, news feeds, or other streaming data. His focus was on a big screen, but it was angled away and Toombs could not see what it was. He lingered in the doorway when he realized that his boss was in conversation with someone, and that it was clearly a video chat.

"Delivery is being arranged, and I think you'll be delighted with the product," said Aydelotte in his usual boisterous and bombastic tone. "Oh yes, it's a rarity. Trust me when I say that none of your friends will have this item."

If there was a reply, Toombs was too far away to hear it. He cleared his throat, and Aydelotte jumped in surprise. He recovered quickly, held up a finger, and finished his call.

"I'll be back in touch later this evening. Yes . . . yes, of course. If you have any questions just text me. Excellent."

He stood up and came over to where Toombs stood.

"How is everything going? Is Shock on her way back?"

Toombs had rehearsed what he would say, but now, in that moment, his mouth went dry, and words failed him.

"I . . . boss . . ." He stopped and shook his head.

"Well, out with it, son. Did everything go smoothly?" Aydelotte grinned broadly and rubbed his palms together in vigorous excitement. "Was Lamech happy with the merchandise? And, more important, did his funds clear?"

"Sir . . . Mr. Aydelotte . . . *Jason* . . ." said Toombs, speaking very slowly so as to get the words past the stricture in his throat. "There's been a problem. It's bad."

Aydelotte's grin faltered. "What kind of problem? Did he renege on the deal? Was he a no-show?"

Toombs told him everything he'd seen and heard through Shock's body cam. Everything. Despite his stoicism, Toombs found his heart beating and his eyes burning.

Aydelotte tried to sit down, his hand flapping behind him for a chair that wasn't there. He fell. Hard. Toombs caught one arm, but Aydelotte was heavy, and his fall was dead weight. Toombs crouched there, holding the arm. He had expected anger and outrage, but this . . .

This was heartbreak. This was grief on a deeper level than Toombs had expected.

"Shock . . . ?"

"She's gone, sir. I'm so sorry, but she's gone."

A sob broke deep in Aydelotte's chest, and tears ran freely down his cheeks. He clung to Toombs, grabbing at the fixer, pulling on him, leaning into him until his hot face was pressed against the man's chest.

"No, no, no, no, no, no, no, no, no. . . ."

The moment stretched and it was terrible.

Toombs knew that Shock was more than an employee. When he had first hired on to Aydelotte's group he thought that Shock was a mistress, but it wasn't that at all. And it was deeper than, say, an uncle and niece. Aydelotte seemed to love Shock as if she were his own daughter. The loss was a bullet fired into the heart of Mr. Miracle. It was painful. Unbearable.

And then Aydelotte snarled in sudden rage. His clinging hands became claws that clasped with terrible strength, the fingertips digging into Toombs's wiry arms. He stared up into the fixer's face, and the light in those eyes was dreadful.

"*Who* did this?"

"I don't know, boss," said Toombs quickly, "but someone inside our organization has to be involved. Those fuckers had the ergot weapon. I'm still not sure how they deployed it, but I watched the effect. It was like a horror show. All at once everyone in the warehouse began acting crazy."

"Shiva? That's impossible," snapped Aydelotte. "There are only four people alive who know what that weapon is and how it works."

"I know," said Toombs, meeting his boss's eyes.

"It's crazy. You have to be wrong about this, Toombs. Only me, Shock, Conti, and you know."

"Yes," said Toombs. "I know."

They stared at each other, and the rest of the room seemed to darken and fall away.

"Only the four of us," echoed Toombs. Shock and me. You. And . . ."

"*Conti*," hissed Aydelotte. "That fucking whore. That cunt. Where is she?"

"I checked her lab on the way here to tell you," said Toombs. "She's not there. I tried her cell. No answer."

Aydelotte grabbed Toombs's shoulder and used it to pull himself to his feet.

"Conti," he said, spitting the word, making it the foulest word ever spoken.

"Conti," said Toombs.

Aydelotte squeezed Toombs's shoulder. "Find her. I don't care what it takes. I don't care who you have to kill. I don't care how much money it takes, Toombs. *Find her.*"

Toombs straightened and stepped back.

"You're goddamn right I'll find her. And I'm going to drag her by her hair and dump her right at your feet."

With that he turned and nearly ran from the office, leaving Aydelotte standing with eyes filled with tears, a mouth twisted into a killer's leer, and fists balled into cold iron. In his chest, his heart had turned to stone.

CHAPTER 101
CAMP 1391, ROUTE 574
BETWEEN KIBBUTZ BARAI AND KIBBUTZ MA'ANIT
NORTHERN ISRAEL

Ayoob Alazaki walked slowly back and forth in the narrow gap between the two trucks his people had brought to this place. He wore a white hazmat suit, but he had been sprayed with a cleanser and now had the hood pulled back to allow him to make a phone call. He listened to it ring five times before it was answered by voice mail. He ended the call without leaving a message and waited. Within sixty seconds there was a call back.

He answered by saying, "It is done."

"Praise Allah," said Harith. "*Mabrouk.* What you have done today will change the world. Generations will praise your name."

"I ask for no praise," replied Alazaki. "My only wish is to be of service to God."

"*Alhamdulillah,*" said Harith, and there was true joy in his tone.

"The devices are being loaded onto the trucks," said Alazaki.

"And the casings?"

"Perfect fit. And three of the devices will fit into the larger truck."

"Excellent."

"The drivers know where to go," said Alazaki. "They have changes of clothes and fresh documents. As you instructed, I picked men who could pass for Jews. Both of the men in that truck can speak Yiddish, Hebrew, and English. They are very bright young men. And their accents are flawless. And they have made the trip many times since their training began. They will do well."

"And God will bless them," said Harith.

"I need to know where the bigger truck will go," said Alazaki. "Can you tell me now, because I would like to be out of here within the half hour."

Harith told him. Alazaki felt alarm leap up in his chest.

"Why there, of all places?" he cried. When one of the men guarding the trucks as they were loaded heard him and turned an inquiring face his way, the schoolteacher waved him off and lowered his own voice. "Why there?" he repeated.

"Because," said Harith, "who would ever think of looking there for these weapons?"

"But is this wise?"

"This is the path of the storm," said Harith. "This is the will of Allah."

The line went dead, and Alazaki turned and rested his back against the door of one of the trucks. He felt very old and tired, and despite everything, there was doubt in his heart. And fear in every cell of his body.

He closed his eyes and murmured a prayer to God. When it was finished, he pushed off the truck and went back to his holy work.

CHAPTER 102
INTERVIEW ROOM C
PHOENIX HOUSE

Russo talked and Wilson listened.

Shiva, he learned, was the name for the ergot bioweapon. Gorgon was the delivery system. Russo told him about the cellulose casings for the weaponized fungi. He could not explain the chemistry or genetic manipulation of the ergotism but gave up a name—Dr. Giada Conti.

Wilson took no notes. One of Bug's team was in the adjoining room, recording everything and parsing out bits of it to other members of the team for deep-dive research.

"How, where, and when will Shiva be deployed?" asked Wilson.

But Russo did not know. Neither threats nor cajoling worked, and Wilson judged that the young Italian really did not know. He just made the weapons but was not on the policy level.

"Who hired you?" asked Wilson. "Who do you work for?"

"I . . . well, at first I worked for a woman. Red-haired chick. Called herself Shock. Don't know her real name."

"At first . . . ?"

"Yeah, I did the RPG upgrades for her and then Gorgon. There was a second person; I heard her call him Toombs. But that's all. Nicknames. No one was using real names around me."

"Keep going. Who else did you work for?"

"This older guy. I never saw him in person. A Muslim. He wore one of those turban things with the scarf part wrapped around his face. He said his name was Harith. But that's all. Then they sent me to Chad to work on something else. Blind Eye."

"You're doing well, Mr. Russo," said Wilson blandly. "Tell me about Blind Eye. And remember that we know a lot already, so I will know if you're lying. And you know what will happen if you lie to me. We're in a place where no one will ever hear your screams."

"Christ, stop saying shit like that. I am telling you."

"And yet you haven't told me anything about Blind Eye."

Russo launched into a lengthy explanation of a new project. Wilson had to work hard to keep all reactions off his face. The truth was that Blind Eye was absolutely new to him, and he knew nothing about it.

"It's a casing," said Russo, "for small to mid-size nukes. The kind fired from jets. Not anything as big as an ICBM. The casing is a foolproof shielding made from lead, porcelain, special polymers, and high-tech screening. Do you know how governments like America, Germany, Great Britain, and others find illegal nukes or nuclear materials? They each have some version of radiological monitoring equipment. Like back in '94 when the cops in Munich intercepted half a kilogram of nuclear-reactor fuel, of which three hundred sixty-three grams was weapons-grade plutonium. Then a few months later the police in Prague nabbed two-point-seven kilograms of highly enriched uranium from a former worker at a Russian nuclear institute. And there's a bunch more. A lot of it was Russians, or former Soviet players trying to move that stuff around because it's worth fifty times its weight in gold on the black market. Everyone from small jihadist groups all the way up to nation-states like Iran and North Korea wanted to buy it."

Wilson nodded but did not interrupt.

"The Americans have been leading the pack to develop sensors and protocols that would allow them to detect any nuclear material being transported. And if you think about how much Cold War nuclear materials are out there . . . it makes you cringe. I know for a fact that bin Laden's people tried to get nuclear material to use in a strike against the US. When they couldn't swing it, they opted for planes instead and, well, that's 9/11."

Another nod.

"The Americans spent a lot of money to develop ways of keeping nuclear materials from crossing the borders. Funny, but people in America are so wrapped up in preventing poor Mexicans from crossing the border when they should be worried about nuclear and radiological materials. Stupid, really."

"Stick to your point," said Wilson.

"Sure, sure. The Americans have developed a whole array of radiation detection sensors. In 2003 they developed the Megaports Initiative, which involved outfitting foreign seaports with equipment capable of detecting nuclear materials hidden in shipping containers. Rotterdam, the Netherlands; Piraeus, Greece; Colombo, Sri Lanka; Algeciras, Spain; Antwerp, Belgium; and Freeport, Bahamas have this stuff. It involves particle scanners, special X-rays, and other gear that measures radioactivity. Now . . . Harith's group asked me to build a casing that makes those sensors blind to any radioactive signal. Hence Blind Eye."

Wilson felt his hands slowly closing into fists, and he had to force his fingers to remain relaxed. It wasn't easy.

"They had me design different sizes. Ones for actual air-to-surface missiles, as I said, but remember that it doesn't take much to build a bomb. I mean, twenty-five kilograms of highly enriched uranium or four kilograms of plutonium-two-thirty-nine are all you need to make a nuclear explosive. And that doesn't even touch on unsophisticated designs of the kind to make a dirty bomb. The isotopes there would be, say, cesium-one-thirty-seven, americium-two-forty-one, iridium-one-ninety-two, californium-two-fifty-two, cobalt-sixty, or strontium-ninety."

"And Blind Eye masks their presence?"

"Yes. Completely. If you put any amount of radioactive material in a Blind Eye casing, you can wheel it down the street and no one would ever know."

Wilson felt his stomach turning to ice.

"Harith wanted this?"

"Yes."

"He is with Boko Haram?"

"Harith is big-time ISIS, as far as I know. Don't know which group, though."

"What are his plans for use of this casing?"

"I don't know." Then, before Wilson could speak, Russo added, "I never know that part of things. I'm just a designer. Software, hardware, and systems. Remember, I'm not on the policy level and I'm not political. I'm in it for the money."

Wilson decided to take a leap and asked, "And in what way is Jason Aydelotte involved in this?"

Russo blinked. "Jason who . . . ?"

CHAPTER 103
COMPUTER SCIENCES DIVISION
PHOENIX HOUSE

It drove Bug crazy that MindReader could not crack Russo's computer. MindReader was designed to be a super-intrusion system. It could waltz into nearly any computer on the planet and, in doing so, rewrite the target computer's security software to remove all traces of the intrusion. Once inside, MindReader could look everywhere, take anything, steal information and secrets, and even destroy or corrupt the host.

But Russo's computer kept fighting back.

Bug sat up well into the night, keeping himself pumped and wired with various mixtures of Mustapha's espresso and Red Bull. Bug's blood pressure was, he was sure, high enough to blow the roof off a stone building. He knew he needed sleep, decaf, maybe a massage. However, all of that could wait until he cracked the damn thing.

The annoying thing was that he could not even use Russo's password—obtained somehow by Scott Wilson—because Yoda had already tried to crack the protections and instead triggered a random password block. It rendered the computer completely inert. A very rare failure for Bug's second-in-command.

Bug would not accept that as a stopping point.

He spent hours approaching the target system from various directions, including sending emails to it in which various kinds of tapeworms were placed. His hope was to remove the password block, or reset it to zero tries.

Then something occurred to him. Russo's system was very similar to MindReader itself, and it fought back the way MindReader itself did. Bug engaged the Calpurnia AI system he had filched from

Zephyr Bain some years back. Calpurnia had created a connection with MindReader that bypassed many levels of cybersecurity.

He set Calpurnia to work, with the task of creating a harmonious link with AI elements written into Russo's overall design. Then he waited.

And waited.

When he came into his lab after watching Scott coerce information out of the young Italian about Blind Eye, Bug was both surprised and delighted to find that Calpurnia had sweet-talked Russo's computer into opening up.

"Damn!" he cried as he dragged his chair over, plopped down on it, and began tearing through the files. It took just under three hours for him to digest all of the Blind Eye information. And one thing jumped out at him. Something Russo had omitted from his confession to Wilson.

He snatched up the phone and got Wilson on the line, then added Church and Joe to the same call. He had to bring Joe up to speed after it was clear Wilson had already made his report to the Big Man.

"Guys," he said, "we got a real problem here."

"Fuck me," said Ledger wearily, "do I really want to know?"

"Want to? Not a chance. Need to? Yeah. Sorry, Joe, but you do."

"Okay, hit me."

"Russo told Scott that he was working on Blind Eye. He told him a lot, but I think maybe he got comfortable and slipped into that same thing he did earlier—telling a lot about some stuff and nothing about something else."

"Oh?" asked Wilson acidly. "What did he fail to tell me?"

"He made it seem like he was working on Blind Eye," said Bug. "But he was pretty much done with it. This Harith cat already has working prototypes. Full-size ones. Big enough for air-to-surface missiles."

There was a long silence on the call as each of the other men let that sink in.

"Well, that's horrible," said Ledger. "My nuts just crawled up inside my chest cavity. Whose nukes, though?"

"That wasn't in any of the files," said Bug. "And if we can believe Russo that he has no idea how, when, or where anything he develops is used, I doubt he'll know what Harith plans for the four casings Russo delivered. Could be a shit-ton of raw materials, could be old Soviet-era nukes. Who knows?"

"Four," breathed Wilson. "Dear god."

CHAPTER 104
EDUCATIONAL BOOK WAREHOUSE
ASHDOD, ISRAEL

I stood in the parking lot, still wearing a hazmat suit that been hosed down with something that smelled like monkey piss, but which a tech had assured me was antiseptic.

The rest of my guys loitered around like a suspicious gang of marshmallows. They were in a cluster near the SUV we'd come in. Violin had vanished entirely.

There were about a million red and blue lights turning the midnight air into a storm of colors. Fire equipment, uncountable ambulances, police cars from at least eight separate divisions including three kinds of military, a troop carrier, and five different kinds of biohazard response vehicles.

Havoc Team was under a no-talk order that came directly from Church. The senior Mossad agent on site did not like that one little bit. He snarled, yelled, and tried to bully us with threats. Let's face it, we're not the right audience for threats. Top wore his charming, warm, fatherly smile that can either be a comfort or aggravate the living shit out of someone. Guess which one he showed to the Mossad chief? Belle might as well have been a statue for all the emotion she showed. Bunny, Remy, and Andrea just stood, and every time someone asked who they were, they pointed to me.

Then someone much higher up the food chain got a call. Not sure if it was from Church directly or from one of his friends inside the government, but the threats and intimidation screeched to a tire-smoking halt. The lower-level cops and agents stopped pestering my guys, and the Mossad chief gave me a look that would have withered the balls of the statue of David.

His name, I learned from Scott Wilson talking in my ear, was

Colonel Lev. He was a power player within Mossad, a former field agent with a lot of wins and citations in his folder. He was known for handling difficult situations with speed, tact, efficiency, and discretion.

Colonel Lev was not having a very good day.

He stood in front of me, close enough for me to smell the Nicorette on his breath. He was close to spraining something by keeping his hands at his side and not around my throat.

"I do not want to have to ask you again," he said slowly, grinding out each word. "Who are the people inside that building?"

"Talk to your commanding officer," I said for maybe the twentieth time.

"I am talking to you."

"And I'm telling you to look elsewhere for answers."

"Who was that man you carried out?"

"What man?" I asked.

Lev stabbed a finger at one of the biohazard trucks. "The one in there. The one two dozen witnesses saw you bring out."

"Talk to your commanding officer."

"Or perhaps I could have that man taken to a special holding facility?" he suggested.

I smiled. I have been told that most of the time my smile is like that of an affable goofball who looks like a gangling, loose-jointed ex-jock. Junie says I sometimes smile exactly like Chris Evans. It wasn't either of those smiles I gave Colonel Lev. I haven't actually *seen* the smile I showed him because I don't practice smiles in the mirror. However, I know what it feels like, and it's one I never show to Junie. Or to anyone I like.

Lev literally took a half-step back.

"You don't want to do that, Colonel," I said.

He stiffened. "Are you threatening me? Seriously? Here? After all this? I lost men in there, goddamn it."

"My heart breaks for you, Colonel, and that's not a joke. That's not me being a smartass. You lost people you know and trust and maybe like. So did I. Maybe if you started acting like we're on the same side, then all of this would go easier. Growling at me and making threats about my people is not exactly the way to win hearts and minds. That man in that truck is not yours to fuck with. He's not political currency, and he's not a bargaining chip. You're going to leave him alone."

"Am I? Or what? What do you think you are going to do?"

My smile got a bit wider. "Maybe we should both find out together."

He studied me. My eyes, my smile. The implications. If his superiors were not already in play, I know we'd have both handled it differently. And maybe he'd be exploring the full extent of his personal health coverage. I saw the exact moment when he realized he was fighting the wrong fight.

He pointed to where Havoc Team stood. "You will wait over there. You are not to leave this area, is that understood?"

I said, "Sure."

With that he turned and stalked away, pulling his cell phone from his pocket.

I sighed. I actually hate bullying someone who was just trying to do his job. As a senior officer within Mossad, he was used to being the dangerous, mysterious guy, and knew he had the full juice of his organization and the Israeli government behind him. I've been there when I was with the DMS and worked for Uncle Sam. Few things suck more than being told you don't have the authority and freedom of movement you think you should.

Maybe he was a decent guy. Probably was. And this was his home turf, and all of us were foreigners kicking up some kind of very scary fuss.

Add to that the fact that *he* was probably frightened. At the very least he had an illegal weapons deal happening on his watch, and at worst the deployment of a bioweapon of some kind. According to all of his training and experience, he should have been able to drop a blanket over all of this, cart the dead and injured to a special biohazard facility, and put anyone still on their feet in holding cells in a black site. It's what I would have done. But his commanding officers were telling him to control the situation and not to mess with the big, blond, not-at-all affable American.

When he spoke, his jaw was clamped so tightly that his lips barely moved. I had to strain to hear him. He was very polite—

sounding. Not *actually* polite, but he shifted to that kind of politeness that everyone in the military and in covert ops learns early on—no transcript would ever contain evidence of anything but full cooperation and respect. Transcripts, of course, do not carry inflection.

There's a real good chance I wouldn't be getting a Hanukkah card from him this year.

CHAPTER 105
LAB 2: "HACK AND SLASH"
COMPUTER SCIENCES DIVISION
PHOENIX HOUSE

Yoda was seldom angry, but at the moment he was thoroughly pissed. And embarrassed.

Never once in his professional career had he mishandled any major project. However, triggering the system lockout on Russo's computers stung.

It stung really bad.

He had the door to his office locked, tuned on a playlist of Irish punk—the Pogues, Flogging Molly, Blood or Whiskey, the Mahones, and Mr. Irish Bastard—dialed all the way up to the point his windows rattled, and was tackling another project.

Even though Bug hadn't dragged him over hot coals for the screwup, Yoda was angry with him. Just because. The fact that Bug's level of trust was still so high that he gave him another major project didn't help.

Not yet, at least. Not until Yoda cracked it.

He had the video camera and the video storage hard drive from the cobra case on his desk. The more he worked on it, though, the more his confidence seemed to quiver and develop new cracks. Joe Ledger had ordered this project and wanted—no, *needed*—an answer that proved the video was somehow faked. Or that a false one had been uploaded.

But try as he might, Yoda could not find a single trace of tampering. Not one trace.

CHAPTER 106
EDUCATIONAL BOOK WAREHOUSE
ASHDOD, ISRAEL

As I headed back to where Havoc Team waited, Church suddenly began talking to me via comms.

"That could have gone better," he said dryly, clearly having eavesdropped via my body cam. For spite I took it off and shoved it into my pocket.

"Lot of things could have gone better tonight," I murmured.

"Toys has been transported to a hospital in Jerusalem. I know some people there who have been briefed on what has likely happened."

"And what would that be, exactly, boss? Because right now I'm pretty short on good intel. Is this the ergot stuff?"

"Yes. A briefing document is being prepped that includes our latest discoveries, theories, and assumptions. Also," he continued, "a prophylactic measure is already in active development. Doc will be able to provide you with syrettes for future field work. That will be rushed to you via courier."

"Will it help Toys and his guys?"

"That will require a somewhat more intense course of treatment."

"I couldn't get details from Toys because he was out of it, and Colonel Lev wouldn't tell me the time of day let alone what his teams are finding inside the warehouse. When I was in there, everybody was crazy or dead. And I don't know the rest of the Wild Hunt. Have you shared descriptions of them with Lev?"

"We did. His people have identified all of them."

"That's good, then, and—"

He cut me off. "Only two are alive, Outlaw."

"Jesus . . ."

"It is not a stretch to say that you very likely saved Toys's life by bringing him out and dropping everyone else with Sandman."

I looked up at the sky, but there was nothing to see but a big black nothing.

"What the hell are we into here, boss?" I asked. "We came here because of two scholars who offed themselves, and I haven't even taken one step in that direction. I mean, there's mission creep and then there's showing up at a Halloween party dressed for the high school prom."

"Despite that, Outlaw," he said calmly, "we have made a great deal of progress in the last few hours. Once you are free from that location and back at the Arklight safe house you'll get a full briefing."

"Tell me this much, at least. Was that Aydelotte in there? Was that him doing this?"

Church paused. "That's something we don't yet know."

I cursed under my breath. "When can we get out of here?"

"Grendel is on the phone with the prime minister right now. The machinery is running, Outlaw. Be patient a little longer."

"What about this bioweapon? Is it going to spread? Is there any danger of a pandemic?"

"No. It's not that kind of thing. In fact, Doc assures me that the fungus should be inactive, either now or soon. Care will still be required, of course."

"That's something," I said grudgingly.

"We take our wins wherever we can."

"Hard to think of any of this as a win. The hazmat suit covered my body cam. You didn't see what it was like in there. It was like walking into a nightmare."

"The members of the Wild Hunt had active body cams. We *did* see it. And your description undersells the horror of it. We will, of course, be sharing all pertinent information and the formula for the prophylactic solution with the Israelis." He paused. "Thank you for what you did tonight. Toys and his people were caught in circumstances beyond their control. Had it been Havoc Team, the outcome would have been the same. We were not prepared for this or anything like it. You saved lives tonight. Good work."

I looked at the steady line of bodies being removed in sealed biohazard bags.

"It doesn't help much," I said to him.

CHAPTER 107
PANERA BREAD
WILLOW GROVE SHOPPING CENTER
WILLOW GROVE, PENNSYLVANIA

"Bug," said Sam Imura, "I've been trying to get in touch with Joe. Is he in the field?"

"Whoa, hey, Sam," said Bug with forced cheer. "How the heck are you?"

The sound of his voice brought back a few of the happier memories of working at the old Department of Military Sciences. That, and it was hard not to like Bug. He was smart, funny, kind, and most of all an apolitical humanist. Sam loathed anyone who brought a party bias to work with them.

"I'm good, Bug."

"I heard you started that company ISS. Nice. Class act, from what I've been reading."

"Reading where?"

A brief pause. "Well, your corporate website and, um, elsewhere."

"Which means you've been using MindReader to snoop." Sam could have said it as an indictment, but Bug was Bug. He had no personal malice. Besides, Bug snooped everyone.

"Well . . ."

"It's okay, Bug. I get it."

"I saw that you were putting together your own PMC field team. The Boy Scouts? Funny name."

"Does raise alarms," said Sam.

"Cool. Anyway," said Bug. "Yes, Joe's in the field. So is Church."

"In Israel? On the Aydelotte case?"

"Um . . . yeah. He told me he shared some of that with you. But, hey, even if you don't work here anymore, you're still part of the family."

"That's kind of you to say."

"Truth."

They let that hang for a short moment.

"Do you need me to pass along a message?"

"I do," said Sam, "though I don't yet know its value."

"Tell me, and maybe I can fill in some gaps."

"Okay, Bug . . . I'm running down Aydelotte's background. Stuff that wouldn't be on the net. Friends and neighbors. Doing interviews, but also putting together the steps that took him from a loner kid in Willow Grove, Pennsylvania, to being Mr. Miracle. I sent some of this to Joe as well, but if he's on an op then he might not have had time to read it."

"Yeah, things have gotten pretty weird."

"I don't want to put you on the spot about sharing classified data—"

"But you will anyway."

"I think I have to. This is a conversation I would have had with Joe. It's about this Jason Aydelotte, this paragon of virtue, this champion of the Christian world. I've uncovered some things that don't square with that image."

"Like what?"

"Like the fact that an old lady in his neighborhood saw him going into a mosque on County Line Road. Willow Grove Masjid."

"That's not too ominous," said Big. "Aydelotte deals with antiquities, and not all of them are Christian. He's into Egyptian, Sumerian, Babylonian, Jewish, and even Roman stuff."

"I knew that much before I hit the streets on this. But I had my own computer guys intrude into the security system at the mosque."

"Who? Jinky or Tam?"

"Tam."

"He's good. Weird, but good."

"Glass houses, Bug."

"Fair enough. What'd Tam find?"

"I had him run an analysis tapeworm with facial and voice recognition, and guess who's turned up time and again?"

"Aydelotte?"

"Yes. Understand, Bug, the Muslim community in the Philadelphia metropolitan area isn't known for radicalism. Rather the reverse. They've been first in line to decry and denounce anything that could even be remotely considered a hate crime. They're good people dealing with the reputation of a very small minority. That said, there is one mosque in the area that has been *suspected* of covertly supporting programs to radicalize disaffected young people. Late teens into college."

"And you're going to tell me that's the mosque Aydelotte has been visiting."

"Thirty-eight times in fifteen years, from the time Aydelotte was fourteen until he moved out of the area and onto the big national stage as Mr. Miracle. Now, I have zero evidence that he *himself* was radicalized, but it's odd enough to bear further investigation. And, good as he is, Tam doesn't have access to MindReader."

"Um, sure, I'll get permission from Scott Wilson to go deeper with that search, but . . . Sam . . . are you suggesting that Aydelotte is a closet jihadist?"

"Bug, all I'm doing is submitting a field report on an anomalous occurrence. Joe hinted that there might be something hinky about Aydelotte, and his former neighbors, school friends, and even some teachers—and granted, they're pretty old now—have been telling me some alarming stories. I sent all this to Joe, but maybe Rudy should take a look, too."

"Okay, Sam," said Bug. "Man, this case keeps getting weirder and more complicated. You'd have to be batshit crazy to make sense of it."

"I'm no psychiatrist, Bug," said Sam, "but from everything I've learned . . . I'm not so sure 'sane' is a label I'd ever hang on this guy. Oh, and Bug . . . ?"

"Yeah?"

"Tell Joe to watch his ass."

Bug almost broke protocol to tell Sam what had happened in Israel, but he did not. Instead, he kept his false cheer in place.

"Will do, Sam. And you watch out, too."

CHAPTER 108
EDUCATIONAL BOOK WAREHOUSE
ASHDOD, ISRAEL

It was a very long night.

The Israelis know their way around situational security. Everyone who wasn't at a certain clearance level was bused off-site and into a holding facility of some kind. Reporters, nonmilitary first responders, all of them. Even some local cops were taken away. There was no shouting, no protests. I guess when you live on what is essentially an island in the middle of a sea of troubles, which is a useful way to view Israel, you understand that security comes first.

We Americans tend to grouse about everything. COVID mask mandates tell that story. People refusing to wear them during a fucking plague because they feel it infringes on their constitutional rights. Please.

Anyway, Colonel Lev showed his skill set as he cleaned up the whole area and locked it down tighter than a church lady's chastity. I stood with Havoc for a couple of hours while all manner of specialists went in and out of the warehouse. We said very little and never once thought we had been forgotten because Lev had six soldiers positioned in a wide ring around us. No one pointed guns at us, but the implication was that staying right there was the smartest play.

Wilson contacted us a couple of hours in and said that they were terminating comms for now because it had become evident that someone—possibly Mossad or another intelligence group—had somehow accessed our signal. Even though we had scramblers, no one wanted to take any chances. Israeli technology was first-rate.

"This is getting old, Outlaw," murmured Bunny.

"Uh huh," I said. And that was probably the longest conversation any of us had.

Finally, Colonel Lev came stalking toward us. He wore a high-end hazmat suit with a pistol belt buckled around it. When he was twenty feet away, he pointed at me and then snapped the finger toward the building. I shrugged and fell into step behind him. We walked in silence over to the side door, and then he stopped, waving away the sentry at the door.

The animosity on his face was flickering at a different frequency, and from the deep lines of tension etched around his mouth I knew that anything he had to tell me wasn't going to be happy news.

"First," he said, "please re-engage your comms."

"What comms would those be?" I asked. The earbud I wore looked like a freckle on the inside of my ear, and the mic was a mole near my mouth.

"I was told you would say something like that. It was suggested that I say this, and I quote, 'Cobbler is sleeping in a patch of sunlight with Bastion.'"

He watched my face as he said it.

Cobbler was my very old, very fat, very lazy marmalade tabby cat. Bastion was Church's Scottish Fold. The statement was a code phrase, and it told me a lot.

"You are Colonel Joseph Ledger and you run Havoc Team," said Lev. "You are a member of Rogue Team International and you work for the Deacon."

"And where does all that take us?" I asked.

He looked suddenly very weary. "Where? In very deep shit."

"Because of this?" I said, gesturing to the warehouse. He turned and looked at the building and shook his head.

"This? This is nothing, Colonel."

And that startled the living hell out of me. I dug a hand into my pocket and thumbed the spark-wheel on the fake lighter, which turned the comms unit on.

"Outlaw," said Church immediately, and I did not like the sense of urgency I heard in his voice. It was out on the ragged edge of emotional stress, and that's not where he ever goes. "Listen to what Colonel Lev has to say. He has been read in on you and everything we know about the Shiva matter. Hear me on this: every other concern is hereby set aside. He will explain."

And the line went dead.

Lev looked more and more like someone had punched him in the face. He spoke like he was trying to hold his shit together, trying to let formality prop him up. And that scared the shit out of me.

"First . . . about this here," said Lev. "Your Dr. Holliday tells me that the ergot spores were likely delivered in some kind of liquid medium. Water or something else. There are no puddles inside, and she said that by now the liquid medium would have evaporated. There is a fine layer of dust over things inside, and that will be collected. She told me to tell you that once the ergot is out of the air it would no longer be dangerous. Even so, we will take precautions. Samples of it will be sent to Phoenix House by our fastest courier."

"That's comforting."

"Not really," he said.

"Colonel," I said, "you look like you're about to have a stroke. Something *else* has happened, so let's cut right to it."

He nodded, but even so he had to take a moment. He rubbed his eyes, and I realized that they were wet.

"There has been another attack," he said at last. "Another ergot attack."

"Where? When? Was it another weapons buy?"

"Buy?" he asked, as if that was nothing more than an amusing distraction. "No. It's much worse than that."

"Worse . . . how? I demanded.

And he told me about the attack on Camp 1391. I felt the ground tilting under my feet. Suddenly there didn't seem to be enough air to breathe anywhere in the world.

Four weapons, he said. And Russo had made those four Blind Eye casings. Now we knew what they were for. Not some old Soviet-era junk. Brand-new Israeli tactical nuclear missiles.

Gone. Taken while everyone at the camp was lost inside their own personal nightmares. The security cameras, remote-accessed by some central command office, got nice, clear footage of the men who came in. They were all wearing hazmat suits. They might as well have been invisible for all the good facial recognition could do.

"Can't you track them? They have to be kicking out strong radio-logical signals and—"

"No," he said, cutting me off. "It's much worse than that, too. None of our trackers can find them. None of the American trackers can, either."

For the second time in two days, I felt a radical, painful, horrible shift in the fabric of reality. Once more for me—and perhaps everyone on planet Earth—the world had changed.

CHAPTER 109
DRIVING TOWARD JERUSALEM

When we were back in the car, I called Church back. We'd all switched to a different comms frequency after Lev dropped the world on us.

"Lev told me," I said. "What do you want me to do?"

"Go to the Arklight house. Clean up. Change out of everything you wore to the warehouse. It's probably clean but be doubly sure. And then, Colonel, you need to catch up on the bulk of intel we've gathered over the last two days. From Sam Imura, Russo, Bug, and Lilith. It's all been sent to you."

"Copy that," I said. "And, boss . . . ?"

"Yes?"

"Clear the path so I can go and visit Toys. I want to do it now rather than later."

"To interrogate him?"

"No," I said. "To see how he's doing. He lost most of his team. He has to be hurting."

Church paused, then said, "You will have full access."

When the call was over, I could feel the eyes of everyone on my team watching me. No one said anything, but Top, who sat behind me, placed a big hand on my shoulder and gave me a squeeze.

CHAPTER 110
HADASSAH EIN KEREM HOSPITAL
KALMAN YA'AKOV MAN STREET
JERUSALEM, ISRAEL

Toys woke from a dream about dreaming.

It was strange. In the dream he was awake, but he kept wandering in and out of other dreams, new and old, never lingering long anywhere because it was clear he was not welcome.

Not welcome anywhere.

He let rejection shove him out of each dream and into the next. Not looking specifically for acceptance but instead for an absence of rejection. An empty dream would have suited him well—a place where he could stop walking, running, fleeing, and just be.

Toys had no idea how long or how far he wandered. Ages. Miles. Forever in both time and distance. Sometimes he wept for the child he had been. Sometimes he screamed hatred at the man he had become. Sometimes he stumbled along, too numb for any intensity of emotion.

He tried to wake up, but no matter how fast he ran toward the door to consciousness it receded from him at a commensurate speed. All he did was grow weary and heartsick, until finally he staggered to a halt and stood at the crossroads of dreams and nightmares.

And then he woke.

It was abrupt, like a switch being flicked by some hand other than his. One moment he was at that crossroads in dreamland and the next he was aware of machines that beeped, of acoustic tile above his upturned face, of a breathing tube fitted into his nostrils, of an IV port in his left arm, and an uncomfortable pillow beneath his head. He was aware of light and the smells of sickness, antiseptic, and circulated air.

Toys gradually became aware that he was not alone.

"No," he said, though he wasn't sure why.

"It's okay," said a voice. "You're safe. You're in a hospital."

It took so much energy to turn his head that he nearly passed out again from the effort. A man sat in a chair beside his bed. The man's back was to the window, and even with the curtains drawn the glare turned the figure into a silhouette. Toys fought to clear his thoughts and to make some sense of the voice he'd heard and the figure he could barely see.

"Sebastian . . . ?" he murmured.

"No," said the voice.

Toys did not look. He didn't want to. He knew that voice. And in a surge of memory, he remembered someone who had rescued him, had lifted him like a child and carried him out of that place.

"Where . . . ?"

"Jerusalem."

Toys processed that. "My team?"

"They are being seen to."

"How . . . how many . . . ?"

"Rugger and Zombie are here."

"Where are . . . the others . . . ?"

"It's just the three of you now. The others didn't make it, and I'm sorry for that."

Toys turned away, not wanting to weep in front of this man. "And

I survived? Me? God almighty." He shook his head back and forth, eyes closed, tears boiling out from under his lashes. "I'm sorry," he breathed, and it was so faint the words were barely there.

"God . . . no . . ." he said, and it was almost a sob. "Go away."

"I just wanted to see how you're doing," said Joe Ledger.

"Please, go away."

There was a soft sound of cloth on vinyl, and a creak as Ledger stood and pushed the visitor chair back.

"For what it's worth, Toys," said Ledger, "nobody could have done that gig any better. There was no way you could have known about the ergot bioweapon. Even if you did know, none of you in that warehouse had the drug that would have saved your asses. If you're tearing yourself apart because you think that any of this is somehow your fault, then don't."

Toys said nothing.

Ledger sighed. "I'm sorry for the loss of so many of your team. I know how that feels. You know that I know. But this was beyond your control. Nothing you said or did could have changed a thing. That's important. Hold on to that."

Toys still said nothing.

"Look, man, we don't like each other and maybe we never will. But we're allies in this war. That means something. And I promise you this, Toys . . . I'll find the bastards who did this. The Wild Hunt is part of the RTI family. That makes all of you *my* family, like it or not. I am going to find whoever did this, and I'm going to tear their lives apart."

Toys kept his eyes closed for a very long time.

When he finally opened them, he was alone in his room. Ledger was gone . . . if he had even been there in the first place. There were sedatives in his system, and he let them—begged them—to take him under. Down into the shadows at the bottom of his soul.

"Boss," said Toombs, "I think we need to have a deeper conversation than we had earlier."

Jason Aydelotte was at his workstation, and he looked up past the big monitor that was turned away so no one but him could see the screen.

"You look upset," Aydelotte said.

"Upset doesn't come within ten thousand miles of how I'm feeling," said Toombs as he stalked into the room. His pale face was more ghostly that ever, and the small muscles at the corners of his jaw kept flexing. "Did you hear the news? All of my contacts in Israel are freaking out; I bet you know why?"

"Yes," said Aydelotte mildly. "Someone stole some nukes from a military base. What of it?"

"What of it . . . ?" growled the salesman, his eyes wide with astonishment. "That's the goddamn base you had me show to Alazaki because we were scaling down weapons sales and you thought he could hit it with a strong force and be over the border to Jordan before the Israeli army descended on them."

"Okay, yes, it's the same base. What of it?"

"Don't act naïve here, boss. We're talking about them stealing a fucking nuke. Maybe more than one. So how the hell are you calm about it like it's nothing?"

Aydelotte leaned back in his chair and folded his arms across his chest. "Speak your piece."

"You hired me to sell arms and ammunition to our buyers. Weapons systems, software, and upgrade tech. At no point in any of our dealings did you say one god damn word about stealing nukes from the Israelis and selling them to fucking ISIS."

"You're making one hell of an assumption, Toombs," said Aydelotte with false calm.

"False? Really? From what my network is telling me, everyone at that base went apeshit. They were still crawling around like lunatics when the cavalry came riding in. I have a guy who keeps close tabs on anything involving military weapons, and he said that one of the junior officers was lucid enough to describe some popping sounds before it all went to shit."

Aydelotte sat there and said nothing.

"Come *on*," snarled Toombs. "Popping sounds and then everyone goes nuts. You know as well as I do what that is. That's our tech. Our products. Shiva and Gorgon are exclusives. They're your proprietary technology. We take a hell of a lot of pains to make sure no one else has it except our clients, and even then this stuff isn't able to be copied. Russo, Conti, and the other eggheads on your payroll made damn sure of that. And now, suddenly someone—and I'm guessing it's Harith al-Wazir—has four of them. Four. You want to tell me how that is even remotely possible?"

"First, stop yelling. Mind your manners."

Toombs took a few threatening steps forward. "*Fuck* manners, Jason. You were pretty quick to throw this all on Conti. But she can't swing anything like this. Not even sure Shock could do it. And I would seriously doubt ISIS could organize a search of their own asses, so no way is it them. If they stole a nuke, they'd blow themselves up trying to figure it out, and you know that as well as I do. So maybe *you* should tell me how this happened."

The moment stretched long and thin before Aydelotte replied. "I may be inadvertently responsible, Toombs," he said wearily. "The truth is that we sold Shiva to a Albanian Mafia team based out of Kosovo. And just the other week I closed a deal for Gorgon launchers to our friends in Russia. I find it hard to believe they conspired to resell the items to Harith."

"You sold that stuff and you're telling me this now?"

Aydelotte bristled. "Why would I need to have told you at all?"

"Because I'm your field sales guy. That's why you hired me."

"Mr. Toombs, let's have some perspective," said Aydelotte, his voice still calm but with sharp edges. He rose slowly to his feet. "I hired you to be a salesman. *A* salesman. I never said or even suggested you were *the* salesman. My organization is a lot bigger than what we've been doing here in the Middle East since you were hired. And let's also be clear that you were hired. By me. I am your employer. How would you ever assume that just because you were in my confidence on some matters that you were privy to everything? Or, for that matter, that you had a right to expect to be involved in everything? You work for me. For me."

Toombs did not wither from the heat emanating from those fierce blue eyes. He stood his ground. "You have me negotiating perpetual or limited-time exclusives with groups of international terrorists. There may be no honor among thieves, but there needs to be trust among business associates. If any of our buyers were to find out about this, they'd lose all trust in me. They'd believe I don't stand behind our products or services, and that they couldn't trust me personally. You'd start receiving me in chunks by parcel post."

Aydelotte smiled. "The deal for Shiva was put into place by Sadiq. Before your time. I worked closely with him on the Gorgon sale to one of Putin's generals and took it over after Sadiq's death in order to strengthen my understanding of a key part of my business. I did not want any hand-holding."

"You're going to look me in the face and swear that you had no idea that they would turn around and sell them to ISIS?"

"I swear to God," said Aydelotte. He placed one hand on his chest and held the other up. "I literally swear to Almighty God that I had nothing to do with that deal. Nor did I, for one minute, think Alazaki had either the brains or balls to steal nuclear weapons. ISIS doesn't have a science team. Frankly, I didn't think he had the balls to even try that base. I had you show it to him as a way of placating him as we backed out of the arms world. I'm shocked, hurt, and alarmed by what's happened. That is the truth. And that, Mr. Toombs, is an explanation I was not required to give, and it will be the very last you can demand of me. Are we very clear on that point?"

Toombs and Aydelotte stood looking at each other for five endless seconds.

"Crystal clear, boss," said Toombs. He showed his employer a lot of very white teeth. After a few more seconds, Aydelotte gave a single curt nod, turned, and walked out of the room.

Toombs stood for a long moment. Then he turned and looked at Aydelotte's monitoring station.

"Well, well," he said softly. He fished in his pocket for a Chameleon, hurried over to the station, made a few guesses as to the best placement, and stuck the bug on a high wall. It began to change from gray to off-white almost at once.

Then Toombs left. His thoughts had turned very dark, and keeping his anger in check was a challenge.

"Bloody bastard," he said to himself.

CHAPTER 112
ARKLIGHT SAFE HOUSE

When we got back, we sat around and watched the news. Ghost whined at the tension in the room and came to me for comfort, but I pulled him close because I needed some, too. Andrea and Belle sat on the couch holding hands like they do. Remy sat near Top, taking his own measure of comfort from the most stable person in that or any room.

But we talked about the warehouse thing first. Deflection, I guess.

"This is bullshit," said Bunny. He crumpled up a paper napkin and threw it at the screen, which showed a sea of flashing emergency and police vehicles, but the news report was shallow on details.

Top gave him a pitying look. "Of *course* it's bullshit, farm boy. What did you expect? It's not like they can say that a Mossad team posing as buyers for illegal weapons, a highly illegal team of reformed criminals—none of whom are Israeli nationals—and a team representing Mr. Miracle, the guy everyone loves, were all blindsided by a person or persons unknown and mostly killed by dancing sickness. You want that on the news?"

"Well, okay, when you put it that way . . ."

Violin sat on the arm of my easy chair

"They aren't saying anything about the nukes," said Remy. "State secret?"

"Politics," observed Andrea. "Imagine the panic if it got out. *Accidenti!* What a mess."

Top glanced at me. "What are *we* hearing?"

"So far, just what I told you. Church wants us all in an ORB in five minutes, though, so I'm hoping that's an update." I looked at my watch. "Might as well head on down."

"It's all set up," said Violin, gesturing toward the door to the basement.

Bunny switched off the TV, and we trooped downstairs. The cellar was much larger than I expected, and likely illegally expanded by Arklight once they made this their safe house. A central hall with small rooms on either side, their doors ajar. I saw an armory with racks of weapons and a sophisticated reloading station. I lingered for a moment, impressed with what I saw. There were several reloading presses, shell holders, plenty of reloading dies in various calibers, containers of case lubricant, primer trays, a powder scale, tricklers and funnels, loading blocks, dial-indicating calipers, case trimmers, deburring tools, and all the rest. Another room was set up as a pistol range with soundproofing materials on all the walls; a manufacturing setup with high-end laser printers and a 3-D printer that was currently printing a handgun out of some tough polymer; a boiler and supply room; and at the end of the hall, the ORB.

ORB is an acronym for Operational Resource Bay. The design was similar to some of the hologram-based conference rooms used in business, but on steroids. It was Doc Holliday's proprietary design. Hundreds of little high-density projectors were set all over the walls and floor, and on the table and chairs.

We came in, and everyone found a seat at the table, leaving three untouched. These seats were marked with blue glowing lights. Violin closed the door, and the lights began dimming. Just as it became too dark to see, the projectors began gradually filling the room with light and shapes. There was a very slight mist projected into the air so that the holograms the system projected could use their water vapor's reflectivity to give mass and apparent substance to the things that appeared. The conference table suddenly became the oak-topped conference table from one of the rooms at Phoenix House. The three empty chairs filled as if by magic so that Church, Bug, and Doc Holliday were there with us.

No one at the table was smiling. Wasn't that kind of day.

Church launched right in. "I am not at Phoenix House. I flew to

Jerusalem last night and am joining you from a portable ORB unit in a friend's office."

We nodded.

"A lot has happened," he said. "Some of it is extreme, so it will be best if we dial down our personal reactions and discuss things one at a time."

"Copy that," I said.

"Let me give you that latest on the warehouse event."

Church, as always, looked clean and tidy, but I knew that was part of his vibe. He always preferred to be a calm fixed point in the storms that tend to surround RTI. When I first met him, I thought it was vanity—the expensive suits, the perfectly combed hair, the tie never askew—but I learned different. Rudy confirmed it. Church is acutely aware of how much the people who work for him need to lean on his stability and borrow both strength and calm for themselves.

"Four of the seven members of the Wild Hunt died at the warehouse," he said. The statement was blunt and clinical, and hard to hear for all that. Even though we didn't know any of them except for Toys, they were still in the extended RTI family. That made it personal. Church continued, "Their deaths, like all of the fatalities at that warehouse, were a mixture of self-harm and murder brought on by exposure to this new weaponized form of ergot. Doc . . . ?"

She was dressed in her usual over-the-top cowgirl couture, but there was no smile or comic animation on her face. She looked grainy and tired, and that added ten or fifteen years to her. Or, possibly, revealed her real age. In any case, there was a leaden quality to her voice.

"Isaac and Ronald did most of the heavy lifting here," she said. "And although we don't yet have samples of the version used last night, the symptoms align with their predictive models. It's a genetically modified version of convulse ergotism married with modified psilocybin. From what we could tell from the body cam footage from the Wild Hunt, the weapon was delivered via small-frame rocket, possibly a modified RPG. The rocket itself burst apart, and still-frame enhancements picked up pieces of what appear to be a plastic shell, though my guess is it will turn out to be cellulose. The rockets burst apart, deploying multiple—for lack of a better word—warheads. These were filled with a liquid medium that would have kept the ergot wet and viable. They were aimed high, detonating beneath the building's ceiling fans, which in turn quickly and uniformly distributed the payload. This new version had some component for ultra-quick onset. Nearly instantaneous. And let me pause here to say that there are cures and treatments that would be of great humanitarian benefit if we knew how to accelerate the rate of effect. Whoever designed this, with a different focus and set of values, could have won a Nobel Prize in chemistry for this. Instead . . ."

She let the rest hang, and there was a disgusted, murderous gleam in her eyes.

"In any case, boys and girls," she continued, "the effect was to give every person in that warehouse an immediate and intensely ugly high. So severe a high that they not only lost touch with reality, but lost all connection to hesitation, restraint, judgment, mercy, and understanding. Even the US Army's experiments with LSD during Vietnam weren't as savage as this. We not only need to stop these pricks, but we also need to hunt down and destroy all traces of this kind of science. It is too easy to use, too certain in its effect, and if used somewhere like on a cruise ship, a jetliner in flight, an indoor concert venue, a school graduation . . . well, there's no bottom to how far down a hole to hell it would dig."

She paused and rubbed her eyes vigorously with her fingers.

"I'm not on the strategic level in this little Cub Scout pack of ours, but if anyone wants my opinion, I hope you shoot the dicks off these cruel, mad-as-fuck sons of bitches. Taking scalps would not go amiss either, as far as I see it." She took a breath. "Here endeth the rant."

"I second that," said Bug.

"Motion is carried," I said.

Church said exactly nothing to contradict that decision.

"Now," he said, "on to the next part. And I'm afraid none of this is good news."

CHAPTER 113
TOOMBS'S OFFICE
PIRATE LAB
UNDISCLOSED LOCATION

Toombs went back to his office and sat heavily in his desk chair. It took a very long time for him to calm down. Self-control was something of pride to him, and he had totally lost it with Aydelotte. That was a mistake.

Then it occurred to him that it might not have *been* a mistake. If Aydelotte was playing games and was doing something very bad behind his back, then maybe the sneaky bastard was spooked enough to reach out to whomever he was in bed with. It was a long shot, but in Toombs's experience longer shots had paid off.

He opened his computer and accessed his encrypted portal that opened up dozens of small screens being fed by his little army of Chameleons. He selected and expanded the one for Aydelotte's monitoring suite.

And . . . Aydelotte was seated at his monitoring station, engaged in a long and convoluted conversation with what sounded like Harith al-Wazir.

"Fuck me," breathed Toombs. He put on a pair of headphones—hardwired instead of the less secure Bluetooth—and adjusted the volume. "Move, you fat fuck, so I can see the screen."

Aydelotte did. He reached to a side table for a bottle of Coke, and in that moment, Toombs saw the screen. Aydelotte sat straight again, but the shift left a good part of the screen visible. After that—and for many long minutes—Toombs sat transfixed as he watched and listened. He could feel the blood draining from his face. He felt his fingers and toes and gut turn to ice.

"Oh, no," said Toombs. "Oh, fuck."

He stood up so quickly it sent his wheeled chair spinning backward until it hit the corner of an area rug and fell over with a crash.

"No," he said, shaking his head. "No, don't fucking do this. Don't you do this to me, god damn it."

He backed away from his own computer, turned, headed for the door, stumbled, and stopped. He swayed there. The room was suddenly far too bright. Sounds, however, seemed weirdly muted, as if his head were inside a bag of cotton.

"No, no, no. Fucking *no*."

Toombs reached for the door handle five separate times, and each time he pulled his hand back.

Where could he go? That tore at him, ripped through. Where could he possibly go?

Whom could he talk to?

Shock was dead and Conti MIA. If she was in her lab, she wasn't in view of any of the Chameleon bugs. There were none in her private lounge, so that was a chance. Long shot, since she hadn't answered her phone or responded to him knocking.

"No, no, no, no . . ."

On the sixth try he grabbed the handle, turned it, pulled the door open, and stepped out into the hall, silent as a ghost. There was no one around. The guards were all on the upper levels. None of them were allowed down there on sub-four. And never on sub-five, where Aydelotte's monitoring room was.

The halls felt unnaturally quiet.

"No," he breathed.

And then, staggering like a drunken man, he crept down the hallway toward Conti's lab in the hope that she had returned. In hope that she could somehow help.

CHAPTER 114
THE ORB
ARKLIGHT SAFE HOUSE
KIRYAT MALAKHI

Church said, "As for the rest of the participants at the weapons buy . . . the Mossad team has two survivors, one of whom is in critical condition. Shock's team was a complete loss."

"Jesus," breathed Remy. He touched the silver dime he wore beneath his clothes.

Top raised his hand. "I don't mean to throw punches at anyone here, but how is it no one knew that Lamech and his team were Mossad?"

Bug fielded that. "Because the Israelis are smart as hell, and they know that systems like MindReader are out there. Not that they were specifically trying to hide from us—though, of course they are—but this is the digital age, and there are high school kids able to hack the CIA using an ordinary laptop."

"Much like someone I know," I said.

He gave a small, rueful grin. "Yeah, well. Point is, there's been a lot more tendency to keep things either contained to intranet that has no Wi-Fi access or exterior landline, on paper, or by word of mouth. With word of mouth being the safest. We can assume that Lamech knew that Aydelotte was tech savvy and kept everything old school. Need to know and spoken, not texted."

"Yeah," said Top, "guess we've seen some of that. Shit."

Bunny nodded. "Would have been nice to know, though."

"And I'm sure Lamech would agree," said Church. "Scott is working through the political knots with Mossad right now."

"Is anyone blaming us for this?" I asked.

"No," said Church. "If the Israelis thought you were dirty in this matter, Colonel Lev would have arrested the lot of you. He almost did just because he was scared and frustrated, and because we don't have permission to run an operation on Israeli soil . . . but cooler heads prevailed."

"Which means you whispered in the right ear," I said.

He spread his hands. "It is useful to have friends in the right places. More can be done in five minutes by two people talking than in a month by a committee."

"Preach," said Top.

"All of that aside, Colonel Lev did an exemplary job containing the situation and controlling the messaging that might have reached the public. As you may have seen on TV, this is being considered a chemical leak with fatalities. Earlier mentions of terrorism have been scrubbed from social media and the mainstream news. And we have Bug to thank for much of that. He made his services available to the Israeli authorities."

Doc Holliday blew him a kiss.

"Where are we on IDing the team that hit the warehouse?" asked Bunny. "Should we assume it's the same Tenth Legion assholes who took a run at us?"

"We do not yet know who deployed that weapon," said Church. "Whoever it is, they were efficient and well prepared. They took all of the weapons meant for Lamech and left no traces other than eyewitness reports from one surviving Mossad agent and Toys, but these are unreliable. The agent said they were 'cloud people,' and Mr. Chismer described them as polar bears. We can infer that the third team wore white hazmat suits."

"Seems reasonable," I said. Church occasionally used Toys's real name. Everyone else called him Toys. I had a few additional nicknames, though. And, to be fair, Toys had a bunch for me.

"But who *are* they, sir?" asked Andrea.

"Got to be the Tenth Legion," said Top. "That attack was done with preparation and procession."

"Which brings us to the next issue," said Church. He turned to Bug. "Want to bring them up to speed?"

"*If* they were Tenth Legion," said Bug, "then they are playing a strange game."

"How so?" I asked.

"While we know that the goon squad that came after you guys at the safe house are—or *were*—Tenth Legion, we don't know for sure if it was them at the book warehouse. Different weapons and tactics. They used a bioweapon instead of going in guns blazing."

"Maybe they learned from their mistake," said Top. "They hit us twice last night, and we spanked 'em pretty hard. So they switched tactics and went with that bioweapon thing."

"Possibly," said Church, "but I'm not convinced. The hit at the warehouse took planning, and it was carried off with remarkable efficiency. Even if Tenth Legion had that technology, the way things were carried out suggests a different tactical philosophy."

Top thought about it, then nodded. "I see where you're going," he said. "Guess I'm just not enthused about there being *another* player in an already crowded game."

"Yes," agreed Church, "the complexity of all this and the number of well-organized and aggressive players is a bit of a microcosm of the Holy Land itself over the last few thousand years. So many groups fighting over the same stretch of desert."

"Can't wait for *that* Hallmark Christmas movie," muttered Bunny.

"*Unholy Land,*" suggested Remy.

"Then why did the Tenth Legion hit us?" I asked. "If they were involved in the warehouse hit, then maybe a separate team was sent to scramble our eggs. They could have thought we were involved and the attack on the safe house was preemptive."

But even as I said it, I didn't like it. I held up a hand to stop any replies.

"No. That's strategically unsound. They could have used that bioweapon on us at the safe house and then just waltzed in and slit our throats while we were all tripping balls."

"Agreed," said Church. "I think we can lean away from the team in the hazmat suits being Tenth Legion."

Belle, who rarely joined in conversations, even strategic ones, said, "If I may, sir, I'd like to change the subject. This Mr. Miracle . . . we know from Toys's meeting yesterday that he is involved. How? Why? I am finding it hard to connect that smiling man with this level of atrocity."

Church glanced at Bug. "Would you take point on this, too?"

Bug pushed his glasses up on his nose. "I'm with you on being confused at Aydelotte being involved at all, Belle. The tendency is to dismiss him as just a self-important jackass trying to play with the big boys. I mean, it'd be like finding out Mr. Rogers ran guns for the cartels. There's no lead-up to it—it's suddenly there and it's weird."

"However," prompted Church.

"However," said Bug, "at your request, Joe, we've been tearing apart Jason Aydelotte's backstory. Actually, I was surprised to learn that you tapped Sam Imura to do some legwork in Pennsylvania. He's been talking to neighbors, family friends, folks from the church he used to go to. Hard to believe he was never a cop. He's good and he's thorough."

"Sam's one of the smartest and least gullible people I ever met," I said. "And despite being a cranky son of a bitch, he comes off as plausible when he wants to. People talk to him. They tell him things they wouldn't tell their husband or their priest."

"Like people do with Rudy," said Bunny, and everyone nodded.

Remy asked, "What's he finding?"

"Hearsay, word of mouth, old neighborhood or church rumors," said Bug. "Nothing you can take to court."

Church made a small impatient gesture with one finger, twirling it in a "get on with it" way. Bug nodded.

"Sam's been building a story that's different from the public Mr. Miracle. He's all sunshine and smiles and good words in public, and it's easy to assume that's how he's always been. But growing up he was really a loner. I asked Rudy, and he said that there are a lot of folks, particularly in the public eye, who appear to be extroverts but that's a mask, it's for show, for business. And it misdirects. People see the smile, hear his jolly voice, and they buy the con that he's a fatuous goof. Even when they know he's sharp at business, their cynicism is defused or even disarmed by the modern Santa Claus persona."

I could tell which parts of that assessment were cribbed from Rudy's own phrasing.

"But . . . ?" I prompted.

"But, like I said, it's a mask. Or maybe it's better to say it's a role. Or a costume."

"What's behind the mask?" asked Belle.

"Depending on how much of what Sam learned is accurate," said Bug, "the guy behind the mask is pretty darn scary. A lady who used to live next door to him told Sam that bad things used to happen to people Jason didn't like. Suspicious fires—a couple of which resulted in deaths. Cars with unexpected brake problems. School rivals and bullies who would get attacked by someone they didn't see—blindside attacks. Thefts in school and from neighbors' houses. Now . . . to be fair, people do tend to make up or exaggerate stories about a local boy who got famous and left without sharing the wealth. Look at any tabloid."

"Happens all the time," said Bunny, whose wife, Lydia, watched every gossip and reality show, and read—god help us all—the *National Enquirer*. She defends it by saying that more than once DMS cases she was part of were the seeds for their outrageous stories.

"So, there's jealousy and whisper-down-the-lane distortions of truths," Bug continued. "But even if we discount like . . . I dunno . . .

seventy-five percent of it, that still leaves a lot of stuff that gives us a completely different take on Jason. I tried to get Rudy to give it a label and all but had to twist his arm. He said that it sounds like some variation of sociopathic behavior."

"The constant self-aggrandizement supports that," said Church. "Even the nickname Mr. Miracle."

"And, for the record, he tried to get his friends in college to call him that because he was practicing magic tricks at the time. He even did stage magic in college. He's all about misdirection and illusion stuff."

I came to point on that and looked at Church.

"Cobras? Could that be stage magic, too?"

"We'll get to that," said Church.

"In business," said Bug, "Jason is the happiest guy in the world. Smiles all the time. I had Nikki do a search to try to find a photo of Jason where he wasn't smiling. Very difficult to find."

"Sociopath," muttered Bunny. "Gosh, didn't see that coming at all."

CHAPTER 115
THE TOC
PHOENIX HOUSE

"Holy shit," yelled one of the technicians who was part of the group monitoring news feeds related to the events at the Ashdod warehouse. He stood up and yelled, "Mr. Wilson!"

Everyone froze and turned to him. Wilson, who was on a call with the Israeli defense minister, looked up in irritation. Once he saw the alarm and agitation on the tech's face, he covered the mouthpiece.

"What's wrong?"

"It's the news."

"What news?"

"*Every* news. We need to get Mr. Church on the phone right now."

CHAPTER 116
THE ORB
ARKLIGHT SAFE HOUSE
KIRYAT MALAKHI

Church said, "I had Bug and his team crack apart Aydelotte's business records, and those of some of his associates."

"Looking for illegal business practices?" I asked. "Is it some kind of tax hanky-panky?"

"Sure," said Bug, "and although he's skating to the edge of thin ice, there is nothing directly illegal. He's under nearly constant audit, as are a lot of corporations as big as his. I mean, we're talking nearly eighty billion in assets globally. And maybe a lot more hidden behind shell corporations, offshore holdings, and squirreled away in numbered accounts. And he has subordinates as CEOs, CFOs, and COOs for his various domestic holdings, and that allows him to let them take the heat for any IRS irregularities. That's not nefarious in itself, because all of the super-rich do that. There's nothing illegal with his signature on it that we've found. He's too careful, and he's terrific at getting top employees to take the blame when something *does* go wrong. A handful of his executives have even gone to jail over the last decade, but you can bet there's a new job and lots of bonuses to pay for the prison time. We all think he's reckless because of being such a public part of that bidding war yesterday Toys was at, but again, there is absolutely nothing we have that will prove he's guilty of anything."

"Excuse me," I said, "but we didn't see that body cam footage."

"Oh, right. You've been busy not getting shot at. Hold on."

Bug ran the footage, speeding up over stuff that was unimportant and showing things like Aydelotte's bizarre demonstration of control when he snapped his fingers and everyone at the bar suddenly stood up.

"He's an attention whore," said Top, making a face.

"It's stage magic," said Remy. "He wanted everyone to look at that so they wouldn't be paying attention to anything else. Big ego and big tricks."

"And nothing visibly illegal," said Bug. "If that ever leaked to social media and anyone called him on it, he'd be able to pass it off as a flash mob thing. Put it on YouTube with a Jay-Z or a Megan Thee Stallion cut and it would trend like crazy."

"Gosh," said Andrea, "isn't life grand?"

"Makes me proud to be a millennial," said Remy.

Bug smiled and then continued. "Once they got up to Aydelotte's hotel room for the auction, there was a jammer in place. We got exactly zilch. We have Toys's word on what happened, but now Toys is in the hospital. And Lamech is dead."

"Cleaning up his own mess?" asked Andrea, but there was doubt in his voice.

"Doesn't make sense, does it?" said Bunny. "Still comes down to that red-haired gal, Shock. The Israelis ran her background, and we know her name was Jennifer Rose, an archaeologist who got caught salting sites. Worked freelance for a bit, and then Aydelotte picked her up six years back, and she's been helping him find antiquities all over hell and gone. Mostly Egypt and the Holy Land, but elsewhere, too. Göbekli Tepe in Turkey, Baalbek in Lebanon, Carthage in Tunisia, and a few other spots. That's how Aydelotte's been able to fill his warehouses to the rafters."

"She's a scientist but now she's selling the Gorgon weapon on Aydelotte's behalf?" mused Top. "Why would Aydelotte send someone that important into a dangerous situation like that?"

"Yeah," said Bunny. "Now she's as dead as her whole team. That can't have been Aydelotte's doing. That would only make sense if he was out of his mind."

"Not sure it would make sense even then," I said.

"Maybe he's making a big play and thinks she might object," I suggested. "If he's in bed with ISIS, I can't see someone dedicated to preserving antiquities, even someone corrupt, accepting that relationship. Perhaps she didn't know but was becoming suspicious, or Aydelotte was afraid of that as a possibility and decided to let her play in traffic."

"That feels likely," said Violin.

"If Aydelotte is as crazy as we're all beginning to think he is," I continued, "then he could be even crazier. Dissociative, which is something we all agree I know something about."

Most of the people on that ORB call were able to meet my eyes when I said that. Only Andrea and Remy looked down at their hands.

I continued. "If the polar bear men were his—and I can't believe I just said that—then his right hand could not be aware of what his left was doing."

"Is that what happened to you?" asked Belle.

"Not entirely," I said. "When the Darkness told hold of me, there was still some part of me that knew what was going on."

"How would you know?" asked Remy. "And I don't mean an insult with that."

"It's okay, kid. The thing is, on some level I *did* know. And I approved. My moral compass was still in play because the Darkness did not hurt any innocents."

"There is one other indicator, Colonel," said Church quietly. "Ghost never left you. Even when the Darkness was in control. Dogs are intuitive like that. If you had become something entirely at odds with your true nature, I think Ghost would either have fled or attacked you."

We all looked at him. I nodded. Ghost was sleeping upstairs, and I suddenly wanted to hug him, rub his belly, and give him lots of treats.

"Colonel," said Church, "Dr. Sanchez has gone to great lengths to forward the view that your condition is unique, even in his experience, and he has worked with PTSD and other forms of trauma since he graduated medical school. This might be a good conversation to have with him."

"Very next time I see him," I said.

"Okay," said Bug, "moving on . . . where were we?"

"We were talking about Jason Aydelotte hiding his criminality," said Church.

"Right. He is a lot smarter than I think we're giving him credit for," said Bug. "I actually *did* talk with Rudy about it, like I said, and he said that self-aware sociopaths are master manipulators. And they can twist relationships so that people are, like, weirdly loyal to them. Even when the IRS came after Aydelotte six years ago for something, his accountant took the full heat. Two years in federal prison. When he got out, Jason hired him back at one of his offshore companies. At double the salary. A *Forbes* reporter asked him about that, and Jason was very upfront, saying that how could a good Christian not forgive someone who confessed to his crime and paid the full debt to society. Social media applauded him for it."

"Clever move," said Remy. "The 'look, I have no secrets' play. Like letting the audience look up his sleeve and in his hat. Nothing to see."

"It's exactly that," said Bug.

"So, Jason Aydelotte is probably a bad guy," I said. "A greedy sociopath who plays cons but whitewashes himself with legit businesses. You can look in any issue of the *Financial Times* or, hell, Congress, and find plenty like that. Where's the link between him and selling weapons?"

"Nikki may have found something," said Church but gestured to Bug to continue.

"Before I go there," Bug said, "the challenge with using Mind-Reader to find stuff like this is that every search we do is illegal. We have no governmental protection. So what we find isn't something any nation's justice department can use to arrest him."

"Understood," I said.

"Okay, so we've gone through a few hundred thousand business transactions all over the world. I won't go into how Nikki puts together her search arguments, but trust me when I say that if there's a pattern, she usually finds it. And the pattern she saw was that large sales of ultra-rare antiquities sold on the dark web are often followed within days or weeks by purchases of illegal weapons. Often in nearly similar amounts. Not exact, of course, but close enough for MindReader to ping them as part of a pattern. Dozens of bank accounts, dozens of shell corporations and straw-man buyers to fool just about everyone who might be looking. We found it *only* because of Nikki and MindReader."

"That's good work."

"There's more," he said. "And this might be the connection to Tenth Legion you were looking for, Joe. The DMS chipped away at Blue Diamond Security a lot over the years. It was fragmenting their corporate structure, and as a result their stock went into the crapper. It was about to collapse completely when someone made a bid to purchase its assets. This was, by the way, the third such company offering private military contractors who went bust and whose stock and assets were bought."

"And you're going to tell us that Jason Aydelotte was writing the checks," I said.

He nodded. "Can't prove it in a court of law because whoever does his cybersecurity is top-notch. And I mean that. As good as most of the people in my own department. But . . . a name keeps popping up. Mr. October. We can't *prove* that it's Mr. Miracle, but the name similarities and the connection to weapons sales in the Middle East are suggestive."

"Suggestive," said Church, "but not conclusive. We have not yet proved that Mr. October is Mr. Miracle. He could just as easily be a vendor or third party selling *to* Aydelotte or brokering on behalf of multiple sellers. It could even be someone trying to rebuild the Kuga organization. The point is to not buy in to a theory while it is merely that."

"Got it," I said.

"But if it is Aydelotte," said Violin, "what does he want with that much muscle?"

"That we don't know."

He was about to say more, but he suddenly held up one hand and with the other touched his earbud.

"Very well, Scott," he said. "We're still in the ORB call. Patch it through."

"What is it?" I asked. "Good news, I hope."

Church gave me a bleak look.

"No," he said, "I think this is going to be very bad news."

CHAPTER 117
ARKLIGHT SAFE HOUSE
KIRYAT MALAKHI

"This is being broadcast on hundreds of global media sites as it is being live-streamed on social media," said Church.

On the inset screen, Bug hit some keys. Suddenly the entire back wall of the room became a holographic screen. At first it showed only the image of a black flag on which was written, in Arabic, *"Ašhadu 'an lā 'ilāha 'illa-llāhu, wa-'ašhadu 'anna muḥammadan rasūlu-llāh."*

Which translates to: "I bear witness that there is no deity but God, and I bear witness that Muhammad is the messenger of God."

"This is live?" asked Bunny.

"Yes," said Church.

"Oh . . . shit," breathed Remy. "Now what?"

"This is never a good thing," said Belle.

"Buckle up," Top advised them all.

The image dissolved into static for a moment and then clarified to show an older middle-aged man with a dark beard shot through with gray. He wore a kaffiyeh that covered his head and he'd wrapped the scarf over his nose and mouth, leaving only the beard below and his eyes above. Those eyes were clear, intelligent, and filled with intensity. When he spoke, it was in English. Very good English, though with a distinct Yemeni accent.

"In the Name of Allah, the Most Gracious, the Most Merciful," he began. He had a measured voice, the kind used to make speeches or give lectures, scholarly in timbre and delivery. "The Almighty said: 'And they thought that their fortresses would defend them from Allah! But Allah's Torment reached them from a place whereof they expected it not, and He cast terror into their hearts.'"

He paused for a moment.

"Are they about to take credit for what happened to Wild Hunt?" asked Top.

"Has to be," said Remy. "This is ISIS, so no way it's about the nukes thing."

Church shook his head and touched a finger to his lips.

We all shut up and listened.

"In a blessed attack for which Allah facilitated the causes for success, a faithful group of the soldiers of the Caliphate have overwhelmed a secret facility in which the Jews have been hiding the tools of Satan." A beat. "Nuclear weapons. Weapons that have defined the excesses of military power that has allowed the West to dominate the world and bully all other nations into accepting their leadership, no matter how misguided and corrupt that leadership is."

"Oh . . . shit," breathed Top.

"Our fighters of holy freedom took possession of those weapons and now they are very far away. They are hidden where no eyes will ever find them. No satellite, no spies, no radar. They are hidden by the grace and the will of Allah.

"Today, this very day, by the grace of God, the Caliphate will prove to the world that the Western powers are not the only peoples who can use such weapons. We will show the entire world that the Caliphate has the will, the courage, and the vision to do this."

He paused, clearly letting that sink in to everyone who was watching. Although this was the first *we* were hearing it, I could only guess how this was playing out on the news and social media. People had to be going out of their fucking minds.

"We do not do this because we wish to harm the Earth. God will heal the scars we, in our need and for our cause, must inflict. It is our choice, though, to do this in a place where few people will be injured. We are not cruel, but we are adamant. We will do this because Allah, in support of His religion and His Prophet, has willed us to do so. The West has left us no recourse. They have hunted and persecuted us for years, and now we will draw a line of fire in the sand."

The image changed to a slightly wobbly view of a rocky expanse of desert.

"This is the Negev desert in the southwestern part of the false nation of Israel." The drone turned in a slow circle to show that there were no people, no structures—just a wasteland. Then the drone began moving upward and backward until it showed an aerial view of a battered old produce truck, and we all leaned in, though none of us knew what we were expecting to see.

Until we saw it.

There was a blinding flash of white. The truck vanished in a microsecond, vaporized along with all of the sand and rocks and stunted shrubs. All of it gone, replaced by an expanding fireball that punched upward as if the devil himself were breaking free from hell. The air shimmered with superheated gases and then it seemed to bulge outward. Then the electromagnetic pulse struck the drone, and its eye went dead.

The screen was blank for a moment. No one spoke. No one could.

And then the man in the mask was back. His eyes were wide as if he, too, was shocked by what had just happened. Then he seemed to gather himself. He leaned closer to the camera, needing the viewers to read his truth, the commitment in those eyes.

"As of this date, as of this day which has altered the course of history, I declare that Daesh is now a nuclear power. You are all witnesses to this truth. You already know, those with eyes and with wisdom, that we are not timid nor faint of heart. We have worn explosive vests and walked into your bases and police stations and churches of false worship. We have never hesitated in our commitment to the will of Allah. Do not think that we will hesitate to follow up today's lesson with actions taken to force the Jews and the Western powers to accept us, make proper and respectful room for us, to stop your persecution of us. A storm has come from the desert, and it is the breath of Allah. What happened today is the first breath of this storm, and it is a clear and certain warning to those who wish to learn."

A beat.

"Honor, power, and glory belong to Allah, and to His Messenger Muhammad, and to the believers."

The camera held on the man's eyes for ten seconds, and then the image dissolved to the black flag and then to nothing at all.

CHAPTER 118
ARKLIGHT SAFE HOUSE
KIRYAT MALAKHI

We sat there. Stunned. Hurt. Shocked. Angry.

Speechless.

We had just witnessed the world change.

I had had two moments already when I felt the world had changed, but I had been wrong. Those were tremors. But this . . .

This was that moment, that pivot point where the world as all of us had ever known it was gone, the slate wiped clean in the flash of a thermonuclear explosion.

I became distantly aware that Violin had gripped my wrist and was squeezing it with terrible force. I let her. I don't know that I had the power or the will to stop her.

Andrea was staring at the blank screen as if his mind had broken. Belle sat caved forward, her face in her hands. I heard her saying prayers in a dangerously fragile voice. Remy kept looking around as if in hope that someone would tell him this was all a joke, or that he'd imagined it. He looked like a terrified six-year-old. Top, seated beside him, looked a hundred years old.

The screen changed, and Church was there again. He looked stunned, but I saw him gather the pieces of himself and piece by piece weld them back in place. I can't even imagine what it took for him to do that.

"Listen to me," he said, and everyone looked up.

Most were startled that he was on the screen because they were staring into their own reactions, their own inner hellscapes.

"This is a terrible moment," said Church. "However, it has happened. This is the truth we must accept right now. The world watched that. The world will be horrified, frightened, confused. That is what ISIS wants. But it is not what we can allow. Not for ourselves."

The room was utterly still.

"In 1945, when America dropped atomic bombs on Hiroshima and Nagasaki, the world *heard* about it, *read* about it, but they did not see it. Not in real time. We are living in an age when we can have front-row seats to all manner of horror. ISIS knows this. They are counting on the enormity of this to cut the legs out from under people like us. They expect the fear—the very natural fear—of what just happened to freeze us in place because this is something that we have all feared but never really expected to happen. But it *has* happened."

We watched him like people turned to stone. I don't even think I was breathing.

"Over the next hours each of us will have to process this," he continued, "but we will need to do it differently than other people. We have to reach a point of acceptance right now. There is no time for a learning curve, no time allowed for us to get up to speed."

"Up to speed to do what?" begged Andrea. "This isn't why we came here. What can we do?"

"We're going to be closed out of this," I said. "This is Israel's catastrophe, but all of their allies will be stepping up to offer service and support. The US for sure. All of the UN. Fuck, maybe even Russia and China. There's a big-ass gap between saber rattling and pushing the big red buttons. They're going to realize that we just entered a new age where nukes get dropped to make political points."

"And that," said Top, "makes me want to crawl into a hole and pull it in after me."

"So yeah," said Bunny, "this is all bigger ticket stuff that we can deal with. So, what *can* we do?"

"We can do the job we came here to do," said Church. "Do not for one moment think that this horrendous action is separate from the case we are following."

"Which case?" asked Bunny. "We got like fifty freaking cases, and none of them make sense."

"I thought that, too," said Church. "But I have come to believe differently. Yoda pulled apart the video equipment associated with the cobra thing. It's real footage, or a deepfake somehow recorded on that camera when it should have been recording the room. That's troubling, but it's secondary. That mission is no longer at the front of the queue."

"No shit," I said.

"The same goes for the case with the scholars who killed themselves," he continued. "Those two cases are likely linked, but they have dropped to low priority."

"Good copy on that," said Top.

"As for Jason Aydelotte," said Church, "after all of what Scott was able to get from Russo, and new information Bug pulled from Russo's computer, I'm leaning toward believing he is involved."

"Tell me how that works," I asked.

"The Gorgon weapon," he said. "Toys has come out of his hallucinogenic phase. He described a popping sound just before Shock and the Mossad team began acting erratic. A similar report came from a lieutenant at the Israeli camp. She was on the fringes of it—drying off after a shower, actually. She heard popping noises, and when she looked out of the window, she saw small bits of debris falling, and droplets glistening in the sunlight. She and a few others who were not in the direct dispersal field ran outside once it became obvious there was a problem. They were attempting to help their fellow soldiers when there was a second round of popping. The officer retreated inside to make an emergency call when the bioweapon—Shiva—affected her. Luckily her dose was mild enough that she was able to recover, call in the attack, and give a reliable report. Bug got the phone and on-scene video footage from Israeli military's computers. He used MindReader because this isn't time for diplomatic red tape. And all of my contacts were naturally in a panic. He turned it over to Doc, who did an ultra-high-res scan of the debris. Her guess is that they used cellulose shells around the Shiva weapon with a minimal burst charge. Nothing that would damage the fragile fungi inside, but enough to spread Shiva in its liquid suspension."

"What the capital F fuck?" I said. "So . . . you're saying ISIS has Gorgon, Shiva, Blind Eye, *and* nukes?"

"Yes."

"And Aydelotte's involved."

"At least as far as selling Gorgon. We know that he tried to sell it to the Mossad agent. We have no idea who else he might have sold it to."

"Okay," said Bunny, "but who made that Shiva stuff? And who made the—what'd you call it? Cellulose?—warheads?"

"I need Havoc Team to go find out."

"Do we have a location on Aydelotte?" I asked. "I mean where he is right now?"

Church nodded. "Bug and Nikki have been working that up since before I sent you to Israel. He has six huge warehouses in America. He has four more in Canada, and three in Mexico. From what Nikki found while tearing through his tax records, there are objects of historical importance that he exported from sites throughout the Middle East. Over the last four years he has sent many, many tons of them to his American warehouses. I have contacted Sam Imura and pulled him off the Aydelotte background gig. I've hired his team, the Boy Scouts, to check the closest warehouse out. It's the one with the most recent shipments from the Holy Land. It might be a long shot, but if there's even a chance he'll find something to connect Aydelotte to ISIS, then it's worth the shot. And I'll add one more thing to the mix, and it might be the most useful."

He told us about Sam Imura discovering that a younger Jason Aydelotte spent a lot of time in a mosque in the Philly suburbs. A mosque known for its connection to radicalization.

"Well, to borrow your favorite expression—now isn't that interesting," I said.

"You hiring Sam to run deep background may have been one of the best moves we've made."

"Thanks, but none of this puts Mr. Fucking Miracle in nut-kicking range. And it doesn't help us find ISIS and their new toys."

"Unless it does, Colonel. Bug found two messages in Russo's emails sent from him to a man named Sadiq. He died some months ago, but he was long suspected as a covert arms dealer selling high-end weapons to various jihadist cells. Bug was able to do some of his computer sorcery and obtain a location from which Sadiq's emails were sent. It was an office building on the outskirts of Jerusalem. This is another long shot, but if Sadiq was selling Russo's weapon designs on behalf of Aydelotte, then some of the math starts to fit."

"And some of the pieces start looking like they're in the same puzzle," I said.

"Agreed. It's the only useful lead that we have. Israel is taking point on this, naturally. We'll follow our part, and if you strike gold, we'll share with the Israelis."

"Works for me. Where's this lab?"

"It's on the other side of the city from where you are now, but you're the closest team, so the mission is yours. Doc Holliday and her team were able to copy and improve upon the formula in the syrettes you found in Chad. I sent them earlier, and the courier is already on his way to you there. Wait for them before you go. Doses last twelve hours, but they begin to weaken after ten. It's the best we could manage in the available time."

He paused.

"There are still three nuclear weapons out there," he said gravely. "The list of potentially useful and politically appealing ISIS targets is huge, but I have to think that if they detonated one in Israel already, then they might keep the others in country. Blind Eye may be able to shield them from sensors, but border crossings are a lot more hands-on. Especially now."

"Oh, no doubt," I said. "So, either the other nukes are already outside of the country, or they are being moved to strategic targets in Israel."

"Whoa, wait a sec," said Top. "There are two things about that I'm not buying."

"Let me guess," I said. "One, why would they waste their best weapons?"

"That, and why would they risk increasing a radiation health hazard when there are a lot of their own people—regular Muslims and radicalized assholes—in the path of potential drift patterns?"

"Valid concerns, Top," said Church, and I nodded. "But this is the only lead we have. If my guess is wrong, *prove* me wrong. If I'm right, find out. We're not operating with the Geneva Conventions in play here. This is the worst nuclear crisis we've ever faced, and my heart tells me there is a clock ticking. Beat that clock." He gave us all a long look. "Good hunting."

CHAPTER 119
ARKLIGHT SAFE HOUSE
KIRYAT MALAKHI

We had what little equipment we were able to bring with us from our own safe house, but Violin peered over my shoulder as I was helping Bunny and Remy lay it out on the floor.

"I can do better than that," she said.

Remy looked up. Despite everything that was going on, the kid's eyes were filled with a blossoming and bottomless adoration for her. Kid has good taste.

She pointed to Remy, Andrea, and Belle. "You three. Come with me."

Andrea and Belle exchanged a look, shrugged and followed. They had to run to catch up with Remy at the cellar door.

That left me upstairs with Top and Bunny.

"Two things," I said. "First, if either of you asks me one more time about how I'm feeling or if the Darkness is sneaking back in, so help me baby Jesus I will kick your ass."

"All good," said Top.

"Five by five," agreed Bunny.

"Second thing, we need to do this right. And I mean a pristine infil. We all have Snelligs and plenty of Sandman. Let's use those because I really, *really* want to have a meaningful discussion with

Aydelotte and anyone he might have on the executive level, and I don't want to have to either do that while they're circling the drain or via a séance."

"Hooah," they said.

"Also, we're likely to hit guards first. They get dosed, too. Everybody take plenty of zip ties with them, because I'd love to be able to give Lev a present."

"After we've had our chats, though," said Bunny. "Right?"

Top elbowed him. "Act your age, farm boy."

Bunny grinned.

A *bing-bong* in my ear alerted us to another call, and a voice said, "Grendel to Outlaw."

"Go for Outlaw."

"I have an update on the package that's on its way to you."

"Hit me."

"Oh, I wish I could," said Doc Holliday, hijacking Wilson's call. "Though . . . more spanking than hitting."

"Behave," I told her. "We're on the clock."

"Okay, okay," she said. "As you've been told, Cuddle-bear and Short-stuff cooked it up. And, yes, I know that's not their official call signs and I don't care."

"Doc . . ."

"These revised syrettes work like an Epipen. Hold it upright blue end to the sky, remove the cap, and slam it into your thigh. You can dose yourself beforehand, but it's strongest if used during active exposure. So, if you get exposed, you may only have moments to do it before you start losing touch with reality. Once that happens there are no guarantees, so keep them handy."

"What's actually in it?"

"We've been working on that nonstop since we got the bloodwork back from what was left of Toys's team. It is clear that this Shiva weapon is some mixture of high-intensity ergot alkaloids.

"LSD on steroids?"

"Kind of," she said. "LSD is one member of a class of molecules that are structurally very similar to serotonin.

"The feel-good hormone?"

"A star for you, sweet cheeks. In normal dosages in the brain, it regulates your mood, sleep, appetite, blood pressure . . . the list goes on. But in high doses it causes serotonin syndrome. LSD and these other drugs in the mix can cause serotonin syndrome almost instantly because they activate the same receptors, only with higher affinity. This can lead to anything from diarrhea to hallucinations and even death because of the effects on blood. Following along?"

"Yes," I said. "Keep going."

"Now, what we have in the new syrettes is mostly a drug called ketanserin. It is a serotonin antagonist. Meaning it blocks the effects of serotonin. It has been shown to block the effects of LSD and psilocybin. There was a clinical trial in 2018 where ketanserin was used to successfully treat intractable visual hallucinations in a patient with schizophrenia. Rudy told us about that paper, and we ran with it. An interesting thing in that paper is that ketanserin significantly reduced the *visual* hallucinations but not *auditory* ones. So, it still might be strange, but hopefully it will be manageable. That would explain what Donnie Darko experienced in Chad. Though I'm surprised more of you didn't see or hear anything."

I will never leave you.

"Interesting," I said tightly. "What happens if we double-dose?"

"God only knows. I wouldn't, though."

"Thanks, Doc. This is great."

"I'll kiss my boys on the head for you."

When she was gone, we went back to filling magazines.

The doorbell rang, and I heard Violin yell up the stairs that it was a friendly. I went and opened the door, and there was Rudy Sanchez.

CHAPTER 120
ARKLIGHT SAFE HOUSE
KIRYAT MALAKHI

I didn't say a word but pulled him inside and nearly broke all of his ribs with a hug. And that big ol' Mexican bear gave as good as he got. Ghost woke up, saw Rudy, and began dancing around and twisting himself in knots.

I finally pushed Rudy back and gave him an up-and-down look. "What in the wide blue fuck are you doing here?"

Rudy knelt and gathered Ghost close, pretending to bite his ears. Then he produced some fresh goat snacks and tossed them to different parts of the room. My large, muscular, combat-veteran man-killer of a dog actually pranced around like a six-week-old puppy. He found all the pieces, brought them over and made a pile, then flattened out on the floor and began delicately eating them. He never took his eyes off Rudy and me, and that big bushy white tail never stopped thumping the carpet.

"Playing delivery boy," he said and gestured to two oversize suitcases standing right outside.

I grabbed the bags and brought them in. Rudy cleared off the long coffee table for me, and I opened them. Inside were a new generation of Snellig gas-powered dart guns, thousands of rounds of Sandman, but many were marked with blue bands. I picked one up and studied it against the light.

"Ketanserin?"

"So I've been told," he said. "The ones with the blue band are that and a bit of Sandman, according to Doc. She called it Sandman-K, or SK for short. Between you and me I get lost in the maze of medical and military code names and acronyms, but I know you fellows love that stuff. Anyway . . . Doc insists this will knock someone down as it usually does, but when they wake, they should be free of the Shiva effects."

"So, you've been in on all of the details about what's happened?"

His dark eyes looked mournful and frightened. "On all of it, including what just happened." He gripped my wrist with a strong brown hand. "Joe, I'm absolutely terrified. Even if ISIS doesn't use the other three weapons, what has happened today changes the world."

"Yes," I said, "it does."

Rudy nodded. "Bug said he spoke with you about Jason Aydelotte. He's your presumed Big Bad? Or, one of them. The name Harith al-Wazir is clearly in the mix now, too, I believe."

"Yup," I said. "Though we don't have much intel on this Harith cat. Nothing that gives us a lead as to where to start looking. Most likely Israel will find him first. They're going to look real damn hard, too. Hamas and other groups firing missiles into Israel is one thing, and we've seen that their idea of payback even pushes my views on tit-for-tat."

"Agreed," Rudy agreed. "They often go to extremes beyond are what I believe is called a proportional response. And while I understand that Israel is an armed camp in a vastly unfriendly—to them, at least—part of the world, the severity of their response often escalates . . . which leads to dead bodies, many of whom are innocents. Martyrdom feeds jihadist goals."

"It does," I said.

"But this?" he continued. "ISIS has now detonated a nuke in Negev, and that will change the math. Everyone is going to escalate."

"Yeah, the Israelis are going to get loud and nasty about it, Rude. Count on that."

"Given the transgressive nature of using a nuclear weapon," said Rudy, "ISIS may well find itself short on allies in the future. This is nearly everyone's line in the sand."

"A literal line in radioactive sand," I said.

"Sadly, yes. There will be more violence. It will be Israel's top priority to find those other three nukes, or there very well might be nuclear war. Limited exchange or not, Joe, it will destroy much and kill many, and we will all live in a changed and ugly world."

"You know me, Rude, I'm not political," I said, "but right now I'm okay with Israel going a little apeshit in order to find that stuff."

He did not reply, just gave a sad shake of his head. Then he shifted the conversational rudder, "About Aydelotte. Bug shared with me everything Sam found, and the things Bug's team dug up."

"So . . . are we talking sociopath?"

"Diagnosing from a distance is always risky."

"Dude, it's not like I'm going to quote you on Instagram."

He almost managed a smile at that. "But, yes, my guess would be that appears to fit the profile of the classic narcissistic sociopath. And, if his recent actions are any indication, he might be racing toward a crisis point. Possibly a fracture."

"From what you've read, do you think Aydelotte could have been involved in some way with either helping ISIS get those nukes, or aiding and abetting through the sale of Shiva and Gorgon?"

He frowned. "I'm no spy or military strategist, Joe, but the collected information we have right now? Well . . . I can't see how it could have happened without his consent or participation. Which leads me to believe that the attack on the weapons buy at that warehouse might be his attempt to cover up his involvement. Making it look like someone else did it, and that's not at all uncommon for a sociopath. They like putting other people in the path of blame so they remain clear."

"My thoughts exactly."

We sat on the couch, except for Ghost. Watching him, but really reading the graffiti painted on the inside walls of our minds.

"Rudy," I said, "there's something else I need to tell you. I've been holding on to it since the attack on the safe house. It's something I've—well, to call a spade a spade—I've been scared to tell anyone. I don't want to be stood down. Especially now that we think we might have a real lead and in twenty minutes I'm out the door with Havoc."

"Today isn't the same day when we had the meeting in Church's office," said Rudy. "It's not the same world. So, tell me, Joe. And if there is any way I can help, I will."

So I told him the full story of hearing Grace in Chad as a preamble to telling him about hearing my dad's voice. Rudy listened. The fear in his eyes changed, showing instead a look of genuine concern.

"That warning saved your life," he said. It hovered in the zone somewhere between a question and a statement.

"It saved my life without doubt. And before you ask, it wasn't me hearing Top or Bunny call a warning. It wasn't over comms, either. It happened. It was my dad, and I'm alive because of it."

He considered that for a bit. We both watched Ghost eat.

"If it happened, Joe, then it happened. We have no proof to the contrary, and you are very much alive."

"You're saying you believe in ghosts?"

"Professionally? No. But I've been a Catholic longer than I've been a shrink, Joe, and Catholics are required to believe in ghosts. And, after all, this is the Holy Land. This is the land of miracles."

We sat with that, each of us considering it.

"Does it frighten you?" he asked.

"Not in the way you think. I don't believe that it is the Darkness."

He nodded. "Nor, by the way, do I."

Ghost finished his treats, came over, and insinuated himself between us on the couch. He laid his head against Rudy's shoulder and thrashed me softly with his tail.

"The world has changed," Rudy said again. "But not all of those changes should be feared."

"I have to get ready soon," I said. "But before I go, let me say this. If I do feel the Darkness coming for me again, I'll let you know. No hesitations, no holdbacks. The Darkness or any other part of me that shouldn't be allowed to speak with my mouth or take control of my hands. I give you my word on that."

"And I accept your word, Joe," he said, and he gave me that kindly smile, that brotherly smile. The smile that reminds me that there is someone who really knows me, gets me, supports me, loves me. Trusts me. "Now," he said, "I believe it's time to get up, gear up, and go do what you know you need to do, and what you *can* do."

CHAPTER 121
DR. CONTI'S LAB
PIRATE LAB
UNDISCLOSED LOCATION

Toombs knocked on the door to Conti's lab.

There was no reply. He bent close and listened. All he could hear was the soft hum of the air conditioners that kept the lab cool and dry. All of the test subjects were long gone. And Conti's staff were working in their own labs on sub-two.

He knocked again.

Nothing.

Toombs felt oddly nervous as he tried the door handle. He was not a man prone to jitters. He had been in too many tense situations, from hostile negotiations with Assad's weapons buyers to knife fights in Malaysia. But he was nervous as hell right then.

What he had seen on Aydelotte's monitor had terrified him. Not just as an employee of the company, but down on an existential level. He needed to talk to someone about it. Someone who might have insight. Someone who he knew was an ally.

He turned the handle, and it opened on silent hinges. Toombs stepped inside, careful not to make a sound, though he did not really understand why he was being so cautious. Instinct, maybe, he thought. The world had just cracked in half for him.

The lab seemed empty. The cubicles were unoccupied, their glass walls clean, all of the restraints put away somewhere. The stainless-steel dissecting table was equally sterile. Chairs at the two workstations were neatly tucked in. The floor had been recently swept and mopped. It all made the lab seem brand-new and at the same time soulless and abandoned.

"Giada . . . ?" he called.

No answer, and even his whispered voice sounded too loud.

He moved slowly through the room, becoming even more convinced that Conti was not there. Or, he thought with a flash of optimism, maybe she was in her little office, sleeping on the couch as she often did.

It was in the far-left corner, and he moved that way, passing the big hot room where all of the variants of Shiva were kept. He paused there, looking at the rows upon rows of vials of the nearly colorless ergot weapon. During the time he'd worked for Aydelotte, Toombs had become gradually aware of his own strange feelings about the bioweapon. Over the years he had sold nearly every kind of gun, bomb, rocket, and missile that was available on the global black market. And even though they had, without a doubt, done tremendous harm to people, and likely to innocents as well, he found Shiva to be more frightening. He wasn't entirely sure why, since it was technically nonlethal, despite the fact that suicide and murder were not at all uncommon.

He began to move away and noticed that on a lower shelf was something he had heard Conti and Jason talk about but had not actually seen yet. They were tiny liquid-filled darts code-named God's Arrows. Where Shiva was terrifying and dangerous, God's Arrows were a concentrated version that was several times stronger.

Toombs backed away as if somehow the darts could leap at him, smash the glass, and tear into his skin.

"I got to get out of this place," he said aloud, and then he paused, listening to his own words. Wondering what he meant. "This place" wasn't Giada Conti's office, and he knew it. He knew that his time with Aydelotte was coming to an end, especially after what he'd seen on the boss's monitor. "Yeah," he told himself, "I really need to get out of this place."

He hurried over to the office door, knocked, waited for a moment even though he had a feeling she wasn't here, and then opened the door and took a single half-step into the room.

"Awwww . . . fuck," he said.

Giada was there. She lay on the couch. On the end table near her was an empty bottle of Colonel E.H. Taylor, Jr. Old Fashioned Sour Mash Kentucky Straight Bourbon Whiskey—a present from Aydelotte when she had perfected Shiva. The boss had bragged about it, saying that it was a $27,000 bottle of booze. Gone now. There were some pills spilled out on the floor near the table. He recognized them as amitriptyline, a prescription antidepressant. What Conti had called her "happy pills."

She lay there, dressed in a blue skirt and charcoal blouse under an immaculate white lab coat. Her hair was done, and her makeup was skillfully applied. The note pinned to her chest was written in a fine Catholic school rolling script.

Sinner

That was all it said, and it said enough.

"Goddamn it, Giada," he said and was surprised that tears stung his eyes.

Toombs backed slowly out of the room. When he was as far as the hot room, he turned and ran for the door.

Sinner.

The word burned in his head.

UNHOLY LAND
PART 5

**One of the illusions of life is that the present
hour is not the critical, decisive one.**

—RALPH WALDO EMERSON

CHAPTER 122

PIRATE LAB
SUBURB OF JERUSALEM

We were mostly silent on the drive.

We took two vehicles: the SUV we stole from Tenth Legion and one of Arklight's. Violin drove the lead car, and Remy was on our six. I was up front with Violin, with Top and Bunny behind me. Ghost was sprawled on their feet pretending he didn't know we were going to a fight. But I saw the tail wags.

Bunny said, "I've been in my full share of firefights, but I don't think I've ever carried this many loaded mags."

"Good, so now I don't have to get you anything for Christmas, farm boy," said Top.

"You probably remember the first Christmas, old man."

I watched Top's face in the rearview. He was smiling. "You ever fall out of a moving vehicle going sixty miles per hour?"

"Close enough. Luckily they teach Marine Force Recon all sorts of tricks."

"They ever teach you to do it with a dose of Sandman in your narrow white ass?"

"No, but it sounds fun."

We drove.

Violin said, "Do you have any jammer drones? I have one, but it's not as good as the ones you have."

I tapped my comms. "Jackpot, the lady wants some jammer drones. No EMPs. Just something to blind exterior video surveillance and motion sensors. A couple of Shrieks ought to do it. But don't activate them until we're ready to go."

"*Qualsiasi cosa per una bella signora,*" he said, clearly directing his comment to her and not me.

Violin replied, "*Un milione grazie.*"

"Coming up on it," said Top.

I tapped the comms again. "Okay, we're five blocks out. Combat call signs only. Jackpot, get the Shrieks in the air. Gator Bait, go around back and find a spot where the car can't be seen. Approach on foot as discussed. Report when you're in position. Stay outside the range of the Shrieks."

"Copy," they said.

"Dialing in the TOC," I said. "Havoc Actual to TOC."

"Reading you, Outlaw," said Wilson. "Sitrep."

I gave it to him.

Church was also on the line. "Proceed with as much haste as caution allows."

"Copy that."

"Jackpot, put some surveillance drones in the air. Keep them out of range, too. Night vision scan first and then go thermal."

Violin drove on a parallel street, which allowed us to glance down side streets as we approached the two-way street where we wanted to park. In situations like this you want all sorts of opportunities for fast flight. I turned in my seat to watch Jackpot and Belle toss handfuls of pigeon drones. They had been repainted to match one of the local species—the amusingly named laughing doves. The wings deployed as soon as they hit the air and, after a brief wobble, they soared upward with such grace that they looked utterly real.

Violin pulled into a wide alley between two buildings that were darkened for the night. A big green dumpster hid the car well enough and gave us some privacy as we piled out and did self and buddy checks on gear. We were not dressed for subtlety. Except for Bunny, we each had an HK416 carbine, 5.56mm, the model with the short-stroke gas piston system that is renowned for its reliability. Violin and Andrea also had M3A1 grease guns slung on their backs, preferring them for close quarters because with the stock folded, they were eight inches shorter. It meant carrying extra .35 ACP magazines, though. Neither seemed bothered by that.

We each had Sig Sauer P226 sidearms tucked into quick-release shoulder holsters; sturdy and reliable, firing 9mm from twenty-round magazines. Slung from our hips were the upgraded Snellig gas dart guns loaded with the new Sandman KS. We'd spent five minutes we could barely spare in the Arklight pistol range in the basement, checking the action and test-firing the guns Rudy brought. Doc and her team had been careful not to make too many modifications because real combat use was not the time to work out the bugs. But the size, weight, and trigger pull were the same. The changes were mostly in barrel length and the ease with which new dart-mags could be added.

One challenge with rounds of that kind is that there isn't a lot of weight to the darts, even filled with liquid. They each weigh less than half of what a bullet of the same caliber does. This reduced mass makes it harder to fire accurately at long range. Kind of like throwing a cooked black-eyed pea at someone. For longer rangers to work, though, it would require a thicker, heavier housing, and that would make the covering less fragile and therefore more likely to simply bounce off without breaking. Contrarily, to keep the cellulose thin but give the projectile that mass would require some extra weight in the form of, say, metal or some other kind of jacketing, which greatly increases the risk of serious or potentially fatal injury to the victim. Lots of challenges, and it would take a mind like Doc's to figure it out.

I held a dart up and turned it over between my fingers and saw the improvements in the aerodynamics and wing structure that would allow it to spin—or drill—through the air in much the same way that the rifling inside a gun barrel does as lead bullets are fired through it. I put it back and saw that there were longer, heavier Sandman darts for Belle's sniper rifle.

I was satisfied. We all were.

We wore back and front armor plates that were a new blend of Kevlar and spider silk. Very tough, and I'd tested mine back home. Most handgun rounds wouldn't punch through, and inner layers of graphene damped foot-pounds of impact so there were fewer broken bones, fewer knockdowns. There was some of the same stuff in the limb pads and ballistic helmets.

We had all the goodies—small but powerful flashlights, Scout glasses, seat-belt cutters; first aid kits with bandages, tourniquets, and the works; weapons-catch bleeder kits on our left hips; two 150-round ammo pouches on each side, and two 100-round ammo pouches across our stomachs. This gave us the ability to carry five hundred rounds, plus whatever was preloaded into our weapons. On our right hips we carried two banger pouches, which would allow us to carry two flash-bangs; and on our right hips we carried two grenade pouches. We had pouches for chem lights, backup comms, blaster-plasters, and lots of high-tech doodads.

Then each of us had our own personal touches. We felt like human U-Haul trucks. Bunny carried the heavy twenty-round drum magazine for his Daewoo USAS-12 twelve-gauge combat shotgun. Belle, over on the dark side of the building, had her SAKO TRG 42 ready. As for blades, Remy had a big-ass Bowie knife on his thigh; Andrea had a double-bladed Adra dagger with one serrated edge. Top and Bunny had Ka-Bars.

I had a Wilson Tactical Combat RRX Rapid Response XL with its lightweight frame and 3.5-inch blade. Many have argued with me that there are better knives out there. None of those people were at the end of my arm when I had that blade in motion. I prefer it because there's almost no drag on my hand when I move, and I move real damn fast.

We looked at one another. All of us looked like something out of a movie or a video game. And maybe all this gear was a bit of overkill, or maybe overpreparedness, but I'd rather bring too many presents to the party than not enough.

"TOC to Havoc Actual," said Wilson. "All body cams and te-lemetry are in the green. We're synced with the drones, and we have clear signals. Jackpot, confirm what you're seeing on your tactical computer."

Andrea already had his computer open and the small, very sharp screen showed an aerial view of the building. He read the data flow.

"Exterior guards. Two pairs on two foot patrols, each with a dog."

By my side, also armored for battle, Ghost listened and gave a single swish of his tail. But I gave him a finger gesture—one of many I've trained into him. Attacking the other dogs was something we'd handle with the KS darts. I hate to kill a dog. I will if I have to, but

I prefer alternate methods. Ghost, on the other hand, had no issue with it at all, but dogfights were loud, and we wanted a whole lot of quiet.

Until we didn't.

"Going thermal," said Andrea. "Building is tough to read. Upper stories have a few signatures. Count four. First floor has eighteen signatures, but I can't tell if they are combatants or not. And then there are sub-basements, but I can't read that deep. No idea how many levels there are."

Belle called from the far side of the building to say that she found a fire escape on a building across the parking lot from our target that would give her a commanding view of the area.

"Get up there," I said. Of all of us she had an extra-long gun, a Snellig MaxShot 811, which is similar but more powerful than the legendary AEA Zeus air rifle. It has a power output of 1,800 PSI and has a thirty-two-inch barrel. I've tried hitting targets with darts using that gun, and I might as well throw rocks. I'm qualified as a marksman on most guns, but I've always been a better handgun fighter. Belle is the third-best sniper I've ever met, following Violin and Sam Imura. We had a sniper back in the DMS days named John Smith who was on a par with Belle, but he was long dead, alas. Violin, who had rescued Belle from sexual imprisonment in a genital mutilation camp in Belle's native Mauritania, had taught her how to shoot. She later told me that Belle was the most natural sniper she'd ever met. That's no joke. She has been handling sniper rifles for five years and is actually that good. Which made her combat call sign of Mother Mercy all the funnier.

Not ha-ha funny, you understand.

I went over the plan of approach with the team, making small modifications based on observed terrain.

"Havoc Team," I said over the comms, "we do this quick and by the numbers. Snelligs are weapon of choice. We need answers more than we need dead bodies. And remember, there is a high probability of noncombatants present. And we don't know if the guards know who they're working for and what's going on. We take them down, but we leave them with a pulse."

"Hooah," they replied.

"Havoc to TOC, cut chatter unless there's something we need to know."

"Copy that," said Wilson.

"Okay, Havoc, let's go to work."

CHAPTER 123
THE TOC
PHOENIX HOUSE

"Scott," said Church from a viewscreen, "if things move the right way, then Havoc Team may need backup."

"The Israelis?" asked Wilson.

"Not yet. I trust them, of course, but the level of anger is bubbling too high right now. We need cooler heads."

"Arklight?"

"Lilith has a small team, and they are ghosting Havoc. Violin can call them in at need. But we need more boots on the ground. Reach out through our whole network and see who else is around."

"Rumor has it our old friend Jack is in Tel Aviv," said Wilson. "He's supposed to be retired, but you know how he is."

"That's excellent. I'll call him," said Church. "Keep looking."

CHAPTER 124
PIRATE LAB
SUBURB OF JERUSALEM

The foot patrols were first on our list.

Top and Bunny went after the team currently doing a slow walk around the east side; Remy and Andrea zeroed in on the team rounding the northwest corner. I hung back with Ghost because those guard dogs would smell him first and mark him as a clear threat.

The building squatted there, pretending to be just another mid-size office building in a neighborhood filled with them in what was essentially a series of interlocking parking lots around dozens of similar structures. Industrial sprawl is the same wherever you go.

There was some lovely and very useful landscaping with dwarf Burford holly shrub hedges instead of fences on two sides and vivid red euonymus burning bush shrubs on the opposing sides, interspersed with tall, emerald-green arborvitae. Nice. Shrubs intended to provide privacy were useful when sneaking up.

We moved into position, each of us checking our Scout glasses for active security traps. As we approached the outside of each hedge wall, we began getting alerts for motion sensors.

"Jackpot, quiet things down."

"Copy, Outlaw," he said; a moment later the Shriek jammers kicked in. Since our last mission in Chad, Doc had replaced the EMP bombs with Shrieks. That allowed us to keep all of our gear intact; and our new comms units were keyed with the Shrieks so they left that alone.

"*Silenzioso come una suora,*" he said softly. "Quiet as a mouse."

"Squads A and B, go," I ordered.

They moved. From my vantage point I could only see Top and Bunny. They moved fast, running low, guns up and out as they approached the edge of the northwest corner from the blind side of the guard team.

"I have the dog," said Mother Mercy, and there was no sound at all. The dog didn't even have time to yelp as the Sandman KS dart took him in the right hip. The guards turned and looked at the dog in surprise. There was no blood visible in the poor light, no sound of a gunshot. They probably thought the dog had just tripped. In the half-second before they could sort things, before they could react, Top and Bunny shot them.

Sandman, even without the KS booster, was like that. No one shakes it off, no one lingers a bit on their feet. You go right down and dream that the sandworms from *Dune* are crawling out of your ass. Or something equally fun.

"Three down," reported Top.

There was a moment's pause, then Jackpot said, "Three down."

"Solid copy," I said. "Squad B, move to the rear loading door. Soft infil if there's a key card reader. Otherwise hold and wait."

Violin had gone with Remy and Andrea, but she tended to cut off and do her own thing. None of what she did was likely to make anyone inside very happy, and she seldom played according to the RTI rulebook. Leaving blood on the walls was more likely than darting people.

I ran over to meet Top and Bunny, with Ghost right with me. All of his playful goofiness was left back at the Arklight house. He was a smart and experienced dog who knew the difference between off duty and on. And he was very much on right now. He moved without sound, with no wandering, no ADHD fascination with squirrels. Just a laser focus cultivated by thousands of hours of training and a lot of field work in real combat.

I love that damn dog.

We edged toward the front doors, aware of the security cameras, and wondering how the guards inside were going to react. I took a black key card from my pocket and swiped it three times very slowly. The first time through it introduced MindReader to the security reader. Second pass made sure the security computer accepted its presence without actually logging the contact. Third pass downloaded a universal top-security code generated by the target. And, again, without leaving a trace.

The door clicked open.

Bunny and I knelt in tandem to one side as Top took the handle and pulled it open. Then we swarmed in. The two guards at the front reception desk were both hunched over the bank of exterior monitors, tapping away at keys to reboot the system. We shot them with KS, and they puddled down. Bunny rushed past me and zip-tied everyone.

When Remy reported that they were also inside, having entered the same way, I ordered them to begin a sweep using the thermal scans from the pigeon drones to help locate targets.

Top tapped my arm and nodded to a wall with—very conveniently—a clipboard on which were marked the names and patrol designations of today's shift of guards. I so love it when the bad guys are courteous like that.

Top scanned the image with his tactical computer and sent it to the rest of the team. It gave us numbers and approximate areas of location, but that left a lot open for random movement, patrol patterns, bathroom and mess hall breaks, and other variables.

We moved like specters through the halls.

When I was ten feet up a hall, Ghost suddenly crouched low and pointed his long, pale muzzle toward a door. It opened, and a guard stepped out, his eyes focused downward at the screen of his cell phone. He was smiling, though, so I knew it wasn't an alarm call. My rifle was slung, and I had the Snellig out, firing at the right side of his chest. He went down. Bunny picked up the cell and showed me the image. A text exchange with the woman he slept with last night. Racy stuff. Junie, who loves a bit of erotica, would have been amused. The bastard on the floor had good use of adjectives and was highly complimentary about the things the woman could do with her mouth. Naughty.

I took the phone from him and plugged in a tiny USB uplink to MindReader, as we had done with the cells belonging to the other guards. Phones are worth a hundred times the value of fingerprints. Despite what you see in a zillion cop shows, fingerprints are actually of little overall use to police. In the whole time I was a detective in Baltimore PD I never once had a case where fingerprints were of any real value. Not one. And that's the case with cops everywhere. DNA? Sure, sometimes. Other forensic evidence? One out of every five thousand cases. Less often, maybe.

You want the truth about what *really* helps cops catch bad guys? Cell phones—legit or captured burners. And Bug loves cracking the so-called uncrackable passwords. Church doesn't hire honorable mentions for his team; only first-chair talent for him.

I had Andrea kill the jammer now that we were inside, and that kicked off the automatic upload process. Nikki was poised to receive the data and begin our decryption process. Knowing her, she had a zillion keywords and phrases ready so she could mine the data to try to find those goddamn bombs.

CHAPTER 125
HADASSAH EIN KEREM HOSPITAL
KALMAN YA'AKOV MAN STREET
JERUSALEM, ISRAEL

Church and Brick were in the office of a doctor friend at the hospital. Each of them was making a series of calls.

Brick Anderson was a very large man who'd lost a leg in combat and had it replaced with a nifty bit of cybernetics courtesy of one of Mr. Church's friends in the industry. Brick was nearly as tall and muscular as Bunny, with more than his share of scars. He was smart, empathetic, good-natured, and wordly. Brick had become Church's personal assistant, confidant, and bodyguard. Apart from Lilith and Aunt Sallie, nobody had a deeper inside track for Church.

It took Church five calls to locate a very old friend of his, a devious and unusual American with whom Church had shared some off-book missions in the pre-DMS days.

The voice on the phone answered, "Deacon? Is that really you?"

"Hello, Jack."

"Jeez, I thought you were dead."

"The rumors of your demise have been equally exaggerated," said Church dryly. "As have the rumors of your retirement."

"Well, retirement isn't all that fun. In fact, it's dull as hell."

"Maybe I can add a little spice to your day."

"Oh?" said Jack, his tone brightening. "We on or off the record?"

"Very much off."

"What's the gig?"

"Highlights are these—Dead Sea Scrolls, ergotism bioweapons, and stolen nuclear weapons. Any interest?"

"The ones ISIS stole?"

"Yes. Any interest?"

"Solo hire or . . . ?"

"Team thing," said Church. "I know you notoriously do not play well with others, but this is likely to break big and break soon. I'm calling in all markers and tapping old friends for something that needs cool heads and few scruples."

"You always say the nicest things."

"Would you prefer I stroke your ego?"

"Christ, no. Who's on point?"

"Joe Ledger."

A beat. "That boy's crazier than I am, and it's not a low bar."

"You both get things done that others often can't or won't even try."

"Didn't Ledger go legit lately? At least that's what I heard."

"He has my trust, and he's way out in front on this, Jack. Can I count on you?"

"Where and when?"

"Jerusalem. Now."

"I'm an hour out. I'll pack light and be on the road in five."

CHAPTER 126
PRIVATE OFFICE
PIRATE LAB
SUBURB OF JERUSALEM

Several floors below, Toombs watched the video feeds from his Chameleon bugs.

Some of the inset windows of his monitor showed the normal stuff—staff winding down for the night. Off-duty guards playing cards or backgammon in the break room. A mix of different staff seated at various tables in the mess. They were watching the local news, following the story about the bomb in Negev. He knew that none of them had even a clue that their beloved boss, Mr. Miracle, had anything to do with it.

Not that they thought Aydelotte was any kind of saint. After all, except for the cooks and maintenance staff, the rest were all involved in some aspect of Aydelotte's less savory business practices. Theft of antiquities; design of Shiva, God's Arrows, and other ergotism variants; autopsies on test subjects and reports on brain chemistry and other effects; and working on packages of RPG upgrades—still a popular item—the Gorgon weapons; and more.

"We're no saints," said Toombs to himself.

Then he leaned closer and studied the images on two other

screens. He enlarged them so they sat side by side, and he felt his heart nearly freeze in his chest. Soldiers in unmarked combat rigs were moving through the first floor. Toombs saw bodies on the ground. He saw them encounter more of the guards and shoot them without hesitation.

"Holy shit," he breathed.

Then he saw them gun down two scientists in lab coats coming out of the mess hall. Toombs saw their coats puff out as rounds took them, but then his frown deepened as he realized there was virtually no blood. Just a dot.

The guns the soldiers were firing were strange, and he zoomed in.

"Snellig dart guns," he said aloud.

There was only one group that he knew of that used them. Not military or even secret police. Not Israelis at all. These were paramilitary shooters, and if he was right, then he was in very, very deep shit.

"Rogue Team," he gasped. "God save my soul."

An odd thing for an atheist to say, and Toombs was aware of it. Any port in a storm, though.

He jerked open his lower desk drawer and took out the Glock 19 and a magazine. He slapped the mag in place, racked the slide, and then sat looking at it.

After nearly five full seconds he released the magazine by actuating the release and removing the magazine, then pulled the slide back and ejected the cartridge in the chamber, which he caught. Then he slowly returned the slide and laid the pistol sideways on the desktop, with the magazine and the single cartridge next to it.

Then he turned to the computer and began composing a message, which he printed two copies of and taped one each to the outer and inner doors of his office. After that he opened a file cabinet, removed a bottle of Knob Creek 100 bourbon and a chunky tumbler. He fetched two cubes from the office fridge and poured himself four fingers of whiskey.

And waited to be arrested.

CHAPTER 127
PIRATE LAB
SUBURB OF JERUSALEM

Things were going well.

Until things went to shit.

That's how it happens. Further proof of the combat golden rule: no plan survives contact with the enemy. This is why training matters so much. Plans are predictions, not clairvoyance. A soldier needs to adapt in the moment, and to use that training along with real-time intel, observation, and common sense to keep the mission under some level of control. Fail to do that, and you can get your team and your own ass shot to pieces. Of which, let's face it, I am no fan.

Ghost alerted me to another threat, but there were actually two of them as, all of a sudden, alarms went off throughout the building, and every door seemed to open, spilling guards out into the halls.

"Light 'em up," I roared as I ran toward the closest guards. They were not easy targets, though, and as one fell from Sandman, two others spun and opened up with Uzis. The air was filled with a frenzy of bullets that tore into the painted drywall, ripped framed certificates and decorative paintings off the walls, shattered potted ficus trees, blew apart overhead fluorescent lights, and ricocheted off the poured concrete floors.

Dart guns are good for most situations where some degree of stealth is possible. Less so by far when squaring off against automatic gunfire.

"Going live," I yelled as I shoved the Snellig into its holster and drew my Sig. I fired fast and took one soldier in the chest, sitting him down spread-legged and gasping on the floor, his hands clamped to mortal center-of-mass wounds.

Bunny, using an open doorway for cover, blasted past me with the shotgun. The .12 Buck tore the remaining guard to rags.

Even as he fell, though, more guards boiled out of a room farther down the hall. Top was behind the entrance to a short service corridor. He and I took turns offering cover as the other leaned out to shoot; calling out to each other when we needed to reload. Ghost hid behind me, waiting for me to find something for him to do.

I could hear more gunfire from somewhere else and knew it to be Remy and Andrea, and Jackpot had his bag of tricks with him.

We were facing down a half dozen guards, and they were using the same kind of cover as us. The fight was already starting to take too much time, so I took a page out of Jackpot's playbook and fished a handful of Killer Bees from a pouch. They are micro-drones just a little larger than an African honeybee. Not particularly fast considering they each carried a payload of Sandman. Old-style, though; we didn't have time to swap their cartridges out with the KS version. Didn't matter, though. They were hard as hell to shoot down because they were small and flew erratically.

"Bees in the air," I yelled and threw six of them in an overhand lob. The responding shots missed my wrist by so little I could feel the hot wind. I snatched my hand back.

There was some wild chatter down the hall—and I noted that it was mostly in unaccented English. Aydelotte didn't seem to hire the locals. No one with an Israeli accent.

Within fifteen seconds the intensity of the gunfire diminished. The Killer Bees have a shared targeting software package that coordinates their attack. Each will lock on to a target and the others will avoid it to find their own. Five of the shooters spilled down onto the floor. The sixth must have swatted his, because he kept shooting after a small pause.

Bunny said, "Drop the gun, asshole." He punctuated it with a blast from the Daewoo.

The guard had a lot more balls than brains, and he stood up and unloaded a full magazine down the hall.

Not sure who killed him because all three of us returned fire.

And then we were in motion, running past the twisted red thing that had been that last guard.

"Jackpot, sitrep," I called.

His voice came back filled with stress. "Heavy resistance in the mess hall."

"You need help?"

"Negative. Our Arklight friend is with us. We're on this."

I tapped Top. "Moving."

As I passed him, he waited until Bunny was in sight and then Top followed. The corridor was choked with bodies, alive and dead. Ghost stepped over the puddles as he was trained to do when there was time to be careful not to leave tracks.

CHAPTER 128
THE STRONGHOLD
OUTSKIRTS OF JERUSALEM

They stood in Jason Aydelotte's office, looking out through the big picture window that was really a massive sheet of two-way mirror. Harith was with him. They watched without being seen as scores of men were hard at work.

Some were busy using heavy-duty forklifts to load a line of trucks. At dawn there had been twenty trucks. Now there were six left, and the largest of the warehouse rooms was looking like a ghost town.

"Will you get it all out?" asked Harith.

"Alas, no," sighed Aydelotte. "I'll get the best stuff. Actually, most of that is already on the first ship or in the States. Been getting this part ready for months."

"You have very efficient people," said the jihadist leader.

"I do. I always use the best people."

"Like Dr. Conti?"

"She had her moments. Sorry she took the coward's way out."

"Before you put a bullet in her head, you mean?"

"Well, sure. But I'd rather have closed out her contract. Tell you the truth," said Aydelotte, "I feel a bit cheated."

Harith nodded soberly. "Sorry about your woman."

"Shock? Yes. That was clumsy."

"There are losses in every war. We both know that."

Aydelotte nodded, and they continued to watch the events below. The stuff being moved out . . . and the items that had been moved in only recently.

"You are leaving much of this too late," said the jihadist.

"They can check my trucks and loads all they want."

"And if they close the ports?"

"If they do, I'll cry a little. Otherwise, it's a write-off. You can't win every time."

Harith grunted. "You know they will figure this out. They may come for you. Even you have to admit that you have made some mistakes."

"Nothing that can't be fixed. Spin control is a favorite game of mine."

"What if it is Mossad?"

"What if it is?"

"What if it is that monster who calls himself Mr. Church?"

"If he comes for me, my brother," said Aydelotte, "or if he sends that freak Ledger, I'll deal with them."

"How?"

Aydelotte looked at him. "You know how."

CHAPTER 129
PIRATE LAB
SUBURB OF JERUSALEM

We picked up our pace as the sounds from the two-pronged attack drew the shooters to us. We used Killer Bees sparingly because we didn't have a lot of them. As the resistance thinned, we were able to switch back to Snelligs, though, and that dropped the noise level down because they are quieter than even the best standard weapon sound suppressor.

"Mother Mercy to Outlaw," called Belle. "Picking up zero signals to local law. No sirens."

"Confirm Mother Mercy on that," agreed Scott at the TOC. "There have been no calls to law enforcement or ambulances. No first responders anywhere have been notified. They're keeping this in house."

"Sucks to be them," said Bunny.

"Tells me they all know they're on the wrong side of this," suggested Top.

"That mean we can play with real toys again?" asked Bunny, waggling his dart gun.

"Can't interview corpses," I said.

Within fifteen minutes all resistance on the first floor was ended. I sent Remy and Andrea upstairs to do cleanup, but as they worked to clear each room on the upper floors, they said that all they were finding were terrified low-level employees.

"Dart and cuff. Nobody stays awake. We can jolt some later."

Jolt was another upgrade by Doc Holliday. It was a stimulant that was effective but not gentle. It blew past the ketamine cocktail in Sandman and pulled the sleeping victim back to consciousness. They woke, almost always threw up, sometimes pissed their pants, and floundered around in pain and confusion. But then their minds cleared, and they were able to answer questions. Most people did, because by then they were pretty sure we were not there to fuck around. Also, they woke bound and helpless while a bunch of big scary people in full combat kit and visored helmets pointed the bad ends of guns in their faces. That kind of thing doesn't inspire trash talk or stubbornness. Most of the time. Some assholes always think they can tough it out. It is occasionally amusing to disabuse them of that notion.

If they were lucky, they had Top's less-is-more approach. If they were not, then they saw me smiling down at them. Top is one of the finest soldiers I've ever known. But I'm crazy and it shows.

"Heading downstairs," I said.

Bunny found the elevator and fire stairs; we opted for the latter. Ghost drifted along in silence, his nails covered with sound-dampening pads. He stayed with me as we paused at each landing to check the corners. One guard tried to ambush us, but I let Ghost have him.

Screams are very loud in a stairwell, and sometimes that's the kind of advance advertising you want. Think about it . . . you're on a basement or sub-basement level of a heavily guarded building, and after a lot of gunfire, no one upstairs is taking calls. How high is your confidence level?

The order I gave Ghost was to bring the man down but not kill him. Being a nice puppy was not part of that order. Ghost left some big bleeders spraying and most of the man's left wrist intact.

We reached the guard long before he could bleed out, applied tourniquets, and when he was stable, I put the blade of my Wilson against his right eyebrow.

"Make smart choices, Sparky," I said. "Tell us who's down there. How many. And where."

He'd had the balls to try and ambush us, but I could see him calculating his payroll and benefits package in the four seconds I gave him. It was clear he didn't think he was getting paid enough for this shit.

He told us everything we needed.

I dosed him with KS. As I was fishing for his cell phone, I found a pack of syrettes nearly identical to those we'd taken from the guards in Chad. I showed it to the other guys.

"Same team for sure," said Top. "Aydelotte's our bad guy."

Bunny held up the syrette and studied it. "Darker than the other formula. Looks like they've been doing modifications, too."

"Take it for Doc," I ordered.

"Also," said Top, "he has this, but the upstairs guards didn't. Labs down here?"

"Makes sense, Pappy. Let's go find out."

CHAPTER 130
PRIVATE LOUNGE
PIRATE LAB
SUBURB OF JERUSALEM

There was surprisingly little fuss as we cleared one sub-basement after another.

One idiot tried to take my head off with a fire axe as we came out of the stairwell. He was a lab geek in a stained white shirt-jacket and an Ed Sheeran haircut. He had no idea what he was doing. I took the axe away from him a lot easier than I ever get Mr. Aardvark away from Ghost at home.

Bunny was going to dart him, but I shook my head and instead dragged him through the open door of his lab. A glance around showed that he was working on preparing slides. His radio was playing, god save my immortal soul, Nickelback.

"I ought to shoot him just for that," muttered Bunny. He took the Echo Dot off the kid's desk, dropped it on the floor, and smashed it under his heel. The young tech watched all of this with wide, terrified blue eyes.

"Where is Jason Aydelotte?" I asked, being nice. I had my visor pushed up so he could see one of my kinder smiles.

"He's not here."

Top, standing behind and above me, said, "Not what the man asked, son."

The kid licked his lips. He was maybe twenty or twenty-two. Fresh out of college and clearly answered the wrong ad on Monster .com.

I squatted down, leaning my chin on the flat part of the axe head between the blade and the pick.

"Do I need to ask the question again?"

"He's. . . . I mean he's at the other place."

"What other place?"

"The warehouse place. They call it the Stronghold."

"Where is this Stronghold?"

"I . . . I don't know."

"Better for you if you did," advised Top.

He started to cry. The tears were real, and he looked to be so far down the policy level that I doubted he knew where the closest bathroom was. So I switched topics and asked about who else was on this floor. He told me about the main lab, the staff lab—which is where at least six other techs were.

"I tried to get in, but they had the door barricaded from inside," he sobbed.

"What else is down here? Make it fast, kid, my fuse is burning."

"Only Dr. Conti's lab, Mr. Aydelotte's monitoring suite—but, like I said, he's not here—and Mr. Toombs's office."

I had him draw me a quick diagram of who was in what room. He did it, though his hand trembled so much it looked like a third grader's work. When he was finished, he cringed back with such abject terror that I actually felt bad for him. But, yeah, he was working for the bad guys, so he only got so much slack. No need for cruelty, though. I dosed him with Sandman, cuffed him and, with Bunny's help, hoisted him onto the threadbare orange couch in the corner.

Before we left, I saw Top studying the kid.

"Just a boy who made a bad choice," he said. "Someone's kid. Someone's brother, maybe. Hope the courts cut him a little grace."

"Nukes, man," said Bunny. "I don't think anyone's skating on this."

Top sighed. "Life's a real prick sometimes."

Neither Bunny nor I could offer contrary opinions. So we all went back to the hall.

The staff lab was, indeed, barricaded. It was a tempting target but would be the hardest nut to crack. So we compromised and set a blaster-plaster across the door seal. Then I banged on the door with the flat side of the axe head.

"You in there," I yelled. "The building is taken and your boss has fled. It's just you in there. The door is rigged with a high explosive charge. If you attempt to leave it'll blow all of you off the planet. Tell me if you can hear me. One knock on the door will do it."

After fifteen seconds and some whispering too low for us to hear, there was that one knock.

"Good. Stay right where you are. We will be back. And between now and then start making good decisions about your future. Your best play is to come quietly with us, no muss and no fuss. Worst option is to let the Israeli army take you, and then no one will ever see you again. I'll give you a few minutes to sort that out."

We left them there.

The monitoring lab was empty, the computers switched off. We took a few moments connecting them to MindReader uplinks. While Top and I were doing that, Bunny went around with an Anteater looking for monitoring bugs.

He found two.

"Hey, guys, check it out." Bunny pointed to a small device that was nearly invisible against the wall behind the computer desk. "There's another by the door. Looks like one of those Chinese gizmos. The Chameleon series."

"What it is," agreed Top. "Question is who put it there? Who's watching the watcher?"

Bunny grunted. "A day ago I'd have said it couldn't be ISIS because they're way behind the tech curve, but . . . they stole nukes from the Israelis, and you don't do that if you're a Luddite. The Israelis are smart and thorough and tough as fuck."

"They are that," I said.

"But now," continued Bunny, "I'm pretty sure they have someone with more brain cells running this op. Maybe this Harith al-Wazir cat. We don't know who he is. Could be a genius of some kind who got radicalized. Someone with a degree in some area of science useful to upgrading more than RPGs. And I'm not talking Russo. Someone higher up the evolutionary scale. And we've met that kind of person before. Way back at the beginning when we all joined. Almirah. The one who developed *seif al din.*"

"Thinking along the same lines," said Top. "Another goddamn mad scientist working for ISIS. Ain't that just a barrel of fucking monkeys."

"Yeah," I said. "Entertaining as hell."

Once we had all the uplinks in place, we left. Bunny took one of the Chameleons with him, leaving the one near the workstation on the off chance that someone—Aydelotte maybe—would slip back in here. But he added one of our own bugs. It was a cockroach that could crawl to wherever the drone driver sent it, and it had superb audio and video pickup.

Ah, the joys of modern science. I wonder if the first guys to be handed crossbows had the same sense of mild confusion and blossoming optimism.

We left.

CHAPTER 131
DR. CONTI'S LAB AND LOUNGE
PIRATE LAB
SUBURB OF JERUSALEM

As we prowled the hall to find the lab of Aydelotte's chief scientist, Dr. Giada Conti, I had Bug run background on her.

"Well," he said after a couple of minutes, "she's a real peach. Top honors in epidemiology from the University of Milan, with her thesis focusing on dangerous fungi."

"Color me all kinds of damned surprised," I said.

"There's more, and here's where it gets good. Despite being top of her grade, she hit the glass ceiling of sexism in Italian research circles at two different universities, and didn't get much further in the private sector. Then about five years ago she fell off the radar after some accusations that she was introducing some compounds to patients without clearing it through proper channels for human trials. No faked suicide like Russo, but definitely off the radar. Even reduced contact with some family."

"So, mystery solved," I said. "Perfect setup for a cultivated asset. Frustrated, brilliant but hitting closed career doors, and willing to take dangerous risks with unsuspecting people in fudged clinical trials. Ideal for this kind of radicalization."

"And Aydelotte snatched her up," said Bug.

"Boy's got a weird but efficient recruiting program," said Top.

We reached her lab door. It stood ajar.

Church said, "We need her alive and awake. Handle with extreme care and extract her ASAP. Top priority. Next to Aydelotte, she is our most important target."

"Copy that."

We moved inside very carefully, spreading out quickly so as not to be framed in the doorway. All of us had dart guns ready, and like me, automatically tapped the pockets where the Jolt was kept. Not that we wanted to use it. But there's that Boy Scout motto we all literally live by—be prepared.

But there was no amount of preparation that was going to help us here. We found her in her lounge, and it was clear we were about four hours too late for her to do us or anyone any damned good at all.

When I called that in, Church made a wordless noise and nothing else.

Wilson said, "Look for this Toombs. If it's who I think it is, then he may be someone I heard of when running with the SAS. Tall, oddly pale, looks like a cartoon villain. Looks like Lurch from the *Addams Family*. But don't be fooled, he's extremely educated, very tough, and definitely savvy. Not to be underestimated."

"What's his job? Enforcer?"

"Negative, Outlaw. Toombs—real name Isaac Tomberland—is one of the smartest salesmen for illegal arms."

Church said, "We want him very badly. If anyone still breathing is likely to know about Blind Eye, it's likely to be him. And he may know the location of the other facility where Aydelotte is hiding."

"Copy that."

We left the dead woman and continued our search.

CHAPTER 132
THE O POD HOTEL
2 KAUFMANN STREET, TEL AVIV

Jack was a man who liked to live simply, travel light, avoid idle conversation, and spend a lot of time with his own thoughts. He also loved being off the grid whenever possible. He did not even have an American Social Security number. Not an official one, though he had two or three dozen top-quality fakes, each with a different name, address, and occupation.

Currently he was in Israel checking into something odd involving reports of miracles of the Old Testament variety.

It made him wonder if the Deacon was pulling at the other end of the same string. That wouldn't be the first—or even the tenth—time that had happened over the years. Jack liked the Deacon and had a pretty good working theory about the man's actual identity. In younger years, before the world got a lot larger and stranger for him, that would have totally freaked him out. But Jack, if nothing else, was a practical guy. Even when the universe kept being wildly *impractical*. Like that early case when he encountered actual *rakoshi* demons. That had nearly fried his brains, but getting through that case and coming out on top changed his perspective about the world forever. It was a larger world.

There were later encounters with the legendary warrior Glaeken and others who were engaged in a very long conflict whose only representation in news and literature was through wild distortions. Funny thing, as Jack saw it, those distortions underplayed it to the point of comedy. In truth it was a close damn call for everyone.

And, no surprise, Jack learned, that Church had some old dealings with the immortal warrior Glaeken in the past. He knew some of those stories, but not all, himself.

Jack wondered how much of this the Deacon told Joe Ledger.

From what he'd heard from hovering on the edges of the Deacon's world, Ledger had walked through some strange shadows. Maybe that's why he was supposed to be out of his goddamn mind.

"Helps in this business," Jack said aloud as he stuffed some goodies into his go-bag.

He paused as he passed the mirror on the inside of his hotel door. Jack liked to be the kind of person other people barely noticed. Average height, average weight and build, average hair and eye color. Nondescript in almost every way. That offered a tremendous freedom of movement.

He shrugged into his backpack, patted down the various pockets of his clothes, including the ones he'd hand-sewn into useful places, gave himself an ironic smile, and then the loner whom people called Repairman Jack went out to get into some trouble.

CHAPTER 133
PRIVATE OFFICE
PIRATE LAB
SUBURB OF JERUSALEM

Toombs turned out to be easy to find. He had a note taped to the outside of his office. It read:

MY NAME IS ISAAC TOMBERLAND.
PEOPLE CALL ME TOOMBS.
    I am in my office holding a hand grenade with the pin out but the spoon in place. That's so I can encourage some consideration instead of someone punching my ticket.
    I have useful intel I am willing to share based on certain conditions.
    The doors are unlocked.
    I will not resist.
    Please do not shoot me. I will take your word on this.
    WE REALLY NEED TO TALK.

We read the note and looked at each other.

"Guy's cool as a penguin with an ice cube up his ass," said Bunny.

Top smiled. "Guy's practical and knows he has one card to play."

"Don't much like the grenade."

"How would you play it?"

"Pretty much the same," said Bunny. "Still don't like it."

"Lot of things going on I don't much like, farm boy."

I knocked on the door, then called through. "Isaac Tomberland."

"I hear you," came the voice from inside.

"You willing to put the pin back in that grenade?"

"You willing to give me your word?"

"Why would you accept my word?"

"Because," he said, "I'm pretty sure you're Colonel Joe Ledger, and despite the fact that everyone says you're crazy as an outhouse owl, they say you'll play fair. I need fair because I am way, way up the creek and I don't have a paddle. All I have is a lot of information in my head that you need, and this here grenade is a conversation starter in any way you want it to be."

"We're not walking in while you're holding a live grenade, Tomberland."

"Please, call me Toombs."

"I'll call you Easter Bunny if you put that pin back in," I said. "I'll call you a hearse if you don't."

I let him think about that.

After a bit, he said, "You want me, that's fine. I can't win this fight. But I want a promise that I get immunity."

"In return for what?"

"I can tell you cowboys two things you need to know. I can show you Harith's face. He's the one with the nukes. And I can tell you where to find him."

"We want Aydelotte, too."

"I can do that."

"Open the door and let's talk."

"Okay, Ledger, putting the pin back," he called. "It's safe now."

"You do *not* want to fuck with me, Toombs."

"No," he said. "I want to live. Come on in."

And we did.

CHAPTER 134
PRIVATE OFFICE
PIRATE LAB
SUBURB OF JERUSALEM

He sat like a statue carved out of marble. White on white on white except for a suit better suited to a midwestern undertaker. A long and lugubrious face that was probably unused to smiling even before three big sons of bitches with guns and a dog with bloodstains all around his mouth crowded into his office.

First thing I saw, though, was an apparently unloaded gun and a grenade with—thank baby Jesus—the pin snugged into place. Toombs sat with his chair pushed back and hands like giant dead albino spiders splayed out on his thighs.

Top covered him while I went around, pulled him roughly to his feet, and gave him the kind of pat-down I used to give wise-guys and gangbangers when I was riding a patrol car in Baltimore. Not as thorough or messy as a body cavity search, but enough to tell me that if he had a wire or anything more dangerous than a butterscotch candy in his pockets, I'd have found it. Toombs did not resist or complain and wore a small philosophical expression throughout.

While I did that, Bunny removed the weapons from the desk, checked them, and stowed them safely away.

I pointed to the chair. "Sit."

Toombs sat.

"So do we have a deal?" he asked, smoothing his tie.

"We don't have shit yet," I said. "Your offer of information is the reason you're still sucking air. Someone associated with the ass-clown you work for blew up a nuke last night, and there are still three missing. Friends of mine are either in the morgue or the hospital, as are a whole bunch of Mossad agents. Your boss is out there with a brain full of spiders and maybe he knows where the three nukes are. You tell me something I can use, and I'll see if I can carve out a sliver of mercy, you ghost-looking motherfucker. But . . . you stall me or misdirect me? And you will spend a lot of time with me in a special room. You think you're tough, and maybe you are, but I have a metric ton of crazy I

JONATHAN MABERRY

haven't even used yet, and don't you begin to think that's a threat you can live with."

Top stood behind me. "Son, look into his eyes and make your best life choice right now."

Toombs did that. He looked into my eyes.

I added, "Your current line of credit is deep in the red, Lurch, so let's see if you can move some of it into the black. If not, I'll let Ghost here munch your nutsack for as long as it takes to get the answers I need."

That actually *did* make him smile.

"Funny as it sounds, Ledger," he said mildly, "I like the way you do business."

"Can't say the same. And that noise you hear is a big-ass clock ticking down to me losing what little patience I have. So . . . that said, no bullshit, no walking us around the park. Start off by telling me things I need to know. If I like what I hear, then all kinds of perks suddenly fall on the table."

"Immunity?"

"Act your age," said Top. "You're going to do time, and we all know it. What kind of time depends on what you say."

Toombs sighed in a way that let me know he already understood the stakes but, as a salesman, had to at least ask.

"I'm not saying this to stall," began Toombs, "but I don't know what you know. Should I assume you're recording this? Yes? Okay, that'll help. And, one preface is . . . the nukes thing was no part of anything I was involved in. When I realized that that's where we went, that became my line in the sand. If Aydelotte was still here I would have blown holes in his kneecaps, dropped a dime, and been halfway to a different hemisphere by now. I could have bugged out after setting this place on fire. And, the thing is, I didn't think I *had* a line I wouldn't cross. I'm not a nice person. I'm not a fine citizen. I'm a career criminal, arms dealer, and total piece of shit by any moral or legal standard."

"Not used to this level of frankness," said Bunny, amused.

"Nor am I," conceded Toombs. "So, here we go."

He went back years. To when Jason Aydelotte first made his move from collecting and selling antiquities to stealing them.

"Far as I know from talking with Shock—do you know about her?"

"Yes. Some," I said.

He nodded. "Nice gal. I liked her. Anyway, he hired her to work on some projects he had lined up using ground-penetrating radar. Likely finds of tombs uncovered, or partially uncovered by sandstorms. You'd be amazed at how much sand a big storm can shift. Anyway, Shock would locate tombs that hadn't been previously found or had only been partially looted. Think about it . . . there were thousands of years of pharaohs, priests, nobles. Modern archaeology has barely scratched the surface, but modern tech is changing that game. Shock was savvy enough to stay current with satellites and ground-penetrating radar and staying hooked into the illegal tomb-raider networks. Jason sold it all. Some legit, of course. And some with provenance that was finessed and fudged by officials willing to take bribes. All of this put Aydelotte on TV in a hundred countries. The fact that he had product no one else did earned him the 'Mr. Miracle' nickname. But it goes deeper than that. He *needs* to be seen as the single best source. He's a narcissist like you've never seen. Clever and sly the way narcissists can be, but with a sociopathic side."

I nodded but didn't interrupt. Everyone on the comms was listening, too.

"From what I got out of Shock—and we became close—a couple of things were happening under the radar. First, Jason made contact with a bedouin who was related to the kids who found the first Dead Sea Scrolls. That guy said that there were a lot of scrolls removed from the cave before the more well-known sales happened that are recorded in all the history books. After some bribes, Jason was able to track down the chain of ownership and pay through the nose for a pretty sizeable bundle. It included a key to the Copper Scroll and . . ." He looked at us. "Am I saying anything you can't follow?"

"No," I said. "Keep going."

"Okay, so there was a key to the Copper Scroll, one that made sense of some of those obscure clues as to where treasure was buried. He had Shock go find them, and aside from some hidden household cash people were hiding from the Romans, there were much larger treasures, including some incredible stuff removed from the Second

Temple. Relics, artifacts, other scrolls. That's how Jason made his first thirty billion, and a *lot* of it was on the black market. Oh, and a lot of the buyers on the dark net are legit antiquities buyers who know it's the only source for things they want for their museums and national treasures."

I nodded.

"Jason went mad for anything related to the Scrolls. He came to believe that there were things of even greater importance. And I guess he wasn't wrong. But here's a plot twist, boys. Shock opened a tomb near Luxor belonging to a lost pharaoh named Siamun. He was the pharaoh during the time of the Jewish enslavement talked about in Exodus. Still follow me?"

"Stop asking. Just talk. If I have questions, I'll cut in. Clock's ticking real loud."

"Fine by me. Here's a bit of good but creepy stuff. In Siamun's tomb they found a sealed lead box about so by so." He gestured with his hands. "Sealed with copper and covered with warnings about how Siamun went mad. Shock and Jason brought that box back here to this lab and turned it over to Dr. Conti. She made one discovery— that the curse warned about on the box was an early form of convulsive ergotism. A very powerful strain that was kept viable in the box because there was moisture sealed with it. There was also another copper scroll in there, sealed to protect it from the moisture."

"What scroll?" I asked.

"One written by the two court magicians working for Siamun. The ones who had that battle with Moses and Aaron. Now the weird part is that the scroll supposedly explains how magic actually worked. Understand," said Toombs, holding a hand up, "I never saw that scroll and I don't believe in magic."

"Where is that scroll?"

"Probably with Jason. Point is, Jason believes that magic is real, and he has been doing something with that scroll. Not here in this place, so I don't know *what* he's doing, but I have a very bad feeling."

"Get to it," said Bunny, gesturing with the fat barrel of his shotgun.

"I am. Now we jump forward a bit to when the Al-zilal splinter group of ISIS does a hit on an Israeli camp and mostly gets killed doing it. Three of their guys fled to Jordan and hid out in a cave in the Qumran area, and bang, one of them falls through the cave floor into a big-ass chamber and finds what is absolutely the largest treasure trove of documents from the invasion of Rome in 66 to 73 CE. Something like a quarter ton of Jewish scrolls and stuff from what Shock said had to come from the burning of the Library of Alexandria in 48 BCE. Before you ask, no, there was no Ark of the Covenant or the Holy Grail. What the jihadists found, though, was a second lead box that was identical in size to the Egyptian one, but this was covered in Hebrew, with a lot of the same warnings. No ergot, though, from what I understand. The leader of Al-zilal, Harith al-Wazir, took possession of it, and all I know about that is that he brought in an expert on Egyptian history and languages. Dr. Hegazy, Egypt's version of Jason Aydelotte. Apparently, the Hebrew box had Aaron's account of that same magical duel, with a similar set of instructions. Now . . . I have no fucking clue as to why those scrolls were made, why they were stored the way they were. Shock didn't know, either. But Jason was over the moon with the whole thing."

"You know anything about cobras attacking a CIA interrogation?" I asked, but Toombs gave me a totally blank stare.

"Cobras?"

"Never mind. Move this along."

"Starting with the hunt for the Scrolls the bedouins sold, Jason began making some dicey legal moves. His big step across the line was striking a deal with ISIS to swap goods for goods. He wanted all of the Scrolls and uncountable tons of statuary and other stuff the jihadists supposedly destroyed as part of their attempt to eradicate polytheism from history. At first he paid good folding money for it, and paid well. Then—and again, I don't have this part of it because the salesman before me, Sadiq, died before I could ask him, and Shock didn't know—Jason started getting his hands on stuff like truckloads of RPGs, LAW rockets, laser targeting systems, and that kind of stuff. My personal guess is that a lot of it was looted during the US pullouts from Iraq and Afghanistan. Sometime after that he made connection with a young but pretty brilliant Italian named Marco Russo."

Toombs explained about Russo designing the targeting upgrades for the RPGs and then moved into an explanation of the Gorgon that matched what Toys had heard from Aydelotte himself at the Lady Stern Hotel. So far, I was impressed with the frankness the big ghoul of a salesman was demonstrating.

Then he moved on to the topic of the Shiva bioweapon Dr. Conti created using the unusually potent ergot strain recovered from Pharaoh Siamun's tomb. He explained that the purpose of it was to allow for what Jason called "soft hits" on hard targets.

"At first I thought it was practical," he said. "Jihadist thugs aren't going to ever go toe-to-toe with Israel regulars. They know that. With a mind-altering bioweapon deployed in nonexplosive airbursts, and with that weapon engineered to be ultra-fast onset, then . . . yeah."

"How and why did Jason test-drive that at his own weapons buy in Ashdod?" I asked.

He cut me a calculating look. "You already know a lot. That's good. It'll help for what's coming next."

"Then get to it."

"I confronted Jason about that. And demanded to know if he had anything to do with the ISIS team that hit the camp. He claimed that the weapons had been sold elsewhere and his non-jihadist clients must have sold the stuff to ISIS."

"Do you believe that?" asked Bunny.

"About as much as I believe Jason Aydelotte is Santa Claus."

"Then how did Harith al-Wazir stroll off with four nukes?" I asked.

"That's where this gets really fucking bad," said Toombs. "And if you think it was bad to begin with, then you're wrong."

CHAPTER 135
INTEGRATED SCIENCES DIVISION
PHOENIX HOUSE

Doc Holliday sat on the edge of a table, her booted feet swinging, eyes bright with false humor.

Ronald Coleman knew how to read her. When she looked like a carefree cowgirl on a Friday night before the bars opened, things were bad. And she was rocking that look hard at the moment.

"God's Arrow . . . ?" she mused. "Well, damn, if it ain't bedbugs it's ants."

"An upgraded version of Shiva?" echoed Isaac.

"Well, I don't know about you boys," said Doc, "but I'm fixing to have me a hissy fit with a tail on it."

Isaac looked at Coleman. "Is that good or bad?"

Coleman knee-nudged him. "What the hell do you think?"

"Bad."

"Yeah."

Doc said, "We sent those boys into this mess with what's already looking like last week's casserole. And, fellows, I have no idea if our super juice is going to do the trick if that Aydelotte freak has something significantly stronger."

"Joe and the guys can double-dose," said Isaac doubtfully.

"And freak out in an entirely different way," said Doc. "And maybe shit their drawers doing it. You know the side effects." She gave him a wicked look. "Telling you now that if you make Joe Ledger drop cargo in his own pants while in a firefight then you'd better shop for real estate on the dark side of the moon."

"Fuck," grumbled Isaac.

Coleman, who sat on a wheeled chair next to him, pushed himself a few feet farther away.

CHAPTER 136
HADASSAH EIN KEREM HOSPITAL
KALMAN YA'AKOV MAN STREET
JERUSALEM, ISRAEL

Church looked up as the office door opened and a pale and ghostly face peered in.

"You should be in bed," said Brick, who was closest.

Toys crept in. He had clearly removed his own IV and wore a pair of scrubs instead of a hospital gown. He looked old and grainy, sick and sad. And angry.

"Something's happening," he said. "I can bloody feel it."

"And what do you think is happening?"

"You're punching back."

Brick, looking amused, smiled at Church. "This boy's never been on the short bus."

"Mr. Chismer," began Church, then he caught himself and changed it. "Toys . . . we are following promising leads. Brick and I are pulling together local unofficial resources."

"I can figure out why," said Toys. "The Israelis will have lost their minds by now."

"Understandably so," agreed Church.

"I want in."

Brick stood and gave him a professional up-and-down inspection. "You don't look like you could beat a six-year-old in an arm-wrestling match."

"I can pull a sodding trigger."

Church asked, "How long since the last hallucination? No lies, no obfuscation. Give me the truth or you'll be benched forever."

"Not since last night, and that is the effing truth. Whatever your doctor friend juiced me with has cleared out all the polka-dot lobsters." Toys let go of the door and walked over to the desk Church was using. "I *need* this. They slaughtered my team. Yes, they were all lowlifes like me, but they were trying their best, and they deserved better. If I don't get to take a bite out of this, I'll never be right. You know it and I know it."

"Have you spoken with Dr. Sanchez?"

"Who do you think found me these scrubs?" asked Toys.

CHAPTER 137
PRIVATE OFFICE
PIRATE LAB
SUBURB OF JERUSALEM

"Before we all die of old age," I said, leaning both palms on the desk, "where is Jason Aydelotte?"

"At the Stronghold," said Toombs. "It's his main warehouse right here in Jerusalem. It was built by the same people who built that camp where ISIS stole the nukes. Same basic layout. Was a police station and training center until they built a newer facility and moved out. Jason bought it, and he's ass-deep in guards over there. It's where he stores and packs all of the antiquities he buys, finds, barters, or steals. He's been there a lot, and from what I've heard he's shipped something like eighty tons of stuff back to the States. The place is working around the clock."

"What's the hurry?" asked Bunny.

Toombs looked at him as if he were dense. "Why . . . nukes, of course."

CHAPTER 138
MIRACLE HOLDINGS AND DISTRIBUTION
TRENTON, NEW JERSEY

Sam Imura sat in the passenger seat of the Escalade and studied the building through binoculars. The driver was a lean young Pakistani woman with eyes that looked very much like those of a hawk—fierce, sharp, focused.

"Hazeema," said Sam, "no time like the present."

"Move closer or stay here?"

Sam turned and glanced at the faces of the four people in the back. Three men and another woman. Each wore a nondescript black suit, white shirt, dark tie over ultra-thin body armor. All wore tinted glasses that were a variation of the Scout glasses designed by a friend of Mr. Church's, and provided as a courtesy by the Big Man.

The team was new, but not so new that any of them were virgins when it came to this sort of thing. All five members of the Boy Scouts were former military. All had seen combat either as employees of Uncle Sam or as PMCs in other companies before Sam scouted them. They were old enough to have wisdom but young enough to move like greased rattlesnakes. Sam, though not a deeply affectionate person by nature, loved them all in his way. They were *his* people.

"Sure," he said, "let's drive right up to the door and knock."

CHAPTER 139
PRIVATE OFFICE
PIRATE LAB
SUBURB OF JERUSALEM

"Do you know for sure that Jason Aydelotte was a participant in helping Harith al-Wazir and ISIS obtain nuclear weapons?" I asked.

"Yes, I do."

"How do you know?

He looked around. "I can show you, but I need to turn on my computer."

I made a small finger gesture, and Ghost rose up and put his front paws on the edge of the desk. When he is on the job, there is nothing cute or charming about my dog. He looks like he has eaten someone for breakfast, enjoyed it, and wants second helpings. Toombs looked like a tough son of a bitch, but no one is all that tough in situations like these. His white face went a deeper shade of pale.

"Show us," I said.

He turned on his computer and, without the slightest bit of exaggeration, absolutely blew our fucking minds.

It wasn't a long video clip, and clearly recorded from a Chameleon. We watched it three times. It showed Jason Aydelotte having a deep conversation with Harith al-Wazir.

"Jesus jumped up Christ on a hoverboard . . ." muttered Bunny.

"Fuck me hard and nasty," said Top.

Toombs looked up at me, his strange eyes hopeful.

I had to fight to keep the Killer in my head from leaping across the desk and doing bad things. My inner Cop was shocked. God only knows what rock the Modern Man part of me crawled under.

I leaned across the desk until my shadow covered Toombs's face. "Where can I find him? Right goddamn now? Where is this Stronghold?"

"Do I get immunity if I tell you?"

"Do not fuck with me, son."

He gave me the address.

"How do we get in?"

Toombs did not need to take another look into my eyes. "There's a key card reader. My card is in my desk drawer, but maybe he changed the code."

"Show me," I said.

He opened the door very carefully and removed a key card on which was printed the logo for Miracle Acquisitions.

"How many men?" asked Top. "How many armed?"

"I don't know. Last time I was there was a week ago. Call it guard force of twenty, and four times as many unarmed warehouse loaders. A dozen office staff. If they're still at it, the loaders are going round the clock. It's late, so the office staff is probably gone for the day. Guards are always there."

He paused and replayed that file.

"But maybe Jason has some other friends there, too."

I leaned back. "Luckily we have some friends, too."

Then I nodded to Top, who shot Toombs in the chest with Sandman KS.

After that, we were all running like sons of bitches for the vehicles.

CHAPTER 140
MIRACLE HOLDINGS AND DISTRIBUTION
TRENTON, NEW JERSEY

"Might as well just brave it out," said Sam.

The Boy Scouts looked like a group of Secret Service agents. They walked right up the flagstone path to the front door. It was locked, and Sam opened a leather ID case and pressed it against the glass at a level where the security guards inside could see it. It said FBI, but that was a lie. One of the pair came over and looked at the card and the badge, frowned and pressed a speaker button.

"You have a warrant?"

"Is this glass bulletproof?" asked Sam.

"What?"

"Open the goddamn door," said Sam, his voice mild but his smile far less so. "National security. Open right now while you have a chance of keeping your pension and not spending the next six weeks being interrogated by that son of a bitch."

He jerked his thumb over his shoulder to the biggest and most obviously frightening of his team, Bear, who was about the size and shape of a grizzly. Sam Imura was very tough, but Bear sold visual threat better. The guard thought about it and began turning to his partner, but Sam rapped sharply on the glass.

"Don't look at him, son," he said. "Look at me. Look at the badge. Open the door."

The guard looked a bit green as he fished for his keys. As soon as the door was unlocked, the Boy Scouts pushed inside. Hazeema and Long Sally swarmed past and took charge of the security desk while the others frisked and zip-cuffed the guards.

"Hey," protested one of them.

Bear grinned down at him from a towering height. "Nice teeth. How many of them can I have?"

The protests died.

Sam kept his own face bland. This was not his usual rhythm—he preferred subtlety and style over brute force—but things were going very quickly south overseas. Not a time for the nice guy routine.

"I'm going to report this," said the first guard. "This isn't right. This is Mr. Aydelotte's private business, and I haven't seen a warrant."

Sam came over to him. "You don't know when you're ahead. Tell me, do you ever have bad dreams?"

"No. What? Bad dreams? The hell are you talking about and what the fuck does that have to do with anything?"

Sam was a long-gun master, but there was no kind of firearm he could not use with speed and ultra-precision. He whipped a Snellig dart gun from his pocket and shot the man in the stomach.

"I'd have said 'sweet dreams,'" murmured Sam as the guard fell. "But . . ."

CHAPTER 141
THE STRONGHOLD
OUTSKIRTS OF JERUSALEM

As we ran to the car, we gathered up the rest of Havoc Team while we went. There was no one left standing inside the building.

Violin seemed to materialize out of nowhere beside the lead vehicle. She was idly cleaning the blades of her matched kukri knives and wore a smile as subtle and beatific as the Mona Lisa.

The others ran to catch up, and they looked tired and sweaty. Belle was the last in, walking backward toward the cars, her sniper rifle covering the parking lot in slow sweeps.

"You all heard?"

"Every word," said Andrea. "*Ostia!*"

"Wow is right," agreed Remy. "This is some Wild West shit right here."

Violin studied my face as we got in. She drove with us this time. "And you believe everything that man said?"

"Oddly, I do."

She nodded. "He seems smart enough to know where his only path lies. He knows what you will do to him if he has deceived you." Violin touched the side of my cheek. "My dear, twisted Joseph. People think you're the boogeyman."

"Cut it out."

She gave me a wicked wink.

Top leaned between the seats. "How far's this Stronghold place?"

Bunny, who had claimed driver's seat, had that up on the GPS. "Twenty-two minutes."

"You planning on taking the slow route?"

"I got old people in the back."

"Farm boy, I swear to god . . ."

But Bunny, laughing, stamped down hard on the gas, and the SUV shot forward like it was fired out of a cannon.

Like it was a missile.

CHAPTER 142

HADASSAH EIN KEREM HOSPITAL
KALMAN YA'AKOV MAN STREET
JERUSALEM, ISRAEL

Brick Anderson punched out of the last of a dozen calls and rubbed his eyes. Then he glanced over at Church, who seemed to be staring a hole through the wall.

"I know it's been a long-ass day," said Brick. "Hell, maybe the longest few days. I know how beat you are 'cause you and I are on the same clock. But . . . I have to tell you, I can't just sit here making calls. I need skin in this game."

Focus came slowly back to Church's eyes, and he gave Brick a faint smile.

"You're reading my mind."

They both stood up.

"I got everything we need down in the car," said Brick.

"I know you do."

CHAPTER 143

THE STRONGHOLD
OUTSKIRTS OF JERUSALEM

It did not take twenty-two minutes.

Bunny had Bug on the line and asked him to plow the road. It was one of the things no one in the car knew how it worked, but Bug could mess with streetlights and reports to local police. Given the crisis rocking all of Israel, what he accomplished that day was borderline sorcery.

They reached the side street a block over from the former police station in fourteen minutes.

"You done good, farm boy," said Top as they got out. "Next time take the training wheels off."

"Bite me, old man."

Top gave a warm chuckle as he pulled his bag of weapons out of the back.

"We waiting for backup?" asked Remy as he trotted up.

"Can't risk it," I said. "We still don't know where those nukes are."

"What's the plan, boss?" asked Bunny.

"Find Aydelotte and get the answers out of him by any means necessary."

"Him and Harith," said Violin, giving me a significant look.

"Yes. Him and Harith."

We were already reloaded and ready. Night had fallen hard over Jerusalem, and that beautiful, troubled old city seemed to tremble around us. As we moved through the shadows, I could feel the weight of it. Invasions, conquest, loss, the screaming echoes of pain the Holocaust survivors brought with them, the hard marks of the foot of Rome, the scars of Babylon. All of it.

And yet there was a grace that transcended all of it. This city meant so much to so many, even to those who were enemies of one another. It was the city. In many ways it was the center of the religious world for billions. Jews, Christians, and Muslims. It was a symbol of endurance, of connection despite all that, of a greater vision than what human eyes could see. I realized I loved this city, and that both filled my heart with something potent and magical—a kind of passion— but it also made me feel so incredibly furious. Aydelotte and Harith and their monstrous weapons threatened everything that the best parts of this city stood for.

I know it's hubris, I know it's absurd, but I could not allow them to win.

None of us could.

We had not fought all this way, over all these years, through countless versions of the Valley of the Shadow of Death to have scum like Aydelotte and Harith destroy everything of value about it.

No. We could not allow that.

I could not allow that.

In my head and heart, the Cop and the Killer were wearing their own versions of combat armor. The Cop was alert, cold, ready. The Killer was unfurling his black flag.

And the Modern Man . . . ? I honest to God think he was praying.

CHAPTER 144
THE STRONGHOLD—EAST SIDE
OUTSKIRTS OF JERUSALEM

The place was huge and built to be the fortress it once was.

It was designed to withstand a siege, but not the right kind of siege. There are walls that can make vast armies smash themselves to red ruin against the walls and gates. There are forts that can take weeks of bombardment without crumbling. There are forts that can protect whole cities against crusaders and hordes.

Protecting against a small team with the most cutting-edge infiltration devices, training, and determination is a whole other kind of warfare. We did not come here to lay siege. We came to Jason Aydelotte's Stronghold to tear him out of the heart of it. High walls, guards, gates, and alarms be damned.

CHAPTER 145
THE STRONGHOLD—NORTH SIDE
OUTSKIRTS OF JERUSALEM

He stood in the inky shadows and studied the fortress.

"Mm," he murmured. "Ominous."

His tone was sour but not dispirited.

Repairman Jack knelt, fished through his backpack, selected the right tools, and set to work. He had to control himself because for some reason he kept wanting to whistle a happy tune.

CHAPTER 146
THE STRONGHOLD—EAST SIDE
OUTSKIRTS OF JERUSALEM

We had night, and we had all of the tech and skills we each possessed. We had the TOC online, an eye-in-the-sky in terms of a satellite belonging to—and this freaks me out—Mr. Church. Don't know how, but I will have to ask one of these days. It was launched during my absence and, Top told me, jammed with MindReader QR tech and the Calpurnia AI system. Sounded to me like the opening act of the new Terminator film, but if so, in this case Skynet was on our side. Any port in a storm.

We went in by waves.

First up were all of the bird drones we had: a lot of them of different sizes and purposes. Some carried small, micro-light EMP poppers, and these perched on the cell and radio towers on the roof. One button push would turn those towers into art installations.

Another set of birds perched on lampposts, tree limbs, or even walked on the ground with the officious strutting of regular pigeons—ready for use but conserving battery power.

We had Killer Bees and Busy Bees—their surveillance-only smaller cousins. We had rat drones, their metal bellies filled with various loads—smoke, tear gas, and explosives packages ranging from bad-burn to meet-your-ancestors.

Plus, Andrea and Remy both carried bags to set up countless configurations of the toy box, but also some one-off gadgets to either slow pursuit or eliminate pursuers. And we could barely run with the weight of ammunition we carried.

The first card down in the game was to see what was on the other side of the big, blocking stone walls.

"Let's take a look, Jackpot," I said as we huddled in the inky cleft between the lead truck and a wall. We were still a block out.

"*Vola via, uccellino*," he said as he tossed another dove into the air. *Fly away, little bird.*

It swooped up and over the wall and flitted about as if looking for beetles to crunch. The eyes were incredible cameras, and they sent continuous files to the satellite, which were taken by Bug's software and transformed into a very detailed 3-D interior model of the courtyard below. What we saw chilled us.

There had to be thirty cars and trucks crammed into the courtyard. Even with all the cars parked outside, these stood out. They were mostly older, dusty and battered, of the kind that saw hard use, indifferent maintenance, and storage without care. The bird began capturing license plates, and not one of them was legit.

As the bird swooped lower, the camera began taking shots of the

JONATHAN MABERRY

men patrolling the courtyard. There were a few standard armed security guards in nondescript brown uniforms. But there were two or three times as many men wearing various kinds of khaki clothes or camos. Every one of them wore a kaffiyeh of the same pattern of blue and brown checks we'd seen before.

"ISIS for sure," said Top.

"Yeah," said Bunny. "Those Al-zilal goons."

"What are they doing here, though?" asked Remy.

"If Aydelotte is pulling up stakes, like that Toombs stiff suggested," offered Top, "then maybe these boys are here to take possession of whatever Mr. Miracle has left to sell. Maybe it's a fire sale. All the Gorgons you can carry."

"If so," I said, "then we take it all away from them."

"Rules of engagement?" asked Top.

"Until we find where they've stashed those nukes, everyone gets to live."

"And after?"

I smiled. "Look into my eyes."

He smiled, too. Not one of his fatherly grins.

I pulled Andrea's arm closer to me so I could study the current image one of his circling drones was sending.

"Look here," I said. "There is an exterior drainpipe forty yards from the corner of the north wall. Lamp glow doesn't reach it, and the camera is on a ninety-second sweep. That's our opening. Mother Mercy, cover that spot. If someone's on the wall and the camera catches them, punch it out."

Her reply was a grunt. A speech for her. Again, John Smith came to mind. He was a good man, gentle and kind despite—or maybe because of—what he did for a living. He died bravely fighting another group who had nukes. The Red Knights. Khalid Shaheed, his best friend and one of the DMS's all-time great warriors, fell in that same battle, far beneath the oil fields in Iran.

Top called the order for climbing. He wanted Gator Bait up first because Remy was light and fit, and gravity never seemed to touch him. He scrambled up like a chipmunk, using only the pipe itself and the friction on the rubber finger-pads of our combat clothes. He anchored a line and then Top sent Bunny up. He was six-six and densely muscled. Slower than everyone when climbing, but once up there he could pull up Andrea, who now had two gear bags and might have had trouble.

And Bunny could hoist Ghost up easier and faster than I could.

Then we were all on the wall.

There were four square towers, and brown-suited guards were visible in each. I had Andrea send two Killer Bees to each but had him wait. We'd use a coordinated hit on them at need.

Then we split up to go hunting.

These moments, we knew, were likely to be the last quiet ones. I just hoped they weren't our last of all moments.

CHAPTER 147
THE STRONGHOLD—NORTH SIDE
OUTSKIRTS OF JERUSALEM

A very small sound made Jack turn very fast. He had a knife in one hand and pistol in the other. His body shifted into the kind of fighting crouch that the unwary would not see the danger in, but which would give a professional serious pause.

"Pax," said a voice as three figures moved out of dense shadow and paused at the edge of weaker gray light. Two of the figures were big, one was smaller and slim and looked sickly.

Jack smiled at the lead man. "What do I call you these days? Deacon. Prester John? Dr. Pope? I've lost track."

"Call sign is Merlin," said the lead man. "But I go by Church."

"Keeps to the theme, I suppose."

Repairman Jack sheathed the knife and shook hands. He was introduced to Brick but before Church could name the third man, Jack pulled his hand back.

"Whoa, wait a minute now," he said. "I know this asshole, and in case you don't, he's not one of us. Doesn't Aunt Sallie do background checks for you anymore?"

"Auntie is retired," said Church. "Stroke."

"Oh. Fuck. I love her."

"I'll tell her."

"But that dickhead is Alexander Chismer. Toys. Worked for Sebastian Gault."

"That was then," said Church. "He's turned a page."

Jack rolled his eyes. "Another one of your lost souls? Good god, you really *ought* to have gone into the priesthood."

"They're better off without me."

Jack studied Toys. "You remember me?"

"Yes," said Toys. "I do."

"Do you recall the last thing I said to you? In Morocco, I think it was?"

"It was Mombasa, and yes, I remember."

Brick looked back and forth and then shifted protectively close to Toys. "There isn't going to be a problem here, is there?"

"I don't know," said Jack. "Is there? Why is he here?"

Church gave him a penetrating look. "Because he's earned his place."

He gave Jack a long time to think about that. Maybe two seconds. Finally, the loner nodded.

"I don't feel like this is a handshake moment, Toys," he said. "You have someone vouching for you whose word matters. I don't want promises from you, but I'll take *his* any day."

"Gosh, thanks," said Toys.

"Fuck with me in any way, though," continued Jack. "Or show the wrong colors, and Church or no, I'll put you down."

Toys gave him a very pleasant smile. "Go fuck yourself. Don't use lube."

"Ain't love grand?" muttered Brick.

The four of them moved off along the inside of the north wall.

CHAPTER 148
THE STRONGHOLD—EAST SIDE
OUTSKIRTS OF JERUSALEM

We descended to the ground level but stayed well back from where the vehicles were clustered. The mixed bag of guards seemed to want to be there, well into the light. And it was obvious there was no mingling. That in itself was interesting. Not one big happy family. Made me wonder about Top's idea of a fire sale being on point.

Teams of them did come out of the south wall of the courtyard carrying metal cases and oversize ammunition cases, which they began to load into the cars.

"Jackpot," I said very quietly. "Tag every car. Nothing gets out of here we can't track."

"You want surprises on them, too?"

"Do it."

He looked *soooo* happy as he removed more micro-drones. Between what he and the rest of us carried, we were lugging about two million dollars' worth of science fiction battle-rattle. And, as with the gear we carried to Chad, anything left behind would self-destruct. It's a damn good thing Church and Bug kept looting the banks of some of the bad guys we took down.

Andrea sent roaches and scorpions to the cars. The roaches climbed up and attached themselves to the inside of the rear fenders away from the gas tank sides. Hard to spot and never the first place someone looks. Th scorpions magnetized themselves to the bottoms of the gas tanks. When triggered, their thermite charges blew upward. In the movies, car gas tanks explode. They rarely do that in real life unless you want them to.

As he finished that, we moved as stealthy as wise cats along the wall until we found doors that no one was using. We entered into Aydelotte's literal stronghold.

We had to rely on the Busy Bees to map the interior, but one small win was that it didn't look like Aydelotte modified it much from the original floor plan from when it was a police station. A few rooms had been knocked together to make studios for cleaning, photographing, and cataloging antiquities. Most of the jail cells had been turned into storage for crates of every kind. There were apartments, lounges, two mess halls, a huge kitchen, and lots of other rooms. Only one basement level that we could so far find.

When Grendel began speaking, I raised my fist, and we all took a knee out of sight.

"Outlaw, be advised two other teams are in play inside," he told us. "Arklight—team of four with Violin on point—is searching the big truck-loading bays. Merlin Team is on the north inner wall moving toward the ops center."

"Merlin Team?"

"Merlin Actual, Iceman, Toys, and Repairman."

Top's expression must have mirrored my own. Surprise, amusement, confusion.

"Copy that," I said dubiously. "We expecting anyone else to this party?"

"Those are our complete resources. Please proceed with caution. Password exchange only at need. Greeting is 'charm school'; response is 'graduate.' Confirm and repeat."

I did.

"You're mission leader," said Church's voice. "You call the shots."

That was a surprise and a bit of a shock. I have never given orders to Church. Nor, for that matter, to Brick Anderson, even though I technically outrank him. And Violin would, I knew, take whichever orders she cared to take.

"This'll be fun," said Bunny, though I wasn't sure if he meant it.

Over the mission channel, I said, "Priority one is to find and secure Jason Aydelotte and Harith al-Wazir. You all know what that means."

"Hooah," came the various responses.

"Whoever gets them needs to secure them where they can be interrogated. Then finding where they've stashed the nukes is the next priority. Bug, Grendel, we need all lines of communication open because once we have a location, we need to turn it over to the Israelis."

"Outlaw," said Wilson, "key players in the government are waiting for that intel. Cool heads, ready for immediate response."

"Good to know." I paused and listened to the ambient noise. The teams loading the cars and trucks were making useful cover noise, and someone had turned on a radio. The somewhat haunting sounds of *mijwiz* music, with its bamboo pipes and that unusual method of playing that involved circular breathing to produce a tone that doesn't require pauses for breath. It went on and on, filling the night with a sinister sweetness.

"Gator Bait to Outlaw," called Remy. "I have cameras set up and am getting live video footage of the brown-suit guards working with the jihadists. This is the evidence we need, isn't it? Can we call the cavalry?"

"We are the cavalry," I said. "The Israelis are looking for the nukes. We're here after the cocksuckers who are trying to figure out who to blow up with them."

"Copy that."

"Jackpot," I said, "keep those EMP bombs handy. If we lose control of this, then we can't let anything out. No cells, no radios, no remote triggers, feel me?"

"Copy that, Outlaw," came the reply. "We're one three-digit code away from sending this whole place back to the Paleolithic."

"Okay, time for everyone to juice up," I said, and removed a ketanserin syrette, took a breath, and jabbed it into my thigh, then gave a smaller canine-adjusted dose to Ghost. He took it in silence because this was a mission. If I'd lightly stepped on his tail at home, I'd have gotten a howling sermon. "Everyone keep aware of your partners. Watch for Shiva effects. Double-dose them if you can, Sandman KS if you can't. No exceptions."

"Hooah."

Using the 3-D models provided by the drones and bees, I split up the building into search grids. I further split Havoc Team, once more sending Remy and Andrea out as a pair. Top and Bunny went looking on the second level, and I took Ghost with me upstairs.

I have often wondered since what would have happened if I had made different choices at that moment.

CHAPTER 149
MIRACLE HOLDINGS AND DISTRIBUTION
TRENTON, NEW JERSEY

Sam Imura and the Boy Scouts went through the Trenton warehouse with speed, aggression, deep curiosity, growing anger, and determination. They were all shooters, but Sam had put each of them through investigative training as well. He wanted his people to be as close to the standard acceptable to Mr. Church. And though he seldom liked to admit it, Sam admired Ledger's background as an investigator. That had helped Ledger make good judgment calls—most of the time—and to make intuitive leaps that saved time and saved lives.

The staff were all shunted into conference rooms, but with jammers in place and cell phones collected. Landlines were removed from their jacks and the instruments carried out. Three times guards tried to make a fuss. Three times Sandman shut them down nicely, and visibly. That went a long way to silencing further pushback.

As Sam went through the various storerooms, he sent body cam images to Nikki Bloom at RTI. Bug, she told him, was doing real-time overwatch for the mission and could not take any calls. As the images flowed to her, Sam could hear her voice getting more excited.

"I'm running these images through MindReader and, god, Sam," she said, "a lot of that stuff is unregistered. If nothing else, we probably got Aydelotte on taxes."

Sam snorted. "I have a feeling Joe wants a bit of heavier judgment on this Mr. Miracle than that."

"No doubt," agreed Nikki. "I bet he wishes you were on his six right now."

"I don't," was Sam's curt reply. "I'm fine where I am. We'll gather up everything that could be useful in court. Remind Grendel that some legit warrants would be useful. I do not relish having to explain things to the IRS or the cops."

"He says to tell you a courier is heading your way right now. Church has a few judges who are—"

"Yeah, yeah, friends in the industry."

CHAPTER 150
THE STRONGHOLD
OUTSKIRTS OF JERUSALEM

Ghost and I went upstairs using a fire stair that was inconveniently placed for common use by the staff. Good for us, though. There was one guard seated on the top step of the second landing, his rifle laid on the concrete beside him and a big falafel sandwich in his hands.

I leaned around the turn and shot him. He twitched, spat out an improbable amount of cilantro and parsley, and fell forward. I caught him before his head could splat on the lower steps, angled his face so if he needed to vomit he could do it without choking, took his cell, zipped his hands to the railing spindles, took his walkie, and moved past him.

Although I was fine not being the angel of death here—and despite rebuke from the Killer in my head—taking these guys out with Sandman and then cuffing them was wasting time.

I could feel a strangeness in my body as the ketanserin worked through me. Not at all pleasant. Kind of like having the first tremors at the beginning of a cold or flu. But nothing crawled out of the walls, so there was that.

Two guards, both brown-suits, were stationed outside of a room with lighted windows. They stood at attention and looked alert. I took the Snellig in a two-handed grip and moved toward them with quick, small, very light steps and shot them as they became aware. They went right down. Had it not been for the music and chatter down in the courtyard, the clatter of their weapons might have been heard. But it wasn't.

I crept up, dragged one farther back from the edge because his arm was hanging over, and very, very carefully took a peek through the lower corner of the window. And I looked right into my own eye.

Two-way glass with the mirror facing out.

Inconvenient, but not a full stop. I removed a small device the size of a pack of Tic Tacs. It stuck to the lower corner of the pane with adhesive strips. Inside the housing was a small circular diamond blade. It cut quickly and very quietly, sacrificing a little of the former to make sure of the latter. When a section of glass smaller than a dime was cut, it pulled the piece into the housing. A counterclockwise turn removed it from the adhesive and I fed in a slender fiber-optic scope. Not much of it, only the tip so as not to present a moving distraction. Peripheral vision is sharper and more alert than many people think it is. When you live in a world of high tension, you become more aware of it. So I was real damn careful.

And there he was.

There *they* were.

Jason Aydelotte in conversation with Harith al-Wazir.

I knew what I would find, but it still jolted me. Aydelotte, dressed in an elegant business suit, sat with a cup of coffee cradled between his palms. On a screen facing him was Harith.

The screen was Aydelotte's big computer monitor.

The screen was turned off.

With it darkened, the surface was reflective. A mirror.

And Aydelotte spoke with the face in that reflection.

CHAPTER 151
THE TOC
PHOENIX HOUSE

Everyone stared at the image on the screen.

It was what Toombs told Ledger, but it changed nothing. In fact, the undeniable truth of it changed the shape of reality.

Jason Aydelotte, the voice of religious antiquities, the hero who saved much of what ISIS tried to destroy, the Mr. Miracle of so many TV shows—from educational documentaries to Hallmark Christmas movies—was one half of a person. His other half, created in some fragmented room of the man's mind, was Harith al-Wazir, the founder and leader of the al-Jilal splinter cell. The felt but never-before-seen master manipulator behind countless increasingly successful arms deals that tore allied planes and helicopters from the sky. The man who had orchestrated one of the greatest crimes in history—the theft of four air-to-surface nuclear missiles from the Israeli army.

It explained everything and nothing.

Only a few people, some of them watching from remote places like the Arklight safe house—Rudy Sanchez and Helmut Deacon—understood. Church understood. Maybe even Repairman Jack understood, since his life was a schism of sorts, too.

Joe Ledger understood.

The rest merely had to accept.

It tied nearly all of the strings of the many cases together. Not all, though. It did not explain the cobras or the bat bites. Everything else, though . . .

Yes.

Shockingly, horribly, yes.

Bug, who was at his big workstation in the TOC, murmured, "We're really in the shit now."

He glanced up at Scott, who was slowly wiping sweat from under his eyes.

"All teams proceed," he said, choking on the words.

CHAPTER 152
THE STRONGHOLD
OUTSKIRTS OF JERUSALEM

Merlin Team moved through a hallway, following a signal indicating the power output of a communications center. Toys lagged behind the others. His face was sallow, and his eyes lacked any trace of his usual confidence.

Brick cut a look at Toys. "Hey, kid, I dig the balls you're showing by coming with us. That says a lot, but this is going to get rough, and you came straight from a hospital bed. You can hang back. You don't need to prove anything."

Toys gave him a look of stinging rebuke. "You don't understand me at all, do you?"

"I—" began Brick but then paused as the image from Ledger's scope came through. They stood, watched, and listened.

"What the *hell*?" asked Jack.

Church explained very quickly what they had come to realize about Aydelotte.

"What are we talking here?" asked Jack, goggling. "Some kind of schizophrenia?"

"Dissociative identity disorder," provided Brick. "Guy had at least two people in his head. We don't know if he's aware of it or not. Either way, both sides of him are scary dangerous."

"One bullet will solve that, won't it?" But then Jack corrected himself. "Let me guess . . . you fellows don't know which part of his brain knows where the nukes are, do you?"

"We don't."

"Shit."

"Life is a bowl of cherries," said Toys. "Haven't you heard?"

"What's the play?"

"Control communications without interrupting anything."

"I get it," said Jack, nodding. "There are forty ways for this to go south if we just go radio silent. Standing orders to push a button if they don't get a regular standby order, and they move on. Or a continuous hold signal transmitted as a kind of dead-man's switch. Like that?"

"Like that," said Church.

"Fun times."

"The war is the war."

"You're still saying that after all these years."

"It's still true after all these years."

Jack sighed. "Yup. Guess it is at that."

CHAPTER 153
THE STRONGHOLD
OUTSKIRTS OF JERUSALEM

I crouched low and crabbed along under the window until I reached the door. The gentlest pressure told me the door was locked.

Shit.

There was no quiet way to get inside. Not through a door that had four windowpanes next to a big two-paned picture window. I looked at the two sleeping, twitching guards. One was about Andrea's size—far too short and thin. The other was closer to my size, but it was hard to say. I'm six foot one and have decent shoulder width. He looked tall enough and fit, but also thinner. But it was worth a try.

I dragged him around a corner and very quickly stripped off everything down to the waist except my thin spider-silk longjohns. Then I removed his shirt and buttoned it up the best I could. Top chest button and throat were no-gos, but I figured a loose knot in the tie, his billed cap, and the uniform color might be enough. All I needed was to get into that room.

Then I stood up, smoothed the shirt, slung his rifle, and went over and just freaking knocked.

There was a sound of movement from within and some murmured words, and I wondered if Aydelotte had to say goodbye to his other half.

"What is it?" he called.

"Sir," I said crisply but not loudly, "we're having engine trouble with one of the trucks."

"Which truck?"

"Um . . . they didn't say, but it's one of the big ones."

"Oh for god's sake, hold on."

There was a heavy movement out of a chair and then the *clickety-click* of a heavy bolt being turned inside. He pulled the door open and stared at me.

"Who the hell are you?" he said.

I was set for it. Not with a gun or a knife.

I had my feet screwed into the floor, my knees, hips, and waist coiled, and as the door opened, I hit him in that zone where the xiphoid process hangs down like a speedbag from the bottom of the sternum. It's what some people incorrectly call the solar plexus. I hit him with all of the anger, fear, and outrage that boiled in my own gut. The blow crushed him in half, and he staggered backward, all of the air whooshing out of his lungs, his eyes bulging with impossible levels of pain and surprise, cheeks darkening, hands thrust forward with fingers splayed like a background dancer in an old Bob Fosse movie. He took a dozen little backward steps, one cheek of his ass against his desk, and sat down hard. His eyes rolled high and white, and he vomited between his splayed thighs, sagged sideways, and passed out.

"I'm Joe Fucking Ledger, asshole," I said.

I came in and closed the door. Ghost bounded around to sniff every corner, but we were alone. Sucked for Aydelotte.

Sucked a lot.

　　　　　　　　　　　　　　　JONATHAN MABERRY

CHAPTER 154
THE STRONGHOLD
OUTSKIRTS OF JERUSALEM

Repairman Jack walked right into the communications room. Unlike everyone else who had invaded the Stronghold, he was dressed the most the like an ordinary citizen. There was a row of handy-looking clipboards on the wall outside, each with some kind of sign-in sheet. He plucked one off, tapped on the glass door with the corner of it, and entered.

"Hey," he said, "I looked for Jimmy on the shift schedule, but he's listed as off. Thought he was on for tonight."

The four men seated at various desks, each wearing headphones, looked up with mild disinterest.

"Jimmy who?" asked one of them. "Smith or Lazlo?"

"Fuck if I know," said Jack and pointed a gun at him. Church and Brick flowed inside immediately, both of them with Snelligs raised. Toys covered the room from the doorway, a pair of Glocks in his hands.

"Hands away from the controls," ordered Brick. "Mouths shut. You fart wrong and this gets ugly."

The four men stared at the newcomers as if they had beamed down from Mars. Three of the four of them were pragmatic enough to raise their hands and push their chairs back from the desks.

But there is usually one person who has what he thinks is a hero gene. Or he's too loyal or too stupid. The fourth man dove for his console and started to yell a warning.

Church was the oldest—by far—of the four of them, and he was farther away than either Brick or Jack, but he reached the foolish one first, and suddenly the man was leaning back in his chair, face contorted in a paroxysm of agony so intense it stole his ability to scream. Church kept pressure on a very specific spot on the side of the man's neck and surveyed the other three with cold, dark eyes.

"You have been given orders," he said mildly.

Toys raised his guns. "Trust me that you want to listen."

The men raised their hands, and Merlin Team went to work on them.

CHAPTER 155
THE STRONGHOLD
OUTSKIRTS OF JERUSALEM

I dragged Aydelotte into the back room, hoisted his bulk onto a couch, zip-cuffed his ankles and wrists, and then gave him a few entertaining slaps to wake him up.

He hadn't gone entirely out, but he was at the edge. There are punches and punches. Do it one way and you knock the wind out of someone. Do it another and you can rupture internal organs. I was shooting for a middle ground. I wanted him able to answer questions, but I sure as hell didn't want him enjoying it.

Understand, I'm not actually cruel—though the Killer part can be. It's just that people were dying, and there were those nukes. Wasn't a Mr. Rogers moment, if you can dig that. I even think Rudy might have approved, though he'd want to go to confession afterward.

Aydelotte's eyes swam slowly back into focus. I let him get a good look into mine. God only knows what he saw. The Cop and the Killer and me looking back.

"L-L-Ledger," he stammered.

"Yeah," I said. "Ain't that fun?"

"You can't be here."

"And yet here I am, jackass."

Ghost, for reasons entirely his own, leaned in and licked some of the vomit off of Aydelotte's chin. Disgusting, unexpected, and yet somehow weirdly effective. Aydelotte turned a disturbing gray-green and was unable to look at my dog again. Maybe he'd seen the wolf behind the eyes of the dog. Others have; few get a chance to walk away from that.

"Listen to me," I said. "I know what you're doing. We're tearing down your entire network, here and in the States. The IRS, Homeland, the CIA, Mossad, and all of the other alphabet groups you don't want giving you a legal prostate exam. But there it is. You're done, you're cooked."

"I'm a businessman," he blurted. "I sell religious antiquities . . ."

"And I'm the Flying Nun. Fuck you. We know what you're doing."

He tried to close his face, to not show anything.

"Okay," I said. "Try this. Gorgon. Shiva. Blind Eye. Lead boxes in tombs. Lead boxes in Cave Thirteen in Qumran. RPG upgrades. God's Arrow. Camp 1391. Four nukes. Shock, dead as fuck. Dr. Conti, a suicide. Toombs, diming you out. Pharaoh Siamun. Ayoob Alazaki. Al-zilal." And I leaned in close for the last one. "Harith al-Wazir."

I let all of that swirl around in his brain as the Cop in me read him, looking for tells, looking for recognition. Searching for a schism between Aydelotte and Harith. Looking for a connection, a shared awareness that I wasn't certain was even there.

When he didn't answer, I leaned closer still and named the mosque in Willow Grove, Pennsylvania. I named people from his childhood that he hurt or possibly killed. I kept turning dials on him, kept driving the mental bamboo shoots up under his fingernails.

His eyes jumped and twitched, and I don't think I have ever seen anyone so comprehensively terrified. Or as confused.

His mouth began to work. Not well, and with nearly no volume to his words.

"My . . . my name is Mr. Miracle," he said in a voice that was almost that of a child. Weak, small, defensive, frightened. Lost. "I'm on TV."

And he began to cry.

CHAPTER 156
THE STRONGHOLD
OUTSKIRTS OF JERUSALEM

Violin and her Arklight sisters moved through the garages at the back of the compound. There was a big bay that opened out into loading docks for tractor-trailers. Brown-shirts with guns stood watch as teams of ISIS fighters moved stacks of metal crates into the back of one truck. The other was full, but the doors were open as men strapped the cargo in place with canvas belts.

Violin did some quick math. The trucks were big—eighteen-wheelers with fifty-three foot bodies capable of holding a max weight of between forty-three and forty-five thousand pounds, or something more than twenty thousand kilograms. Each of the boxes she could see was familiar—the kind used to store RPGs, LAW rockets, and similar man-portable weapons. And many newer, sleeker cases of the kind she had seen in the video footage from the book warehouse: Gorgons.

That much firepower, even if they were not loaded with Shiva, would give Al-zilal the ability to do untold harm.

She turned to her companions, and in the silent, flowing sign language unique to Arklight, told them that they could not allow those trucks to leave. She sent two women down to slip under each truck and do something to disable them.

Then she used a keypad on her tactical computer to relay the information to the TOC, to her mother, and to the rest of the team.

Word came back at once from Scott Wilson to hold until Aydelotte was confirmed secured and intel was acquired about the nukes.

Violin passed this along, and she and her sisters waited. Watching the jihadists who, unlike so many, many Muslim men and women they knew and trusted, were living according to an ugly and twisted interpretation of the Quran. Their hatred toward learning, toward women, toward freedom of thought was no different to the Arklight women than were the brutal policies of the Red Knights.

The hatred of those four women for the ISIS fighters was no different than it had been for those knights. Those dead and butchered knights. Hatred, like revenge, was a dish best served cold, and there was nothing but ice in the hearts of Violin and her sisters.

Witches in the dark.

Silent and patient as spiders.

CHAPTER 157
THE STRONGHOLD
OUTSKIRTS OF JERUSALEM

Top and Bunny walked right into trouble.

Sometimes it happens that way. Even with all the experience they had individually and collectively, and with all of the tech support and caution in the world, sometimes things just go south.

They were moving soundlessly down a hall when a man came out of a side room. He didn't walk out, but caught his foot on something and tripped. He yelled as he fell, and a tray heavy with six cups of coffee flew from his hands, hit the top rung of a metal pipe rail, clanged improbably loudly, tilted over, and dropped six porcelain mugs, the hot coffee, a dish of sugar packets, an open box of power bars, a metal pot of milk, and a lot of spoons over the edge and down onto the main courtyard where the cars were being loaded.

Immediately everyone down there stopped working and looked up.

The man who tripped, at that moment, saw Top Sims. Big, black man in combat armor and guns.

He screamed very, very loudly in the half second before Top dosed him with Sandman.

But the damage was done, and such things can never be undone.

Below, dozens of men dropped what they were carrying and dove for their rifles.

"Shit, shit, shit," cried Bunny as he grabbed Top by the shoulder and jerked him back just as the first fusillade began chewing up the walkway. The man who'd dropped the tray was torn apart, though by then the Sandman had lulled him into a protective sleep from which he would never awaken.

"Havoc, Havoc, Havoc," called Bunny. "Shit's hit the fan. We're compromised."

By then there was no part of the Stronghold that did not echo with automatic gunfire. All because one guard forgot to tie a loose set of laces.

Worlds turn very badly on such moments.

Worlds have burned for less.

CHAPTER 158
THE STRONGHOLD
OUTSKIRTS OF JERUSALEM

I heard the gunfire and knew the poop had hit the propellers. Didn't matter who or why.

I took Aydelotte's face between the fingers of one hand and gave his jaws and cheeks a bit of a lobster pinch. Cute when you do that with a laughing kid on his birthday. Far less so when a killer is doing it to you during an interrogation.

"Where. Are. The. Nukes?" I asked, pinching a little harder with each word.

"I . . . don't know . . ." he wailed. "I don't have them. I sell—"

"If the next word out of your mouth is 'antiquities' you're going to lose teeth."

"But I . . . I . . ."

"If Jason Aydelotte can't tell me," I whispered, "then let me talk to Harith."

No, I really don't know if that sort of thing works. It does in bad movies. It's even been tried on me early on, by a colleague of Rudy's who was later scolded for it by my friend. But what else did I have to try?

I watched his eyes. Those blueberry blue eyes could look so innocent in the right light, and they used lighting to good effect when he was on TV. In this light, though, they looked darker, ominous, and I caught something there. Still Aydelotte, I think, but it was the worm wriggling in his mind. The Aydelotte who sent Shock to the book warehouse. The Aydelotte who hired Toombs and Giada Conti.

"I can see you," I said, and my voice was that of the Cop. Inflexible, knowing, cynical, and wise. "You know where the nukes are. You, Jason Aydelotte. You know. You gave the Blind Eye casings to Ayoob Alazaki, didn't you? That's what Toombs thinks. Maybe you don't know you're also Harith, but I don't think that's true. You see, I've got other people in my head, too. One of them really, *really* wants to come out to play. I don't care how many scary Old Testament stories you read about wrath, but real wrath is right here. Right at the ends of my fingers. I can keep you alive for a long, long, long time, Jason. And there won't be one single second of it that won't be screaming hell. And I want to. God damn it, I want to."

His mouth, still between my lobster pinch, trembled. His eyes filled with tears, more of hate than fear, but that was fine. Fear was in there, too. Plenty of it.

"Tell me where the nukes are, Jason. Tell me, and I will keep the monster locked up in my head."

"Go to hell," he said in a voice that was cold and clear and accented. Not at all his own.

"Harith," I said. "Tell me. You're in there, too. You can feel pain, too."

"God burn you."

"God's not on your side, Harith. You're pissing on your own people, your own faith. You're bringing harm *to* them."

"I am going to free them. I am going to free everyone."

"Okay. Sure. Give me the speech. Tell me why and how. Fuck, I'm crazy, too. Maybe you have a point."

He laughed at that, as I expected.

"People like you have made war here for thousands of years," he said. "And who has been served by it? By Crusaders? By Babylon and Rome and all the other conquerors? By Britain and the Americans? By the Jews who came and went, came and went while we Arabs have seen our lands devastated, stolen, occupied, defiled."

"Yeah, and ISIS is doing such a swell job of restoring and protecting these lands. You blew up a nuclear bomb yesterday."

He grinned as best he could from between my fingers. "Yes. To open the eyes of the world. To draw the eye and sharpen the ear."

His diction as Harith was so startlingly different from Aydelotte's that it really was like talking to two people. Even a nutcase like me was unnerved. In my own head the Cop and the Killer were distortions of my own inner voice. When they spoke through my mouth, anyone could still tell it was me. Not here, though. Harith and Aydelotte were different people entirely.

"What's the point of all this?" I demanded. "No matter what you do, Israel will still be here. The holy places you all fight over and have fought over for all these years will still be here. All you can do is cause death and pain and dial up the fighting. People will fight harder here if you do something stupid. You know that. This is not a pathway to understanding, and it'll never free your people. Not this way."

"I know," he said. "That has always been the problem."

"Then what is your fucking point? Do you think you can hide those nukes from Israel and its allies forever? They will find them, and when they do, the concept of *revenge* is going to take on a whole new meaning. You'll hurt everyone you think you're trying to save."

"Not if there is nothing left to fight for," he said.

And each of those nine words hit me like punches. Like bullets. My heart nearly stopped. My lungs did.

I let go of his face and stared at him.

"What have you done?" I asked, my voice returning in a whisper filled with such horror that he knew that I knew. That I was right there with him. That the madness in me was able to understand the mad desperation in him.

"They are right here," he said, his mouth smiling but his eyes swirling with mad lights. No . . . with holy purpose. "In this building. One of them. Soon it will go to the Temple Mount. One is already parked near the Western Wall, and the third is in the parking lot of the Church of the Holy Sepulchre."

"What . . . ?" I gasped, and my heart lurched with shocking pain in my chest.

"What need will there be for war when the wrath of Allah cleanses the trappings of conflicted faith. And Mecca . . . even beloved Mecca. What are stones and artwork, paint and tilework to the will of God? What is any of it except an excuse to fight forever over the same bloody ground that has tasted the blood of the infidel and the holy for all these millennia? I, Harith al-Wazir, have dug like a lion in the dirt and unearthed the weapons of God's purity, and with them I will end the wars of the Holy Land for all time. This I do for my people and for the greater glory of Allah."

CHAPTER 159
THE STRONGHOLD
OUTSKIRTS OF JERUSALEM

Andrea and Remy heard the gunfire and began running for cover, leaving behind several toy box areas. But as they ran, they heard what Aydelotte/Harith was telling Joe Ledger.

Remy shot a look at Andrea.

"This can't be real, can it?"

His face was filled with such honest fear that it stole away his adult veneer and left a terrified young boy. Andrea tried to give him a reassuring smile, but what assurance can one give after news like that? Three nukes about to blow, and they were in the thick of it.

"We'll be fine," he lied. "The colonel and Mr. Church will figure it out."

Remy did not know Joe Ledger very well, and Church hardly at all. A madman and a mystery man. His confidence cracked more with every step.

A group of jihadists and one brown-shirt rounded the corner ahead of them and began yelling and firing, and then there was no time to think.

Somewhere nearby a voice was screaming a single, terrible word.

"*Fail-safe.*"

"God," breathed Remy, "don't let that be the bomb. Don't let that be the bomb."

And, all at once and with no apparently reasonable explanation, the overhead sprinklers kicked on and showered everything with water.

It burst from the units with unusually intense force, and there was a subtle golden tint to the spray. It smelled, too. Like old socks.

Like fungus.

And God's Arrow was among them.

CHAPTER 160
THE STRONGHOLD
OUTSKIRTS OF JERUSALEM

I heard the screams and gunfire, but it was hard to look away from those mad blue eyes.

There was such . . . *peace* in them.

Peace. Acceptance. Belief.

Jason Aydelotte was mad as the moon. Harith al-Wazir was a visionary willing to change the face of the Holy Land forever, and in doing so, change the world. These were the trembles I'd been feeling as, bit by bit, the fabric of reality that I understood began to change into a new pattern that no one could yet understand. Harith had, like a true believer, set himself on a course to immolation with the rest of us. With his land and the structures of the faiths of the Muslims, Christians, and Jews.

His desire was, in its own way, pure.

The crazy, ugly, funny thing was that in many ways he might be right. Not that I could permit him to impose that will, but without these contested places, these markers to draw the eye and the ire, what would happen?

Israel might crumble, or what was left of it—and there would be a lot left—would likely overrun all adjoining areas in a retributive land grab to replace what was stolen.

Pilgrims could no longer come to Mecca. So where would they go? After a disaster of this scale, would pilgrimages as a whole falter and fail?

Where would the US stand? Would they allow Israel to retaliate, which they would want and need to do? Or would the Americans try to be the voice of reason? Of peace?

Given the state of Congress and the national temperature there over the last decade, I had serious doubts. Same went for England, France, Russia, Germany, and the other countries. Would Ethiopia try to rise, embracing more dramatically their claim that they were one of the Lost Tribes of Israel?

Would there be a New Mecca, a New Jerusalem? Would all Christian pilgrimages turn to the Vatican or some other place?

What would the world be without the Holy Land? Even for atheists, it was a political area too important to be written off.

I grabbed the man with both hands.

"Where are the bombs? Tell me exactly where they are."

Aydelotte's personality swam into view, and it was sly and cruel. "You never broke Mr. Russo, did you?" he mocked. "You don't even know how Blind Eye works. God in his heaven, it's like playing with children."

In my ear I heard Grendel give a sick cry, then he squeezed out two words. "On it."

I tried to give Aydelotte my own arrogant smirk, but it never gelled, and he didn't buy it.

"Fail-safe!" someone yelled from outside. Then a dozen voices picked up the chorus.

"Your time is up, Colonel Ledger," said Aydelotte. But there was a bit of Harith in there, too.

Directly over our heads the sprinklers kicked on and soaked us with Shiva.

CHAPTER 161
THE STRONGHOLD
OUTSKIRTS OF JERUSALEM

Brick Anderson caught Church under the arm and dragged him out from under the fierce spray from the sprinklers overhead.

"I saw a main down the hall," snapped Toys. "Maybe it's the cutoff." He whirled and staggered from the room, arms over his head in a vain attempt to block the spray.

"You're dosed," Brick said to Church. "It's okay, boss, you're dosed."

Even so, Church tore at his pocket for a fresh syrette.

"You're dosed, boss."

Church looked at him. A soft smile formed on his face, sweet and sad, as he held out the syrette. "But, Auntie," he said reasonably, "you haven't had your medications today."

Brick froze. "Boss, it's me. Iceman. It's Brick. Aunt Sallie's not here."

Repairman Jack, lingering in the doorway, watched the byplay. "Oh . . . shit . . . are you sure he got that juice stuff?"

"Yes."

"Auntie," said Church. "You need your blood pressure medicine. You can't keep skipping it."

"Awwww . . . shit," breathed Brick.

"Can't you dose him again?" cried Jack.

Brick reached for a syrette, and in that moment the face of Mr. Church changed. It lost all softness and went as dead as a mask. He slapped the syrette from Brick's hand with a movement so fast neither Brick nor Jack saw his hand move.

And then Mr. Church attacked them.

———

Top and Bunny kept spitting the liquid from their mouths as they fought.

Both of them had Snelligs, but the distance down the hall was too great and the downpour of water knocked the darts to the ground, where they smashed.

"We're going to die up here," snarled Bunny.

"Fuck no we ain't," said Top. He crammed back against the wall, holstered his dart gun, and swung his rifle into place. "Time to stop fucking around. You with me, farm boy?"

"Now until the end, Dad."

Top cut him a questioning look. "What?"

Bunny blinked. "No . . . not Dad. That's wrong. That's stupid. Old man."

Top grabbed a powerful fistful of the front of Bunny's combat harness and banged the younger man off the wall. Not hard, but hard enough.

"You *good*, farm boy?"

"I . . . I . . ." Bunny swallowed, then flinched as bullets burned through the air. "I'm good, Top."

In his ears Doc Holliday was yelling at them to take a second dose.

Neither man could understand the language in which she spoke. It sounded like opera to Top and dolphins to Bunny. And neither was aware of it.

———

Violin was not under the spray of the sprinklers. She was tucked into a niche between two stacks of boxes, and the water did not fall directly on her. The two under the truck were safe, too. But the fourth—Alza—was caught directly below the cascading water.

Violin watched her and the jihadists.

The men seemed untouched by the Shiva in the sprinklers. But Alza was dancing. She threw her guns away and tore off her balaclava and was spinning with gorgeous turns as nearly on pointe as her combat boots would allow.

The men stopped and watched her, mesmerized by such an anomalous thing. Alza was a dark-skinned woman from Gabon on the Atlantic coast of Africa. Daughter of a mother rescued from the Red Knight pits. Granddaughter and great granddaughter of women raised in horror. And now she danced in front of men who hated everything her freedom in that moment—the sensuality and expression of dance, the acceptance and celebration of her own sexuality and power—represented.

Grinning, they closed on her.

And Violin came out of hiding.

She did not use her gun because Alza was in the center of them. Instead, she drew her matched kukri knives, the heavy-bladed bone-cutting weapons of the Gurkhas Nepal. Matched knives Mr. Church had given her many years before, and which her mother had taught her to use.

As the Shiva rain fell on her, Violin entered into the dance. She was still herself. She was that, yet.

She was also a dancer in her own way, but that was part of who she was. The blades lifted and moved, silver fire cutting through the fall of amber droplets. Slicing them and spattering them in the moments before the razor edges met flesh and bone, sinew and vein, tendon and artery.

Through it all, Alza danced.

———

Toys found the main and tried to turn it. It gave an inch one way, and the spray jumped higher in pressure, soaking him to the skin.

"Bloody hell," he snarled and hauled on it the other way.

It was hard to do, especially when the knobbed wheel grew hands and grabbed him by the wrists.

———

I held onto Aydelotte, confident in the power of Doc Holliday's drug to keep me steady.

I shook him and slapped him and yelled in his face, demanding to know what he meant about Russo. Demanding to know where the bombs were.

The water fell on him, running down his face and into his eyes and nose and ears and mouth. His smile never varied. It was as if his mind had locked halfway between both parts of who he was. Madman and visionary; killer and savior; corrupt businessman and zealot for his version of God.

Then I started punching him.

I didn't mean to. I sure as hell did not want to. I needed him.

But my first blow came out of nowhere and hit him in the mouth. I could *hear* teeth break even with the alarms going and the sprinklers hissing.

His eyes changed then, lighting up with pain and shock. Maybe he was snapping out of the complacency of certain victory. So I hit him again and again.

"Joe, you have to stop."

The voice was behind me. Her voice.

It wasn't Violin.

It wasn't Grace Courtland, either.

I paused and looked over my shoulder and saw her.

As she was when we were fifteen. She stood in the doorway in torn jeans and a blouse ripped away from a plain white bra that was stained with grass and blood. Her blood. Her dark hair was in disarray, and her lips were bruised.

"Helen . . ." I breathed. "Oh my god . . . Helen . . ."

Top forced the sound of opera from his thoughts, afraid of what it was and what it meant.

The team of shooters was running toward him, bold in their certainty that Shiva had no power over them.

Top said something in a language he did not even know and opened up. Once, a long time ago and on another mission, someone had taken over his mind and made him do terrible things to the innocent. Back on the Kill Switch case. Top remembered that. He thought about what it felt like to be invaded, violated, used as a weapon. He prayed about it on his bad days and used it on his good ones to build up who he was.

As the Shiva fought to take hold of him and once more turn him into some warped monster, Bradley "Top" Sims fought back. He let the strange words fall from his lips. They didn't matter as long as his finger kept pulling the trigger. He fired with all those years as a Tier One soldier, as a man who fought for family, brothers in arms, freedom.

He turned the falling water into a storm of crimson.

Andrea and Remy ran.

More than a dozen jihadists followed. Gunfire was a constant storm, but as they went, both men shot out the lights and made wild turns. Once they were in darkness, they flipped down their visors and went to night vision.

And then they were in the first toy box.

Andrea slapped a small panel he'd stuck to the wall, and behind them a series of waist-high charges exploded all along the path their enemies followed. The blasts cut five men in half. It tore the front leg off a sixth.

Then Remy grabbed him and pulled him into an alcove.

"I'm feeling it, man," said the young Cajun. "I'm hearing birds."

Andrea shoved him against the wall, tore a syrette from a pocket, and slammed it into the younger man's leg. He tried to do the same to himself, but there were too many fingers on his hand and none of them had joints. He dropped the syrette. Remy bent to grab it, and Andrea kneed him in the face.

"Your mother wants my eyes," yelled Andrea. *"She can't have them."*

He yelled it in English and Italian and in some language spoken nowhere on Earth. And it made so much sense to him.

Remy's nose exploded, his Scout glasses and night-vision burst apart, and he sagged down on the floor. Andrea began kicking him, but at the same time the Italian was firing his handgun down the hall. Somehow, impossibly, there were screams as round after round hit flesh.

━━━━━

Brick Anderson was a very big man. Nearly as tall as Bunny, as solid as Top, and almost as fast as Joe Ledger. But he was nothing beneath the onslaught of Mr. Church.

He had seen his employer fight before. He'd fought alongside him more than once. That, though, was nothing like this. It was like fighting a machine. There was no emotion on Church's face, no wicked joy or anger or maliciousness. Only a coldness so profound that Brick felt it in his own soul.

The blows came in with incredible speed and accuracy. Brick could feel his face break apart. He felt his left collarbone shatter. One eye went totally dark.

He fought back, but it was like trying to fistfight a tornado. Nothing in Brick's entire life prepared him for anything like this. In the extremes of it, as his mind was beginning to go dark, he fumbled for his gun. The Snellig fell from his grip, and he thrashed for his Sig Sauer.

Then a shot rang out.

He lifted his pistol, but he knew he hadn't fired.

Mr. Church staggered backward, his cold face flickering with pain and with doubt. He looked down at his chest. At the hot red blood that poured from a bullet wound.

He and Brick turned toward the man who held the gun.

Repairman Jack stood there with a Glock in his hands. "I promised Glaeken I wouldn't move against you, Rasolom, but he's gone and your ass is mine. The Lady knows. She needs me to do this. She does."

Brick's knees buckled and he collapsed down and then fell face-forward without making a single effort to break that fall. Church looked down at him and then at the torn flesh on his own knuckles. At the blood. Most of it was not his. Most of it was Brick's.

Church stared in absolute horror as understanding smashed through Shiva's distortions and forced him to see the damage he had caused. He turned back to Repairman Jack.

"I--" he began, but that was all he got out before the gun spoke.

Repairman Jack fired.

Again and again.

CHAPTER 162
THE TOC
PHOENIX HOUSE

Russo screeched as Scott Wilson kicked the door open.

"What?" he cried.

Wilson was not very big and did not look strong, but he grabbed Russo with both hands, hauled him completely off the floor, and slammed him down atop the interview table. He clamped one hand around Russo's throat and with the other took a huge, scrunching, twisting fistful of his crotch.

"Blind Eye," he roared. *"How do we fucking well stop it?"*

Bug and Doc Holliday were in the TOC, yelling into the comms, begging them all to take a second dose.

Isaac and Coleman were pawing at them, urging them to get the message through.

"The stuff in the sprinklers," cried Coleman. "It must be that God's Arrow stuff. A fail-safe in case someone like us came for them. They were prepared. They were prepared."

"Shut up!" bellowed Doc, shoving the men back. "All teams, listen to me. Dose up. Dose up. Do it now. That is an order. Dose up!"

CHAPTER 163
THE STRONGHOLD
OUTSKIRTS OF JERUSALEM

I stared at Helen.

She was the way she had been on that terrible day when we were kids. When those older teens beat me half to death and raped and brutalized her. I remember the look on her face. When the boys had gone, she crawled over to me, pressing trembling hands to my many cuts. Trying to stop me from bleeding even as she bled worse. Apologizing to me as if anything of what happened could ever have been her fault.

I remembered the hot tears that fell on my upturned face. And the drops of blood.

"I'm so sorry, Joey," she said. "I'm sorry."

Joey. She had been one of the very few people ever to call me that. And after that day no one did. I was Joe or Joseph or Cowboy. Now I was Colonel or Ledger or Outlaw.

Joey.

"You can't hurt people, Joey," she said, gesturing back to Aydelotte, who was sagged sideways, blood and broken teeth sliding from his rubbery, torn lips.

I reached for her. I stumbled past Ghost, who sat transfixed, confused, staring as if somehow he could see her, too. He whined but did not move.

I lost balance and went down on my knees, fell forward, and

wrapped my arms around Helen's waist. Her clothes were torn, and I spent foolish minutes trying to put the pieces back in place, as if by doing something like that I could rebuild her into who she had been before the teens tore that from her. My hands were fast and diligent, but the pieces fell away, revealing bruised, scratched, and bitten flesh that was no one's to see but whom Helen chose. Except for parts of her glimpsed around a bathing suit on the beach, I had never seen her naked. And I did not want to see a forced nakedness that was in no way a gift. Certainly not to me, who had failed to protect her.

I buried my face against her hip and cried so hard I could feel my chest break. It tore my fragile heart loose and dropped it into darkness.

Darkness.

But not *that* Darkness.

In my head the Cop closed his eyes and turned away, remembering too many times when he had been called to the scene of a rape, knowing that there was nothing in law or power or justice that could give back to those girls and women what had been stolen. Cops, like field agents of the kind I am now, are reactive. We can't go looking for fights. We have to come in response to screams, to sirens, to desperate cries.

I knew that, and even knowing it, I condemned the Cop I had been and the agent I was for not possessing prescience. For being too human to stop all hurt and harm.

The Killer dropped to his knees, threw back his head, and howled. Those teenagers had never been identified. Helen said she recognized none of them; they had been strangers to me, and I never found them again. And, oh, I looked, scouring the streets and parks as soon as I was out of the hospital. I had no martial arts training back then, so I stole a gun from my dad and went hunting.

Never found them. Never learned a name.

The Killer cried out in unbearable frustration because he, too, was unable to either protect his tribe or avenge it.

But the Modern Man stood there. The weakest part of me, I'd always thought. The civilized and ordinary person who might have been, had that dreadful day in the park never happened. He stood there, and he—only he—had the courage, or perhaps the purest love, to look Helen in the eye.

"I'm sorry I wasn't strong enough to save you," he told her.

"I know, Joey," she said. "I don't blame you. There was nothing you could have done."

A young girl's face, but a woman's voice.

Then she bent and whispered into my ear. Five names.

The names of five boys.

I looked up at her in shock and alarm.

But I was alone.

Except for Ghost, who looked terrified and confused. Except for Aydelotte, who looked half dead.

Five names in my ear. In my mind.

———

Repairman Jack shot past Church. He shot all three of the technicians behind the man.

He shot the console.

He shot the floor.

Then he looked at the gun as if it were a slimy, crawling thing in his hand and flung it away. He shook his head like a drunk fighting to come away after a car crash. Jack grabbed Brick as the man fell and lowered him to the floor, then immediately began pawing at Brick's pockets for syrettes.

Church stood above him, swaying, bleeding.

Dying.

"I'm sorry, Sallie," he said. "You deserved better."

And he fell.

———

I turned back to Aydelotte.

He lay there, flickering and changing.

One moment he was Mr. Miracle, though dressed like a department store Santa, with bright red clothes bordered in snowy white. The damage to his face was there, but it seemed artfully concealed beneath stage makeup and greasepaint. A pair of smiling young women dressed as elves perched on the arms of the chair, and when they laughed, black blood poured out over their lips. I could see maggots squirming in the goo.

One of them had an eerily familiar Chinese face. She winked at me and whispered, "Sometimes you have to burn to shine."

It was Mother Night—once a coworker and friend named Artemisia Bliss. A protégé of Doc's predecessor, Dr. Bill Hu. Brilliant, lost, corrupt. And dead. She'd stolen the *seif al din* pathogen and released it during Dragon Con, the huge pop-culture convention held in Atlanta over Labor Day weekend. The DMS and local law had stopped what could have been a doomsday spread of the prion-based bioweapon conjured in a lab by Amirah at the behest of Sebastian Gault. I'd shot her and watched her body fall from a high balcony. Watched it smash on the floor. Saw her scraped up and shoveled into a body bag, and now she was either bones in the ground or frozen meat in some covert bioweapons lab. So I knew this couldn't be her.

I wanted to shoot her again. At the same time, I felt a strange desire to apologize. Maybe for not spotting the warning signs as she lost her faith in our overall mission and began embracing her dark thoughts. Not sure if that was really on me, but I have a foolish compulsion to pick up other people's emotional baggage. At this point I could open a luggage store.

The other elf was a stranger at first, but as Mother Night coalesced, so did the other woman. She became almost—*almost*—Grace Courtland again. But it was a distortion. This was another woman who looked so achingly like Grace, but it was not her. I'd met her only once, during a solo mission that should have been a nothing-burger time filler, but which led to the discovery of a black market genetics lab. There, I met an agent from Barrier named Felicity Hope.

We fought side by side against horrifying mutations, and then she vanished, slipping into the water, and was never seen again. And it turned out she never officially existed.

This version of Felicity Hope watched me with eyes that looked too round and dark. Fishlike.

"I'll be seeing you soon, Joe," she said. "*If* you get out of this. But . . . dress warm. It's *soooo* cold down there. Very cold and very dark. But there are lights. Oh, yes, Joe, there are some beautiful lights down there."

Water—smelling of sea and salt—ran down her face.

"You're not here," I yelled. "Neither of you."

They smiled at me and then melted away, leaving Jason Aydelotte wearing the face of a different man. Maybe it was the face he saw in the shadowy screen of his turned-off monitor. Maybe it was the face of Harith that was in his mind. Generic, straight from the casting office for when they needed a dignified, wise-looking, heavily bearded Arab who could play a true believer and leader of jihadists.

"I admire your determination, Colonel Ledger," he said. "But it is far too late."

"Can't be," I said. "You're not going to blow yourself up. Worse case is that these nukes are on timers to give you time to leave."

Harith shrugged.

"Jason Aydelotte believes he will escape. He has spent months moving the majority of his stock out of the country. Out of the Middle East. Once the bombs go off, there will be far fewer places to obtain such objects, and he will become very much wealthier exploiting the paucity of goods that only he can fill." He made a disapproving noise. "He was never a believer. Not in anything. Not for all of his speeches. Jason is merely a fatuous, foolish, sneaky, greedy man who does not believe anyone is as real as he is."

It was a startling insight, and one whose truth I didn't for a moment dispute.

"And what about you, Harith al-Wazir?"

His smile was oddly human, even vulnerable. "I have been fighting for a long time, Colonel. I have grown old in this war, and I know that I will never see its true end. Once the bombs have spoken, it will be time for younger men to carry on the fight. Old men like me will be the ones the world can blame, and I have no wish—perhaps not enough remaining courage—to stand trial."

"Meaning what?"

"Meaning that Jason does not control the bombs," he said. "*I* do."

CHAPTER 164
THE STRONGHOLD
OUTSKIRTS OF JERUSALEM

Violin moved through the dance, following the music, finding beauty in everything.

Her knives moved with such grace that she could watch them and be entertained, enchanted, by the slowing lines the silver steel carved through the air. The blades left a trail that sparkled and vanished slowly.

And the blood.

Never was the blood of evil men cast in so pure a light. Each droplet became a delicately carved and faceted ruby. Each face caught a fragment of some other light, some color pulled from crates and trucks, from prismatic grease puddles on the floor to pinup calendars on the walls. Taking those shades and hues and creating true art.

Bullets burned past her, but the choreography of the dance did not allow them to interrupt anything. She saw Alza miss a step, though, and that allowed a bullet to find her.

Even that was beautiful, because it caught Alza as she rose, and it tilted her into a final, forever arabesque. She swanned to the floor, arms spread as if it were merely the little death at the end of passion rather than her actual spiritual passion. Alza's eyes remained open, as did her mouth, as she watched her older sister continue with the ballet of perfect slaughter.

There was machine-gun fire from under two trucks, but they became percussion to counterpoint Violin's every step. The bullets burst the feet and shins of the running jihadists, and as they fell, more bullets found their screaming mouths, silencing their discordant shouts.

———

Toys fought and fought to free his hands, but the big valve wheel had him. Nearby, a fire hose smashed out of its glass box, and the heavy nozzle *thunk*ed to the floor as seemingly endless yards of white canvas hosing coiled down around it.

Toys stared at it, aware that he was losing his mind again.

"Don't," he begged. "Please don't."

There was a lot of God's Arrow in the watery air that swirled around him.

There was a lot of ketanserin still in his bloodstream. He knew that. He needed to know it. And Toys forced that truth into the front of his mind as he fought for what little control God was willing to provide.

He prayed as he fought.

As had happened so often over the last years, he knew God was listening. It was simply that Toys did not know if God cared about him anymore.

———

"Your mother wants my eyes," yelled Andrea over and over as Remy collapsed on the floor. Then the words faltered. "Your . . . mother . . . ?"

He paused.

"*Macché!*" he breathed. He leaned back from the brutalized Cajun, seeing him again but seeing his reality. He looked down at his thigh and saw Remy's hand clamped around a syrette, the needle still in the muscle. Even as he'd beaten the boy down, Remy had dosed him. The second injection of KS was like boiling oil in his bloodstream, and there were Vaseline smears at the corners of his vision, but Andrea could feel himself coming back together. "Gator Bait . . . Remy . . . ?"

The younger man was badly hurt, but all of the damage seemed to be on his face. Nose and lips, a split eyebrow, dazed lights and pain.

Bullets still chopped and chewed at the corner of the niche into which they were tucked. Andrea shook Remy, but the kid was still too dazed.

"It's okay, kid," said Andrea. "I'll get us out of this."

He unslung his rifle, checked that it had a full magazine, took a breath, prayed to God, and leaned around as he opened fire. The jihadists had been creeping up under the cover of their fusillade, and Andrea's barrel was nine inches from the closest man's face when he pulled the trigger.

CHAPTER 165
THE TOC
PHOENIX HOUSE

Russo screamed.

And screamed.

"They'll kill me," he pleaded. "God! My balls. What are you doing? I told you everything I . . ."

Wilson leaned so close that when he spoke spit from his mouth flecked into Russo's.

"You built Blind Eye to hide those bombs, you pathetic little cunt," he snarled. "Don't try to tell me that you can't switch it off. Don't you *dare* try and tell me you can't find them again."

"But *they'll kill me!*"

The Eton-educated former soldier turned diplomat turned COO of RTI smiled down at Russo. "I try to be a better man," he said. "To uphold the values of restraint, compassion, tolerance, and mercy."

Wilson head-butted him, splattering Russo's nose.

The Italian screamed in fresh pain.

Wilson grabbed him by the hair, pulled him back off the desk, and punched him five times. Very hard and very fast. Breaking things. He felt a knuckle in his own right hand crack badly, but he did not care. It made him punch all the harder next time.

"Millions of people are going to die," he said, pausing between savage blows. Blood and spittle from his own bitten lips bubbled on his chin. His hair was in disarray, and there was nothing remotely civilized in his eyes, and no trace of it in his heart. Except it was that memory of civilization, of civility itself, of the driving forces in people like him who came to the life more as a civil servant than a killer. It was a perspective from which he could see the small, daily cracks in the structure of the orderly world he treasured. And here he was with someone who wanted to bring carnage and destruction and waste to replace peace and order.

It did not break his mind. Even in the extremes of the moment, he was clear. However, it was breaking his heart. The crack, the split was tearing him apart.

"You want to ruin it all," said Wilson. "You think ISIS will get you? They are hundreds of miles away and you are here. With me.

In this small room. I can make you last and last. You will be put on public display, and every book that will be written from now on will list you as one of the worst traitors to humanity. You'll die a failure. A monster. A Judas."

"No . . . no . . . no . . ."

"Or you can tell me how to turn off Blind Eye. Right. Fucking. Now."

CHAPTER 166
THE STRONGHOLD
OUTSKIRTS OF JERUSALEM

Repairman Jack knelt over Church and Brick. Panic exploded like artillery shells in his chest. He had two syrettes in each hand.

"Here goes nothing," he said. He heard the words, but they sounded like he was speaking in some frog language. It made sense, though.

A sound in the hall made him pause and turn. He saw his long-time love, Gia, and her daughter, screaming. He saw them running, with a big shaggy *rakoshi* chasing close behind. They screamed his name.

It took an incredible amount of willpower—as much as he had ever used when battling Rasolom—to keep focused, to not respond, to accept one truth at a time, to be where he was and to do what he needed to do.

With a savage roar, he raised both fists and then slapped down with the syrettes. Two into each—Mr. Church and Brick Anderson. The orders had been to dose them with, at most, two.

Fuck the rules, though. In all his years, Repairman Jack had seldom felt that any rules applied to him. Less so, right now.

Top and Bunny were positive they had each taken a second dose.

They were 100 percent sure. They swore to each other; they swore they'd seen the syrettes jab home. That they could feel the KS clearing their thoughts.

"We're good, old man," said Bunny.

"God damn right we are," said Top. "Now let's get our shit wired tight and go get some."

"Hoo-fucking-ah."

They swapped in new magazines, adjusted their gear, tossed grenades around the corner to clear the way.

And then the two of them, stalking shoulder to shoulder, went hunting for the man who caused all this. The mad son of a bitch who was trying to end the world. They thought they knew where he was hiding. He was upstairs.

"We're going to kill that cocksucker and *end* this," said Top.

"Yeah, we are."

And they began climbing the stairs to find and kill Colonel Joe Ledger.

———

I could feel myself losing my grip.

It came and went.

So did hallucinations. Some of them were bizarre and terrifying and, if they carried meaning, I could not grasp it. My boyhood friend, Wheatie, appeared and told me rumors about my dead sister-in-law, Ally. He was still a kid, looking the way he had when he died.

Once I could feel hands on my shoulders from behind, and I let them turn me. And Mom was there.

That nearly broke me. I'd been at her hospital bedside when cancer burned the last light from her eyes. She looked now like she had then, but there was a ghostly image overlaying her aspect that showed how she'd been the summer before. Strong and healthy, bright with sunlight on her face, and her hair in that sloppy bun she wore. I cringed, froze, waiting for her to be another monster, to say or do something to chip away the last little bits of control that I owned.

But she didn't. Instead she cupped my face, stood on tiptoes, and kissed me.

"I love you, Joe," she said. "And I'm so proud of you. We all are."

As she said that I saw them all standing behind her, looking at me through the open door to Aydelotte's office. Dad was there, wearing his uniform from when he retired as the commissioner of the Baltimore Police Department, right before he ran for mayor. Sean, dressed in his BPD blues, too. Holding hands with Ally, who was plump with the pregnancy that she'd taken with her to the grave. Now, in that moment, she was lovely and whole. As were the two kids—Em and Lefty. All of them buried in Maryland soil. All of them here.

"They're coming for you, Joe," said Dad.

"Yeah, big brother," agreed Sean with a smirk. "Now if you were smart, you'd dose up."

"Dose up . . . ?" I didn't know what that meant.

"You'll figure it out, Uncle Joe," said Lefty.

Then they were gone. The warm touch of my mother's hands lingered longest.

I turned back to the man—*men*—I'd come to see. Harith was still there, watching me with amused eyes.

He said to me, "I have accepted death. You cannot force me to break my trust with God."

"That," I said as I moved toward him once more, "will depend on whose side God stands."

And that, for the first time, made his belief flicker. Not a lot. A little.

There was a lot I could do with a little.

As I approached, though, something niggled at me. He had already told me something. Something important. But what the hell was it?

I guess I would have to make him tell me again.

CHAPTER 167
THE STRONGHOLD
OUTSKIRTS OF JERUSALEM

She entered through a back door.

There were four guards back there. Two brown-shirts, two jihadists. They had a small glimpse of her. Just a moment. A form materializing from nowhere. Slim, tall, regal. Powerful in ways not one of those men could ever understand.

She walked without apparent haste. Almost floating. Like a ghost, like a dream.

One of the men raised a hand to stop her.

He blinked, and there was no hand on the end of his wrist. Just a small geyser of red. Then the world went red before blackness painted it all in silence. He was dead before he saw what Lilith did to his companions. Their screams followed him down, down, down all the way.

When she stepped into the rear loading bay, the first thing she saw was Alza, sprawled dead in an artless heap. Lilith's heart was ice, but that made it feel colder.

Two brown-shirts ran at her from an oblique angle, trying to blindside her with automatic gunfire. Lilith turned with a grace that made Even Violin look clumsy. She fired two shots from a slim Walther PPQ M1 handgun. She fired twice, and each man went down.

Then Lilith went to rescue her daughter from herself.

———

There were so many screams in that room.

Top and Bunny ran along the halls and up the stairs.

Jihadists were everywhere, firing, trying to ambush, but they were both having what soldiers called a John Wayne day. They seemed unable to miss. Bullets were unable to find them. Grenades thrown their way took bad bounces and either fell over and down into the loading bay or rebounded and blew the legs off the men trying to stop the killers.

Bunny walked without haste, the stock of the Daewoo shotgun snugged against his hip as he burned through one round after another of alternating buckshot, explosive rounds, armor-piercing, and even porcelain deadbolt-destroying Shockloc rounds. No matter how many tried to stand their ground, he blew them to rags.

Top walked beside him and a half-pace back, away from the muzzle blast of the shotgun. He'd switched from rifle to sidearm and was doing terrible damage with spaced shots that seemed to want to find their targets.

As they marched forward, killing and killing, they were both singing with good harmony and pitch. They thought they were singing "Get Down with the Sickness." They weren't. It was "God Rest Ye Merry, Gentlemen."

They ignored the blue cats that ran past them. That seemed perfectly normal for moments like these.

———

Andrea pulled Remy to his feet and they stood swaying, hurt and bleeding.

"Are you *you*?" asked Andrea, not knowing how, in the moment, to say it better.

Remy nodded. "I think . . . I . . . yes . . ."

There was less gunfire, and the sprinkler tanks seemed to be emptying. Everything dripped. Everything was painted in watery red. The hallways on either side of them were filled with dead men. And a camel, but as Andrea glared at it, the thing melted into nothingness.

He almost asked Remy if *he* had seen the animal but withheld the question.

They moved to the rail and looked down at a scene that made each of them question whether the second dose was doing any good at all. Men were fighting one another down there. With guns and knives, fists and tools. One beat on another with a fire extinguisher. Another man sat in the saddle of a forklift and chased whoever was closest with the long steel arms.

Remy, whose mangled mouth made talking difficult, mumbled, "Do they have it . . . ?"

Andrea wasn't sure. Not at first.

"Maybe they don't all have the right syrettes."

He leaned over the rail and made an obscene gesture while shouting, "*Vaffanculo a chi t'è morto.*"

Two of the men below—both brown-shirts—wheeled and fired up at them.

Remy grabbed Andrea to pull him back.

He was one half second too late.

———

Belle could not bear to wait. She heard the screams, saw the carnage on the screen of her tactical computer, and knew that she was doing no one any good outside. She jammed a second dose of KS into her thigh, then scampered and slid and climbed and dropped to the parking lot ground and ran, rifle at port arms, her dark skin helping her vanish.

The first open door led to the main loading bay. It stood ajar, and when she paused there, she saw brown-shirted guards and jihadists engaged in a massive bloody brawl. Dozens of them. Many dead, all wounded.

A rattle of gunfire drew her eye, and she looked up to see a slender figure bow slowly forward over the pipe handrail on the second floor. Belle felt her heart turn to ice and then crack into despair as Andrea toppled over and plummeted to the unforgiving concrete. He landed badly.

So badly.

Belle had few real friends in life. Violin and Andrea. Everyone else was a comrade in arms, but not a deep friend. And now she had lost the person dearest to her. Andrea, who accepted everything about her, sheltered her when she needed it, took shelter when she offered, and could always make her laugh. No one else could do that.

Her rifle moved in her hands before she was aware she was doing it. Firing. Working the bolt. Firing.

Missing nothing.

Except joy. Except hope.

———

Repairman Jack knelt over Church, pressing a folded piece of torn shirt to the sucking chest wound.

"Sorry, Deacon," he said. "I . . . I . . . fuck. I'm so sorry."

Church's hand fluttered and rose slowly. Then his eyes opened. In the struggle he'd lost his tinted eyeglasses, and it occurred to Jack that it was only the second time since 1990 that he had seen his old friend's eyes. They were different from the rest of him. Softer, far more human. Even readable, to some degree.

There was pain in those eyes.

"Brick . . . ?" asked Church faintly. "Did I . . . how badly did I . . . ?"

They both turned to look at Brick, who lay very still. Church's voice trailed off into a terrible silence. Awareness, like understanding, was sometimes a terrible thing. A monster.

"I . . . don't know," said Jack, his voice filled with a shared despair. "He was still breathing when I dosed you both. But that last dose did something to him. Convulsions, and then he passed out."

"It's not the drug," mumbled Church, his voice heavy with pain but sharp with that cruel understanding. "I did this . . . "

His hand flopped down and reached for Brick's outstretched left arm. He pressed the pads of his fingers against the strong brown wrist, listening through touch.

There was a pulse. Very light, very fast. Too shallow.

Fading, though.

Slowing.

Until all Mr. Church could feel was silence.

———

I was ready for another round with Harith or Aydelotte or whoever the hell was in there at the moment.

I kept thinking about the word "dose," though. Trying to make sense of it. Ghost was in the doorway behind me, barking so loudly it was putting cracks in the wall. There were cracks appearing on my hands, too. I could see them.

It froze me.

There was something very wrong about those cracks. They weren't dry and ashy like dead skin; nor did they bleed. Not blood, anyway.

What I saw swirling like tiny rivers in my skin was blackness. Like looking at flowing oil from a great distance. I could see tiny bits of light sparkling on wavelets of the blackness.

Only I knew it wasn't oil.

It wasn't blackness that I was seeing inside those cracks, inside me.

It was the Darkness.

Returning. Coming out. Breaking through.

———

"He's up there," said Top. "See him? Right there."

He pointed to the big, mirrored window next to an open door on the level above. Some big white dog stood in the doorway, but they both thought he looked fake. A statue. Some kind of oddball taxidermy.

Beyond the fake dog there was a man in combat armor. He was all in black. He *was* black. Not skin color. Not properly black like that.

Both of them knew and understood what they were seeing.

The Darkness. It made sense to them now. They loved Joe Ledger, but it was clear that the Darkness had come back, and it owned him. Body and soul.

"We can't save him, can we?" asked Bunny.

"No, farm boy, we cannot."

They looked down at the battle below. Belle was there, and she was killing people like she'd been appointed the new Angel of Death. Remy clung to a railing, screaming and shooting. And Andrea. . . .

"No," cried Bunny.

The body had clearly fallen, and it seemed to have landed just below the part of the railing below Aydelotte's office.

"Joe killed him," Bunny said.

"Nah, farm boy," said Top. "It was the Darkness that killed him. And now we got to nut up and do what's right. We got to stop the Darkness before it kills all the cows."

"Cows . . . ?"

Top blinked twice. "You know what I mean."

Bunny nodded, and they picked up their pace.

———

"Daughter," said Lilith, that single word sharp and clear as a whip-crack.

Violin paused in the midst of a turn, one arm swinging around with a bloody blade. Lilith checked it with a flat, hard palm.

"I love you," said the older woman, and some meaning and understanding flickered in Violin's eyes. Lilith jabbed her with a syrette. "Own yourself."

Violin's knees bent, and she began to collapse, but Lilith caught her and roughly hauled her upright.

"Own yourself," she snapped and then gave her daughter a single sharp slap across the face. "This is war."

CHAPTER 168
THE STRONGHOLD
OUTSKIRTS OF JERUSALEM

The building was falling quiet now. Too many people were dead or dying or lost in hellscapes to wage war.

I bent over Aydelotte, cringing and mewling as I did it because the Darkness was trying so damned hard to take me.

Ghost was behind me, growling softly. He must have seen it, too, though I didn't dare look back. After all we had been through a year ago, I knew—I feared—that he would not allow the Darkness to take me again. Not the dog he was, or the wolf within. He would try to stop me.

He would kill me to save me.

I knew that I could not let him stop me. Not until Harith told me exactly where the bombs were. If I had to, I would . . .

I would.

"Ghost," I sobbed.

His growl turned into something deeper and heavier. More sinister.

I reached for my pistol.

"Please, Ghost . . . " I begged.

Harith was staring at my face. He was looking deeper. I think in that moment he saw me. The Darkness that was stealing me away.

The Killer howled and threw his full weight against the inside of my head. Screaming in his feral, paleolithic grunts that predated any human speech. Ranting for the safety of the tribe. Afraid of the destructive power of the Darkness but also willing to die to stop it from winning. The Cop stood there with his hand on the gun.

"No," cried the Modern Man. "It's not what you think."

He said it to all of us. Not to Aydelotte or Harith. The Modern Man spoke to the scattered parts of me in the voice of my deepest damage, my deepest hate.

Aydelotte looked into my eyes.

"God protect me . . . " he gasped.

When I spoke to Harith, the voice was mine but not. It was so much older. Deeper, heavy enough to shake the building.

"I am not God," I said in the voice of Darkness.

"What . . . are . . . you . . . ?"

I felt my mouth smile. It opened far too wide. I could feel too many teeth in there, and they were all sharp. My tongue flicked out like a snake.

"*I am Iblis,*" I said. "*I am al-Shaytān. I al-Rajim the Accursed. I am the truest monotheist and I reject you and your works, Harith al-Wazir. I would not prostrate myself before Adam and I will not bow to your heresy.*"

The words hit him so much harder than any punches I could deliver. Ghost was barking now, and its pitch was rising to a frenzy.

I bent close to Harith to let the Darkness speak. "Tell me where you hid your weapons. Only that can save your soul. Only that can save Islam. Only that can save your people."

I leaned closer still, and he began to speak.

Which is when Top Sims shot me in the back.

CHAPTER 169
THE TOC
PHOENIX HOUSE

They saw the shot.

Heard it.

Bug and Doc. Nikki and Yoda. Isaac and Coleman. All the others.

Scott Wilson saw it as he staggered in to join the others. He was sweating and bloody. His glasses were gone, his shirt torn, and his arms were red to the elbows. He had begun to yell as he came in.

The shot, though.

The shot stopped every word.

CHAPTER 170
THE STRONGHOLD
OUTSKIRTS OF JERUSALEM

I fell forward onto Harith.

Even with body armor I felt cut in half. I hit Harith, rebounded, slid to my knees.

Ghost was snarling, and there was someone screaming. Not me, though I wanted to. I toppled over and turned, finally getting my gun out.

Top stood there with his pistol aimed at me, smoke curling out of the barrel.

"Can't let you win," he said in a voice that sounded entirely too reasonable. "Can't let Joe go like this. Not if it means you get to take his place."

He fired again.

The second bullet hit my side, shattering the pouch of syrettes. I felt the pain—and that is far too shallow and pale a word for it—but none of the heat. On some distant shelf of awareness, I knew that the spider-silk undergarment and the plates in my running gear had stopped entry. They were supposed to slough off most of the foot-pounds of impact, too.

It sure as fuck did not feel like that.

I coughed out a plea, but my voice was thick and wrong. I sounded like a monster. I sounded like the Darkness.

And yet, on some level I knew I *wasn't*.

Not really. This wasn't that. I had to believe it. This was Shiva. This was God's Arrow. This was my own madness warped by those drugs.

Harith was gasping on the couch, babbling in English and Arabic and Latin and Greek. Word salad, spilling out of him. When I glanced at him, there was no sanity—not one trace of it—left in his eyes.

I heard bits and pieces in those few seconds before Top fired his gun for the third time. Places. Streets.

"Top!" I yelled. "No. Not now. Christ, not *now*."

He fired again. I saw his finger move, and I twisted, returning fire as I fell sideways. His round missed my head by one inch, and behind me there was a soft *uggghh* sound.

I risked one fast look and saw fresh blood pumping from Harith's chest.

Ghost had Bunny down and was tearing through his forearm limb pads. There was blood—fresh blood—on both of them.

"Top . . . *No!*"

We fired at each other.

Maybe on some level there was still enough of each of us left inside. We aimed center mass, but that's where the Kevlar plates and the spider silk was strongest.

We fired and fired from ten feet away.

Blood flecked his lips, and I knew bones were breaking.

I felt my own breaking.

As was my heart.

Then Ghost left Bunny and slammed his bulk into Top, knocking him out of the office and into the hall. Top lost his gun, which went skittering down the hall, and had to clamp hands on the rail to keep from going over. Ghost nipped and slashed at him, and Top lashed out with a boot, catching Ghost in the ribs. That sent my dog halfway down the hall and tore a cry from him. So I charged out and grabbed Top by the shoulder, spun him around and hit him in the belly and face and throat and inner thigh.

He turned with the blows and counter-fought with the clinical precision of a man who had turned a boyhood hobby of karate into the skill set of a master soldier. The armor and gear we wore soaked up a lot of it, but we both knew how to hit and hurt.

Aside from combat drills and sparring, we had only ever fought once before. Years ago, on the day Church put a bunch of testosterone-soaked alpha males in a room and told us to sort out who would lead Echo Team. I'd been on my feet at the end of it, but I'd had to sucker him and Bunny and two other guys.

This wasn't that kind of fight.

Top was older than me, but he had the moves, and I could tell from the look in his eyes that he thought he was on the side of the angels. And that I was decidedly not. Although the spray had stopped now, the damage was done. I had no syrettes left for him. None for me. All there was for us was this fight.

We fought.

Most fights are a few seconds long. Most fights aren't two men wearing this much gear. Two men whacked out of their minds by designer drugs. Two men already injured.

We fought and fought.

A jihadist appeared as if by magic, looking confused. He raised an

AK-47 at us and then . . . died. I don't know how or why. Someone did something, and he pitched headlong and crashed into Top.

That gave me a moment.

I needed to get back into that room before Harith was dead. He had been saying things I knew with all my heart that I needed to hear.

I staggered back, giving Top a final short heel kick under the chin. I said something. Maybe it was an apology. God only knows what language it was in. Then I whirled, staggered, stumbled into the room.

Bunny was on his feet. He was bleeding, and there was a mad vacuity to his eyes. He was forcing a new drum into his shotgun. Body armor wasn't going to save me from the 12-gauge dispersal pattern of buckshot. So I ducked low and drove my shoulder into his middle. It was like hitting a wall, but we both moved. He struck the mirror, and his massive bulk smashed through it.

I looked around. There was a small room behind Aydelotte's desk, so I grabbed him and dragged his bleeding body through and kicked the door shut. While he lay there, I summoned what strength I had and shoved a desk and a file cabinet in front of the door. Harith was talking the whole time, moving from language to language. Speaking in broken fragments.

I tapped my comms.

"Outlaw to TOC," I gasped. "Tell me you heard any of that."

There was no answer.

I heard gunshots out in the hall. Coming my way.

CHAPTER 171
THE STRONGHOLD
OUTSKIRTS OF JERUSALEM

I hid in the shadows and tried not to scream.

Tried.

Failed sometimes, and then I had to bury my mouth in the crook of my arm and muffle the sounds.

Things were bad. I was hurt. Bleeding in more places than I could count. Pretty sure something was broken inside. In my body. In my head.

I crouched there on one side of a door.

They were on the other side.

I had my knife. I had my combat dog, Ghost. I had a pistol with two bullets. Maybe I could use them to take the first two down. Or maybe I should save them. One for Ghost. One for me.

My head was filled with monsters, and I couldn't think straight.

There were monsters on the other side of the door, too. Some of them used to be people I knew. People I loved and trusted. Top and Bunny. Or what had once been Top and Bunny.

Pounding on the door.

The wood was splintering. My time was running out.

The pounding was getting louder.

I stood. Blood flowed down my arms and legs and body. The world spun, and I knew that I was at the end of what strength I had. Maybe there was enough for one more fight. One last try.

The door began to buckle. Ghost got shakily, weakly to his feet. His white fur was painted in red. He looked up at me, at his master, his pack leader. Looking for comfort, for direction, for strength.

"It'll be okay, boy," I said.

He knew I was lying. It wasn't going to be okay. The wood around the lock began to splinter.

I raised the gun.

"Come on," I growled. "*Come on!*"

And, damn it to hell, they came.

CHAPTER 172
THE STRONGHOLD
OUTSKIRTS OF JERUSALEM

I slipped in a puddle of blood and went down.

One man stood in the doorway.

Not Top. Not Bunny.

He wore torn, sodden clothes. His face was puffed and bruised.

One eye was swollen shut, and there were two important-looking teeth missing from the side of his crooked smile.

He held a fire axe in his hands. I reached over my shoulder for the one I'd brought with me all the way from the Pirate Lab. One I'd forgotten I even had. It was gone. He held it.

Him.

Toys.

"Ledger," he said, gasping with simple syllables, "you incredible tosser. You stupid wanker."

In my ear I heard Scott Wilson.

"Grendel to Outlaw," he said, and he sounded as winded and worn out as the rest of us. There was horror in his voice, I thought. Hurt and despair.

God damn.

"Go for Outlaw," I said, not wanting to. There was so much I could not bear to hear.

"We heard it," said Wilson.

"What?" I had to ask three times because my mind was slipping gears.

"We heard what Harith said. The nukes. We know where they are. All three."

"I . . . I . . ."

"Russo is giving us the ID codes to shut them down. Outlaw, do you hear and understand?"

I looked at Toys. Past him. Top Sims and Bunny lay outside, both of them covered in blood.

"We stopped the nukes," insisted Wilson.

The axe fell from Toys's hands, and he sat down next to me. We were both so broken, so beat. Ghost came and stood in the doorway, watching us. He sat down, then lay down and put his bloody head on his paws.

I began to cry.

Toys looked at me for a long time. Then he put his arm around my shoulders.

"I got you, brother," he said. "I got you."

EPILOGUE

I woke up in the hospital.

Wasn't sure which hospital. Hell, I wasn't sure of anything. Took me a good ten minutes lying there to remember my name. Other details stumbled along into my consciousness at their own pace, and none of them made me happy to be awake.

Then the images came.

The ones I saw for sure. The ones that maybe I saw. Not sure I can doubt any of them completely; and there were too many I did not want to believe.

"Joe?" said a voice, and I turned my head on a neck made of burning wires and debris. Junie was there, and it was only then that I realized she was holding my hand.

"Are . . . are you real?" I asked.

Her smile was the clearest thing in all the world. She rose and kissed my battered face. She kissed my lips and my eyes.

"I love you," she said.

That was all the reality I needed.

-2-

There was a steady stream of people in and out of that hospital room.

Rudy and Church came in next.

Church was in a wheelchair. Rudy said he'd been shot in the chest, but Church looked like he had maybe a bad cold. Guy was a freak. He'd been shot before and recovered more quickly than I do from a hangnail. I did not then and do not now need to know how.

They were not smiling. There was no glow of victory. What I saw was sadness. Deep. The kind of hurt that isn't global or cultural or historic.

This was a personal hurt.

It took every bit of what little strength and courage I had left to ask.

"Who?"

"Top and Bunny are in intensive care," said Rudy. "Toys used the flat part of an axe to take them down. He said it was very hard to do, and for a lot of reasons."

That took a ton of weight off my heart. But I had to steel myself for the next question.

"Ghost . . . ?"

"Junie took him to her apartment. JM is flying out with a vet to take him to Phoenix House."

I waited, knowing there was more.

"We lost Andrea," said Church softly. "And Brick."

His voice broke just a little when he said his friend's name. Church and Brick had become very close over the years. Brick was one of a very small handful that had Church's complete trust. A level I've never reached. But then again, Brick was a better man than me. Many are.

"How'd Brick go out?" I asked.

Church looked away out the window for a long time. I saw his hands begin to tremble, and then there was a shudder in his chest. It was a while before he could answer my question.

Then he told me. He told me everything that had happened with him, Repairman Jack, and Brick. Every goddamn thing.

I closed my eyes.

"No . . . " I murmured.

"God forgive me," said Church.

They were family. They were friends. Brothers in arms who had helped save the world. But they were not official military. Their names would never be in the papers. No books or movies would be written about them. Real heroes are often like that. The ones who don't do it for glory or praise. The ones who have the kind of integrity that runs miles deep. The ones who really are heroes. Not defined as such by themselves, but everyone around them knows it.

We sat in silence, perhaps in vigil, for almost an hour.

"I will fly to Italy to see Andrea's husband and family," said Church. "Then I will go to Detroit. Brick has a grandmother and some cousins."

"When you can fly," said Rudy gently.

Church ignored that.

"And the rest?"

Rudy measured out a sliver of a bad smile. "This entire wing is filled with our people."

"Toys . . . ?"

Church studied me. "He's here, too. He's sitting with the survivors of *his* team."

I dabbed at my eyes.

"And the world?" I asked, saving it until the end.

"The nukes are back with the Israelis," said Church, his voice hushed and thick. "We are letting them take all the credit."

"Sure," I said.

We sat with that.

"Aydelotte?"

"He died of wounds sustained," said Church. I have never heard such bitter coldness in any person's voice.

I turned away and looked out the window. It was a brilliant blue sky filled with white clouds and birds.

"Good."

-3-

As I healed and tried to put the pieces together, I asked about Church's mysterious friend, the one they called Repairman Jack.

"Who *is* he?" I asked Church.

"Someone important," said Church after a long time to consider the question. Then he smiled faintly. "He's you, had you walked a different path."

Church didn't elaborate, and I have never asked.

-4-

"This isn't over yet," I said to Church a few days later. He'd taken to sitting in his wheelchair in my room, neither of us saying very much, which said it all. "You know that, right? There's more to this."

He looked up from his phone, where he had been texting someone. Lilith was my guess. I wondered if they ever used emojis. Probably not. And if they did, I was pretty sure I didn't want to know which ones. If there was an eggplant or a peach, I think I'd lose my shit.

Church looked at me, waiting for me to continue.

"The bat bites," I said. "The two lead boxes. Egyptian and Hebrew sorcery. The cobras. Tenth Legion. That's what brought us into this, but we didn't really figure out any of it."

"No."

"What does that mean? Is the Aydelotte-Harith thing still in motion? Is there more to do?"

"I rather think it's more like being in a sea battle," said Church. "We fought a big ship-to-ship action and won, but in the light of that gunfire we glimpsed other enemy ships going in elsewhere, bent on different missions."

"What missions?"

"How can we possibly know that yet?" he asked. "We are sharp, Colonel, but we lack true prescience. I am disturbed by those other events but comforted in that we are—for once—not entirely unaware of gathering forces. Bug and his team are already at work looking for anything that will sharpen them in our view."

"That stuff scares me, boss."

"Fear is the whetstone on which we sharpen our knives, Colonel."

I looked up at him from the nest of my hospital bed. "The war is the war."

"Sadly," he said, "yes." There were ghosts in his eyes and in his voice.

With that, he patted me warmly on the shoulder, and wheeled himself out.

-5-

David White flew from Israel to Hartsfield-Jackson Atlanta International Airport and then took a feeder flight to Dothan Regional. A woman met him at baggage, and it was clear that she recognized him. She waited a dozen yards back until he picked up his bag. She was medium height, stocky, with a hard face and eyes the color of gin—pale, nearly colorless.

He walked over to her, pulling his case.

She nodded and said, "What's your favorite month?"

"October."

"And what advice can you give me?"

David licked his lips. "'Sometimes you have to burn to shine,'" he said.

Karen offered her hand, and her shake was hard and brief. David found it odd that her voice sounded almost masculine and vaguely familiar. It was the same cadence and nearly the same tone as Mr. October's. He wondered if she was somehow related.

"The rest of the guys are in a DHL truck in the parking lot. Forty miles to the Inferno."

They walked together outside and climbed into the back of the car. The driver looked like a retired offensive guard who had taken too many hits to the face. He said absolutely nothing, then or later.

Once they were on the road, David risked a question. "What's *in* that casket thing we're supposed to fetch?"

Karen turned her head and looked up into his face. She did not answer his question. Instead, she smiled. And as she did so, they passed beneath a line of trees, and sunshine cast dappled shadows across her face. It created an optical illusion that he found quite unnerving. Her eyes seemed to change color. For just a moment they swirled with odd colors—sickly greens and browns. But when the car passed out of the dappled sunlight, they were pale and clear again.

David did not repeat his question.

Instead, he looked out at the green trees and wished that he were somewhere else. Anywhere else.

And, in the privacy of his own thoughts, he began to recite an old prayer he had spoken many, many times as a child. A prayer he had thought he left behind. A prayer to Mary.

Pray for us sinners, now and at the hour of our death.

He did not dare look again into that woman's eyes.

ACKNOWLEDGMENTS

The Joe Ledger novels could not be undertaken without the help of a lot of talented and generous people. In no particular order: Many thanks to Dr. John Cmar, Director, Division of Infectious Diseases, Sinai Hospital of Baltimore; Dr. Ronald Coleman, Principal Scientist, International Stem Cell Corporation; Chelsea Shimer Neddo; Jason Aydelotte; Debra Getts; Amira El Taggi; and Ammar Habib.

Thanks to my friends in the International Thriller Writers, International Association of Media Tie-in Writers, the Mystery Writers of America, and the Horror Writers Association. Thanks to my literary agent, Sara Crowe of Sara Crowe Literary; my stalwart editor at St. Martin's Griffin, Michael Homler; Robert Allen and the crew at Macmillan Audio; and my film agent, Dana Spector of Creative Artists Agency. Special thanks to F. Paul Wilson for allowing me to use his wonderful character, Repairman Jack. And very special thanks to my brilliant audiobook reader, Ray Porter.

ABOUT THE AUTHOR

Sara Jo West

JONATHAN MABERRY is a *New York Times* bestselling, Inkpot-winning, five-time Bram Stoker Award–winning author of *Relentless, Ink, Patient Zero, Rot & Ruin, Dead of Night,* the Pine Deep Trilogy, *The Wolfman, Zombie CSU,* and *They Bite,* among others. His V-Wars series has been adapted by Netflix, and his work for Marvel Comics includes the Punisher, Wolverine, Doomwar, Marvel Zombies Return, and Black Panther series. He is the editor of *Weird Tales* magazine and has also edited many anthologies, including *Aliens vs. Predators, Nights of the Living Dead* (with George A. Romero), *Don't Turn Out the Lights,* and others.

LISTEN TO JONATHAN MABERRY'S
ROGUE TEAM INTERNATIONAL SERIES

READ BY THE AUDIE AWARD–WINNING
NARRATOR OF THE JOE LEDGER SERIES
RAY PORTER

"Ray Porter is the perfect book narrator. He submerges so completely into each character that they come alive as individuals. . . . It's to the point that I hear his voice in my head when I'm writing."

—JONATHAN MABERRY

"[Ray Porter's] perfect tonal qualities for Joe give a sense of humor to a basically damaged person. Listeners will find themselves entranced by Porter's terrific narration."

—AUDIOFILE ON THE DRAGON FACTORY
(EARPHONES AWARD WINNER)

"Porter is a perfect narrator for these action-packed thrillers."

—AUDIOFILE ON JOE LEDGER: THE MISSING FILES
(EARPHONES AWARD WINNER)

Visit MacmillanAudio.com for audio samples and more!
Follow us on Facebook, Instagram, and Twitter.